D0998760

LINCOLN
LIBRARY

DARK PARADISE

Also by Lono Waiwaiole

Wiley's Lament (2003)
Wiley's Shuffle (2004)
Wiley's Refrain (2005)

DARK PARADISE

LONO WAIWAIOLE

Dennis McMillan Publications 2009

FIRST EDITION
Published January 2009

Dustjacket and interior artwork by
Michael Kellner.

ISBN 978-0-939767-61-8

Dennis McMillan Publications
4460 N. Hacienda del Sol (Guest House)
Tucson, Arizona 85718
Tel. (520)-529-6636 email: dennismcmillan@aol.com
website: http://www.dennismcmillan.com

For Skippy Iolane, who sang this story long before I wrote it; and for Daddy Blue Bug, who is willing to read anything but the writing on the wall. . . .

"Believin' somethin' don' make it true."

—Elmer, in *Wiley's Lament*

"Without his measure of poison, any man will flatly refuse his invitation to dance."

—Charles Willeford, *Something About a Soldier*

DARK PARADISE

Chapter One
Pre-game Warm-ups

1

The first time Happy Dixon died, Geronimo Souza breathed life back into him at Isaac Hale Park on the Puna side of the island. Everyone blamed Junior Silva for the accident because it was Junior's board that ran upside Happy's hard head, but the truth was Happy had a habit of sticking his head where it didn't belong.

Geronimo had been at the beach that day only because his yearlong pursuit of Lahapa Wong had yet to bear fruit. His plan had been to take the SAT that morning, but he jumped to Plan B as soon as Lahapa called in search of a ride to the beach. He felt like he was making solid progress, too; Lahapa's sweet tongue was halfway down his throat when all hell broke loose. By the time he'd saved Happy's sorry life and got back to the blanket, Lahapa had chilled down by several degrees and was ready to head for home.

Funny how much can turn on the tiniest twist of fate, Geronimo thought as his memories of that day more than two decades ago flooded through his mind. He never did get with Lahapa, who eventually married a *haole* and lived in Pasadena now, and he ended up in the Navy instead of the university. Which Geronimo had no complaints about, because the Navy had led directly to where he was standing right now—at the scene of a fatal accident on Highway 11 about halfway between Mountain View and Volcano, Geronimo the one who had arrived at the scene in a Ford Explorer, which now had a blinking blue light on the roof, and Happy Dixon the one with his hard head stuck through the windshield of an overturned Toyota Corolla.

Geronimo called the accident in and went about the job of laying out flares in each direction. "Jeezus Christ, Happy," he said aloud, even though he knew Happy wouldn't have listened to him even if he were still alive. It was a single-car accident, thank god, the Corolla off the road in the thick ginger simply because Happy could drink a helluva lot better than he could drive.

Louie Yamamoto arrived just as Geronimo finished with the flares, the ambulance Happy didn't really need right behind him. Louie's blue light was flashing on top of a new Land Rover. The new rig made Geronimo think briefly about replacing his Explorer, but he knew the way his finances were going the numbers would never add up—even with the departmental allowance all the Big Island cops earned for using their personal cars on the job.

"Oh, fock," Louie said as soon as he took a close look at the wreck. "Ain't that Happy Dixon?"

"Yeah," Geronimo said. "And I think he's really dead this time."

"Whaddaya mean?" Louie said, because Louie had been in elementary school the first time Happy Dixon died and was as ignorant about Geronimo's generation as Geronimo was about Louie's.

"It's a long story," Geronimo said. "Can you take this the rest of the way?"

"Too good now for traffic action, yeah?" Louie said through a grin, a reference to Geronimo's transfer to the drug task force the previous year and to Criminal Investigations five years before that. "We get a helluva lot more traffic deaths than anything, you know."

"That's why we need a real cop on this, Louie," Geronimo said, a grin of his own flirting around the edges of his broad brown face. "Plus you're the one on duty here."

"That, too," Louie said, his grin jumping suddenly to a high chuckle. "I got it, brah, no problem."

Five minutes later, Geronimo was headed into the wet night again, the irony of the situation rolling around in his mind unimpeded while he drove through a light rain.

Just like the last time Happy Dixon died, Geronimo was only at the scene because of a woman. This time, though, the scenario was a little more complicated—the woman he had just left in Volcano was not the same one he was headed home to when he happened on the accident.

"I'm late, I'm late, for a very important date," he recited under his breath, followed by immediately wondering where the fuck that had come from. It was only half true, anyway. He was late, but he had no important date with Denise in front of him and hadn't had one behind him for as far back as he could remember.

You fucked this up good, he said to himself, thinking back to the way things had been when the two of them had started together, him chiseled *koa* fresh out of the SEALS and her by far the hottest *wahine* in Hilo High's graduating class that year.

Fifteen years disappearing down the fucking drain, Geronimo thought. *You satisfied yet?*

2

"What the fock kinda system you got here, homes?" Jesus Fernandez said finally, the beer ad now beaming out of the television screens not holding his attention to the same degree as the game that the ad had interrupted.

Buddy Kai had been waiting for the better part of an hour to hear something come out of the guy's mouth not related to the fucking game, something that had even the remotest connection to the reason they were both in a bar at the Honolulu airport. *And this is the best the moddafockah can do?* Buddy thought.

The Los Angeles connection was the problem, of course, Jesus having flown all the way from LA that morning just to bleed Laker blue while Detroit kicked the collective butts of his home-boys in the first game of the NBA championship series. Jesus had followed the action on four or five different television screens in the bar, but they all told the same sad tale.

"Not *my* system, you know," Buddy said quietly. He had hopped over from Hilo for this meeting, but so far it hadn't been worth the energy required to cross the street. For a moment he even began to second-guess his decision to move toward the Mexicans in the first place, but it didn't take him long to remember that the Mexicans had done most of the moving and he had never been offered much of a choice.

"Well, it's focked," Jesus said. Buddy couldn't argue with that, so he didn't bother to comment. Instead, he leaned back in his chair and began to inventory the gold Jesus was flashing in front of him—three or four necklaces, a bracelet on one arm and a watch on the other, several rings on the fingers of both hands, and many of these pieces encrusted with precious gems of one kind or another.

"How much money you wearin'?" Buddy asked.

"If I know the answer to that question," Jesus said, "it's too much."

Too much eithah way, Buddy thought.

"The sheet been sittin' here for two weeks already," Jesus said, referring to the Honda Accord stuffed with crystal methamphet-amine Jesus had sent from LA to Buddy on the Big Island—only it was still sitting on Oahu, waiting for an inter-island barge.

"Put the shit in your suitcase, brah," Buddy said, "you gonna get it here way quickah, I promise."

"You think this sheet is funny, homes?" Jesus said, his face broadcasting clearly his own opinion on the subject.

Kinda, Buddy thought, but what he said was this: "Comin' ovah this week, you know. Soon as we get it, we gonna sell it."

"Anything goes wrong, *ese,* you ain' gonna be laughin' no more."

"Not laughin' now, you know. Just more used to it."

"Whatever," Jesus said. "I still say the system is focked."

"Saved you from payin' good money to see that fockin' game, you know."

"True," Jesus said. "But ain' gonna be no more games like that, believe me."

"I wondah," Buddy said.

"Believe me, homes," Jesus said. "The Lakers got all the horses in this fockin' race."

"Not," Buddy said. "I wondah 'bout this deal. Anyt'ing goes wrong, you gonna be pissed. Not'ing goes wrong, the Japs gonna be pissed."

"Let us worry about the Japs," Jesus said. "All you gotta do is move the fockin' sheet."

"No problem," Buddy said, but what he was thinking was this: *On my end of this fockin' deal, I gotta worry 'bout everyt'ing.*

3

Jay-Jay Johnson perked up considerably as soon as Jolene and Kapua walked through the door of his party house off Ainaola, Kapua the primary object of his carefully calculated attentions since the first time Jolene had brought her around two or three weeks earlier.

Jay-Jay had a serious yen for brown beauties like Kapua, but she was a lot better than most and way better than the skank Jolene had become over the past twelve months—Jolene all skin and bones now, and to make it worse the skin gray and pasty like she had died without even knowing it.

That was the thing about Kapua—she was still ripe, still juicy, still something you could sink your teeth into. Jay-Jay had been sucking on the best of his own weed for most of the night, so he knew he was looking at the girl through a warm, mellow haze. But even after adjusting for his buzz, Jay-Jay began to believe the girl was the best thing he had seen for months, if not longer. His blue eyes began to dance behind his innocuous granny glasses while he sat in his chair at the battered kitchen table and watched Jolene guide the princess through the throng of partiers to say hello.

"Hey, sweetheart," Jay-Jay said as he and Jolene kissed each other on the cheek, Jay-Jay sticking to his chair so Jolene had to bend in his direction to do it. "I was hoping you'd come by."

He could see that Jolene was chafing to cut to the chase—as usual, she had no time to waste on small talk—but he turned his attention to Kapua to repeat the same greeting he had shared with Jolene. The princess had come into the room behind some interesting cleavage, but she flashed a lot more of it when she leaned down to peck Jay-Jay on the cheek.

God is so fucking good, Jay-Jay thought. The girl looked younger up close than she had from across the room, which was fine with Jay-Jay—the fresher the fruit, the sweeter the juice. Jay-Jay had a good eye for judging the age of these princesses; this one was 15 or 16, no more, and Jay-Jay had a bar of iron between his legs by the time he finished inhaling her sweet scent and kissing her discreetly on her smooth dark cheek.

The princess was rigid where Jay-Jay's hand rested briefly on her shoulder, like her guard was up, and he knew there had been nothing extra in the touch of her lips to his cheek. It was all enough to make Jay-Jay smile, so that's what he did.

"Wassup, Kapua?" he asked innocently, brushing a blonde dreadlock away from his forehead with the hand that had been on her shoulder.

The princess hesitated, as though she suddenly couldn't recall why she was standing in Jay-Jay's kitchen, but Jay-Jay just sat there behind his gentle smile and waited until the reason came back to her.

"You have more ice?" she said finally, her eyes down like Jay-Jay might see straight into her mind if she made eye contact with him. Jay-Jay smiled even more broadly at that; he had started reading her mind from the first moment he laid eyes on her—her mind and her future, too. Everything had been laid out in front of him as soon as she walked in the door.

"You know I do," Jay-Jay said. "How much you want?"

"Don't have much money," the princess said, looking up very much like she had that first night to try to fend off what she still feared was coming next.

"Please," Jay-Jay said. "You know I don't want your money, sweetheart."

"Not gonna do not'ing for it, you know," she said with a little toss of her head, her back straight and her arms folded protectively across her chest.

"Do I still seem like that kind of a guy to you?" he asked.

Kapua shook her head shyly, as though embarrassed to have suggested such a thing. Jay-Jay looked at her closely, and then at Jolene almost foaming at the mouth next to her. He had their full attention, that was obvious. *What a piece of cake this business is, he said to himself. Sooner or later, sweet princess, you'll do anything for this shit—any fucking thing I say. Right now, though, it's time to ratchet this delightful little game up a notch.*

"Actually," Jay-Jay said, "I do need a favor from you, Kapua." He was staring straight into her deep brown eyes now, and she was staring back; he watched as her gaze turned suddenly more wary, as though the other shoe she had always feared might drop was right now beginning to do exactly that. *Which it is,* Jay-Jay said to himself, *but you won't recognize it at first.*

"What kind of favor?" she said.

"Would you stop coming here?"

"What?" she asked, after a mental double-take that Jay-Jay could see just behind her eyes.

"Would you stop coming here?" he said again.

"Why?" she asked, already thinking exactly the wrong thing, already set up perfectly for the curve.

"Because I can't stand it anymore," he said earnestly, his own eyes beaming out what he hoped was just the right amount of his private misery.

"What do you mean?"

Jay-Jay looked away before he replied, as though embarrassed by what he had to say. "I'm afraid I'll do something inappropriate, Kapua, and we both know you don't want me to do that."

The girl stared at him like he was speaking a foreign language, and he let the stare percolate for a while before he continued. "You don't know how you make me feel, girl," he said when he thought the time was right. "You're so fucking gorgeous, Kapua. Do you realize I'm hard right now, just from looking at you? I've never experienced anything like you before."

Jay-Jay said this with the same note of earnest certainty he had started on, but he glanced at Jolene for an instant while he did it because Jolene had heard it all before. She looked back at him blankly and didn't say a thing. *We're cool, huh, baby?* Jay-Jay said to her silently. *Long as I keep the fucking ice coming, we way cool.*

"I don't understand," Kapua said, which Jay-Jay thought might be the truest words the girl had ever spoken.

"You don't want to be around me when I'm like this," he said soberly. "I'm thinking things you shouldn't have to deal with." Then he watched her carefully, counting to himself as he read her reaction in her eyes. He reached eight before she seemed about to speak again, and he spoke first.

"Don't worry about the shit, Kapua," he said. "I'll still take care of you, I'm not saying that. Just tell Jolene when you want something, and she can come over and get it for you. Is that okay with you, Jolene?"

"Shuah," Jolene said, looking nowhere in particular but the word flowing as though its path had been greased in advance. "No problem, Pua."

"There's no reason why you should have to suffer because of the way I feel," Jay-Jay added.

He watched the relief flood over Kapua's face, the mystified expression still there but buried to a significant degree. *Long as the shit keeps coming,* Jay-Jay thought. *Ain't that right, my gorgeous princess?*

4

Dominic Rosario knew it was all over as soon as Kobe Bryant buried the three-pointer from the parking lot to send the game into overtime—the entire series, not just the second game, the stupid Pistons fucked now for giving Dominic's Lakers new life.

Once you got 'em down, Dominic said to himself, *you gotta crush da moddafockahs.* Just like the Lakers were doing when the phone rang, Kobe leading them through the extra period like the Grim Reaper on speed.

"Dominic?" a tentative voice said into Dominic's ear.

"Who's fockin' numbah you called?" Dominic said.

"Yours."

"Den who da fock you t'ink it is?"

"This is your cousin Karl from Matson's," the voice said next, the speaker apparently believing that Dominic's last question had answered itself.

"What you want?" Dominic said gruffly, but he wasn't feeling the same way he sounded. *Tell me somet'ing I wanna hear,* he said to himself.

"I might have something for you."

"Fockin' spit it out."

"We have a car coming in for Edith Kealoha Thursday."

"What da kine I fockin' wen tell you fo' watch?"

"Buddy Kai or Sonnyboy Akaka."

"Exactly."

"Yeah," Karl said. "But Edith Kealoha is Sonnyboy's aunty."

Dominic let his mind run until he got a hit. "Old, old one live in Panaewa?" he asked.

"Yeah," Karl said.

"No way she in da fockin' business, you know."

"I know," Karl said quickly. "The only thing is, she doesn't drive, either. I wonder what she wants with a new car."

For the second time that night, Dominic knew it was all over—this time as soon as the words were out of Karl's timid mouth. It was still a long shot, sure, but this long shot was going to hit just like Kobe's, and Dominic could already feel it snapping through the net.

"Way to fockin' go, Cuz," Dominic said before he cut the connection with Karl and substituted it for a new one. He listened to three rings before the woman's voice came through.

"Yes?" she said.

"Dis da fockin' drug bitch, yeah?" Dominic asked.

"You have a rude mouth, Dominic," the woman said.

"Yeah," Dominic said. "But you fockin' gonna love what I gotta say."

5

One, two, three, Robbie Tsubamoto hummed under his breath. *That's how element'ry it's gonna be. Come on, let's fall in love, it's easy; don't just stand there like a baby.*

Robbie loved all those old soul tunes from the Sixties, and just about anything could set one to popping in his head—just like this meeting here, the three of them in Hilo's best hotel room: the old man, of course; Kitano, there because the old man couldn't or wouldn't speak English; and Robbie, the one who actually lived on the Big Island and the only one there with his ass totally on the line.

There were several more people within a stone's throw of the door to the room, the old man and his crew having taken over more than one room on this wing of the floor. All of these people were armed and dangerous, Robbie knew, but he could still have come up with an appropriate tune to accommodate the entire assemblage if pressed to do so. He was not so pressed, however; for better or for worse, he was now at the point where he had to deal directly with the old man—directly, that is, if you didn't count Kitano.

When the old man finally rattled something off in his guttural Japanese, Robbie let the old soul tune on his mind dry up and blow away. He needed to stay on top of this situation, if staying on top of it turned out to be humanly possible.

"He wants to know how much you know about this cop," Kitano said, referring to the account way past due that Robbie had known coming in was going to catch the old man's eye.

"Everything," Robbie said after thinking it over for a moment.

Kitano said something in Japanese, and Robbie saw the old man blink once as though a blink of his eyes was the same as an affirmative nod of the head for a normal person. Then the old man said something else.

"Is he good for this debt?" Kitano asked next, the exact question Robbie had known would be asked and the one he didn't really have an answer for—even though he had grown up with the cop in question and had already claimed that he knew everything about the guy.

"This is one touchy kinda guy," Robbie said. "But I think so, yeah."

"Ten thousand dollars is a lot of money," Kitano said.

"Not gonna cost *you* anything either way, you know," Robbie said.

Kitano rattled something else off and the old man responded, Robbie cursing himself silently once again for failing to learn how to speak the language that went with his surname when he had been given the opportunity as a kid. Kitano nodded slowly in the old man's direction, and the old man blinked his eyes again.

"How much did he win yesterday?" Kitano asked.

"Five hundred," Robbie said, reviewing in the back of his mind how the cop had finally hit a winner when the Lakers turned back the Pistons in Game Two.

"Encourage him to increase his bets to get even," Kitano said. "The deeper he gets, the better."

Robbie's heart sank as he absorbed these words, even though they were what he had expected. He nodded to indicate that he understood the message, but he didn't agree with it. He hated to see this come down on his old friend, but there were things Robbie hated a lot more and the old man was capable of making many of them occur. So if Robbie had to climb up his old friend's back to get on top of this situation, Robbie was ready to make the footprints.

That's how element'ry it's gonna be, he thought, already working out in his head how to make his old friend think the whole thing was his old friend's own idea until the old man spoke again.

"He wants to know about the other thing," Kitano said.

"That's not my thing, you know," Robbie said, but he had said the same thing the first time they brought the subject up. Neither Kitano nor the old man responded; Robbie couldn't tell by looking at them if they had even heard the words. What they did instead was stare at him like the shit was going to hit the fan if he didn't answer the question pretty fucking soon.

"Buddy guys gonna win, they go head to head," Robbie said. "Dominic's weaker overall, I think, but what the fuck do I know?"

Kitano translated that, but the names Robbie had offered floated through the Japanese words like flagships on a foreign sea. The old man listened, and thought, and spoke.

"Something happens to Buddy, who takes over?" Kitano asked.

Robbie wanted to say again he wasn't qualified to answer these questions, but he swallowed that desire and answered anyway. "Sonnyboy, I think," he said simply, wondering while he said it where all of this local drug shit was coming from and what it all meant to him.

Chapter Two
Game time

Geronimo
1

Zero for three, Geronimo thought for the millionth time as he turned on Shower Drive into Hawaiian Paradise Park. It's not a park, it sure as hell isn't paradise, and it's not even all that Hawaiian anymore.

He turned again on Sixteenth, and a minute or two later he was home. He parked the Explorer on the cinder driveway next to Denise's Suzuki—Denise had transformed the carport into the *lanai* they didn't have—then walked around the picnic table and let himself into the house.

"You're late again," Denise said as he entered the kitchen. She was sitting on the loveseat in the living room in front of a muted television set, smoking a Kool and staring at him like her face might break if he said the wrong thing.

There was room for two on the loveseat if you sat a certain way, but Geronimo couldn't help notice that wasn't the way Denise was sitting. "Late for what?" he asked, suddenly not caring what happened to her face.

"You fockin' bastahd," she said quietly, punctuating it with a long drag from her cigarette. She exhaled slowly, and when she finished she started talking through the smoke.

"Could I smell da slut on you if I tried, Gerry? I went down on you right now, would I fockin' taste her?"

"Like that would ever happen," Geronimo said, a statement he had a lot of recent history to support.

"I fockin' dare you to come over here," she said. "I fockin' dare you to!"

"Don't be ridiculous," Geronimo said, but he couldn't afford to call her bluff, and he was reasonably certain that she knew it. He noted once again that the trace of pidgin in her speech rubbed him the wrong way, even though he had grown up speaking it himself and still heard it every day on the job.

Why is it that it pisses me off every time I hear it come out of her mouth? he wondered. He dropped his keys on the kitchen counter, opened the refrigerator door, snatched the last long-necked Silver Bullet, twisted off the cap, tossed the cap into the garbage under the sink, and slowly sucked the beer down as though he could actually taste it.

Denise watched this entire sequence through a silent cloud of smoke, but Geronimo knew the smoke would last a lot longer than the silence. "I fockin' hate you, Gerry," she said finally.

"No, you don't," he said.

"With all my heart I do, I fockin' promise."

"If you hated me, you wouldn't still be here. We don't hate each other, Denise."

That's when her face did break, tears washing across it as though she had a dozen crying eyes instead of two. Geronimo was moved by her grief; he imagined that it was very similar to his own. He set the empty beer bottle on the counter next to his keys and moved across the room to the loveseat.

"Come here," he said softly, bending down to place a hand on each of her elbows. She buried her face in her hands and continued to weep.

"Come here," he said again, tugging lightly on her elbows until she rose into his arms. She buried her face in his chest and continued to cry without a sound, her shoulders trembling within the close confines of his embrace.

"What happened to us, Gerry?" she asked after several minutes of silence had unraveled around them. "You used to love me, yeah?"

"I still love you," Geronimo said softly, for some reason thinking of the woman in Volcano while he cradled Denise in his arms. *This fucking shit wouldn't hurt otherwise,* he thought. *Would it?*

2

"When the Saints Come Marching In" started trilling from the phone on Geronimo's belt at about the same time Denise finished drying her face on his shirt. He kept one arm around her shoulders while he reached for the phone with the other.

"Yeah," he said.

"Need to see you tomorrow, Gerry," the voice from the other end of the line said into his ear.

"Tomorrow's not good," Geronimo said.

"Tomorrow," the voice said again.

"Or what?" Geronimo asked. "You trying to threaten me now, Robbie?"

"Not," Robbie said. "I answer to people on my end, yeah? They're the ones callin' the shots here now, you know."

"I'll be even by the end of the series," Geronimo said. "You don't want my action anymore, I'll take it somewhere else."

"No can do, Gerry! You have to go all the way to Vegas to find another book now."

"Bump me up to five grand for Sunday. The fucking Pistons can't do it again."

"Five grand? They won't take that kind of weight on top of what you owe."

"They don't want to take it, tell 'em they can forget what I owe."

"You don't wanna say that, brah, believe me."

"Now you know what I wanna say and what I don't?" Geronimo said. "Five grand on the Lakers, Robbie, or fuck all of you."

For a moment, Geronimo thought the phone had gone dead, but Robbie's voice was back in his ear after the moment was over. "You gotta give one point," Robbie said, "if you go with the Lakahs."

"Fuck the spread. The Lakers'll blow 'em all the way to Canada this time."

"They're not gonna like this, Gerry."

"You t'ink I give a fock what dey like, brah?" Geronimo said before he cut the connection, wondering at the slip into pidgin that had just spilled out of his mouth.

Where the fuck did that come from? he thought, but Denise didn't give him much time to ponder the question.

"How bad is it now?" she asked quietly, still standing close enough to speak directly into his heart.

"Don't worry about it," he said. "It sounds worse than it is."

"How bad?" she asked again.

"I'll be back to even by next week. Don't worry about it."

Denise stiffened and stepped away from him. He watched her pick up her Kools and the Bic that went with them, and then he watched her walk to the kitchen counter and pick up her purse. She spent a moment putting the purse and the Kools and the lighter together somehow, and then she came out of the purse with her car keys.

"You're killin' us, Gerry, one dollar and one fockin' slut at a time," she said, staring at him sadly from the same spot he had been standing in when he had first come in the door. "Don't you see that?"

No, Geronimo said, but Denise couldn't hear it from where he said it so she walked out the same door Geronimo had come in without an answer to her question.

3

How would the old Apache chief whose fucking name I carry have handled this situation? Geronimo wondered, but he didn't know enough about Apaches to answer the question.

Too bad I can't ask dear old Dad—he was the big Apache expert; he was the one with a hard on about the name so big he just had to stick it on his only son.

Geronimo was stretched out on the bed he occasionally shared with Denise, although this was not one of those occasions because he had just driven her out of the house. But his mind had drifted from Denise to the dad who had departed after eating and drinking himself to death nearly a decade ago, and he did nothing to redirect it.

Kainoa Souza was the angriest man Geronimo had ever known. His rage was Hawaiian first and Portuguese second; in his twisted mind, the islands had been stolen from his people twice. That's what Kainoa liked about Geronimo—the "fockin' *haoles*" had stolen Geronimo's land, too, but the Apache had at least made them pay in blood before he rolled over and gave it up.

No question how dear old Dad would handle this situation, Geronimo thought. *With the back of his hand, and then with his fist if the back of his hand didn't work.* Geronimo knew this with certainty because he had seen Kainoa use both on Geronimo's mother until his mother finally learned to submit without objection no matter what her husband demanded.

At least I can still say I have never raised my hand to Denise, Geronimo thought. *At least I can still say that.* Now that he was thinking about Denise again, Geronimo got up and padded into the living room. The television was still on, its flickering message still streaming soundlessly into the room even though no one had been there to receive it. He found the remote where Denise had left it next to the loveseat and canceled the mute.

The first thing he heard was John Wayne in mid-tangle with an Irish spitfire, the issue being her shame at having a man who wouldn't stand up and fight for her—and fuck the fact that John Wayne had already killed a man with his fists and no longer desired to hit people for any reason. The Irish spitfire didn't know that at first, of course, nor did she ever say or think the word "fuck" or even its Irish equivalent.

Geronimo knew the movie and loved it well, but it shed no new light on his present situation. According to the film, the Irish loved a good fistfight almost as much as his own people, but Geronimo could never quite relate to the joy either of these groups seemed to derive from that activity. He sometimes thought this was why he had become a cop, but at other times he noticed that many of his colleagues on the force were just as slaphappy as everyone else. He couldn't think of any reason for his decision at those times, or confirm beyond a doubt that it had been a conscious decision at all.

Whatever the why, Geronimo loved the what. His certainty about this was bone-deep; his work was the one thing about his life that he found completely satisfying. This had been true from the very beginning, and that early satisfaction had been squared or possibly even cubed as soon as he earned the move to Criminal Investigations. Geronimo had all the characteristics of a good investigator and he knew it, even though he was unable to apply many of them to any area of his life outside of his job. He was patient in his work, methodical, insightful, a good listener and a keen observer, all overlaid by a nearly fanatical ability to focus on the case in front of him. This made him hard to live with, which he also knew, but he rationalized it easily since he couldn't see himself actually living at all any other way.

He found himself in need of comfort from time to time, fanatical at work or not, and he took that comfort where he found it almost as a matter of course—as though it was his due and beyond a second thought. If that meant a woman in Volcano, so be it; if that meant the spice of a wager on a game now and then, so be that. And fuck Denise and everyone like her if they couldn't deal with it.

Geronimo ran this line of thinking around his head for a while, and he liked it as far as it went. But while the Duke and the Irish spitfire went on with their wrangle in the film on the tube, Geronimo couldn't help noticing that his line of thinking did nothing to bridge the hole slowly growing in his heart.

4

Geronimo was more than two hours ahead of the morning commuter traffic by the time he hit Highway 11 again, so he was downtown in 20 minutes max in spite of the steady rain. He parked his rig at headquarters and walked in on a two-ring circus and a gaggle of celebrating clowns, the clowns all tripping over each other as they passed congratulations back and forth. Geronimo picked his way through the crowd to join his boss at the back of the room, acknowledging the Hilo cops he met along the way with a nod or a quiet word and walking by the feds as though they had been sketched into the scene with invisible ink.

The briefing began as soon as Geronimo reached Ralph Benedetto's side, so he turned toward the front of the room and listened to a gray-haired *chicana* lay out the situation. The woman had DON'T EVEN THINK OF FUCKING WITH ME written all over her, but Geronimo figured she had probably needed that to make it this far with the feds. Hell, he thought ruefully, she would have needed the same thing to make it with us.

The situation was apparently the biggest drug bust in the history of the Big Island—"one point three million dollars on the street," the woman said—found in the form of crystal methamphetamine packed into the interior panels of a two-year-old Honda Accord fresh off an inter-island barge at Matson's.

Geronimo glanced at Ralph when he heard the number, and his boss was looking back with his eyebrows raised slightly. Now the plan was to follow the car as far up the leadership ladder of the organization involved as possible, and the drug task force had been called in to support and assist.

"Your local insight and connections will be invaluable as we proceed from this point," the woman said in conclusion, which was the first hint of bullshit Geronimo had detected in her presentation.

Not too bad for a fed, Geronimo said to himself.

"Are there any questions?" the woman asked.

"How you know da cah been hot?" the chief asked, lacing the question with a little pidgin for the benefit of the feds. Geronimo found this slightly amusing—as did the rest of the chief's men in the room, Geronimo imagined—because the chief used only standard English for everyone but the feds.

"We got a tip," the woman said.

"Who from?" the chief asked.

"A *confidential* informant," the woman said, the word confidential coming out with some extra *salsa.*

"Had to be somebody dirty, yeah?" the chief said.

"Any other questions?" the woman asked, her voice suddenly a lot colder than *salsa.*

"Who was the car goin' to?" Ralph asked.

"Edith Kealoha," the woman said after referring to the papers on the podium in front of her.

"You know her?" Ralph asked, turning toward Geronimo.

"Yeah," Geronimo said. "But I don't think she drives."

"She knows somebody who drives, I assure you," the woman said.

"She's Sonnyboy Akaka's aunty," Geronimo said. "He drives."

"That's Buddy Kai's cousin, yeah?" Ralph said, and Geronimo nodded in confirmation.

"According to our informant," the woman said, "these were Buddy Kai's drugs. We hope to follow the car to him today."

Good luck with that, Geronimo thought. *Sonnyboy doesn't come from the dumbass side of the family—if he did, Buddy wouldn't have picked him for this job.* He kept the thought to himself, however, because he had already taken the message written all over the woman to heart.

"That makes your informant Dominic Rosario, right?" Geronimo asked, dropping it in offhandedly as though an answer was neither needed nor expected.

"What makes you say that?" the woman said.

Because Dominic is Buddy's primary rival, maybe? Geronimo said to himself, but he put his voice on a different set of words. "Shot in the dark," he said aloud.

"If there's nothing else," the woman said, "the chief will explain the electronic surveillance and announce your assignments."

When no one seemed to have anything else to say, Geronimo reconsidered his reluctance to elaborate. "Actually," he said, "I have one question."

"Yes?" the woman asked.

"You seem to know a lot about where the drugs were going. What do you know about where they were coming from?"

"The car was shipped from LA," the woman said.

"That's it?" Geronimo asked. "Who put the fucking ice in it?"

"We have people working that end in LA," the woman said. "That's not really our concern here."

"You aren't in much of a position to determine what my concern here is," Geronimo said, his disinclination to mix it up with this woman beginning to fade beyond recognition.

"What's your point?"

In for a penny, Geronimo thought, *in for a fucking pound.* "If this is Japanese shit," he said, "it came the long way around, didn't it?"

"And if it isn't Japanese?" the woman asked.

"Then we're talking Pearl Harbor all over again, only this time it's the Japanese getting bombed."

"You don't see that as a good thing?"

"I might, if I didn't live in the fucking drop zone."

The woman didn't respond to that immediately, and no one in the room apparently felt like interjecting anything because no one said a word until the woman finally spoke.

"I see," she said. "All I can tell you at this point is that the likelihood of this shipment originating with a Mexican organization is extremely high."

"Gracias," Geronimo said, even though he knew the Spanish word for "fuck" and was sorely tempted to use it. Everyone started breathing again and the chief took over the podium. Ralph, Geronimo and two feds Geronimo didn't know drew a post on Kawili with their noses pointed at Highway 11, where they were supposed to pull out and follow if the target car passed by.

After an hour of milling around the squad room like idiots and five minutes of driving to their location, they were parked half in and half out of the right-turn lane next to the Nissan dealership because there turned out to be no shoulder on that side of Kawili.

You've got to be kidding me, Geronimo thought as whatever traffic came up their butts on Kawili had to work its way around them, but he kept the thought to himself because he already knew that no one in the entire operation was kidding no matter how big a joke the operation turned out to be.

They sat there like lame ducks for almost four hours, at the end of which Geronimo had a head full of his own problems again. He could have focused on the bullshit the feds in the front seat were laying on them, but the feds usually rubbed him raw and these guys were no exception.

Geronimo perked up when the radio announced the arrival of Sonnyboy and Aunty Edith at Matson's, followed a few minutes later by their departure from the lot and their turn in the right direction on Highway 11. When the Honda finally flashed by, Geronimo felt like flagging it down and kissing both Sonnyboy and his aunty on the lips.

The fed behind the wheel of their car got them out into the traffic three or four vehicles behind Sonnyboy and a couple of cars behind the primary tail. They all proceeded in an orderly fashion until the Honda suddenly switched to the left-turn lane in front of the Borders store, which prompted a similar sudden switch to the new lane for the followers.

"Fuck," Geronimo said quietly.

"You got somethin' to say?" the driver asked.

"We're blown, is all," Geronimo said.

"I suppose you could have done better, what with your fuckin' local knowledge and shit."

"I doubt it," Geronimo said, keeping his temper tamped down reasonably well while he said it. "We needed a driver a lot dumber than Sonnyboy to make this work."

All three cars got through on the same left-turn light and rolled east as though Sonnyboy had designs on either the Wal-Mart on the left or the mall on the right. But he drove straight through, past the KFC and the Home Depot construction site, and the tails that had been reasonably subtle in the traffic on the highway suddenly began to stand out on the less-traveled side road like they were made of neon.

When Sonnyboy turned right on Railroad Avenue, the primary tail turned left to get out of the picture. *Too little, too late,* Geronimo said to himself as the car he was in stayed with Sonnyboy. The Honda turned right at the next street, which brought them back to the mall from the opposite side, and then it turned right again into the mall parking lot between a Macy's store on one side and a Safeway on the other.

That lot was jammed, as usual, and Sonnyboy had to cruise down two rows and up one before he found a spot to park. Then he got out of the car, walked around the front, helped Aunty Edith disembark, and sauntered lackadaisically toward the Macy's arm-in-arm with the old woman.

"They're out of the car and headed for Macy's," the fed in the front passenger seat said into the radio. "Please advise."

"Stay with the car," a voice from the radio replied. "If you're not really blown, you can pick 'em up again when they come back out."

"If you still want to see where he goes next," Geronimo said as he watched Sonnyboy and his aunty disappear into the store, "you better tell them to get some cars at the other mall exits. He won't be coming back out this way."

"We want your fuckin' opinion," the driver said curtly, "we'll send you an interagency memo to that effect."

Geronimo opened his door and climbed out of the car, the rain a cool relief on a face a lot hotter than it had been a moment or two earlier.

"Where you goin', brah?" Ralph asked.

"To get some fucking lunch," Geronimo said. "We're going to be here a while."

5

Geronimo had roller coasters on his mind as he moved quietly through his empty house, turning off lights as he went. When he got to his bedroom, he stretched out fully dressed on top of the bed, his home phone on the nightstand to his right and his cell phone resting comfortably on his chest.

He settled back to review the roller coasters one at a time, starting with the one he was on that had emptied his house. He hadn't heard from Denise all day, nor had she heard from him. This was not normal; he wondered what it might mean. He could talk to her, of course, and probably discover the meaning—it wasn't like he didn't know where to reach her. But that would be work, he knew, and he didn't feel up to it.

These thoughts inevitably led him to the money he owed Robbie—or Robbie's associates, apparently—a situation he knew was part of the bumpy ride with Denise. He had never been in a hole like the one he was in now, that much he couldn't even begin to dispute. And if the Lakers pulled another disappearing act on Sunday, the hole he was in now would look like a mountaintop in comparison—he couldn't dispute that, either.

Not that the Lakers were much of a question. They had the players, some of the best ever assembled; they weren't going to keep losing to a bunch of wannabes in Detroit, for chrissakes. No, the only thing that really bothered him about the situation with Robbie was Robbie's new associates—those were the only players in the game Geronimo didn't know, and his ignorance made him uneasy whenever he allowed himself to think about it.

Such as now, early Friday night in a house a lot emptier than it had been when he first moved into it. There was a house Geronimo could probably visit in Volcano more inhabited than his own, and he briefly contemplated using one of his phones to call that residence. The woman there was a genuine find, no question; but she was work, too. The more he thought about the work, the less tempting the call became, until the temptation dissipated entirely.

Which led to the roller-coaster ride underway at work. The "biggest drug bust in the island's history" was going to make great reading in the local paper, but Geronimo got a case of the shakes every time he thought about the continuing potential for catastrophe inherent in that situation.

That was really his biggest issue with the feds—even more than the air of superiority they seemed to breathe all over everyone. They weren't part of the community; they didn't appreciate the context of the drug problem as experienced by this particular set of people. The feds thought playing Dominic off against Buddy was part of the solution to the problem, or pitting Japanese gangsters against a bunch of whacked-out Mexicans; but Geronimo saw these as serious intensifications of the problem, adjuncts requiring more immediate attention than the original problem they were all trying to solve.

Which brought Geronimo back to his silent telephones and Buddy Kai. Geronimo had been lucky that afternoon, walking from the mall to the residence of one of Sonnyboy's cousins in Panaewa and finding Sonnyboy eating lunch in the cousin's carport. Geronimo was reasonably certain that the message he had left for Buddy would be delivered, but so far it had not had the desired result.

Hit one of these numbers, Buddy, Geronimo said to himself, and then he settled down to wait until Buddy did exactly that.

6

Geronimo watched Buddy park in the driveway behind the Explorer, power down the windows in both of his front doors and sit back in his seat. The dark air streaming through the open window in front of Geronimo's face was damp but the rain had stopped; Geronimo could see stars now and then as the clouds beyond and above Buddy's car slowly broke ranks with each other. Geronimo drifted out of his house after a moment or two of watching and filled the empty seat next to Buddy. "Wassup?" he said.

"You're the one who wanted to talk, yeah?" Buddy said.

"Yeah," Geronimo said, but he was in no hurry to start. He stared at Buddy quietly, as though close examination might influence what he wanted to say, and Buddy let him do it without comment.

"I need you to hold off on Dominic for a while," Geronimo said finally.

"Dominic?"

"We both know he dropped the dime, Buddy. Don't waste our time here."

"Why would I care what you need?" Buddy asked, back on point as though he had never detoured from it.

"You might benefit from doing it," Geronimo said. "You get the two families fighting, neither one of you can win."

"The moddafockah goin' down if we fight, you know."

"Then what? How do you absorb his people if it goes down like that?" Now it was Buddy's turn to stare, and this time Geronimo sat there without a word while Buddy attempted to discern how Geronimo had read his mind. "What happens if I wait?" Buddy asked when his stare had run its course.

"I take a shot at him," Geronimo said.

"Why would you do that?"

"It's my job," Geronimo said. "Just like you are."

"You're workin' me overtime, brah."

"That's why it's Dominic's turn."

"How long would I have to wait?" Buddy asked after another moment of silent deliberation.

"I can't promise it will be fast," Geronimo said. "But you're more likely to end up with what you want if you wait."

"I'll think about it, brah," Buddy said.

"Good," Geronimo said.

"One thing, Gerry. We've got players in this game ain't gonna listen to me, you know."

"Who?"

"Somebody shipped those drugs over here, yeah? Maybe they're some crazy moddafockahs."

"Whatever," Geronimo said. "I'll work just as fast as I can."

"Isn't it easier to just let us shoot it out?"

"How many of the wrong people end up getting shot that way?"

Buddy nodded slowly and cranked the car to life. Geronimo opened the passenger door and stepped out, then closed it and leaned inside the open window.

"They want Sonnyboy downtown, Buddy," he said.

"Why didn't you take him in today?"

"I'm not the one who wants him."

"How do you work with those fockers?"

"You like everyone you work with?" Geronimo asked.

"First thing tomorrow," Buddy said with a smile. "Our lawyer's bringin' him in."

Geronimo straightened up and stepped away from the car. He watched Buddy back out and drive down Sixteenth toward Shower, and all the while he wrestled with the questions he had yet to answer about Buddy's busted drugs:

Where'd you get the kind of money it takes to move that much shit, Buddy? he asked himself. *And how long before the guy you got the shit from shows up?*

Buddy

1

Even though Buddy had been a criminal all his life, he thought of himself as the most law-abiding citizen on the island—the laws he abided by being the laws of supply and demand. He had never been able to rub two dimes together in 37 penny-ante years until he discovered ice, but now he had all the dimes he wanted and was anxious to jump to quarters or even higher.

That jump might have already occurred if Buddy knew the first thing about chemistry. If you listened to the media, anyone could turn household chemicals and cold medicine into crystal meth, but Buddy couldn't do it and didn't know many people who could. He had a hippie to handle the chemistry right now, though, and he was willing to wait for that connection to come through.

As long as it doesn't take too much longer, Buddy said to himself. The hippie had his head in a cloud of chronic half the time, which Buddy didn't really appreciate, but the other half of the time the guy was in the makeshift lab where his kitchen used to be turning next-to-nothing into gold.

Not that the hippie was the ultimate answer to the question of supply. He was a stopgap measure, pure and simple, although more important than usual now that Buddy's biggest shipment ever had drawn federal badges like the shit had suddenly been magnetized.

Everything Buddy didn't know about chemistry he did know about economics. He understood that demand for ice on the Big Island was going to go nowhere but up because the shit created its own demand when given half a chance. It could turn casual samplers into permanent consumers even faster than crack, and it was dirt cheap in comparison to the other available highs—an important consideration at the bottom end of the Big Island's economy.

The sky was the limit on demand, Buddy knew for certain, but supply— supply was another story. You could make it from scratch, sure, like the hippie was doing that very moment, but you couldn't do it fast enough if you wanted to corner the market on the island.

And why the fuck would you enter a market you didn't want to corner? Buddy asked himself. It would take a lab in half the houses on the island to feed the demand the drug would create when Buddy really got it rolling, so he knew he had to stay connected to either the Japanese or the Mexicans as far into the future as he could see.

But how far is that gonna be? Buddy thought. He had known going into the deal that the Japanese wouldn't like it, but now that he had lost the drugs the Mexicans weren't going to like it, either. The Mexicans had been hungry enough for a shot at the Japs to front him the ice, but Buddy knew for certain what they were going to be hungry for now.

He was sitting in Kea`au on a picnic table outside Verna's Drive-in, sipping coffee from a plastic cup while he waited for the hippie to come up with something. He could have been sitting in the driveway next to the hippie's broken-down VW bus instead of nine miles down the road, but Buddy didn't like to be anywhere near the drugs. He wouldn't have been even this close if Sonnyboy hadn't become a marked man when he arrived to pick up the car at Matson's that morning.

The thing with Sonnyboy pissed Buddy off almost as bad as losing the car full of ice. The kid was a keeper, as he had proved again that morning when he parked the heat at the mall instead of dumping the whole mess in Buddy's lap like the feds had wanted him to. And when Geronimo Souza had come around to the house in Panaewa, the kid was smart enough to go with that flow, too.

Now the kid would be in custody soon and off the board for a while. Buddy liked his chances of springing the kid on bail, but this entire event was a huge step in the absolutely wrong direction and he hated like hell having to take it.

And on top of everything else, Geronimo needed attention. Buddy sensed an opportunity there, but an opportunity for what, exactly? Geronimo's transfer to the drug task force had been a serious blow, because Geronimo knew his way around Buddy's family much too well—which he had just proved again when he walked up on Sonnyboy in Panaewa like he was following a tracking beam.

Might be a bright side to Geronimo Souza, Buddy thought, but I still gotta do what I gotta do, yeah?

One thing Buddy knew beyond a doubt was who had dropped the dime; that was obvious. What he needed to find out was how Dominic had done it. Something had to be done about Dominic, and soon, no matter what Geronimo had to say; and something similar had to be done even sooner about the member of Buddy's family in Dominic's fucking pocket.

2

Buddy's problem was sprouting new shoots like one of those huge banyan trees down on Hilo's hotel row. The root, Dominic Rosario, was one thing—in Buddy's mind, that was clear and straightforward. Buddy had to rip Rosario right out of the ground, and found he was actually looking forward to doing it. But the affiliated problems were much thornier than the root.

For one thing, Buddy was a general without an army. This was a problem on the supply side, too, because good help was hard to find on the Big Island. He had his own family to draw on, but that pool wasn't deep enough to float the operation Buddy wanted to build—especially since some of his relatives were stupid-crook stories waiting to happen and others actually objected to his business and wanted nothing to do with it.

So starting a war with Dominic would be easy, but fighting it would be hard with the number of soldiers Buddy could bring to the field. Buddy could see a way around that—he could mount a surgical strike against Dominic singlehandedly—but once you got rid of him, how did you absorb his business? It looked to Buddy like whatever move he made had to end up with Dominic's sales force on Buddy's team, which was ticklish because Dominic's organization was also populated primarily by family members.

And speaking of family members, Buddy was totally stymied in his quest to identify the member of his own family who had tipped Dominic about the ice shipment in the first place. What made this problem thorny was the shortage of possible culprits, because Buddy was not loose with that kind of information and could think of very few people who could have done the deed and none at all who would have done it.

Which is why he was in an almost-empty movie theater at the mall while a film he had no interest in unreeled in front of his face. "You got another way to see this?" he asked, his voice so low he could barely hear it himself.

"Maybe," Sonnyboy said from the next seat.

"How?" Buddy asked.

"Maybe nobody did it," Sonnyboy said. "Maybe he got somebody at Matson's."

"What good would that do? We didn't tell Matson's, brah."

"If the moddafockah knows this family good enough, he might make one educated guess."

Buddy nodded his head in the dark, seeing the possibility. This was why he valued Sonnyboy; the kid brought much more than muscle to the operation, and any curtailment of the kid's participation as a result of this current fiasco was going to hurt.

"You talk to Geronimo yet?" Sonnyboy asked.

"Not," Buddy said. "But I'm goin' to."

This time it was Sonnyboy's turn to nod in the dark, and Buddy wondered as he watched him do it how long they would dance around the subject neither of them wanted to discuss.

"Get down on the Pistons Sunday," Sonnyboy said next.

"The experts all have it the other way, brah."

"Fock 'em," Sonnyboy said. "Tell Robbie gimme five hundred, fock the spread. You gonna call him, too?"

"Yeah," Buddy said. "I'm gonna call him."

"I go in tomorrow, yeah?" Sonnyboy said finally. He knew Buddy had already made the arrangements—Sonnyboy and their lawyer were going to police headquarters first thing in the morning.

"Yeah," Buddy said. "I think you'll get bail, no problem."

"I go in Saturday, I gotta stay in over the weekend."

"Yeah," Buddy said. "But it's gonna be better if they don't pick you up, brah."

"If I'm inside," Sonnyboy said, "I can't get your back, you know."

"No need," Buddy said. "The fockin' Mexicans will try to get their money back before they do anything drastic."

Buddy rose from his seat, leaned down, embraced his cousin warmly, and walked out of the theater. When he reached the pay phones near the door to the parking lot, he stopped and brought one to life.

"Yeah?" Geronimo said on his end of the line.

"You alone, brah?" Buddy asked.

"Yeah," Geronimo said.

"I'm comin' over," Buddy said, and then he hung up the phone and went out the door.

Sonnyboy

1

Sonnyboy was sitting at the table in his second cousin's carport in Panaewa eating pork *adobo* from a takeout container when Geronimo walked into the driveway like he had dropped by for lunch.

"Aunty Edith had a lot of shopping to do?" Geronimo asked.

"More than me, brah," Sonny said, brandishing his takeout container. "This is all I needed."

"I like it, too," Geronimo said. "I think it might be the best *adobo* on the island."

"You want some?" Sonnyboy said.

"Nah," Geronimo said. "I ate while the feds were waiting for you to come back out."

"But I never did, yeah?" Sonny said through a grin. Instead, he had made two calls from a pay phone in the mall, one to Buddy with the bad news about the bust and the other to a cousin to come pick up Aunty Edith. After his cousin arrived, Sonny purchased his lunch in the food court and walked the 15 minutes from the mall to the carport he was sitting in now. The walk would only have taken ten minutes if he had come out the same door in the mall he had entered, but he didn't mind the extra steps at all; he would have walked twice as far for a chance to give the feds a hard time.

"You seem to be taking it pretty well," Geronimo said. "That was a helluva hit."

Sonnyboy looked at Geronimo over the lip of his lunch container, but the only response he made was to snatch another piece of pork with his fork and deposit it where the others had gone.

"Buddy know yet?" Geronimo asked, and when Sonny stuck with the same response as before, Geronimo settled in to wait for an answer. When the *adobo* was gone, Sonny set the container and the fork on the floor of the carport next to his chair.

"Where are the feds now, brah?" Sonny said finally.

"They'll be here eventually," Geronimo said. "They didn't know where to look."

"Why didn't you tell 'em?"

"I wanted this chance to sit here while you pretend all you did was take Aunty Edith to the mall."

"What do you want, Gee?"

"It's more what I don't want," Geronimo said. "I don't want a war to start because of this."

"Already started, brah."

"No," Geronimo said. "You just got hit. It won't be a war unless you hit back."

"You talkin' to da wrong *kanaka,* Gee. I'm just one drivah, yeah?"

"Tell Buddy I wanna talk, and what I wanna talk about."

"We gotta hit back, you know. No way we can let this slide."

"Tell him, Sonny. I want a shot at this situation before it all turns to shit."

"Why do you care, brah? If we kill each other, isn't that better for you?"

"If you could all shoot straight, I might go with that."

Sonnyboy nodded at that, then picked up the residue from his lunch and rose from the chair. "You takin' me in?" he asked.

"What for? Driving your aunty to the mall?"

"Hey, Gee," he said through a grin. "How'd you know where to find me so quick?"

"Closest cousin I could think of," Geronimo said through a grin of his own. "It was worth a shot."

"If you didn't find me here, how far were you gonna walk?"

"Ralph is picking me up. I needed to get away from those fuckin' feds for a while."

"Me, too," Sonny said. Then he walked into the house while Geronimo leaned back in his chair and waited for his ride to appear.

2

Sonnyboy stayed in his seat until the movie ended, even though he wasn't really watching the film. The dark theater was a better place to think than many, and he used it for that purpose until the lights came on.

He had a lot on his mind. He had the trip to the police station in the morning, of course, but he had finished thinking about that several hours earlier.

What he was working on now was a little farther down the line—farther, he was afraid, than Buddy was thinking.

Sonnyboy loved his cousin, but he didn't let those feelings get in the way of the wheels that turned in his head. Buddy's recent drive to make his business grow underscored a couple of issues for Sonny, and he had yet to work either of them out.

He left the theater as the cleanup crew came in, and a minute or two later he left the mall as well. The parking lot was quiet as he walked to the car he had borrowed from another cousin that afternoon, and he allowed himself to be sidetracked into the beginnings of a grin while he did it.

I didn't even leave the neighborhood, he thought, *and the fockahs still never found me.* He was unable to maintain the grin as he drove out of the lot, however, because the Wal-Mart across the street reminded him of one of the questions on his mind.

After decades of a mom-and-pop economic system on the Big Island, Wal-Mart had moved in and plucked the local retail market like a ripe papaya. It had happened almost overnight, Sonny remembered, in spite of all the people he knew who claimed they would never step foot in the Wal-Mart. The place was jammed from morning to night, so Sonny knew someone's feet were stepping in there on a regular basis.

The same thing had happened in the ice market, first with the Japanese and now with the move by the Mexicans. And so far, Sonny had not seen a way to get out from under the weight of this phenomenon. The best he could foresee for any of the local operations on the island was chief of local distribution for the big boys who had moved in on them—which was the role to which both Buddy and Dominic apparently aspired.

Sonnyboy's question was this: how much investment was control of the ice equivalent of the local Wal-Mart actually worth, especially when the capital required in this equivalent included blood as well as money?

Not that Sonny had an aversion to blood, particularly. He had a reputation for cracking heads, and he had earned it honestly. But he had no thirst for blood; he knew he would suffer no withdrawal symptoms if he never spilled another drop.

He continued to turn these thoughts over in his head as he drove across the highway and leisurely wound his way to Anna's apartment near the university. He unlocked her door with the key in his pocket that matched the one he had given her when she moved in.

"Is that you, baby?" Anna asked from the bedroom.

"You're focked if the answer is no," he said as he closed the door behind him.

"Or yes, I hope," she said, looking up from what she was doing on the bed when he entered the room. "Wanna join me, baby?"

The answer on the tip of Sonny's tongue was not what he said when he saw her fumbling with the pipe. "What the fock are you doin'?" he said as he slapped the pipe out of her hands and off the wall next to the bed.

"Sonny!" she shouted, the look on her face screaming that she couldn't believe her eyes. "Why'd you do that?"

"Don't fock with that shit!" he said.

"What the fuck is wrong with you?" she asked. "You know I'll be careful with it!"

Sonny felt the heat flee from his body and his heart fall out of his chest as he looked down on the angry college girl sitting in front of him, her perfect white breasts rising and falling under a filmy wrap that he had given her even before she had moved into the apartment.

"Ain't no such fockin' thing, I promise," he said quietly, knowing it was already much too late for words.

"I can't believe you think I'm that stupid," she said. "I can control it, Sonny. I'm not one of those fucked-up ice whores you're used to."

Until now, you know, Sonny said to himself. *The others didn't start that way, either.* He took his keys out of his pocket, removed the one to the apartment door, and set it on the nightstand next to the bed.

"The rent's comin' due next month," he said. "Stay or go, whatevah."

"Sonny! This is crazy!"

"Don' fock with that shit, I'm tellin' you."

"Why are you acting like this? You're the one who sells the shit, not me!"

"So far," Sonny said. "Sooner or later, you'll be sellin' everything you've got, girl. Don' fock with that shit."

"Sonny!" she said one more time, and the word stretched out

all the way from the bedroom to the apartment door. It echoed in Sonny's head as he retraced his steps to his cousin's car in the parking lot.

This was the other problem bugging Sonnyboy—the long-term effect of the product they were selling increasingly sickened him. He had no desire for ice himself, nor did he want anyone he cared about to mess with the stuff now that he had seen where messing with it ultimately ended.

So how many people did Sonny actually care about? How far away from himself was he willing to draw the line?

Buddy also avoided their product, and Sonny understood the way Buddy used basic economic analysis to resolve this contradiction—someone was going to supply the stuff as long as the demand for it existed, so why not them? This line of reasoning made sense on a certain level and had initially worked just fine for Sonny, but it conveniently overlooked the fact that their product produced its own demand.

Makes one fockin' difference, he said to himself. *Makes all da fockin' difference, I t'ink.*

He continued to ponder this question as he drove down to the bay. He pulled over and parked when he couldn't drive any farther and continued on foot until he was across the bridge and onto Coconut Island.

The tiny island was deserted, if you didn't count the ghosts of people past or the shifting shadows thrown down on the island's namesake trees by an on-again, off-again moon. The ground was soaked even though the rain had stopped, but Sonny didn't mind getting his feet wet. He wandered to his favorite vantage point for staring out at the water and hunkered down for a while, content to breathe in the damp air and watch the gentle roll of the waves.

Could be my grandfaddah, Sonny said to himself, *or my grandfaddah's grandfaddah. How fah back we got da trees and da watah heah?* He didn't know the answer to this question—not exactly, anyway, not like he knew the answer to how long his people had needed crystal methamphetamine just to get through another day in their ancestral paradise.

Can't do this shit much longer, Cuz, he thought, and then he watched the moonlight dance in front of him without thinking for a while, the gentle waves washing onto the rocks just as they had done for all of his ancestors before him.

Dominic

1

Dominic was wired. He was less than halfway through the best day of his life, which meant there was still plenty of time left for his good fortune to expand even more.

It had started days before, actually, when he stumbled on the information he had relayed to the feds. With any additional luck, Buddy would be working overtime to find out who leaked Dominic the information—that would be frosting on the fucking cake.

Dominic was pressing 380 pounds on the bench in his carport, a total close enough to his max to make him work on most days. Today he felt like he could rip off 25 or 30 reps before he broke a sweat; that's how pumped he was.

Dominic didn't lift to increase his strength—he had been born strong and had gotten stronger every day of his life. He lifted because he liked the discipline of it, the way his lungs expanded and contracted with his breathing while his muscles burned, and then the lingering memory in his body in the hours that followed the exertion.

He was a big man, but short for his size, which he thought of as his penalty for having Filipino genes mixed in with the Hawaiian. He was careful to work his lower body with the weights as much as the upper; he understood that he needed strong legs to move all his muscles from one place to another. And the place he had moved to in the last day or two was as close to dead-center perfect as he had ever been in his life.

Actually, Dominic's good fortune was nothing new. It had washed over him without interruption for three years, starting with the day he killed his wife and got away with it.

Fockin' frigid Filipino bitch, he thought while he racked the bar over his head and rose from the bench. *Da one save herself fo' fockin' Jesus in heaven, yeah?* Which is exactly where Dominic had dispatched her, although he hadn't exactly planned it that way.

What happened was a simple surge of anger, the last of many his wife had sparked in him during their 13 years of marriage. The three of them were in the boat, though, so she didn't have many places to fall when he lost his temper and cracked her a good one on the side of her head.

The force of Dominic's blow had literally lifted his wife off her feet and turned her in the air, and when she came down she hit her head on the edge of the tackle box just exactly right. By the time Dominic moved over to see why she refused to get up again, she was gone to that better world she had been dreaming of since the night Dominic consummated their marriage by brutally laying claim to every orifice on her body.

Dominic had dodged the consequences of this fatal outburst of anger because the witness supported his version of the event—the boat had hit a swell suddenly, causing his wife to lose her balance and fall. The tragic result was officially ruled an accident, and he had managed the role of grieving husband reasonably well all the way through the official inquiry and the funeral which followed it.

The witness had done the same with her role—the grieving daughter— although her performance required less acting than his. Dominic knew Nalani's grief was genuine, but he also understood it was nothing new; Nalani had been grieving for her mother quite possibly since the moment of Nalani's conception during the long night Dominic had become a husband.

Good t'ing I come in dat cold bitch's cunt, yeah? Dominic thought. It had taken thirteen long years for that good fortune to blossom fully, but there was no denying that Nalani was part of what made this new day so perfect.

It had been so simple, too, which made it even sweeter. He had said nothing to Nalani in the boat that day—all he had to do was look at her hard, and he could see in her eyes that she knew what she had to do. He did say one thing to her that night, but that probably could have remained unsaid as well.

"Now you da woman in dis house," he had said when he came to her bed, and she had known instinctively what he meant by that, too.

"You one lucky bruddah," Dominic said aloud as he walked through the laundry room and into the kitchen. He opened the refrigerator, removed the ice water, and began to drink directly from the pitcher. When he had drunk his fill, he returned the pitcher to its spot in the fridge and leaned with his thick arms folded on the kitchen counter.

He needed a shower, but he didn't need it immediately. He stood in his kitchen and savored life as he had recently come to know it. "You goin' down, Buddy," he said, and he said it aloud so he could hear it as well as think it. "You goin' down hahd, I promise."

Dominic's mind flashed back to the exact moment he had discovered when Buddy's shipment was coming in, and he started to grin. Once he started, he couldn't stop, and the grin soon graduated to a deep laugh that spilled out of him as easily as the rain rolled off his metal roof.

That had been simple, too. After many unsuccessful attempts to turn someone in Buddy's organization, Dominic had experienced an epiphany of sorts—all he had to do was turn someone at Matson's. If someone there let him know when someone in

Buddy's inner circle was due to receive a shipment— someone like Sonnyboy Akaka's Aunty Edith, for example, who turned out to have a car coming in from the mainland even though she hadn't driven a day in her long life—then he could play the Buddy Kai lottery with the feds. And maybe win. Big. Which is exactly what he had done, and now he was the only major player in the Big Island ice market with product and undoubtedly number one with the Japanese.

Which is why he was laughing out loud in his kitchen, and why he couldn't wait for the woman of his house to get home from her basketball workout to put the finishing touches on the best day of his life.

2

Dominic found himself dragged down by business Friday evening, which was simultaneously good and bad. He knew you had to do business to be in business, he had no problem with that, but some of the fools involved drove him nuts.

The fact that Dominic was directly related to most of the fools in question made the situation even worse. Take Jose Lopez, for example, who was on the phone when Nalani came in from her workout.

"Break yo' fockin' neck, I promise!" Dominic was saying as Nalani strode through the kitchen. Dominic waved in her direction, and she veered over and kissed him discreetly on the cheek before she disappeared down the hallway to her room.

"No need, Cuz," Jose said. "You know I gonna get it."

"Get what?" Dominic said. "Mo' pussy? You fockin' trade da kine fo' pussy, how you fockin' pay me? Gonna give me one fock, too?"

"She gonna get paid, you know. I gonna get paid right aftah."

Nevah fockin' fails, Dominic thought. *You keep it cash an' carry, no problem. You get one credit customah, you get one fockin' mess.*

Dominic wouldn't put up with Jose's shit for a minute if he had a better alternative, but he knew good help was hard to find. Finding competent people he could trust to retail his drugs was almost more work than it was worth.

Almost, but not quite, because there was more money than aggravation in this business—a lot more. Which was more than Dominic could say about his legitimate business.

Dominic liked his birds and always had, but he knew there was no bounce in the cock-fighting business. He wasn't particularly put off by the fact that the actual fighting was illegal now, but he knew the revenue from raising the fighting cocks was unlikely to increase over time. That was fine; he needed a legitimate occupation. He liked raising the birds and raising them was at least still legal. But the income potential of ice—especially if Dominic swept Buddy off the charts—made raising fighting cocks look like a retirement hobby.

Dominic worked the phone most of the evening, pushing his dealers to poach as many of Buddy's people as possible in the next few days. Dominic knew this would be simple as soon as today's bust hit the news, because ice addicts were loyal only to their next high and distributors weren't much better—unless related to their source by blood as well as commerce—but Dominic had no intention of waiting until the word got around to get started.

You been focked, Buddy Kai, he thought with a smile as he chewed on another cousin who didn't know up from down. *You been focked real good da kine.*

Nalani brought him a plate of stew halfway through the evening as though she knew by some form of telepathy when he was hungry, but otherwise she stuck to her area of the house. This was their usual pattern, and Dominic was happy with it. He was proud of his circumspection—he played the role of fanatical father religiously from one end of the day almost to the other.

Dominic heard Nalani start a shower around the same time

Sportscenter flashed for the zillionth time the highlights of the Lakers being served their lunch the previous night by a bunch of no-names who had no business being on the same court.

Dominic didn't understand how this fluke had occurred, but he didn't belabor the question for long. The basketball player on his mind by the time the report was over didn't play for the Lakers or the Detroit Pistons—she was down his own hallway in the first room on the left.

Nalani

1

Nalani Rosario was halfway through her workout, the sweat pouring off her body freely just the way she liked it. Her hair hung out of the way in one thick black braid down her back, which was also the way she liked it, and Coach was delivering the ball directly into her shooting pocket exactly the way she liked that, too.

She had started on the blocks with her back to the basket 30 minutes previously, first on the right and then on the left, pouring in bank shots off crisp drop-steps followed by jump hooks off moves to the middle. Then she had slowly moved away from the basket, catching Coach's perfect passes and redirecting them like she had a rail laid in the air all the way to the hoop.

After catching and shooting for five minutes at each spot, she spent five minutes at each spot shooting off one hard dribble. All these shots had the same result, mostly; all Coach had to do was catch the ball coming out of the net and throw it back to her.

When she finally reached the three-point line, the misses became more common. This was the newest part of her offensive game, and in some ways the most important.

Nalani was just a fraction under 5'7", which was not really short on the Big Island. And she was a lot stronger than most people guessed when looking at her wiry frame, so she had no trouble scoring down low on most of the girls on the island no matter how big they were. But Coach was right, she knew; she needed an outside game to play at the next level. She was building it, too, the same way she had built the inside game she already had—one day of hard, joyful work at a time.

She occasionally questioned her devotion to basketball, but the answer always boiled down to the same word—joy. She loved the game and everything that went with learning to play it, and she believed she deserved that joy in her life in spite of the realities of the situation she was growing into at home.

"You goin' nowheah, you know," Dominic had said the first time she brought up college basketball. "You no need da kine."

Which was true, as far as it went. It was just something she wanted, but Nalani was determined to move what she wanted much higher on the list of priorities in her life very soon.

"Up!" Coach shouted every time her shot was short, and then he ran down the rebound and snapped the ball back to her again. She liked the way he reminded her, the way he brought her back to where she needed to be at that moment. She planted the following shot more firmly on the floor, concentrated on the bounce off the balls of her feet and lifted the shot away with more arch, and almost always her reward for this renewed focus was a ball ripping through the net just like she wanted it to.

As soon as she worked her way to the end of her allotted time, Nalani allowed that iron focus to soften slightly. She studied Coach surreptitiously while she mopped her face with a towel, and she knew her radar had been right after a moment or two of watching him idly bouncing the ball while he waited for her to finish. There was a new vibe in the air; she could feel it.

Now Coach wants some, too, she said to herself. *Fockin' men are all the same, you know?* Coach was three times her age with a wife and a family, but she knew the truth in her bones: *Makes no fockin' difference, I promise. Now he wants it, too.*

This realization saddened Nalani a little, but not much. She didn't think badly of Coach as a result; in fact, she gave him credit for keeping this vibe out of their work together for as long as he had. She could not explain this glaring weakness in the male of the species; she did not pretend to understand it. But she knew it existed the same way she knew the tide came in every day—regular repetition eventually makes every phenomenon predictable.

Nalani stored this new knowledge away where she kept all the knowledge like it, somewhere slightly below the surface where she could call it up if she ever needed it. Which she would do, without hesitation, if she ever did really need it, because Nalani also knew in her bones that this predictable weakness in men was simultaneously a source of tremendous power for anyone strong enough to use it.

"Thanks, Coach," she said as she draped the towel over her shoulders and picked up her bag.

"Good job," Coach said.

"Not," she said lightly. "The three-pointahs are still junk, Coach."

"Da t'rees gonna be deah, I promise. You got one ride?"

"I got my license now, Coach," Nalani said. "Finally. No more rides for me."

"Dat's good," Coach said, but Nalani knew better than he did that somewhere deep he was disappointed with this revelation. "See you Monday, den?"

"I'll be here, Coach," she said, and then she walked out of the gym with her bag slung over her shoulder. She knew he was watching her as she made her way to the rusty old Datsun Dominic had given her, but she changed nothing about the way she moved in response to Coach's new interest.

You can look, you know, she said to herself as she climbed into the car. *But you wanna touch this shit, you gotta fockin' wait in line.* Then she cranked the car up and began the drive to the house where she knew the first man in that line was already waiting.

As soon as Nalani started thinking about her father again, she started visualizing the fully loaded Glock wrapped in an old towel under the driver's seat of her car. This was happening more and more frequently, she noted—she'd start out thinking about her father and her mind would jump right to the gun. It was one of Dominic's handguns, actually, one of dozens, but so far he hadn't missed it or the ammo she pilfered occasionally to practice with it.

She knew something had to be done about Dominic, and done soon. She thought about it as she drove, the new freedom of driving herself around washing over her while she thought—even contributing to the shape of those thoughts, maybe. It wasn't like she had suddenly turned a corner when she got the license; the change had been slowly coming on for years, perhaps from the very beginning. She had been scared shitless at the start, no question, her mother dead on the boat at her feet and her father looking at her hard like Nalani could easily be next.

But the change probably began that very night, when Dominic made his first visit to her bed. That scared her, too, but beneath the fear she instinctively understood *that* truth, as well—that she had something he wanted much more than she wanted it, and in that fact there was power enough to make her stronger than Dominic no matter how big his muscles became.

Not that she knew how to use this power at first, or really trusted it, or was familiar enough with its limitations. But three years were a long time, and she learned as she went. Which was more than she could say for Dominic, who had learned nothing from those years and was still exactly as weak as he had been when they started.

Which was why something had to be done about Dominic, and why Nalani was going to have to be the one to do it.

2

Nalani's cell phone rang while she was sitting in the drive-through at Taco Bell, a detour she had decided she deserved after her workout. She knew without a glance at the phone that the call was bad news because no one she actually wanted to talk to knew her phone number. *The only thing wrong with sixteen,* she thought, *is you're surrounded by fockin' kids all the time.* Nalani had never been a kid, and certainly wasn't one now, but she spent a significant portion of every day in a world populated primarily by teenaged children.

This might have been only a small problem at most except for the instinctive desire that drove these kids to congregate in packs. Nalani knew she had little choice but to conform to this condition—the alternative left her alone, with insufficient camouflage to escape the kind of attention she could not afford to attract. She tried to limit this infringement as much as possible, but she could not escape it entirely.

Consequently, Nalani knew without looking that her caller was one of the girls from the clique of athletes to which she ostensibly belonged, or one of the boys from the same clique, or a member of her extended family—all of these possibilities devoid of a bright side, although each with its own set of problems.

The family was the farthest of these groups from Nalani's affection simply because her relatives had been closer to her situation for longer than the others. She understood the myth of *ohana,* but she thought of it as a basic tenet of Hawaiian cultural propaganda and the cruelest cut she had endured so far. Sure, you had all these relatives everywhere you turned, but what good were they? They hadn't done a thing for her mother, who had been slowly beaten to death right in front of everyone for 13 years, and they were doing nothing for Nalani now.

On the other hand, they were dangerous. She knew some of them wanted the same thing Dominic did, so she had that to deal with, and some of them might muck everything up trying to do the right thing if they ever did open their eyes and see what was going on in her house. The last thing Nalani needed now was Child Welfare Services turning her life inside out.

The boys were a different problem entirely, but if there were a button to push that would flush them all off the face of the earth, Nalani would hit it without a second thought. For some reason, the same people driven to move in packs were also compelled to couple, and the pack eyed anyone disinclined to participate in this ritual with suspicion. This was further complicated by the fact that these people talked incessantly among themselves about everything each of them did or might have done, which made boys and what you did or did not do with them another minefield Nalani had to navigate.

No matter how dimly she viewed her family and the boys in her circle, however, she recognized the girls to be the biggest threat on her horizon. She thought the girls were generally as clueless as the boys, but the girls were considerably more dangerous because their access was much greater.

Nalani was diligent in her response to these conditions, but she resented it deeply. *The sooner I get away from this shit, the better,* she thought, but she accepted the fact that her getaway moment would not arrive before she had to answer her cell.

The ringing phone triggered the flash of all this information across her mind, but it didn't take long to process because it had not been far from the surface. She glanced at the phone long enough to identify the caller, then picked it up and put it to work.

"Wassup, girl?" she said.

"Nothing," Kapua said into her ear, which Nalani knew for sure was not the case.

"You get the physics homework?" she asked, even though she

knew Kapua's call had nothing to do with physics—or if it did, it had nothing to do with the homework for their summer-school physics class.

"Got it, I promise," Kapua said. "Don't need it until Monday, yeah?"

"Thanks," Nalani said.

"Where are you?" Kapua asked.

"Taco Bell. I'm starvin', girl. Coach worked me plenty hard today."

"You goin' to Pono's party?" Kapua asked next, which was what Nalani had figured was behind this particular call.

"No can," she said. "My father'll freak if I do."

"Your father doesn't need to know, girl," Kapua said. "Why don't you stay at my house tomorrow, yeah?"

"Maybe I can do that," Nalani said as she eased her Datsun up to the drive-through window to pick up the burrito and drink she had ordered before the phone began to ring. "Girl, I call you mo' latah. Gotta go feed da face."

"You gotta come, Lani. You're gonna like it, I promise."

"I'll try," Nalani said, even though the prospect of Pono's party would ultimately make her physically sick if she allowed her mind to dwell on it. "I'll call you after I ask. See you, sistah."

"You bettah, girl. Dis one gonna be crackin', you know."

"I'll try, Kapua. Now get offa da phone, yeah? I stahvin' ovah heah!"

As soon as the connection with Kapua was finally terminated, Nalani dropped the phone on the seat next to her and drove from the window to an empty spot in the parking lot overlooking the highway. Her appetite had vanished long before that point, but she ate the burrito anyway while her mind chewed on the latest situation she now had to finesse.

One thing after another, she thought, and then she started thinking hard about the moves she could make to leave the world of children behind her for good.

3

Nalani completed her preparations when she heard Dominic hit the shower in the room he had previously shared with her mother—not that Nalani had much more to do. She had recently showered herself, which he liked, and her long black hair was recently brushed and hanging loose, which he also liked.

And she was already nude, of course, which had become mandatory over the years, and the lamp next to her bed was already on so Dominic could savor this mandatory nudity. All Nalani had to do now was open the drawer in her nightstand and extract the bottle of lubricant.

Nalani no longer really minded these visits from Dominic; they had stopped actually hurting as soon as she discovered the lubricant. She opened the bottle and let it drool between her legs for a moment, guiding the liquid over her genitals with the fingers of her right hand. When she was certain she was slick enough, she closed the bottle and returned it to the drawer.

Dominic entered her room a moment later, still running a bath towel over his massive frame. Nalani loved the solid bulk of his muscles; it thrilled her to know that the considerable power his body wielded was insignificant compared to her own. She rose from her narrow bed and stood meekly next to it while he moved across the room and replaced her, then she straddled his legs and slowly bent her head over his groin.

Dominic was already erect, which was usually the case, and she let her long hair softly tease his erection for a while. He was pumped, she could tell, and she proceeded cautiously because of it—if he finished too quickly, she knew he would immediately want to do it again. She skipped the oral stimulation she knew he loved but probably wouldn't be able to tolerate today; instead, she moved up over his hips, took his erection in her hand and carefully inserted it into her vagina.

Dominic slid inside her easily, and as soon as she was comfortable around him Nalani leaned forward with one hand on each side of his big head. She was certain her small breasts didn't measure up to the ones in the magazines in Dominic's room, but she knew from experience that he loved these particular small breasts anyway. She brought one to his lips and then the other, and as she rotated back and forth she rolled her hips up and down on his penis. She monitored his reaction carefully, and when he seemed to be getting close she stopped her movements until his breathing returned to something similar to normal.

After several moments of these on-again, off-again ministrations, Dominic cupped her bottom with both of his hands and put an end to her careful regulatory process. "Yo' fockin' moddah mo' like you," he said, looking up at her with genuine regard in his glassy eyes, "she fockin' be alive right now, you know."

Whatevah, Nalani said where Dominic couldn't hear it, her hips rising and falling to whatever rhythm his big hands demanded. *But then you'd be one dead moddafockah by now, I fockin' promise.*

Chapter Three
Game On

Robbie

1

"About the cop," Kitano said. "How much did he put on Sunday's game?"

Robbie was trying to talk on the phone and stay on top of his stir-fry at the same time, and he was making a mess of both processes. He finally moved the stir-fry off the heat and answered the question because Kitano wasn't the kind of guy you put on hold.

"Five big ones," Robbie said.

"How big?"

"Thousands."

Kitano replied to that in Japanese, which threw Robbie for a loop until he realized Kitano was talking to the old man. The old man said something, too, and then Kitano switched back to English. "Try to get him to go all the way if he loses Sunday," Kitano said.

"He might get off the hook, you know," Robbie said.

"He's a loser," Kitano said. "Encourage him to try to get even with one bet."

"No fockin' problem," Robbie said. "He's gonna be beggin' for it, I promise."

"Good," Kitano said. Then he terminated the connection, leaving Robbie standing in front of his stove with stir-fry past its prime and the sinking feeling that his old friend Geronimo was about to become the next thing over the flame.

2

Business was brisk on Sunday's game, calls coming in steadily from every corner of the island, and Robbie noticed the anomaly about halfway through the day—the people he knew to be part of Buddy's organization generally favored the Pistons, and those affiliated with Dominic seemed to lean toward the Lakers.

What's that say? he wondered, but no explanation leaped out at him. He had no opinion on the outcome of the game himself, or the series of which the game was a part. Actually, Robbie didn't like sports and almost never watched them—if his book happened to be significantly out of balance on a particular event, he might feel compelled to keep an eye on it, but that was more a phenomenon of his earlier days; now that he was hooked up with the Japanese, it was easy to lay off action like that.

No, Robbie would rather watch a concert than a game any day, which is exactly what he planned to do that very night. The only question was how to use his two remaining tickets—play it safe or take a chance? Robbie didn't like to gamble any more than he liked sports, which is why he was a bookie rather than a bettor, but he knew he had very little to lose in the scenario on his mind and he was sorely tempted to roll the dice.

He was locked down solid for the night himself, of course, which was part of the temptation to take a chance. His latest flame was a music lover, too, and extremely likely to be insatiable in bed later on no matter what happened with the other two tickets. The buzz Robbie felt as he savored that prospect made him generous; he thought everyone should have the opportunity to feel the same way, especially two of his oldest friends, and it didn't take long with that thought in his head before he found himself on the phone.

Geronimo

1

"You've got to be kidding," Geronimo said.

"Not," Ralph replied, shaking his head as though he could hardly believe it himself.

"The whole fucking crop?"

"The whole thing, brah."

No wonder people think we should legalize all this fucking shit, Geronimo thought. *What percentage of the theft running rampant on this island is directly related to drugs?*

It was first thing Saturday morning at headquarters downtown, and Ralph was sharing the latest horror story from the trenches of the ice war. Apparently a local banana farmer had come back from a short trip to Maui to find his entire crop stolen right off his trees.

"What's it going to be next?" Geronimo wondered, aloud this time, but Ralph just shook his head like he didn't want to even think about it.

"Sonny should be coming in first thing this morning," Geronimo said. "Can you cover me here while everybody celebrates?"

"Wassup?"

"I'm gonna rattle Rosario's cage."

"No problem, brah," Ralph said with a grin. "If they want your autograph, I'll fockin' forge it."

"Yeah," Geronimo said through a grin of his own, but the grin was gone by the time he was out the door.

Twenty minutes later, he parked behind an old Datsun in Dominic's driveway. He was climbing out of his Explorer when a Polynesian poster girl walked out of the house and into the carport.

The girl literally struck Geronimo dumb for a moment, and looking back on it much later he was unable to explain why. He had seen a similar degree of beauty wrapped around a woman before, although rarely, but there was something extra about this girl that briefly stopped his breath in his chest.

The girl looked back at him as she moved deliberately through the carport. She stopped when she reached the Datsun, her eyes suggesting that she knew him in a way Geronimo believed to be impossible.

"You must be Nalani," he said as soon as he could.

She didn't respond to that except to brush a lock of her long hair away from her face, a movement which seemed to Geronimo to underscore both the lithe beauty of her long, muscular limbs and the subtle message in her knowing eyes.

"I haven't seen you for a while," Geronimo said, as though that might explain his state of shock, but he immediately hoped the comment didn't sound as lame to the girl as it did to him.

"Am I under arrest?" she said, the trace of a smile on her lips.

"Should you be?" Geronimo asked, starting to regain his stride.

"Not," she said. "Unless thinking is a crime."

Geronimo found the comment to be provocative, and his first reaction was to wonder why the girl felt compelled to provoke him in this way. He looked at her some more, but this time from a perspective more professional than before. She continued to look back at him, her perspective still a mystery.

Geronimo's second reaction was to wonder how the girl knew he was a cop. "Do you know me?" he asked.

"The cop with the funny name," she said. "Everybody knows you."

"Not really," Geronimo said. "I'm kind of surprised that you do."

"I can go, yeah?" she said with a shrug, her eyes mildly mocking him.

"Yeah," Geronimo said. "Of course."

"You gonna move, maybe?" she said as she opened the rusty door of the Datsun.

Jeezus Christ, Geronimo thought as he climbed back into his rig, cranked it up and backed it out of the way. *Why do I feel like a fucking kid?*

The girl tossed a gym bag inside the car and followed it gracefully. Geronimo didn't recall seeing the bag before that moment, although she must have been holding it in the hand that had not touched her face. *And you're a fucking trained observer,* he thought.

He watched her start the car, back it in a half-circle that skirted around his Explorer, and drive to the road. At that point, she honked at a Chevy pickup turning in as she departed, and Geronimo suddenly had something else to watch.

He climbed back out of his rig as Dominic did the same, but Dominic's movements had an intensity to them totally absent from Geronimo's.

"What you fockin' wen do wit' my daughtah?" Dominic said, closing fast on Geronimo, his eyes a little too big for everyday activity and the veins throbbing in his thick neck much too well defined.

"Slow down," Geronimo said, but when the words didn't seem to penetrate far enough to accomplish their mission, Geronimo tried his department-issue Smith & Wesson instead. He had it up and extended in time for Dominic to run right into it, and when Dominic felt the blunt barrel trying to make a hole in his forehead, he finally put on the brakes.

"Back the fuck off, Dominic," Geronimo said.

Dominic blinked two or three times and stepped back; in response to that, Geronimo lowered the arm with the nine on one end and waited for further developments.

"Da fock you want?" Dominic said, as though his earlier question had never been spoken.

"It's more what I don't want," Geronimo said. "I don't want you thinking we like Buddy better than you."

"T'ink you love dat moddafockah, yeah?" Dominic said, his face suddenly fracturing into a grin. "You nevah fo' fock me da kine."

"It's not over," Geronimo said. "We're holding plenty back for you."

"Fock you, Gerry. Check da fockin' feds you wanna come flashin' down heah, brah."

Geronimo felt his face grow hotter as Dominic's words worked their way under his skin. He returned the nine to the holster on his right hip, but he kept his eyes locked on Dominic while he did it.

"How long have you known me, Dominic?" he asked.

"Fo' fockin' evah, yeah?"

"Yeah. But it sounds like you don't know me as well as you should."

"I know you mo' boddah Nalani, I break yo' fockin' neck like not'ing, I promise."

"Why would I bother Nalani?"

"You no got one warrant, Gerry, get da fock outta heah."

"You're probable cause, by definition. I don't need a warrant for you."

"What you mean?"

"Call your fucking *federales,"* Geronimo said as he climbed into the Explorer. "Maybe they can explain it to you." Then he started the rig and let it roll him away from the spot Dominic was standing in, Dominic's bulging muscles and his angry eyes clenching in tandem like one had been told to find the other something to hit.

Geronimo reviewed his encounter with both Rosarios as he drove toward town, but he could make little sense of either. It bothered him that Dominic was bopping around like he didn't have a care in the world—other than the protection of his beautiful daughter—and the beautiful daughter bothered him some more all by herself.

"What the fuck was that all about?" he said, but he was the only one who heard the question so no one hooked an answer to it.

2

Geronimo was late; by the time he found a place to park, his watch pointed at seven straight up. His tardiness was unintentional—he loved Taj Mahal, with or without the mainland bluesman's celebrated interest in island music, and he could think of no finer location in Hilo for the show than the auditorium at the university.

He could blame his delay on the gray-haired woman from the DEA, but it wouldn't be fair—and Robbie was unlikely to give a rip, anyway. The woman had asked Geronimo to observe while the feds interrogated Sonnyboy Akaka, and he had consented even though he could foresee no benefit to anyone from doing so. His premonition had been correct, but he was more curious about the woman now than he had been before—there was something to her he hadn't found in feds previously, and whatever it was genuinely intrigued him.

She had run three teams of agents at Sonnyboy throughout the afternoon, but had not participated in the interrogation herself. Instead, she had taken a seat in the observation room with Geronimo and a few others and observed— although it seemed to Geronimo that she did so on a higher level than the others, himself included.

Actually, Geronimo had spent most of the time with his eyes on the woman rather than Sonnyboy; he had assumed the feds would be in over their collective heads with Sonny, and he lost interest in the interrogation as soon as he confirmed that his assumption was justified.

The woman, however, held up very well under sustained observation. It was nothing physical, whatever it was that attracted him. She was all angles instead of curves, all bones and no meat, and her attitude was unfortunately much the same—nothing soft or endearing there, either. But she had an electric intensity radiating from her that set off sparks in Geronimo, who was thinking about those unusual points of light as he hurried across the parking lot.

Robbie was waiting for him at the ticket entry, a ticket for each of them in his hand. "Sorry," Geronimo said. "This is going to blow your seat selection, Robbie."

"Not," Robbie said with a grin. "I sent the others ahead."

"What others?"

"Our dates, brah."

"Please tell me you're kidding," Geronimo said. "I have way too many women already, Robbie."

"I didn't say anything about *wahines,"* Robbie said, his grin almost jumping off his face. "I got a nice *mahu* fella for you this time."

"One of your castoffs, I suppose."

"Not. That would be way too hard on you."

"I hope you like this fucking concert," Geronimo said as they walked down the side of the packed auditorium, "because you are not going to live through this night."

"What a way to go, yeah?" Robbie said. He stopped when they reached the second row from the front, and Geronimo ran his eyes down that row when he got to it. There were two empty seats at dead solid center, a guy Geronimo didn't know on one side of them and a woman he was quite familiar with on the other.

Geronimo was immediately torn between saying something appropriately sharp to Robbie or wringing his scrawny neck, but the house lights started coming down and he didn't have a decent shot at either of those options. What he did instead was hustle down the row until he reached the seat next to Denise.

"This is John," Robbie said behind him, and Geronimo turned and shook the hand John was extending in his direction. "This is Geronimo, John."

"You have my sincerest condolences," Geronimo said softly as he leaned over to embrace Robbie's date.

"I think you know Denise," Robbie said, also softly, motioning in the opposite direction. Geronimo turned that way and settled into his seat just as the band came on the stage.

"Did you know?" Geronimo whispered. Denise shook her head slightly, a small smile lurking around the edges of her mouth. Someone came out to introduce Taj Mahal, but Geronimo continued to look directly at his wife. He tried to remember a moment when she had looked more beautiful, but none came to mind.

Geronimo did glance at the stage when Taj Mahal kicked into his first song, which the old bluesman did with a characteristic flourish, and Geronimo discovered quickly that he was twice blessed—both the performers and the audience knew what they were there for and got right to it.

Or maybe Geronimo was thrice blessed, because he also had Denise in the next seat and Denise seemed on the verge of setting that seat on fire all night. Taj Mahal was threatening the same thing on the stage, so Geronimo kept his eyes moving from the musician throwing down an electric vibe to the woman next to him receiving it like it had belonged to her all along.

Denise was wearing a short, sleeveless shift that allowed ample amounts of her to spill out of it at both ends, a situation Geronimo found himself enjoying in a way simultaneously fresh and familiar. He brushed against the long brown arm next to him occasionally, and he wanted to do the same to the long brown leg draped over a knee and keeping perfect time with the music. Both of these limbs had the same fine skin over musculature with just the right amount of tone, and it wasn't long before Geronimo was recalling occasions when they both had been wrapped around him lovingly.

What the fuck ever happened to those days? Geronimo wondered, but the answer came to him almost immediately and he tried to think of something else. The music helped in that regard, because the headliner was not the only capable musician on the stage. Taj Mahal's Hula Blues Band was eight players deep, including one who frequently played two instruments simultaneously, and they kicked ass from one end of the show to the other.

Near the end of the performance, however, the music brought Geronimo directly back to the thoughts he was trying to escape. "Shouldn't nobody still be sittin' in their seats," the singer said in the middle of a particularly funky groove, and women all over the room jumped to their feet in response.

One of them was Denise, who knew how to move and immediately began to demonstrate some of that knowledge. It was a restrained performance, Geronimo knew from sweet experience, but the restraint did nothing to obscure the fiery potential beneath it. Denise let her hips roll to the beat, but only slightly, and her arms and shoulders moved with the same subdued abandon as her hips. Geronimo leaned back in his seat and savored the sight, even though it reminded him of how far from grace he had fallen.

Everyone in the auditorium had risen by the time the band played its final note, and Geronimo imagined everyone was filing outside through the crowd waiting for the second show with a sense of satisfaction similar to his own.

"Gonna kill me now, brah?" Robbie asked as the four of them strolled toward the parking lot.

"Nah," Geronimo said. "It was so good I think I'll just hurt you really bad."

"Thought you might like it," Robbie said, but he didn't have much more to say after that—he and John seemed anxious to continue their date at another location. After a moment or two more, Denise and Geronimo were alone.

The pavement in the parking lot was wet, but the sky was mostly clear and the night air warm. "Let me walk you to your car," Geronimo said.

"No need," Denise said quietly. "I can find my own way, you know."

"Yeah," Geronimo said. "I do know that. Let me do it anyway."

"Not," she said. "If I walk away, maybe you'll see something you're fockin' gonna miss."

"I saw that all night, Denise."

"Good," she said, and then she did walk away, her hips rolling just the right amount under the thin shift and her long brown legs stretching enticingly all the way to the ground.

Jeezus Christ, you fucking idiot, Geronimo said to himself as he watched her go. *Is this really what you fucking want?*

3

Geronimo was the fifth blue light to pull into Dominic's driveway, and Ralph piloted the sixth one in right behind him.

"Looks like a cop convention, yeah?" Ralph said when they were both out of their cars and walking toward a crime scene illuminated haphazardly with headlights and whatever spilled out of Dominic's carport.

"Yeah," Geronimo said glumly, swiping the back of his right hand across the light sweat breaking out on his forehead in spite of the cool night air.

"I thought you said Buddy was gonna think about holdin' off," Ralph said.

"He did."

"You call this holdin' off?"

"He did say that," Geronimo said. "Not even twenty-four hours ago, as a matter of fact."

"Shoulda done it, brah," Ralph said, and Geronimo answered that with a silent shrug. They walked to the edge of the small throng that had already accumulated in the vicinity of the body, but neither of them spent much time peering at Buddy Kai's remains.

"Jeezus," Ralph said, which about summed it up for Geronimo, too. Geronimo turned his focus to Dominic and the two feds standing next to him in the front of the carport—the same pair of feds Geronimo and Ralph had ridden with during the fruitless pursuit of Edith Kealoha and her loaded Honda Accord.

"What the fuck are they doing here?" Geronimo said.

"Guess we know for sure who dropped the dime on Buddy," Ralph said as soon as he figured out the objects of Geronimo's comment.

"Was there ever any doubt?" Geronimo said.

"Not," Ralph said. Then he wandered in Dominic's direction, picking a route that didn't disrupt the work being done on the scene, while Geronimo stayed put and watched the activity from where he was standing.

He discovered that he could see a lot from that vantage point—the mass of brains, bone and blood that had once been Buddy's head; the gun clasped in Buddy's lifeless hands; the bullet hole in the side of Dominic's truck; the bloody baseball bat; and the gravel rake laying on the ground between the body and the carport.

A short, muscular detective with a salt-and-pepper brush cut walked up while Geronimo catalogued this information. "Quite a mess, yeah?" he said.

"Hey, Stefano," Geronimo said. "How you been?"

"Up and down," Stefano said. "Right now I'm a little down."

"You the primary?"

"Yeah."

"What's the story?"

"Buddy jumped him, they fought, Buddy lost."

"Pretty hard to argue with any of that."

"No shit."

"Have to wonder how it all played out, though."

"Yeah," Stefano said. "Unfortunately, Dominic's the only one around who can offer a version of that."

"Which is what?"

"Haven't heard all the details yet, actually. Guy was traumatized by the experience, you know. His little nursemaids over there wanted to hold his hand for a while first."

"When did they show up?"

"Before I did."

"He called them first?" Geronimo asked.

"Kinda looks like it," Stefano said.

"Must be nice to have your own nursemaids at a time like this."

"I guess," Stefano said. "It was me, I'd rather suffer on my own than have those fuckers around."

"I heard that."

"Wanna listen in?"

"I'd buy a ticket and wait in line to hear this one."

"No shit? How much would you pay?"

"Please don't make me hurt you," Geronimo said with a grin. "You're already a little down, remember?"

"Come," Stefano said, and Geronimo went. They followed a path similar to Ralph's before them, and when they got to the carport, Geronimo took a close look at Dominic's face. A liberal patina of blood had dried over most of it, and one side of his mouth was noticeably swollen, but Dominic was relatively unscathed—relative to Buddy, for sure.

"You got someplace else to stay?" Stefano asked. "We won't be done here for a while."

"My birds heah," Dominic said. "Wheah I gonna go?"

"You sayin' you give a fuck about these birds?" Geronimo said.

"What you t'ink?" Dominic said. "How I gonna make one livin' wit'out 'em?"

"Right," Geronimo said. "What was I thinking?"

"We'll get him a room downtown," one of the feds said. "Will tonight be enough?"

"Probably," Stefano said. "You ready to make a statement?" The first word was directed at the fed, the rest at Dominic.

"Isn't it obvious what happened?" the fed said.

"I'm sorry," Stefano said, everything directed at the fed now. "I still don't get what this has to do with you."

Dominic was sitting in a canvas chair, his legs stretched out in front of him and his head cradled back against his hands. He had a grin plastered on his face as he moved his eyes back and forth between Stefano and the fed.

"Take my word for it," the fed said. "This has a lot to do with us."

"Fine," Stefano said. "Just keep your mouths shut unless you saw what went down here."

"You know da kine," Dominic said through his grin.

"I know I have a couple of questions," Stefano said.

"Whatevah," Dominic said with a shrug.

"Looks like you kicked the fuckin' shit out of him."

"Dat's one question?"

"The question is how he ended up with the gun in his hands after the beating he took."

"Fockah got some haht, dat's why. No wanna quit."

"So he gave you no choice but to beat his brains in with the bat."

"No choice whatsoevah."

"I guess the bat just happened to be layin' around somewhere handy."

"Lucky, yeah?" Dominic said.

"Yeah," Stefano said. "You always have been one lucky guy."

"Luckiest evah, brah. You don' even know."

"Yeah, well, there's lots of things I don't know," Stefano said, looking first at Ralph and then at Geronimo. "You guys got anything?"

"Where's your daughter?" Geronimo asked after Ralph shook his head slightly.

"Why da fock you ask da kine?" Dominic said, his face starting to turn as red beneath the skin as it had probably been on the outside before the blood on his face had dried.

"Thought maybe she might have seen what happened," Geronimo said quietly.

"She nevah wen see not'ing!"

"Where is she?"

Dominic began to rise out of his chair, but the fed standing closest to him dropped a hand on his shoulder and Dominic settled back down again. "One sleepovah," he said.

"Sounds like she's lucky, too, then," Geronimo said.

"You got anyt'ing else?" Dominic asked.

"Not really," Geronimo said, and Dominic rose from his chair and turned toward the back of the carport with a fed on each side. "Just the rake, is all."

"What?" Dominic said, suddenly turning back in Geronimo's direction.

"The rake," Geronimo said. "I was just wondering what you used the rake for."

"What you t'ink I use it fo'?"

"I wasn't here, Dominic. That's why I'm asking you."

"Why you t'ink you can fock wit' me? I fockin' break yo' neck like not'ing."

"You keep sayin' that."

"Do it, too."

"Like you did poor Buddy here?"

"Not," Dominic said. "Him I beat his fockin' brains out. I go eidah way wit' you, no problem."

"You ever do, it won't go down like this one."

"You t'ink so?"

"I have a gun in my hands like Buddy here, you're gonna have some new holes in your body when it's over."

"Whatevah," Dominic said as he turned in the direction of his door again. "Just fockin' stay away from me."

Ralph and Stefano both looked from Dominic to Geronimo with their eyebrows raised in almost exactly the same way. "Guess you been told, brah," Stefano said.

"Yeah," Geronimo said. "I been told about everything but the fucking gravel rake."

Jesus

Jesus had nothing to do for a moment but think, so he stood near the curb in front of the terminal and let his mind work while Manuel waited for their luggage and Jaime crossed the street to sign out the rental car.

Hilo International Airport, my ass, was the first thing Jesus thought. *Every fockin' flight here starts in Honolulu.* The more he looked around, though, the more he had to acknowledge the convenience that came with the size of the place. *Can fockin' spit from the baggage carousel to the rental car,* he thought next. *Not many places you can say that about.*

But it didn't take Jesus long to get to the third thing he thought, because the first two were throwaways easily cleared out of the way. Jesus actually had only one thing on his mind, and it had been there since the phone call about the bust had reached him in Waikiki. It was the thought that had driven him to hit the next flight to Hilo, and it was the thought turning the wheels in his head as he stood with the sun in his face and waited for the car.

I'm not sure who yet, he said to himself as he focused on his missing drugs, *but someone around here is gonna pay me for my fockin' sheet.*

"You got the guns worked out yet, *ese?*" Manuel said from behind him. Jesus turned slightly to the left and regarded the dark man with the Ray-Bans standing there with the luggage at his feet.

"Si," Jesus said, even though they both knew that he didn't have to explain shit to Manuel. But he also knew Manuel didn't like walking around without some functioning hardware within easy reach, a feeling Jesus completely understood because he felt the same way.

"Ortega's gonna hook us up at the hotel," Jesus added.

"I thought you sent him to the Kona side," Manuel said, referring to the crew Jesus had dispatched from Honolulu as an early precaution the previous week—long before the feds had scored his drugs and forced him to make his own trip to the Big Island.

"I did," Jesus said. "But you can drive all the way around this focker in five hours, homes. The Kona side ain't that far away."

"Bueno," Manuel said, and then they both settled into a still silence that lasted until Jaime drove a Chrysler Sebring up to the curb four or five minutes later.

Buddy

1

Buddy knew something was up with Jay-Jay Johnson as soon as the bespectacled *haole* failed to walk his blond dreadlocks into Ken's House of Pancakes at the agreed-upon time. Not only had Jay-Jay been crying for product all week, but Buddy was buying the breakfast—and Jay-Jay had never passed up a free meal in his life.

The no-show meant Buddy had to find Jay-Jay, but he didn't race right out of the restaurant to do it. He finished eating slowly, turning this development over in his mind while he chewed on his food.

He started by imagining what he would do in Dominic's position, and after a couple of minutes he knew what was going on.

The fockin' troops are already restless, he said to himself, certain that Jay-Jay—and who knew how many others—was lining up with Dominic for product.

Once Buddy got out on the road, Jay-Jay turned out to be only two stops away. Buddy came up empty at Dotty's down by the water, but Jay-Jay was jitterbugging across the parking lot at Don's Grill like a mongoose on hot lava when Buddy pulled in there. They immediately moved in opposite directions, Buddy with an eye on getting out of his car and Jay-Jay focused on getting into his.

Buddy was the quicker of the two—he caught Jay-Jay at the door of a white Suburban and immediately slammed him off the side of the car. Jay-Jay tried to roll into a ball as soon as he hit the ground, but Buddy grabbed a handful of dreadlocks with one hand and the seat of Jay-Jay's surfer shorts with the other and bounced him head-first off the side of the Suburban again. He repeated this maneuver twice more, denting the door significantly and slightly changing its color, but after that he lost interest in it.

Jay-Jay was piled in a heap on the ground, and the first thing he saw after spitting the blood out of his mouth was the redesign of his door. "Fuck, Buddy," he said. "Look what you did to my ride!"

Buddy looked, but didn't feel compelled to say anything about what he had done to Jay-Jay's ride.

"Couldn't you have fuckin' bounced my head off the ground or something?" Jay-Jay asked.

"Still can, you know," Buddy said.

"What's the point? We already know you can kick my ass."

"You didn't give me a choice, Jay-Jay. What'd you think was gonna happen?"

"I gotta have product, Buddy."

"What? You think you're an independent contractor? You're workin' for me, you stupid fockah."

"I ain't workin' at all without product."

"Got your product, brah. Gimme the money, and everything's cool."

"What are you talking about? I gave the money to Rosario's guy, and he gave me the shit!"

"You wanna use Dominic's shit, Jay-Jay, fine with me. Just gimme my money."

"I can't pay twice for the same shit!"

"Sure you can. Three times, too, or four or whatevah the fock I say."

Jay-Jay ran out of words at that point. He stared up at Buddy through glasses that had somehow remained intact throughout the close encounter with the Suburban's door, and the sight of those glasses sitting there undisturbed infuriated Buddy so suddenly that he kicked Jay-Jay in the face before he had a conscious thought of doing it. The glasses flew one way and Jay-Jay's head the other, his head dragging the rest of him behind it like a last-minute addition to the process.

"Would you fucking stop, Buddy?" Jay-Jay said. "Jesus Christ!"

"Give me your cash," Buddy said.

"I have a lot more than I fucking owe you!"

"Not," Buddy said. "I'm chargin' fockin mileage for chasing you all ovah town."

"The town ain't that fucking big, Buddy."

"Maybe you should remember that," Buddy said as he snatched the cash from Jay-Jay's hand, "you fockin' try to run on me again." Then he put the cash in his pocket, returned to his rig, and slowly drove past the old Japanese couple standing at the door of the restaurant with their mouths open.

2

Buddy rolled up on the house he had been raised in around noon, even though he knew he would regret it long before he left. *Fockin' regret it now,* he said to himself as he stopped in front of the carport.

The house was nothing special, although it easily could have been. Buddy had offered to remodel the dump so many times he had been tempted to record the offer for easy replay, but his mother refused to even consider the idea.

Buddy got hot every time he thought about it, but he knew his anger really had nothing to do with his mother, so he always tried to turn it in another direction. The house was actually his, of course, because he was more than a quarter Hawaiian and his mother was less than that; it had been passed down to him after his half-Hawaiian father died.

Hawaiian homelands my fockin' ass, he thought, the Department of Hawaiian Homelands being the source of the blood restrictions on the property. *The whole fockin' island's my homeland, you know.*

So the house was essentially the same as it had been during Buddy's childhood, only older and more worn down. Just like most of the houses on their street, Buddy noticed every time he made this trip. And on every other street in Keaukaha, for that matter, Keaukaha being a little slice of worn-down paradise carved out for native Hawaiians between the airport and the beach—not including the actual beachfront property, of course.

Buddy's mother was a lot like the house—essentially the same as she had been during his childhood, only older and more worn down. He could have alleviated that to some degree and wanted to, but his mother was nothing if not consistent—she refused to take a dime of drug money from him, and every dime Buddy had to his name was drug money.

Buddy's mother was hanging wet laundry on the lines stretched across the carport, lines Buddy had offered to replace with a dryer more times than he could count. He leaned against the front of his rig and watched her work for a moment.

A lot of the laundry would have fit a five-year-old boy, which was no coincidence—a five-year-old boy was the only reason Buddy ever made this trip. "He in the house?" Buddy asked finally.

His mother nodded as she continued to work, shaking each garment briskly and then pinning it to the line. She was a small woman, much more Chinese than Hawaiian from the outside but actually the opposite from the inside looking out.

"Has his mother been by?" Buddy asked, and his mother responded with another nod. Buddy couldn't stand the boy's mother anymore, but he knew he was lucky with her—she loved their boy and never failed to show it, even though she was incapable of caring for him.

Not that Buddy's capabilities in that department were much greater, which is why the boy was with Buddy's mother. Buddy was lucky there, too, although the fact that his mother refused to speak to him as long as he continued in the drug business significantly dampened his enthusiasm for that arrangement.

Buddy was about to move inside the house when the boy bounced out. He was a chunky kid with intelligent, cautious eyes that saw most of what was going on around him and sent the message that he regarded it all carefully. He wandered through the hanging laundry until he saw Buddy, and then he stopped moving and started seeing and regarding for all he was worth.

"Howzit, brah?" Buddy asked after he had absorbed as much of the boy's careful consideration as he could stand.

"Good," the boy said, moving as he spoke until he was standing in front of his father. Buddy reached down and picked him up effortlessly, the boy settling into the crook of Buddy's left arm like it had been built for him.

"Peanut butter for lunch, yeah?" Buddy said as he kissed the boy on the forehead.

"How you know?" the boy asked.

"Missed some, that's why," Buddy said. He wet the tip of his right thumb and swiped away the smudge from the boy's lunch lingering on his cheek, the boy dodging under the assault in a futile effort to escape.

"That tickles, you know," the boy said.

"Yeah," Buddy said, "I know. You been good for Tutu?"

"Yeah," the boy said, and Buddy believed it; this was a very good boy.

"Then get in the car," Buddy said. "Take you for one ride." He lowered the boy back to the ground, and the boy did the rest on his own. He was belted into the backseat a moment later, ready to roll.

"Be back soon," Buddy said to his mother, who had finished with the laundry and was standing there with one hand on her hip and the other holding the empty laundry basket.

His mother nodded silently, but Buddy saw the flash of something warm in her dark eyes. *It's not gonna get any better than that,* he said to himself as he climbed behind the wheel of his rig, closed the door, and backed out of the driveway his father had graveled back in the days when his father was still alive and his mother still spoke to him.

3

Buddy reached under his seat for his .45 as soon as he saw the open gate, so the gun was already in his hand when he parked next to the rental car in his driveway and climbed out of his rig.

"What did you do to my dog?" he asked.

"Had to shoot him," Jesus said. "Focker wouldn't back off at all."

Buddy could hear Jesus better than he could see him, Jesus leaning in the dark against the pole supporting a basketball hoop

Buddy had stuck in the ground a couple of years earlier. But Buddy didn't like what he could hear any better than he liked what he could see.

"Who the fock you think you are?" he asked.

"I'm the messenger," Jesus said. "You have until Monday, *ese.*"

"Or what?" Buddy said.

"Or you get what I gave your dog."

"You're gonna be lucky if you're still breathing by then, you know."

"It don't have to be me, *amigo.* There's lots of guys where I came from."

Buddy sagged a little under the weight of those words, which he knew to be true. But they weren't the only true words he knew, so he linked a few together for a message of his own.

"You kill me Monday," he said, "you're gonna lose the fockin' money."

"True," Jesus said. "But all your fren's will know not to fock with us."

"They're not the ones fockin' with you," Buddy said. "You wanna send that message, hit the moddafockah dropped the dime."

"You wanna take the lead on that, *ese,* we might give you a little more time on the cash."

"How much?"

"Friday, maybe."

"You make a lot of decisions for a messenger, Jesus."

"Everything was decided long ago, homes. Don' you know that?"

"Not everything," Buddy said, putting a little wiggle into the .45 in his hand. "I'm decidin' right now how much longer you're gonna live."

"Not really," Jesus said, and two more figures drifted into Buddy's peripheral vision while Jesus said it, one at the corner of the house nearest the driveway and the other from the far side of the rental car. "All you're decidin' there is how long you're gonna live."

"You owe me for the dog, you know," Buddy said.

"Fair enough. Subtract it from the total."

"Where is he?"

"Up by the gate."

"I'm takin' off fo' the chain lock, too," Buddy said.

"Fine."

"Plus I need another shipment, Jesus."

"You make it through next week, that would be a possibility."

"This is all part of takin' on the Japs, you know. You can't put it all on me."

"We know," Jesus said. "But you gotta be able to handle this sheet, homes, or we gotta go another direction."

"Can so far," Buddy said, "but there's a lot more comin'."

"We know that," Jesus said. "You handle this end, we'll do what needs to be done at the other end."

"Shoulda done it already, you know."

"Whatever," Jesus said with a shrug.

"I'm pissed about the dog, I promise," Buddy said.

"I know," Jesus said. "I didn't do it, the focker be hangin' from my throat right now."

"Fine with me."

"See you Monday or Friday, depending," Jesus said.

"Likewise."

"No," Jesus said. "That's what you got to remember, homes. You'll only see me if it's Friday." Then he walked away from the hoop, crossed the driveway, and climbed into the back seat of the rental car. His two companions took the front seats, and a moment later Buddy was standing alone in front of his carport. He watched without moving until the car was no longer visible, then traded his .45 for a shovel and headed slowly up the driveway toward his gate. "One of us fockin' goin' down, Dominic," he said, spilling the words into the night air even though he was the only one around who could hear them. "Who da fock you t'ink I gonna choose?"

Kapuanani

1

Kapuanani knew exactly what she wanted and exactly where to go to get it, but knowing this and doing it were two totally different things.

It all could have been so much easier—if Jolene would answer her phone, if Nalani were not due to arrive in a couple of hours, if Kapua had some fucking money for a change and didn't need to deal with Jay-Jay, or if Jay-Jay hadn't put this bullshit prohibition on her. But none of these conditions had been met so far, and the clock was ticking.

Of course, Kapua could abandon her plan to get crushed at Pono's party that night, which would pull the plug on the whole problem. But Kapua had no intention of doing that—none, zip, zero, absolutely out of the question. She had been looking forward to this high all week, and waiting any longer was totally unfair, totally wrong, totally impossible.

She tried Jolene's number again, but that phone was no more in service now than it had been earlier. She looked at her watch again, and at her mother's car in the driveway, and at the keys on the kitchen table that went with her mother's car in the driveway. Then she punched in a different number on her phone.

"Hey, princess," Jay-Jay said into her ear after the fourth ring. "Wassup?" This threw her off-stride for a moment, him knowing who was calling, until she realized his phone had identified her.

"You got something today?" she asked, rushing to get it out before she lost her nerve.

"Of course," Jay-Jay said. "Just send Jolene over to pick it up."

"Actually," she said, "I can't get her on the phone."

"No problem. I'll be around later on."

"Only thing is, I need to get it now, that's why."

"Oh," Jay-Jay said, his voice getting sad on her. "That's not so good."

Kapua took a deep breath as soon as she noticed that she was standing there without breathing, but her voice was freezing in her chest and she wasn't sure what to say even if her voice thawed out.

"You know how much you want to get your hands on some shit right now?" Jay-Jay said.

"Yeah," Kapua said, because she knew what to say to that and her voice was still flexible enough to wrap around one word at a time.

"That's what it's gonna be like for me if I see you, princess. Fuck—that's how I feel right now, just talking to you on the phone. I'm getting hard here just off the sound of your voice. Believe me, you don't want to be here. I'm not cool when I'm like this."

"I know," she said, which she did; he had explained most of this before, when the bullshit prohibition was introduced.

"If you come over," he said, his voice trailing off a little before it came back. "Well, that's just not fair to me, Kapua. You can hit the shit you get from me to get the high you want, but nothing on this earth can do that for me except you."

Fockin' bullshit, she thought, which is what she had said from the beginning, but the thought began to turn on her as she stood there with the phone to her ear—unless it had started turning even before she had dialed his number.

Maybe it's kinda sweet, you think about it, she said to herself.

"Sorry, princess," he said. "You reach Jolene in time, send her over, and I'll fix you up."

Jay-Jay was nothing but nice to her, that's for sure—he hadn't asked for a dime, hadn't asked for anything in exchange for the shit he gave her. The only exception was this prohibition on coming around in person, which he needed because seeing her just drove him crazy. How bad was that, really?

Maybe give him something, she thought. *Nothing much, nothing complicated. How hard could that be?*

"Are you still there, princess?" he asked.

"Yeah," she said.

"It's all up to you," he said softly. "You are totally in charge, you know."

He's nothing but nice to me, yeah? she thought. *Maybe give him something.*

"Can't do too much, you know," she said, finding it not quite as hard to say as she had imagined. "Anything," he said. "Whatever you say, Kapua, whatever you're comfortable with. I'm like a fucking kid over here."

I've gone with plenty of kids before, she said to herself. *How hard could this possibly be?*

"Can trust you, yeah?" she asked.

"You know you can," he said.

"I'm comin' over, then," she said, her mind already racing ahead to Pono's party. *Gonna fockin' be flyin' tonight,* she thought as she picked up the keys to her mother's car in the driveway and walked out the door.

2

Kapua barely got the car back in the driveway before her mother and her mother's boyfriend returned, and those two barely got back before Nalani rolled in.

Kapua tried to avoid her mother's boyfriend as much as possible because the sight of him turned her stomach. He was always all over her mother, and how her mother could stand it was something Kapua had yet to figure out.

Fock it, Kapua thought. *Gonna fockin' be flyin' tonight, I promise.*

Jay-Jay had been exceedingly generous; in addition to the ice for tonight, she had two jumbo joints to help her get through the afternoon—provided she could keep Nalani from freaking out on her long enough to enjoy the fucking grass. *Didn't do a thing for it, either,* she thought, her recollections of the scene with Jay-Jay actually warm and fuzzy. Well, she did something, sure, but not much—nothing, really. Jay-Jay had wanted to kiss her, and she had let him do that for a while even though his face was all busted to hell and she had no desire to kiss him back. After the while was over, that changed—Jay-Jay could fucking kiss, and Kapua had no trouble getting into it after a while.

Then Jay-Jay had wanted to touch her breasts, and when his hands began to slide under her shirt she let them wander freely for another while. Jay-Jay could fucking touch, too, and after that while she had no objection when her shirt and bra were out of the way and he was suckling her breasts like his life depended on them—avid, yeah, eager like the teenagers she knew, but somehow soft and fluttery at the same time in a way far beyond anything she had experienced before.

After all of these whiles had passed, Kapua's skin was tingling and she was aching for something between her legs. Still, she brushed Jay-Jay's hand away when he moved it there, and he honored that just like he had said he would. He went back to her breasts with renewed conviction, and she rode on top of that warm stimulation until time ran out on her.

Jay-Jay had been glowing when she lifted his head away from her chest. "*Mahalo,* princess," he said, and Kapua knew he meant it. He had watched her get dressed avidly, too, like she was good to the very last glimpse, and Kapua smiled to herself as she recalled the look on his face.

"What are you thinking?" Nalani asked. She was sprawled across Kapua's bed, watching closely as Kapua fussed with her hair in front of the long, skinny mirror leaning against her bedroom wall as though waiting for someone to come by to fix the crack that ran down the middle of it.

"Nothing," Kapua said, alarmed that her thoughts were not quite as private as she had imagined.

"You look like the cat that ate the canary," Nalani said. "Nothing, my *okole.*"

Kapua turned toward her guest, her critical eyes drawn directly to the *okole* in question. Nalani was on her stomach now, her long brown legs streaming perfectly from a pair of shorts that accentuated a butt Kapua would have killed for. Kapua was plenty fine, she knew, but she could see that her own dimensions were a little too thick to match the standard set by her flawless friend.

Fockin' fat, she thought. *Gonna lose it, I promise.*

"Got something to show you," Kapua said. "Come." She led the way out of her room, through the overstuffed living room and out the front door, a path that avoided the *lanai* where her mother and the disgusting boyfriend were tag-teaming a short case of Bud Light.

They walked down the driveway side by side, past the house in front of Kapua's and all the way to the road. They turned to the right for a block or so, then veered off to a small clump of pine trees when they reached an overgrown stretch of lots without houses.

"What?" Nalani said. "You killin' me ovah heah." Kapua removed a plastic container from her purse, the container used for tampons in a previous life but perfect for its new function. She popped the lid and carefully drew out one of the joints, then replaced the lid and returned the container to her purse.

"Nice, eh?" she said, brandishing the joint like a prize.

Nalani's face began to turn to stone right before Kapua's eyes. "Where did you get that stuff?" Nalani asked.

"One guy I know," Kapua said. "Jolene hooked me up."

"Jolene's a loser," Nalani said. "How did you pay for it?"

"Not," Kapua said, the heat coming up in her cheeks as she said it. "I didn't have to."

"Sooner or later, you're paying something, I promise."

"Not everybody is a fockin' queen like you, you know," Kapua said. "Some of us need this shit."

"Whatevah," Nalani said. "Who is this guy?"

"Jay-Jay," Kapua said, watching closely for a sign that the name meant something to her friend but seeing none.

"I can't believe this," Nalani said.

"You're the fockin' All-Star, Lani. You're the one playin' summer ball. Why can't I smoke it?"

"You can, you know," Nalani said. "You can do whatevah you like, Kapua. Why would I care what you do?"

"I thought you were my friend, that's why."

"A friend would tell you to flush that shit. But no way are you gonna listen to that, yeah? What else did this Jay-Jay give you?"

"Nothing! Just the weed, I promise!"

"Why are you lying? I'm not your mother, Kapua."

"Then why are you on my fockin' case like one mother!" Kapua asked, even though she knew the answer.

Nalani didn't reply; she stood there in the trees behind her hard face without a word for a while. Then she moved around Kapua and strode back to the street, Kapua standing alone in her wake with the unlit joint still in her hand.

Jay-Jay

"God, how I love this game!" Jay-Jay said as he put the phone on his table and picked up the bag of ice—this ice the kind made out of frozen water—and applied it to his battered face. "She's coming over."

"Can turn my fockin' phone back on, yeah?" Jolene said.

"By all means," Jay-Jay said, grinning in spite of the fact that the slightest contortion of his face hurt like hell. "You were right about today—she really wants it bad."

"Whatevah," Jolene said, more than ready to move on to the next phase of this operation. "You fockin' sick, you know."

"Oh, yeah," Jay-Jay said. "Gloriously so."

"Can cop heah?" Jolene asked, brandishing a small baggie filled with the kind of ice that only melts in front of a flame.

"Hell, no," Jay-Jay said. "You need to get the fuck out of here. I don't want to spook my little princess this early in the game."

Jolene was out the door a moment later, and Jay-Jay's painful grin spread even wider as he watched her go. *God is so very, very good,* he thought. *He put that fucking beating on me this morning, sure, but now He sends the sweetest of all balms to soothe me.*

Jay-Jay knew he could have scored this princess the first night he had seen her. Pop her the right pill and he could have done anything he wanted to her. But this way was the very best—this way was foreplay, really, extended over weeks instead of minutes, a mind game as well as a physical one, and so much more delicious for it!

What a wonderful fucking business this is, he thought as he began to prepare for the next phase in the protracted unveiling of precious Princess Kapua.

Nalani

1

Nalani had a reputation for religion that she cultivated carefully. She didn't believe in God, of course—the non-existence of some benign higher power had been proven dramatically during her lifetime and was regularly reconfirmed—but she loved the Catholic rituals she had learned from her mother, and she adhered to them faithfully.

This was more than a tribute to her mother's memory, however. The church was part of the wall she had built between herself and the boys who churned around her like starving sharks, and it had functioned reasonably well. *That's a sin,* she had always been able to say. *Why would you ask me to do that?*

Ironically, her father was the other part of that wall. Nalani had a keen appreciation of this irony—the antichrist combining with the Catholic Church to keep her pure in her relations with the boys lusting for her, her father playing the part of fanatical single parent devoted to his daughter's moral sanctity as though born to the role. He had been reasonably effective, too, his intimidating presence alone enough to curtail the number of boys in the hunt.

This screen filtered out the least challenging of the boys first, unfortunately, leaving only the strongest and most confident: the ones treated like minor deities, the ones accustomed to getting whatever they wanted, the leaders of the pack. Boys like Pono, who had finally risen to the status of serious problem. Nalani had nothing against Pono; actually, she liked him. And she hadn't really minded the way they had been dancing around each other since the onset of puberty, she the undisputed queen of their circle and he the king, but the two of them never quite aligned as Nalani skillfully played her father and her devotion to her church to keep him at bay.

Pono hadn't waited for her, of course, but neither had he ever lost interest in her. Every time he was rebuffed, he moved off in another direction, but when he eventually came back, he was stronger than he had been the time before. Now Pono was loose again, and Nalani had no illusions about who would be the total focus of his attention if she attended his party tonight.

Which everyone wanted her to do, just as everyone in their circle actually wanted her and Pono to hook up. Even the boys and girls each of them had turned away wanted this, as though only the union of Pono and Nalani would explain to the satisfaction of all why the others had been found wanting.

Nalani pondered the question of Pono and the new information about the policeman with the funny name while she drove toward the same church she had attended with her mother, the object of the drive this time her weekly confession. Not that Nalani ever actually confessed her sins, the confessions just another set of things that had to be handled with care. But she missed this weekly ritual no more frequently than her mother had before her; she derived a feeling of constancy from the experience and some vague satisfaction from the meaningless penances imposed on her for her fabricated transgressions. About the cop, Nalani was uncertain what to think. Was it good or bad to have Geronimo Souza struck speechless in front of her? One thing Nalani knew for sure—a member of the drug task force was extremely vulnerable to her right now. But vulnerable how? There was something different in the vibe than she was used to, something unfamiliar.

What is that all about? she asked herself. *Wassup with Geronimo Souza?*

2

Now what? Nalani wondered. She had spent most of the afternoon in the water at Richardson's and most of the evening watching the light drain out of the sky on the beach, but now it was time to move. Go to the fockin' party? Go home? Go somewhere else?

The thing with Kapua bothered her very little as far as Kapua herself was concerned. The two were considered the closest of friends by the people they knew, but Nalani knew better—she had no real feelings for Kapua and little concern for what Kapua did or did not do. But Nalani was more than bothered by the possible significance of Kapua's new fascination with drugs in her own careful life—no, bothered was not nearly the word. Another last thing she needed was to get tripped up by someone else's drug use.

Nalani was a sponge for information about her father's business dealings, and she had absorbed a lot of that information during the past three years. Her father had no inkling of this, which had been Nalani's desire; she believed knowledge was a powerful thing and should be hoarded like precious stones. Consequently, she knew her father's real income was not derived from raising fighting cocks, which meant she knew that consumers like Kapua were underwriting her own standard of living. But she avoided drugs with the same dedication she would devote to outrunning a *tsunami*—she had no intention of ever getting caught up in those roiling waters. And now that Kapua was obviously getting her feet wet, Nalani needed to cut the connection between herself and Kapua immediately and irreversibly.

But how, exactly? A split of this magnitude would reverberate through their circle in ways difficult to predict and control, so the question of how to manage it had burned in Nalani's mind since the moment she had left Kapua standing in the pine trees with a fat one in her hand.

It was seven straight up by the time she saw what she had to do, which was still plenty of time to switch gears and get ready for Pono's party. It was simple, really, nothing but the most natural of wedges between two girls in their world—what Nalani needed now, for the first time in her life, was a boyfriend.

The first step in Nalani's new direction was actually a step back, but she had no difficulty with that apparent contradiction. She knew that the shortest distance between two points was rarely a straight line—or perhaps that the straight lines, while shorter, were rarely navigable.

Nalani pointed the Datsun in Kapua's direction and got on her phone. "What do you want?" Kapua said when the phone stopped ringing, her voice strained as though coming from another archipelago entirely.

"Sorry, girl," Nalani said. "I was just freakin' out, that's why. You gonna forgive me?"

"You hurt me, you know," Kapua said.

"Sorry, sistah. Really, I promise."

"Where are you?"

"Keaukaha-side," Nalani said, "but I'm comin' ovah, yeah?"

"You bettah," Kapua said, her voice back to normal almost, the reconstruction of the facade Nalani wanted well underway.

"I'll be there in ten minutes, fifteen max," Nalani said into the phone, but what she said to herself was this: *Fool Kapua, fockin' fool 'em all, you know.*

Nalani's estimate was accurate—twelve minutes later, she and Kapua were embracing in front of the mirror with the crack down the middle, Nalani selling it hard and Kapua buying.

"You lookin' good, girl," Nalani said when they finished, an appraisal she knew would be shared by everyone they saw that night. Although Kapua's basic outfit would be replicated many times at the party, not many girls would wear it with such telling effect—Kapua's long legs made the short skirt particularly enticing and her tight midriff actually looked good exposed by the skimpy halter.

"You think so?" Kapua asked, a look in her eyes telling Nalani that Kapua wasn't able to read the message in the mirror on her own.

"No way I'm walkin' in with you, I promise," Nalani said, which brought a smile to Kapua's face even though she knew Nalani need fear juxtaposition to no one. "Get in the fockin' shower," Kapua said. "I'm ready to pah-tay!"

3

Pono's party was rolling full throttle at Mana's house in Kurtistown rather than Pono's in Panaewa because Mana was the one with parents in Honolulu for the weekend. Nalani walked in with Kapua, in spite of her proclamation to the contrary, and the two of them turned every head in their vicinity, male as well as female, the perspectives somewhat different according to gender but the interest equally profound either way.

Nalani and Kapua surfed expertly along the curl of this attention from the front door of the house all the way to the back edge of the long lot. They greeted everyone they knew with warm cordiality, male or female, and were greeted in return the same way.

'Gotta go pee," Kapua said as they entered the house for the second time, a pronouncement Nalani had been expecting but didn't believe. "Be right back."

Nalani nodded and kept moving, skirting the makeshift dance floor filled with couples freaking to hip-hop music. *She's gonna hit something, I promise,* Nalani said to herself as she scanned the room for a glimpse of Pono.

Nalani didn't like the music or the dancing that went with it, the former too devoid of melody and the latter too close to what she had to do on her bed with Dominic, but her survey of the crowd seemed to indicate that she was in a minority of one. The beat by itself was enough for everyone else, everyone grinding to it as though orgasm might be just around the next verse.

She didn't see Pono during her initial scan, and she wouldn't have seen him during the second if the crowd hadn't shifted a little at just the right time. Melanie Ferraro was flat on her back on the floor, Pono looming over her on his hands while their hips moved together in time to the music. Nalani watched until the throng shifted again and she could no longer see the couple.

"Want a beeah?" Mana said at her elbow, leaning in close to her ear to be heard through the din of the music.

"No, thanks," Nalani said, using the same technique as Mana.

"Pono's gonna be glad you're here," Mana said.

"It's gonna be hard for him to notice," Nalani said.

"Not," Mana said with a grin. "They gotta come up for air sooner or later."

"Sooner is better then later, I promise."

"Get some *pupus,* yeah?" Mana said with a grin. "I'll tell him you're here."

Nalani drifted in the direction of the table piled high with finger food on the *lanai,* but for some reason the thought of eating turned her stomach. Three or four minutes later, Pono showed up at her side.

"Hey," he said softly, looking down on her from his six feet plus an inch or two with what Nalani guessed was sincere appreciation.

"Hey," she said, but she didn't look up at him the same way he was looking down at her. Pono noticed this and smiled broadly in response, an expression Nalani had to admit looked very good on him.

"That Melanie can really freak, yeah?" he said.

"Way better then me, you know," Nalani said. "I'm never gonna do that, Pono."

"And Melanie's never gonna be you, girl."

"Good one," Nalani said through a smile of her own. "Give you one point for that one."

"How many points I gonna need?"

"I'll let you know when you have enough."

"Gonna keep track of your points, then?"

"No need," Nalani said. "I have plenty of points already."

Pono laughed at that, a warm and musical sound that Nalani had always liked and especially liked at that particular moment.

"You gonna be one trip, Nalani," Pono said when his laughter subsided enough to allow speech.

"You have no idea," Nalani said. She reached toward him with her right hand, and when he responded by extending his left, she led him off the *lanai* and into the yard. They strolled aimlessly hand-in-hand, responding politely to the approval emanating from the friends they encountered along their way, until they eventually found a space they could momentarily call their own.

"You nevah been kissed, yeah?" Pono said when they stopped moving.

"How do you know that?" Nalani asked.

"You've been waitin' for me."

"You get a minus one for that. You're back to zero, I promise."

"Not," Pono said. "Give you one kiss, gonna get double points, you know."

"Double minus, maybe."

Pono laughed out loud again, warm and quiet in the space next to Nalani, and then he leaned toward her face. She ducked her head at the last moment, and he kissed her on the side of her nose.

"I don't know anything, Pono," she said.

"Yeah," he said, cupping her chin gently with his right hand and tipping her face upwards a little. "Gonna teach you everything." Then he leaned toward her again and kissed her softly on the lips.

Fockin' boys, Nalani thought as she returned Pono's kiss a little. *It's a good thing they don't know how fockin' funny they are.*

Dominic

Dominic's run of good fortune was tested twice Saturday night, once early and once late. The first test came at Aurelio's dice game, where Dominic couldn't hit shit with the bones and had to settle for putting a dent in Francisco Gomez's face for laughing out loud when Francisco should have kept his fucking mouth shut.

Dominic was consequently in a foul mood when he found Buddy Kai in his driveway later that night. "Da fock you want?" he said as he climbed out of his truck.

"Your fockin' ass," Buddy said, which turned out to be a couple of words too many. As soon as he got a glimpse of the .45 in Buddy's hand, Dominic dropped like he'd already been shot. The gun coughed through a silencer and the bullet pinged the side of the truck, but Dominic hit the ground rolling and swept Buddy's feet out from under him before Buddy got off another shot.

Buddy was nimble-footed, but the gun popped loose and skittered under the truck while he scrambled to regain his balance. When they both came up empty-handed, Dominic broke into a grin.

"You focked now, you know," he said, but Buddy was initially unconvinced. He came in with two short lefts and a very good right, but Dominic waded through all three of the blows until he was close enough to wrap Buddy in a bear hug.

Once he had his arms around Buddy, Dominic began to squeeze the air out of him. He continued to grin as he watched Buddy struggle against the pressure, but when the process began to seem too slow Dominic slammed the top of his forehead into the bridge of Buddy's nose.

Blood sprayed in Dominic's face, but that only encouraged him to follow immediately with another shot just like the first one. When Buddy's eyes glazed over, Dominic dropped him on the ground and squatted next to him.

"Wake up," he said softly, and then he waited patiently while Buddy's eyes slowly cleared.

"No done wit' you yet, you know," he said. Buddy rolled up on his hands and knees, then struggled to his feet. Dominic rose with him, and when they were both standing again he ripped a short left into Buddy's midsection. Dominic had his hip in the blow and it knocked loose whatever air Buddy had accumulated while on the ground. Buddy dropped like loose laundry, his body suddenly lost inside his clothes.

"Get up," Dominic said, squatting again. "Show me you got

some fockin' haht." Buddy's eyes were the only part of him that responded, but Dominic noted the heat there with approval. "Dat's right," he said. "Dat's what we wanna see, yeah?"

Dominic stood and walked into his carport, where he rummaged around for a minute or two. He came back out with an aluminum baseball bat in one hand and a gravel rake in the other. He leaned the bat against the side of his truck and used the rake to chase Buddy's gun back where Buddy could get his hands on it again.

Not that Buddy's hands were up to a function of that complexity at first. Dominic had to wait for what seemed like several minutes before Buddy actually reached for the gun, and then he had to wait some more while Buddy fumbled around with it.

His patience was finally rewarded, however, and Buddy eventually had both hands wrapped around the weapon. At that point, Dominic picked up the bat and tried his best to grand-slam Buddy's head from the driveway to the carport. He fell considerably short of that objective—Buddy's head refused to abandon the rest of Buddy's body and consequently didn't go very far at all—but Dominic tried once more just in case. When he met with essentially the same result, he dropped the bat on what remained of Buddy Kai and reached for his cell phone. He punched in a number and waited.

"Yes?" someone said.

"Dis da drug bitch, yeah?" Dominic said.

"Are you trying to hurt my feelings, Dominic," the someone said, "or are you just retarded?"

"T'ought you'd like to know I got Buddy Kai ovah heah," Dominic said.

"So?"

"So he dead, dat's why," Dominic said, which shut the woman up for a moment.

"He's no good to me dead," she said finally.

"Fockah no good to you eidah way, I promise."

"Don't assume you know anything about what's good for me."

"Just get somebody da fock out heah," Dominic said. Then he terminated the call, waited five minutes, and punched in nine-one-one.

Chapter Four
Quarter Break

Geronimo
1

Geronimo hit the brakes as he went by Nalani's old Datsun without a conscious thought—one moment he was driving into the night with his head full of bleak conjecture about what the death of Buddy Kai might ultimately mean, and the next moment the Datsun flashed by and Geronimo stopped dead in the road.

Why the fuck did I do that? he wondered as he watched Nalani do exactly the same thing in his rearview mirror. As soon as her brake lights came on, Geronimo slipped the Explorer into reverse and rolled backwards until his door was lined up with hers.

Nalani was looking up at him through her open window while she waited for his window to come down, an inferior position forced on her by the relative height of her ride. Geronimo was oddly moved by this juxtaposition—it reminded him of his responsibility to her in any interaction between them.

He could barely see the outline of her face in the Datsun's dim interior, and he imagined her view of him was similarly insufficient. He switched on the Explorer's dome light and the emergency flashers, and she responded with the same maneuvers in the Datsun. The new light gave him access to Nalani's eyes, which burned up at him with an intensity he had not seen Saturday morning.

"Do you know what's going on?" he said as soon as his window was out of the way.

Nalani shook her head slowly, as if a rapid movement might somehow unravel the tenuous connection between them.

"Someone tried to kill your dad tonight," Geronimo said, his eyes locked on hers.

"Who?" Nalani said, her voice exactly loud enough to reach Geronimo with nothing left over.

"Buddy Kai," Geronimo said, and then he watched without a word for a moment or two while Nalani processed that information. She turned her eyes away from him and stared through her windshield, revealing that her profile was every bit as perfect as the full-front view of her face.

What is it about this girl? Geronimo wondered while he waited, but he had no answer in mind when Nalani finally turned in his direction again.

"He's dead, yeah?" she said.

"Buddy?" Geronimo asked, and Nalani nodded almost imperceptibly.

"Yeah," Geronimo said. "Buddy's dead."

The girl seemed to drift off somewhere with this information, and Geronimo watched her go. She began to drum her fingers on the Datsun's steering wheel while the wheels in her head rolled in a direction Geronimo could not decipher.

What is it about this girl? he asked himself again.

"Don't worry," he said after he got tired of the silent churning of Nalani's mind. "It's all over now."

"Is it?" Nalani asked, her eyes suddenly crackling again.

"You don't have to worry," he said. "There's a couple of feds at the house to keep an eye on everything."

"They won't be there much longer, I promise," Nalani said, the heat draining out of her eyes just as quickly as it had come.

"What do you mean?" Geronimo said.

Nalani stared at him blankly, and Geronimo wondered again

what she was thinking behind her empty gaze. Finally, she tossed her head slightly, as though physically banishing the thoughts from her mind.

"Nothing," she said aloud.

"I think you meant something, Nalani," Geronimo said.

"Nothing I want you to know," Nalani said.

"Then why bring it up?"

Nalani said nothing in response to that question. Instead, she looked over her shoulder into Geronimo's eyes as if she had never seen anything like them before.

"If you ever change your mind about that," he said after another silent moment or two, "call me."

"Whatevah," Nalani said softly. Geronimo continued to stare at her, but it seemed to him that neither of them recognized the vibe coursing freely between them. *What is it about this girl,* Geronimo thought again, and the more he looked at her, the more he sensed that she was thinking the same thing about him.

"I think you're going into town for the night," he said next. "You better get on home."

"Shuah," she said softly as she reached up and doused the dome light. "I fockin' better get on home, yeah?" Then she cut her emergency lights, slipped the Datsun into gear, and eased into the darkness, leaving Geronimo alone in the road with nothing but triangular questions and circular answers careening around in his head

2

Dawn was sneaking into the night sky behind two or three shades of blue by the time Geronimo finally got with Sonnyboy Akaka, and it would have been a lot later than that if the shift commander at the holding facility hadn't been an old friend.

"Kinda early for visitors, yeah?" Sonny said, looking up from his cot like he had stretched out on it every night of his life. Geronimo looked at him through the bars and shrugged.

"I don't know. Maybe it's late."

"Maybe," Sonny said through a grin.

"Buddy's gone," Geronimo said abruptly, and Sonnyboy's grin disappeared as soon as the words were out of Geronimo's mouth.

"The fockin' Mexicans?" he asked.

"No. Not directly, anyway."

"He fockin' went after Dominic?"

"Yeah."

"That's why I'm here, you know. He wanted me out of the fockin' way."

"You're here because the feds wanted you."

"We waited until they found me, I'd be out there another week or two, I promise."

"You sure as shit would have been out there last night, I grant you that."

Sonny rose from the cot and moved to the bars. Geronimo was standing sideways, one shoulder propped against the cell door from the outside, and Sonny adopted the same position from his side of the door so they wouldn't need much volume to hear each other.

"What do you want, Gee?" Sonny said.

"You know what I want."

"No way this shit's gonna fockin' evaporate, brah."

"Don't act like we're talkin' the laws of nature here, Sonny. You can control what you do next."

"Dominic's goin' down, with me or without me."

"The Mexicans?"

"I think they'll hit the fockin' Japanese behind Dominic, too. These moddafockahs don' play, I promise."

"That brings us right back to you, doesn't it?"

"What do you mean?"

"The Mexicans do all this shit, then what? Who's their guy after that?"

Sonny nodded, but he didn't say anything for a while. Geronimo watched him closely, but he couldn't see any more than he could hear so he continued to lean against the bars and wait.

"Would have been me," Sonny said finally.

"What's that mean?"

"I think I'm done, Gee. I fockin' hate ice, you know?"

"You're done with Dominic, too?"

"No fockin' way. The Mexicans fock that up, I'm gonna drop-kick that moddafockah."

"The Mexicans gonna let you walk?"

Sonny shrugged. "If they're smart," he said.

"Are they smart?"

Sonny shrugged again, moved back to the cot, and stretched out on his back with his hands behind his head and his ankles crossed. "We're about to find that out, yeah?" he said, his grin back on his face.

Geronimo nodded, and neither of them spoke for a moment while Geronimo stood there and thought. "If it all goes down like you just said," he said finally, "who's next in line around here?"

"There won't really be a line," Sonny said. "Fockah gonna be wide open."

"Somebody's gonna step in there, Sonny. Give me your best guess."

"We don't have anybody, I promise. Gonna be from Dominic's side, I think."

"Who? I don't see that they have anyone, either."

"Dominic's daughter, maybe, if she finds the right help."

"Get serious, Sonny. Nalani?"

"You watch her close, Gee, you're gonna see more than you think. Fockin' girl scares me, I promise."

"She's a fuckin' kid."

"Yeah," Sonnyboy said. "Fockin' Dominic's kid."

3

The woman from the DEA was leaning against the door on the driver's side of Geronimo's Explorer when he left the building, and she was still there after he crossed the parking lot.

"Is your boy taking over?" she asked when he got close enough for conversation.

"Don't misinterpret his name," Geronimo said. "Sonny is nobody's boy."

The woman looked at him soberly for a moment and Geronimo looked back the same way. "I didn't mean it like that," she said finally.

"Whatever," Geronimo said with a shrug. The morning sun was streaking the clouds with several shades of red now, and he stared at the woman in that half-light. He saw exactly what he had expected to see—the woman was generating a significant amount of light on her own.

"Well?" she asked.

"Well what?"

"Is he taking over now?"

"I don't think so."

"Why not?"

"He said he hates ice."

"Really?"

"No," Geronimo said. "I'm makin' this shit up."

That stopped the woman again, but only briefly. "Kind of touchy this morning," she said. "Long night?"

Nights are all the same length around here, Geronimo thought, but he kept his voice off the words because he recognized that the woman was right—for some reason, he *was* kind of touchy this morning.

"I never heard a dealer say that before, is all," the woman said.

"You didn't hear this one say it, either."

"Look," the woman said. "Drop the fucking attitude, okay? I recognize what you can bring to this party—that's why we're having this conversation."

"Swell," Geronimo said. "I feel so much better now."

"Fucking locals," the woman said. "Always the same, no matter where you go."

"If that's the case, maybe you should stay home more."

"Aren't you overlooking something here?" the woman said. "We just took a lot of shit off the street that would be rolling through the system right now if we hadn't done it."

Yeah, Geronimo thought. *I have been overlooking that.* "Good point," he said.

"So who's next in line if Sonnyboy drops out?" the woman said.

"Nobody," Geronimo said. "He said there won't even be a line after your boy is out of the picture."

"Rosario?"

"Dominic is gone," Geronimo said. "Forget Dominic."

"Dominic is under our protection. He's not going anywhere."

"He's going down. If the Mexicans don't do it, Sonny will."

"Is he that bad?" the woman asked quietly.

Geronimo felt like shrugging again, but he resisted the impulse because this woman was hard to shrug off. "I guess we're about to find out," he said. "If the Mexicans aren't bad enough, that is."

"Some are badder than others. I'd like to know who we're talking about here, exactly."

"Maybe you can ask them when they come around for Dominic. Exchange business cards, maybe, get all their numbers in your little black book."

"Do people around here think you're funny?" the woman asked.

"Not lately," Geronimo said, his mind jumping to Denise. "Not for quite a while, actually."

"If I were in just the right mood, I might think you are."

"Let me guess," Geronimo said. "You're never in that particular mood."

"Exactly."

"If you move away from my door, I might be able to get out of here."

"If everything comes down like Sonnyboy says, they'll still need someone to step up around here."

No shit, Geronimo thought, but he kept the thought to himself and answered with a silent nod instead.

"He had no suggestions about that?"

"No," Geronimo lied.

"If there really is no one else, what makes him think the Mexicans will let him walk?"

"The limitations of force, maybe."

"What?"

"If you're willing to die," Geronimo said, "you can't be forced to do shit."

The woman raised her eyebrows slightly at that. "Interesting," she said. "I never thought of it like that, exactly."

Imagine that, Geronimo thought, but he kept the thought to himself while he stood in front of the woman and waited. After a silent moment or two, she opened the door to the Explorer and stepped out of his way. He slipped behind the wheel, fastened his seatbelt, and cranked the rig to life.

The woman lowered the driver's side window before she slammed the door shut. "About Rosario," she said. "Any advice?"

"Why the fuck do you care what happens to him now? He already gave you what you wanted."

"Until we wipe Buddy's organization all the way off the scoreboard, Dominic might be able to do the same thing another time or two."

"Meanwhile, you're making a giant out of the fucker."

"I do this for a living, Souza," the woman said, her voice softer than usual. "I know how to do it."

Geronimo was surprised at her use of his name—the word sounded odd coming out of her mouth. "Wow," he said. "I didn't know you knew my name."

"I imagine there are many things you don't know about me," she said, the words soft again, like she had suddenly come to the conclusion that she didn't need to be hard in front of him.

"He'd be a lot easier to protect if he was smart enough to be afraid," Geronimo said, going back to her original question. "Stupid prick thinks he's invincible."

"Judging from last night, I'd say he *is* pretty tough."

"Whatever."

"Not tough enough?"

"Nobody is, you get right down to it," Geronimo said as he slipped the Explorer into gear. "You bring enough fire, everybody burns."

"I guess we'll try to keep the fire down."

"Yeah," Geronimo said. "Good luck on that." Then he drove off and left the woman standing alone in the parking lot.

4

"Had breakfast yet?" Geronimo said into his phone.

"No," the woman in Volcano said softly. "I hardly ever eat while I'm sleeping."

"Sounds like you're awake now."

"Yeah, you big meanie."

"I can have your breakfast there in forty-five minutes."

"I'm not that kind of hungry."

"Then I can be there in thirty minutes."

"You might have to wake me up again."

"I think I can handle that."

"Me, too," the woman said before she cut the connection.

Geronimo killed his phone, too, tossed it on the empty seat next to him, pointed the Explorer *mauka* and drove. Twenty-six minutes later, he let himself into the woman's small cabin.

The woman's latest canvas dominated the room he entered. He stopped to study it, even though he had done exactly the same thing on his last visit. The woman had made significant progress since then, but Geronimo still had no idea what he was looking at. He was drawn to it, though, as he was to all of her work—there was something deeply seductive about the curve of her lines and the heat of her colors that he responded to physically.

After a few moments of quiet observation, he moved to the cabin's single bedroom. The woman was sprawled on her back on top of her sheets, her legs spread apart under a thin white nightgown and her right hand cupping her genitals under the gown's lacy edge.

Geronimo stood in the doorway and observed the artist like he had studied the art in the other room. She was not a beautiful woman, and there was nothing about the features she did have that had ever appealed to Geronimo before—she was too thin, too long, too pale. But he responded to the woman the same way he responded to her art—just looking at her never failed to raise a spark in him, just as it was doing at that moment.

The woman's fingers began to caress her genitals gently, and she opened her pale blue eyes and regarded Geronimo for a moment. "Hey," she said finally, her voice dreamy and quiet as it drew the word out a little.

"Hey," Geronimo said.

"Couldn't get back to sleep," she said slowly. "So I started without you."

"Hope I'm not too late," Geronimo said.

"It's not like I have a limit or something," she said. "Long as you get here, you can't really be late." Geronimo replied to that by disrobing, a process which revealed his erection. "Oh, my," the woman said with a quiet smile. "You started early, too."

"Your art makes me hard," Geronimo said.

"Come over here," she said. "Let me see if I can make you soft." Geronimo went, and the woman eventually did. When they were both finished, she leaned her arms on his chest and stared into his eyes for a while.

Geronimo rested beneath her and stared back. "Something changed," she said finally. "It was different this time."

"It's different every time."

"Not like this."

"I don't know what you're talking about."

"Sure you do," the woman said. "Spit it out."

"Things have changed at work, I guess. All hell is gonna break loose around here."

"I don't give a fuck about that, Geronimo. What happened?"

"Denise walked out on me after I got back the other night."

The woman blinked once, her probing eyes hidden for a moment. "I see," she said when her eyes were locked in on his again. "Can't really blame her, can you?"

"No," Geronimo said. "But that doesn't mean I have to like it."

"If you don't like it, you should do something about it."

"I don't think I'll like what I have to do, either."

"Ah!" the woman said. "The eternal quandary of life."

"What is that supposed to mean?"

"Some things are mutually exclusive, Gee. We can't always have everything we want."

"If that's what you think, what the fuck am I doing here?"

"I'm not the one with a problem. I like it when you drop by now and then."

"Just as long as it's not all the time."

"Yes," the woman said, her voice low and throaty. "I tried to make that clear from the start."

"You did."

"Well, there you go, then. It's all up to you now, big boy."

"In that case, roll over."

The woman did as he asked, and Geronimo rolled with her until their positions were reversed. The white nightgown was bunched around her shoulders, exposing her small white breasts. Geronimo tongued one of the hard ruby tips and then the other, repeating the maneuver until he was erect again and she was urging him inside her.

"Denise thinks you're a fucking slut," he said when he was thoroughly mounted.

"Can't really blame her for that, either," she said, her hips moving with the same slow insistence as his. "I do fuck her husband every chance I get."

"Does that mean you agree with her?"

"No. Not at all."

"Why not?" Geronimo said, ratcheting up the power of his thrusts a notch or two.

The woman wrapped her long pale legs around him before she answered, using the added leverage to generate a significant thrust of her own. "Because you're the slut in this relationship, Gee," she said when her rhythm was rocking in perfect time with his. "But don't let that bother you—a good slut can be a wonderful thing."

Then neither of them spoke for a long, hot interlude while Geronimo proved the woman right.

5

Geronimo parked three or four car lengths from the top of Haili Street, the nose of the Explorer pointed at the bay below. The sky was clear and blue, and so was the ocean, but Geronimo noted this only in passing. He trained his eyes about halfway down the hill and waited.

It didn't take long. People started streaming out of the church no more than 10 minutes after his arrival on the street, and he saw Denise and her mother emerge from the building as soon as the flow of departures slowed down to a trickle.

Last one out, Geronimo thought. *Nothing better to do, is there?*

Even from this distance, Denise stood out. There was nothing remarkable about her attire, but the light dress she was wearing somehow hung differently on her than the similar dresses on everyone else.

Her stride is different, too, isn't it? Geronimo said to himself as he watched her cross the street. *There has always been something special about the way she moves.*

Denise walked around her Suzuki and held the passenger door open for her mother; when that task was completed, she retraced her steps and tucked herself behind the steering wheel. A moment later, the Suzuki pulled away from the curb and proceeded down the hill.

Geronimo eased the Explorer into the street about two blocks behind his wife and followed. He maintained the distance he had started with until she stopped at the intersection with Kinoole Street. He pulled up behind the Suzuki and watched Denise step out of the car and walk in his direction. When she reached the side of the Explorer, he lowered his window.

"What you want, Gerry?" she asked, her voice quiet and steady and her eyes a close match for her voice. Geronimo looked back at her dumbly until another car rolled up behind him.

"Breakfast," he said finally, and he thought he saw the shadow of a grin flash through Denise's brown eyes when he said it.

"Got my mom, you know," she said.

"I can do breakfast with your mom," Geronimo said.

"Then follow me a little more, big boy," she said, and this time there was no question about the grin in her eyes.

6

"What brings you back to the scene of the crime?" Stefano said through a crooked smile as Geronimo joined him at the front of Dominic's carport.

"What crime is that?" Geronimo said.

"Yeah, that's the problem."

"I didn't think you'd still be here."

"I just got back. Wanted to take one more look around."

"This shit bothers me, too," Geronimo said. "It didn't come down quite like we were told, that's for sure."

"Nope," Stefano said. "It did not."

"What I was wondering," Geronimo said, looking around the carport. "How deep did you dig around here? You know, in the course of your investigation."

"I know what you're getting at. We went as deep as we reasonably could, Gee. I didn't see any signs of Dominic's business out here."

"Too bad all this didn't come down inside. I'd love to poke around in the house for a while."

"What good would it do you? The way he's hooked up with the feds right now, whatever we came up with would disappear at the top, anyway."

"You're probably right," Geronimo said. "I'm chasing my fucking tail out here."

"What's up your butt about this? There's nothing new about this shit."

"This thing with Buddy is only the first round, Stef. We're gonna have fucking bodies all over the place before it's over."

"How many of these fuckers are we really gonna miss, though?"

"They won't spend much time worrying about collateral damage," Geronimo said. "If things bounce just a little wrong, we could be grieving a lot more than we want to."

"I hear you," Stefano said.

"And it's not just that. This isn't LA or Tokyo—fuck, this isn't even Honolulu. This is the Big Island. This fucking shit isn't supposed to be happening here."

"Ain't nothin' new about that, either, Gee."

"What? We just bend over for these fucks and take it up the ass?"

"Where you been? We've been ass-fucked for centuries now."

"Maybe that's why I'm tired of it."

"Maybe," Stefano said softly, looking deep into Geronimo's eyes as he said it. "But you know you can't stop the tide from comin' in, Gee. Sooner or later, you'll be in over your head."

"I've been in over my head for as long as I can remember," Geronimo said. "Nothin' new about that, either."

"Maybe it's time to turn around and head back to the beach."

"What the fuck are you, now, fucking Dr. Phil or Oprah Winfrey?"

"Right. That's exactly who I am."

"Fuck you," Geronimo said, grinning ruefully and shaking his head slightly.

"Like I was saying," Stefano said gently, "you gotta stand in line to do that, brah."

7

Robbie rolled up Geronimo's driveway almost immediately after the Pistons finished schooling the Lakers for the third time in the series. Geronimo stood in the doorway between his kitchen and his carport and watched Robbie climb out of a new Mustang and walk in his direction.

Geronimo had given his position with Robbie some serious

thought during the final few minutes of the game, but nothing that came to mind did anything to ease the grip of the cold fingers slowly clenching in his gut.

"You didn't waste much time, did you?" Geronimo said.

"Gonna invite me in, brah?" Robbie said when he reached the doorway. Geronimo stepped aside without a word, and Robbie walked past him the same way. Robbie strolled into the living room like he knew where it was, which he did, and he sat in the loveseat like he had done it before, which he had. Geronimo followed behind him and took a seat on the sofa that matched the loveseat.

"I didn't see Denise's car," Robbie said.

"It wasn't there."

"You guys watched hoops together back in the day, yeah?"

"So you're my guide down Memory Lane now, Robbie?" Geronimo asked, although it occurred to him while he said it that Robbie was uniquely qualified for the position if Geronimo ever wanted to fill it.

"I think you need one," Robbie said, as though the same thought was running through his mind.

"So what's the word?" Geronimo asked. "Your guys cutting me off?"

"I wish," Robbie said quietly.

"What?"

"You've got the green light, brah."

"Really?" Geronimo asked, and the question was genuine. The sudden turnaround by Robbie's people and Robbie's strained reaction to it did nothing to ease the fist in Geronimo's intestines.

"They love you to death now, I promise."

"Why?"

"Good question," Robbie said. He leaned back a little in the loveseat and closed his eyes for a moment, and Geronimo sat back on the sofa and watched him do it. Robbie still looked a lot like he had in high school, Geronimo noted, which was more than most of his classmates could say. But it was a mixed blessing—there were times when the island's designated bookie didn't want to look like a kid, and this might have been one of them.

"Spit it out, Robbie," Geronimo said after a moment or two.

"You got the fifteen grand?" Robbie asked.

"Yes and no," Geronimo said. "I could dig it up if I wanted to bad enough."

"Do it, brah."

"Why? If they keep taking my bets, it's only a matter of time before I'm out from under this weight."

"You're sick if you think time's on your side, Gee. You're riskin' more than money here."

"What's my limit?" Geronimo asked.

"No fockin' limit. You've got the green light all the way now."

"They'll go the entire fifteen?"

"They'll love it, brah."

"Why?" he asked again.

"Because they know how to fockin' count," Robbie said, his eyes definitely open again. "Thirty is twice as good as fifteen."

"That's if I lose," Geronimo said. "Those fucking no-names can't beat the Lakers again."

"You're talkin' to the wrong guy, Gee. You go on, you goin' without me."

"Fine. Get 'em on the phone."

Robbie produced a cell phone and punched some numbers into it. "He wants to talk," he said into it when the numbers did their job. Then he held the phone in Geronimo's direction.

Geronimo got up from the sofa, stepped across the room, and took the phone out of Robbie's hand. "Are we going to do more business, Mr. Souza?" a voice asked after a moment passed by without anyone saying anything. Geronimo didn't recognize the voice and didn't really like the question.

"That depends on what the business is," Geronimo said.

"We have a lot of businesses," the voice said. "What business do you want it to be?"

"I'm only interested in one."

"Fine."

"Put fifteen on the Lakers."

"That line is even right now."

"Fine," Geronimo said. "When the Lakers win, we're square. Right?"

"That's right, Mr. Souza. When the Lakers win."

"Fine," Geronimo said again. "Here's Robbie."

"No need," the voice said. "From now on, Mr. Souza, you deal with us directly. Robbie will give you the number."

Geronimo extended the phone back in Robbie's direction, and Robbie took it from his hand. "He said you'd give me his number," Geronimo said.

"Yeah," Robbie said. "Already gave him *your* number, you know."

"This will be over Tuesday night, Robbie. The Pistons can't do this shit again."

"Gerry," Robbie said softly while he rose from the loveseat, "this is not about hoops, brah. You don' know that?"

No, Geronimo thought, *I don't.* But the fist in his gut and the nagging doubt in the back of his mind argued otherwise while he walked his old friend to the new Mustang in the driveway.

Jesus

"How many with the focker?" Jesus asked.

"Dos," Manuel said, his thin lips barely moving and whatever expression might have glimmered in his hard eyes covered by the Ray-Bans he never seemed to take off his face.

"You take those fockers off in the shower?" Jaime asked from the other side of the room, apparently chewing on the same question about the sunglasses as Jesus.

"Why don' you jump in the tub with me," Manuel said slowly, his voice as flat as the surface of the Ray-Bans, "you really wanna know. Maybe you scrub my ass, or soap my fockin' *cajones.*"

"Can't believe they've got the focker right here in our hotel," Jesus said, redirecting the conversation before his hired help wandered any farther down the detour in front of them.

"Pissant town's only got three," Jaime said.

"Quatro," Manuel said, "you count the one down by the place the kids always jumping in the water off the focking fence."

"Whatever," Jesus said. "How solid is our information, *ese?*"

"As a focking rock," Manuel said. "This *pendejo* put Buddy down, no question."

"And now he's right down the hall."

"Si."

"With a couple of feds."

"Si."

"And what? His daughter?"

Manuel nodded silently, his Ray-Bans barely moving.

"Fock," Jesus said. "Gotta let him slide for now."

"¿Por que?" Jaime asked. "He's here, we're here."

"I want more than his ass," Jesus said. "We hit him here, how do we get paid for the shit we lost?"

"Let whoever takes Buddy's place pay for that."

"We do it here," Manuel said, "we have to hit the fockin' feds."

"And maybe the daughter," Jesus added. "Then we'd still have to get off this fockin' rock. No way this is the time and the place."

"What about the Japs?" Jaime said. "We got them fockers right down the street."

Jesus took his time before he answered; he could see that Jaime was wound a little too tight for the situation they were facing. "A *tsunami* would take care of both ends, wouldn't it?" he said lightly.

"Us, too," Manuel said.

"Sí," Jesus said. "So what we do is, we pick at the edges of this thing for a while."

"Starting with the *señorita,* maybe?" Manuel said, a little more edge to his voice than usual.

"Maybe," Jesus said slowly, as though the word had traveled a great distance before it drifted from his mouth. "Maybe the *señorita* is just the place to start."

Kitano

1

Kitano was stretched out on a lounge chair by the hotel's pool in the middle of the afternoon. The sun was out for a change, and his skin was getting hot; if the weather didn't flip again in the next few minutes, he was going to hit the water for a while—providing he didn't die of boredom first, which was always a distinct possibility in Hilo.

The old man was in the chair next to Kitano, his hungry eyes hidden by dark glasses while they feasted on the kids splashing in the pool. There were three of them, a boy and two girls, apparently siblings who shared a connection with the tall blonde woman who had picked a chair on the opposite side of the pool. Kitano wondered idly which of the three the old man favored, although he knew it didn't really matter—even the old man wouldn't mess with a tourist kid from the same hotel.

Kitano was growing weary of the old man, and the old man's insatiable appetite for tender flesh was only one of the reasons. It was not impossible to feed that hunger on the Big Island, thank the gods, but it was more difficult here than in Honolulu and much more complicated in both than at home.

Kitano could think of better ways to spend his time than procuring the objects of the old man's lust, but he knew that neither of them would even be on the island if not for the old man's thirst for exotic delicacies. This ice thing could have been handled by a telephone call, for example, but the old man was going to tie up the better part of a week before deciding to do the exact same thing Kitano would have done by phone—pop this fucking Buddy Kai's balloon for going to the Mexicans, and let the Akaka kid choose between the same fate or moving the whole family business over to Rosario.

To be fair, though, the old man was cute with this thing with the cop. Kitano loved the idea of having a handle on someone from the drug task force, and they were only two meaningless basketball games away from a handle big enough to drag this cop's sorry ass from one end of the island to the other.

2

The old man was standing at the window in front of a panoramic view of the bay, but Kitano knew he wasn't perusing it because the old man's distance vision wasn't worth shit. Kitano stretched out his legs in front of him, leaned back in the plushest of the suite's armchairs, and waited.

Takes you too fucking long to think, old man, Kitano said where only he could hear it. Kitano had already processed the information on the table—the temporary incarceration of Sonnyboy Akaka, the death of Buddy Kai, and the apparent ascendancy of Dominic Rosario—and already knew what the next move had to be.

The old man finally spoke, starting a brief flurry of short, staccato bursts of Japanese scuttling between the two of them. Then the old man turned away from the window, walked to the suite's master bedroom, and disappeared inside.

Kitano picked up the phone next to his chair when the old man was gone and punched in the required number. The phone rang twice before it was answered.

"This is Robbie," the bookie said into Kitano's ear.

"The old man wants to see you," Kitano said, and then he cut the connection and put the phone back where he had found it.

Robbie

1

"You're up kinda late, brah," Robbie said into his phone. He could see the digital clock flashing 4:05 on his stove from where he was sitting at his dining-room table, which was either very late or much too early for words.

"Sounds like you da kine, too," Dominic said.

"Always up the night before a big game."

"Dat's what I t'ought."

"You wanna get down on da Lakers, yeah?"

"How you know dat?"

"All you guys like the Lakers."

"What guys?" Dominic said, the agitation level in his voice rising much too fast to suit Robbie. "What kine guys you talkin' 'bout, Robbie?"

"Guys you know," Robbie said quickly. "Relatives, friends, whatevah."

"Don' fock wit' me, Robbie."

"I would never, Dominic. You know me."

"Yeah," Dominic said. "But do you fockin' know me?"

"You know I do."

"You nevah heard yet, yeah?"

"Heard what?"

"Buddy Kai wen try take me out tonight."

"Why?" Robbie asked, even though he was fairly certain that he already knew the answer.

"Fockin' stupid, dat's why."

"Where?"

"Right in my fockin' driveway."

"How is he?"

"What you t'ink?"

Robbie's belly began to tighten in spite of the fact that he wanted to believe with all his heart that this news had nothing to do with him. He got up and paced from the dining room to the kitchen and back again, stopping at the window that provided a view of his front yard.

"He's dead, yeah?"

"No shit."

"Now what?" Robbie said, thinking of Kitano and the old man even though Dominic had no way of knowing that and therefore was unlikely to address that thought.

"Now you no wanna fock wit' me, Robbie."

"You know that's never gonna happen, Dee."

"Gimme t'ree t'ousand on da Lakahs."

"You gotta give one point."

"Fock da spread. Da Lakahs gonna kick Detroit all da way to Canada dis time, I promise."

"I've been hearin' that a lot," Robbie said, his mind flashing to a particular mutual acquaintance who had said exactly the same thing.

"Now you can fockin' believe it," Dominic said before he terminated the connection between them.

Robbie lowered the phone slowly, his eyes wandering around in his yard as he stared out his window but his mind totally locked on Dominic and his Japanese associates. The first thing he noticed was that he had been wrong before—his belly hadn't really tightened earlier, because he could feel a pair of icy fists methodically coiling his intestines while he was standing there completely powerless to do a thing about it.

Why the fock does this drug shit keep comin' up around me? he asked himself. *And what the fock am I gonna do about it?*

2

"I thought you didn't like to gamble," John said soberly. He was flat on his back on Robbie's king-sized bed, his hands behind his head in a way that accentuated the lean musculature of his honey-colored arms.

"I love your skin, you know," Robbie said.

"Don't try to change the subject."

"You're right. I don't like to gamble."

"You're talkin' about one helluva risk here."

"Yes and no."

"What's that supposed to mean?"

"Risky, yeah. But you can't stand still—you gotta keep movin' in this fockin' business."

"What business are you talking about? You aren't even in that fucking business."

"I'm not sayin' I'm gonna make this kind of move. I just wanna be ready to move."

"I think you're nuts."

"The fockin' shit keeps comin' up all the time, I promise. Anything these guys are fockin' into, I'm into almost automatically."

"Nuts or not," John said, "I'm down with you, if that's what you're asking."

"That's exactly what I'm askin', brah."

"One thing, though," John said slowly, his beautiful round eyes clouding over suddenly.

"What?"

"Tell me this isn't the reason you hooked up with me."

"No way, sweetheart. I wanna lick the fockin' honey off every time I look at you, that's why."

"That shit doesn't come off, you know."

"I know," Robbie said as he moved on top of John's trim body. "But that's never gonna stop me from tryin', brah."

3

"You said Buddy Kai was going to win," Kitano said.

"Not," Robbie said, looking from Kitano in the armchair to the old man standing in front of the window overlooking the bay.

"Not?" Kitano said.

"I didn't say anything about Buddy himself. This thing isn't over, brah."

"The Akaka kid is in jail."

"Not for much longer."

Kitano nodded his head slightly and said something quick in Japanese. The old man said something, too, and then they both turned their attention back to Robbie.

"So the Akaka kid will come at him, federal protection and all?"

"This is not my thing, you know," Robbie said, even though he knew it would do no good.

"You know all the players," Kitano said.

Yeah, Robbie said to himself. *And now I know you fockahs, too.* "Nobody else does it," he said out loud, "yeah. Sonnyboy'll come at him hard."

"Who else gives a fuck?" Kitano asked.

"Whoever fronted the shit the feds busted."

"The Mexicans? They're walking around here dead and don't even know it. You don't have to think about the fucking Mexicans."

No need to think about any of you, Robbie thought, *but I'm doin' it. Again.* "Whatevah," he said. "Plenty of life left in Sonnyboy, I promise."

"That can be corrected pretty easily, I would think."

"Not," Robbie said, but it struck him as soon as the word was out of his mouth that he might have been saying it too often.

"You don't think so?"

"You can do it, yeah, but no way is it gonna be easy."

Kitano shrugged his shoulders slightly and shot a little more Japanese in the old man's direction. The old man blinked once and motioned toward the door with his head.

"You can go," Kitano said, and Robbie went, the wheels turning relentlessly in his mind every step of the way.

4

Robbie's phone rang as soon as he cleared Geronimo's driveway, and after a quick look at the identity of the caller he almost didn't answer it.

"Who the fock is callin' from the lockup?" he asked himself, and he finally hit the phone to find out.

"Sonnyboy?" he said.

"How'd you know that?" Sonny asked.

"Only customer I have inside, brah. I'm gonna pay up when you get out, you know."

"Yeah," Sonny said. "But how are you gonna pay what you owe Buddy?"

"You didn't hear?"

"I heard. That's why I'm callin'."

"If Buddy can't collect, I can't pay, you know."

"Pay his boy, Robbie. He's gonna need it."

"How would I do that?"

"He stays with his *tutu,*" Sonny said. "But she won't take the money, you try to give it to her."

"How 'bout I give it to you? Maybe you can get it to the kid."

"I can do that. Thanks, brah."

"When will I see you?"

"Gonna get out tomorrow mornin', but I don't need it right away. Maybe you can let it all ride—me and Buddy's both?"

"Dead men can't bet, you know."

"How much do you owe him?"

"A grand."

"Put me down for fifteen hundred. I can still bet, yeah?"

"You want the Pistons again?"

"No question. Dis t'ing gonna be *pau* Tuesday night."

"Pistons might be favored," Robbie said.

"Fock the spread," Sonny said. "The Lakers can't beat these fockin' guys."

"Already beat 'em once, yeah?"

"Yeah, a fockin' gift from God. He ain't comin' down with a miracle again."

"No way God is watchin' this shit."

"That's what I'm sayin', brah. Fifteen hundred, whatever the points."

"You got it," Robbie said before he traded talking for driving without words. He stopped at the highway and eyed the traffic coming from his left carefully. He knew that people occasionally died trying to move from Shower Drive into the flow of cars headed for Hilo, but even with that knowledge he had trouble keeping his mind focused on what his eyes were watching.

Fockin' phone's gonna ring off the hook, he thought while he waited for a hole in the traffic. *Too bad I have to think about this other fockin' thing.* He finally punched the Mustang onto the highway and drove, the wheels in his mind turning every bit as fast as the wheels on his car.

5

Robbie's cell went off as he was flashing by the sprawling new high school in Kea`au. "Wassup?" he said as soon as he got the phone close enough to his mouth to talk into it.

"You coming back soon?" John asked, his voice tighter than Robbie was used to.

"On my way now, brah," Robbie said.

"Good," John said.

"What?" Robbie asked.

"I said good."

"You know what I mean."

"We've got some company."

"Who?"

"I don't know, exactly. They speak Spanish pretty well, though."

"What the fock?"

"You'll see when you get here," John said, which is exactly what Robbie did ten minutes later when he parked behind the new Chrysler Sebring that didn't belong in his driveway.

The company inside his house went three deep, one sitting in an armchair opposite John on the divan and two leaning against the counter on the kitchen island. Robbie looked briefly in all three brown faces, but was not rewarded for the effort. He turned his attention to John, who had the same tightness in his face that Robbie had heard in his voice on the phone.

"Wassup?" Robbie said to no one in particular.

"We need a favor, homes," the one in the armchair replied.

"Why the fock would I care what you need?" Robbie asked, a little hot around the edges and getting hotter by the second with these guys draped all over his house.

The man in the armchair did not reply immediately; what he did was sit back in the chair and look at Robbie through eyes cold enough to freeze the blood in Robbie's veins. "You care, homes," the man said finally, "maybe you live longer than you don' care."

"We're not homeboys, moddafockah," Robbie said.

"Si," the man in the chair said slowly. "Maybe you should keep that in mind."

"How'd you get here?"

"We keep one eye on the Japs. You been in an' out a lot."

"You been fockin' followin' me?"

"We do whatever the fock we wan', homes. *Comprende?*"

"What do you want?"

"A guide."

"What?"

"A guide. A local expert to point us in the right direction from time to time."

"I can show you the way to LA right now."

The man in the chair smiled at that, but it was the coldest smile Robbie had ever seen. The man made a motion with his head, a motion so slight Robbie was not certain the man had moved his head at all. Then one of his compatriots at the kitchen counter, the one standing implacably behind a pair of Ray-Bans, moved to the divan and kicked John flush in the face.

John bounced back and then off to the right, blood spraying from his nose as he rolled onto the tile floor. Robbie could see traces of dark red smeared across the divan in John's wake, and he could see the same color as John rose slowly to his feet with his face in his hands.

"You shouldn't have done that," John said, but he said it oddly. There was no heat in his voice, no sentiment of any stripe; he could have been commenting on the weather or his horoscope for the day. He walked past the counter, drew a dishtowel out of a drawer, ran water over the towel in the sink, and then stepped to the refrigerator and extracted a handful of ice cubes from the dispenser in the door. Then he wrapped the ice in the wet towel and positioned it over his nose.

Robbie watched the entire sequence without a word, and when it was over, he was staring at something hard in John's eyes that hadn't been there before.

"Tell me about this fockin' Rosario's kid," the man in the chair said.

"What do you wanna know?" Robbie said.

6

"You're the ones with all the fockin' shooters," Robbie said. "What the fock are you guys good for if you don' deal with this kind of shit?"

Robbie sounded a little hotter than he actually was, but this was the level of heat he imagined they would expect in this situation, so he tried to hit it right on the nose. Kitano looked at the old man, but the old man was standing at his window again with his back to all three of them—Kitano, Robbie and John, John having trailed into the room with his busted face to illustrate exactly what kind of shit Robbie meant.

"You're a big boy," Kitano said finally. "We expect you to be able to take care of yourself."

"I can, you know. But then why do we need you moddafockahs?"

"Calm yourself down. You're asking questions now that you already know the answer to."

"I'm plenty calm, I promise. You need to watch the Mexicans—the fockahs are makin' a move on Rosario right now."

"We know that. We think the same thing about him that we think about you."

"Nothing, yeah?"

"He's an even bigger boy. He should be able to take care of himself, too."

"He goes down, you just work with whoever's left?"

"Exactly."

"What if the focking Mexicans are the only ones standing?"

The old man suddenly turned at the window and fired a short burst of Japanese at Kitano, who answered just as briefly before bringing his focus back to Robbie.

"It won't be the Mexicans," Kitano said quietly. "The Mexicans aren't getting off this fucking rock alive, I assure you."

"He focking understands English, yeah?" Robbie asked.

"Does he?" Kitano said.

Robbie looked at Kitano, leaning back now in his armchair as though confident nothing more would transpire which might require him to sit up on the edge of his seat; at the old man, his back to everyone again so he could resume his examination of the view from the window; and at John, who was leaning silently next to the door with his lethal hands in his pockets while the others conversed.

"Whatevah," Robbie said when he was finished with his survey of the room and its occupants, a little more disgust in his voice than he actually felt—or maybe a lot more, considering he had found out what he wanted to know and had the beginning of an idea about how he might want to put that new knowledge to work.

Nalani

1

I fockin' hate him, I promise, Nalani mumbled to herself as she pointed her Datsun in the general direction of Pahoa and drove.

She had just watched Kapua skip through her yard and into the house, the culmination of a process which had killed most of the hour since Dominic's call had interrupted her night—fifteen minutes just to find Kapua in a bedroom at the back of the house, another fifteen to get her untangled from Mana and into the car, and the rest of the time to drive back to Kapua's side of Hilo from Mana's side of Kurtistown.

Kapua's response to the sudden departure was frosty, to say the least, but she overcame that reaction rapidly when Nalani threatened to leave her there without a ride she could count on to be available with no strings attached. Kapua was virtually silent on the way back to her house, and Nalani understood this silence perfectly—the gap between the two of them was growing wider by the minute, and it wouldn't be long before they stopped trying to bridge it.

Consequently, Kapua was in and out of Nalani's head quickly as she drove. Dominic, on the other hand, lingered like a bad head cold. He had offered no explanation of the order to return, but Nalani had heard his motivation humming in the thin outer edges of his voice over the phone—he was wired again, without a doubt. She had been strangely infuriated by the call, as though Dominic had somehow crossed an invisible line that neither of them had known existed.

She wondered about this sudden fury as she drove, but she came up with no easy explanation for it. Being called away from the party had nothing to do with it, she knew for sure—she had been tired of the party even before she and Kapua had arrived there—and she could say the same of her first night as Pono's new girl, an experience she found exhausting. Not Pono himself, who was occasionally engaging, but the careful monitoring which the situation demanded—not too much, not too soon, the pace entirely Nalani's responsibility.

Fockin' unfair, you know, she said to herself, but she immediately saw the triviality of this new complaint in comparison to all of the injustices already stacked up in her life. The insight almost made her laugh on top of her anger, but not quite.

And speaking of anger, she knew she would find some at the far end of this drive. Dominic would be counting the minutes as they ticked by, and too many had elapsed already if she had been where she was supposed to be when she received the call.

She didn't fear Dominic's anger; she knew she could do whatever she wanted with it—drain it away, build it up, whatever served her best. But she knew she had to take the anger into account, and on this particular night that seemed like another unreasonable imposition on her life.

Fock him, she thought. Or maybe don't fock him this time. How would he like that? She knew the answer to that question just as soon as the question insinuated itself into her thoughts—Dominic would take it if she didn't give it up, no question there at all, especially as pumped as he had sounded on the phone. But could that be useful to her somehow?

What would happen if someone should come to the house an hour or so after she told her father to fuck himself, after she fought for as long as she could, after she accumulated the physical evidence of the beating and her father was who knew where in the process which would ultimately and most certainly follow? Could that be made to happen, and what would it be like if it did?

Where the fock is this comin' from? she said to herself. *Much too fockin' public, way too fockin' complicated. But fockin' sweet, yeah, the fockin' bastard busted for raping his daughter?*

She was turning this over in her mind when the ambulance went by, no siren, no flashing lights; then a short procession of cars with unblinking blue lights on the roofs, nobody in a hurry, everybody pointed in the direction from which she had come.

What the fock? she thought, and then she thought it again when the last car under a blue light—the Ford Explorer she had seen in her driveway Saturday morning—stopped in the road as soon as Nalani drove by.

2

Nalani had never been this furious in her life, but she had the anger buried so deep that she was the only person in the room with access to it. This was by design; she had repressed her earlier fantasy about picking a fight with her father. Instead, she was lying on her back with her legs splayed apart while he hammered his way to his second orgasm of the morning.

They were in the bedroom of a suite they didn't need, the feds under the impression that she would require more privacy than was actually the case. Her father was ostensibly inhabiting the front room of the suite, the one with the ocean view, but the ocean had been the farthest thing from his mind as soon as the feds walked out, and Nalani knew it was nowhere in his fucking thoughts now.

When Dominic finally finished, he rolled on his side and grinned at her like a cat that had swallowed every drop of milk in Cheshire. The grin intensified her fury; she had to make a conscious effort to restrain herself from trying to gouge his eyes out of their sockets.

"I wen kill da fockah, girl," he said, beaming behind the words like he had never heard anything better. "I wen fockin' killum."

Nalani made no audible response to this pronouncement, and she labored diligently to make no physical response, either. Her mind ran free, however, and what it came up with was this: *Can do the same thing to you, you know—can do it any night I fockin' feel like it. Then who's gonna flash one fockin' grin?*

3

Nalani tried to walk her morning queasiness off, but she heaved halfway across the bridge to Coconut Island. She spit her vomit over the side and into the water below, attracting a glare or two from the early-morning fishermen who had beat her to the bridge. She looked behind her quickly to measure the reaction of the fed who had followed her out of the hotel, but he was leaning over the railing like his fishing pole had just slipped out of his clumsy *haole* hands.

She walked the rest of the way to the island with her head down and her stomach still rolling. *Mana's fockin' pupus,* she thought, although she recalled as she was walking that she hadn't felt much like eating at the party.

She continued her long strides after crossing the bridge, moving across the cleared area and through the trees until she ran out of ground. The breeze off the bay seemed to soothe her, so she breathed in deeply and focused on the breakwater looming in the distance.

I need one of those, she thought, trying to imagine what it would be like if someone built a wall between herself and her father capable of breaking the force of his seething lust in the same way the breakwater protected Hilo from the ocean.

The thought flitted away from her as quickly as it had come, and she turned her mind to possibilities more likely to occur. She could still feel the impact of her father's most recent assault between her legs, the result of being dragged into town without her bottle of lubricant. She was glad for the lingering pain, though; it helped keep her mind where she wanted it.

How much more you gonna take, girl? she wondered, and the answer followed the question without the slightest hesitation: *No more, I fockin' promise.*

This sequence led directly to another question: *What the fock you gonna do?* She stood at the edge of the water and wrestled with the answer to that one until her stomach jumped up through her mouth again and she had to focus her attention on keeping her vomit from splashing on her feet.

4

"Wheah da fock you t'ink you goin'?" Dominic asked.

"Mass," Nalani said.

"Fock dat," Dominic said. "We got t'ings to do heah."

Nalani walked out the door into the carport without a word, leaving the door open behind her. She was almost to the side of the old Datsun before Dominic's voice caught up with her.

"Who da fock you t'ink you is?" he shouted.

"Your fockin' daughter," she said as she opened the door of her car.

"Bettah staht actin' like one daughtah, den!" he said.

"You really wan' da kine?" Nalani said, glaring at him before she slipped behind the wheel, started the car, and backed away from the house.

"I didn't think so," she said softly as she looped around until she was pointed at the road. Then she drove away without another word to her father or herself.

Kapuanani

Kapua hadn't been able to sleep at all. *Sleep?* she thought as she wandered into the cluttered living room. *I can't fockin' sit still.*

She drifted to the front of the darkened room, lifted the dusty sheet draped over the window, and glared outside. The morning was well underway on the far side of the glass, even if it had failed to penetrate through the sheet. Kapua dropped the makeshift curtain and restored the darkness in the room, her right foot tapping as she stood there like a bird searching for a branch to land on.

Maybe a shower, she said to herself, thinking a hot soak would be even better but knowing the house didn't have a tub. *Fockin' dump,* she thought, as she picked her way to the bathroom.

There had been a hook-and-eye lock on the bathroom door in the recent past, before the latest boyfriend kicked the door in when Kapua's mom made the mistake of locking it in front of him one night. Now the jamb was splintered where the eye had torn out and the door wouldn't close all the way.

Kapua paused in the doorway, running the benefits against the risks. *The fockah awake, he's comin' in on me,* she thought. She moved quietly to the door of her mother's room and listened intently; she heard nothing but her mother's steady snore.

After a moment or two, she slipped into the bathroom, closed the door as best she could, stripped out of the clothes she had been wearing since the party, and stepped into the shower stall. The water came out cold, but Kapua stood and took it in her face until it gradually ran hot. Then she stuck her head under the streaming water and started the long process of shampooing her hair.

She was standing with her back to the spray, her eyes closed and her head tipped back when she heard the bathroom door swing open. She froze as the shower curtain slid open in front of her, the pig of a boyfriend standing where the curtain had been in boxer shorts and fat.

"Oh, yeah," he said, a sick grin spreading across his thick face until it engulfed everything except his hard eyes.

Kapua made no attempt to hide or cover herself; instead, she screamed at the top of her lungs. The boyfriend pulled the curtain shut and staggered to the toilet, where she could hear him draining off the waste of last night's beer.

Kapua heard her mom's voice next, coming from the bathroom doorway. "What, Pua?" she asked.

"Get that fockah outta here!" Kapua said.

"What I'm gonna do, piss on da flo'?" the boyfriend asked.

"You scare me to deat', girl! He nevah mean not'ing—he gotta go, he gotta go."

Kapua did not respond to her mother; she stood under the water and waited. She listened to the flushing of the toilet and the footsteps moving out of the room, then the closing of the bedroom door. She turned off the water and listened some more, water continuing to stream down her cheeks long after the shower dried up around her.

Chapter Five
Halftime

Sonny
1

It took the Japanese lawyer less than 45 minutes to clear Sonny out of the Japanese judge's courtroom once the bail hearing got started—*gotta fight fire with fire,* Sonny said to himself as he watched the proceedings—but as soon as he was out on the sidewalk he wouldn't have minded picking up a Japanese companion or two.

"You wanna ride, *ese?*" said a dark guy decked out in bright jewelry leaning on the side of a new Chrysler, right next to the open passenger door. Sonny saw another guy at the wheel and someone else behind a pair of Ray-Bans coiled against the front fender like a cobra.

"Do I have a choice?" Sonny said.

"Si," the guy replied, "but some choices is better than others."

"Shuah," Sonny said. "I can use one ride." He moved past the guy and slid across the back seat; the guy followed him while the cobra with the Ray-Bans took the spot next to the driver.

"Where to?" the guy asked.

"Keaukaha."

"Where the fock is that?"

"Drive down to the bay and turn right."

"How far?" asked the guy in the driver's seat. "We got somewhere else to be in a while."

"Not far," Sonny said, his body turned away from his window

slightly so he could give the guy in the seat next to him his full attention.

"You heard about Buddy?" the guy said.

"Yeah," Sonny said.

"What you gonna do?"

"Nothing."

"Really?"

Sonny saw no overwhelming reason to repeat himself, so he sat there and watched the guy without a word.

"I don' think so, homes," the guy said.

"Think whatever you want."

"I think you're gonna pay for the shit Buddy lost, that's what I think."

"Like I said, brah. Think whatever you want."

"What I wanna know, are you thinkin' what I'm thinkin'?"

"Fock no."

"Maybe you wake up dead, you don' do it."

"Maybe, maybe not. Anybody can die, you know."

"I was jus' bein' polite, homes," the guy said. "You gonna die for sure, I don' get paid."

"Either way, you don' get paid shit by me."

The guy blinked at that, then stared at Sonny for a quiet minute or two. Sonny stared back; he could think of nothing further that needed to be said.

"You gonna let this motherfocker did Buddy walk?" the guy asked finally.

"Fock no," Sonny said again. "You don' do something, I'm gonna punch his fockin' ticket."

"Why would I do something?"

"You da one wants to muscle in on da Japs. 'Dis how you show what kine muscle you got."

"Say we do that. Rosario and Buddy both gone, who's gonna be our man on the ground here?"

"Good question."

"Why wouldn't it be you?"

"I'm out, that's why."

"What if I say you're still in?"

"Then you're talkin' to yourself, brah."

"You talk like you got a death wish, *ese.*"

"Maybe I'm harder to kill than you think."

The guy shook his head slowly. "It's easy to kill someone, believe me," he said. "Manuel could do it right now, no problem."

"Not," Sonny said.

"Show him," the guy said, and Manuel turned in his seat next to the driver and poked a nine in Sonny's face like it had been a natural extension of his arm all along.

"See, the jet lag's fockin' with your thinkin', brah," Sonny said "He pulls the trigger, you've got shit all over your rental car. Big fockin' problem, I promise."

"So we pull over someplace first."

"This is fockin' Hilo, yeah? How you gonna know where to go?"

"I'm sure we can find a place."

"Plus, we get out of the car, I'm gonna kick that Glock down his moddahfockin' throat. Another fockin' problem, yeah?"

"You can do that," the guy said, "it would be a problem, yeah."

"But I don' think you can do it, *cabron,*" Manuel said quietly, still looking over the top of the Glock at Sonny.

"You don't get that thing outta my face," Sonny said, "you're gonna find out more sooner than later."

Manuel glanced at the guy next to Sonny briefly; the guy nodded slightly and Manuel turned back around in his seat as though nothing had actually transpired during the previous minute or two.

"Go straight through," Sonny said when he noticed that the Chrysler was approaching the intersection with Highway 11, and the driver followed that instruction and a couple more until the car stopped at a house where a five-year-old boy lived with an old woman who had missed her last chance to speak to her only son.

"I be back in touch," the guy said as Sonny climbed out of the car.

"No need," Sonny said. "Nothin's gonna change, you know."

"That's where you're wrong, homes," the guy said. "Things change all the fockin' time."

"Some do," Sonny said as he slammed the door shut. He stood there impassively until the Chrysler drove away, and then he finished his previous thought even though the guy could no longer hear him: "And some don't, I fockin' promise."

2

Sonny sat on an old sofa, the boy tucked up snug along his side. Sonny had one arm wrapped around the boy and both hands on the book in front of them, and the boy studied each picture avidly as Sonny read the book out loud.

Sonny liked every Dr. Seuss book he had ever seen, and this one was no exception. What Sonny liked about them was the way the good doctor twisted the words around so they always rhymed, sometimes even making up new words when he needed them. *Gotta do the same fockin' thing myself,* he thought as he read, but he wasn't thinking about a children's story when he thought it.

He had been at Buddy's house in Keaukaha all day, starting when the Mexicans had dropped him there, and he sensed that Buddy's mother appreciated his presence even though she had said nothing to confirm that suspicion. She had said nothing at all, in fact, opening the door for him in silence and going about the business of caring for the boy as though every word in her vocabulary had been burned with the trash one morning and never replaced.

The boy hadn't said much, either, but he had been glued to Sonny's side from the moment Sonny arrived. Sonny had seen immediately that the boy's *tutu* had been informed of Buddy's death—he could see the silent grief in her dark eyes as soon as she opened the door—but he wasn't sure about the boy. Even if he had been told, Sonny wasn't sure five-year-olds were capable of understanding the concept of death.

Sonny wasn't sure he understood it himself. *One moment Buddy was here, the next moment he was gone,* he said to himself. *What the fock is up with that?*

He finished the book while he pondered his quiet questions, but the boy just looked up at him and waited.

"Again?" Sonny asked.

"Again," the boy said, and Sonny flipped the pages back to the beginning and spread his voice on top of the words one more time. The good thing about the process was it didn't engage his mind, so Sonny's thoughts continued to roam as he read. Or maybe that was a bad thing, because most of his thoughts were less than comforting.

He could feel something heavy coming down before this thing with the Mexicans and the Japanese was finally resolved, and he accepted it calmly even though that conflict seemed likely to spill over on him. After that, though, what? He envied the boy at his side, in a way, even though the boy had just lost his father; the boy still had everything he might ever want to be stretched out in front of him.

Sonny remembered the days before he started with Buddy, days filled with nothing but long, languorous hours punctuated by moments of aimless activity; things happened in those days, but not very often and always without purpose or effect. No matter how much the drug business eventually rubbed him the wrong way, it had at least given some structure and meaning to what he did every day.

Now what? he wondered, looking up from the book briefly as the boy's *tutu* sat down in a rocker on the opposite side of the room. The woman returned his glance approvingly, but a thought simmering in the back of his mind suddenly boiled over as soon as their eyes met.

Why is no one calling? he said to himself. "The phone okay, Aunty?" he said.

"Turned it off," the woman said. "No wanna talk to nobody."

"No worries," Sonny said. "I'll handle everything, you know."

"T'anks," the woman said quietly, leaning back in her chair and closing her eyes while she breathed the word out of her mouth.

The boy squirmed at Sonny's side, looking at his *tutu* and then back at Sonny. "Read," he said, nudging Sonny slightly with his elbow.

Sonny rubbed the boy's head playfully, rewrapped his arm around him, and started to read again.

Jesus

1

Jesus knew a lot of green was flashing by outside the window on the far side of the girl, but he couldn't focus on the scenery at all with the girl sitting there in front of it. He watched her lean her head against the back of her seat and slowly close her eyes, a picture worthy of a frame, the girl's unusual poise pouring into the space between them until Jesus was swimming in it.

"You need to make a call," Jesus said. "How far to the next pay phone?"

The girl opened her eyes and looked out the window for a moment. "There's a store in Kurtistown pretty quick," she said.

"Got that?" Jesus said.

"Yeah," Jaime said from the front seat, and two minutes later Jesus was standing next to the girl at a phone.

"It's me," the girl said into the receiver, idly playing with a lock of hair that had escaped from her long braid as she listened quietly for a moment. Jesus thought the girl could have wandered into the gym where they had found her from a travel poster or a Nike billboard, everything not covered by her workout gear knockout fine and everything else screaming for exploration. Even so, the visuals were not what fascinated him about the girl.

Why is she not afraid? Jesus wondered as he watched her.

"Not," she said next. "I'm fine, I promise. Really, I'm fine. One of them wants to talk to you."

Jesus took the phone when the girl handed it to him, and he could hear the voice from the other end long before he had the phone close enough to talk into it. "Shut the fuck up," he said as soon as he had a reasonable opportunity to be heard.

"What da fock you wen do to my daughtah?" the voice said, the words coming complete with the kind of tremors Jesus had learned in Los Angeles to associate with an imminent earthquake.

Jesus responded by cutting the connection, his eyes totally involved with the steady browns the girl had trained in his direction. "Focker don' follow directions very well, does he?" he said.

"Not," the girl said.

"That bodes ill for you, *señorita.*"

The girl said nothing to that, and neither did her eyes. She continued to observe him quietly, Jesus eventually thinking he could hear the invisible wheels turning methodically in her mind even though he couldn't see them.

When he thought the time might be right, Jesus repunched the number the girl had used. "Yeah?" the voice said, still bristling with anger but on a shorter leash.

"I talk," Jesus said. "You listen."

"So talk," the voice said.

"You owe me for the shit you fingered for the feds," Jesus said, but the voice made no reply.

"This is where you ask how much," Jesus said.

"I fockin' talk now?" the voice asked.

"Si."

"Fock you."

"That response may be a little hard on your beautiful daughter, homes."

"My daughtah got not'ing to do wit' da kine!" the voice said, the heat rising in it quickly.

"Sure she does," Jesus said. "We don' reach the right understanding, she gonna have a whole lot to do with it."

"What da fock you want from me?" the voice asked.

"Restitution," Jesus said. "Or something better."

"Like what?"

"You popped our guy. Maybe you wanna take his place."

"Why da fock I wanna do dat?"

"You part of the team, homes, you don' owe us nothin' no more."

"Don' fockin' owe you not'ing now!" the voice said, the intensity surging again.

Touchy motherfocker, Jesus thought, but he kept that thought to himself. "You take that position," he said into the phone, "what you think happens to the *señorita?"*

"Do anyt'ing," the voice said, slipping the restraints entirely now, "I break yo' fockin' neck, I promise!"

"Maybe you need some time to consider the situation," Jesus said. "Maybe we jus' play with your little girl for a while." Then he cut the connection again, lowered the phone, and contemplated the girl's steady brown eyes. He saw no antagonism there; no surrender, either. He found her eyes perplexing, actually; quite possibly the most perplexing he had ever seen.

"What are you thinkin' behin' those eyes?" he said.

"My thoughts belong to me, yeah?" she said.

"I can force 'em out of you, though. You understand that, *si?"*

"Why are you talking to my father?" she said, looking at him steadily still. "My fockin' father's a dead man."

"Your father ain' dead," Jesus said. "I was jus' talkin' to him on the phone."

"He died," the girl said. "He jus' don' know it, yet."

"But you do?"

The girl nodded slowly, then finally looked away. Jesus knew the girl was quite probably right about her father, but he was amazed that the girl knew it— and that the prospect appeared to be no cause for grief.

"You ain' gonna cry at the funeral?" he asked.

He watched her briefly survey the cars streaming by on the highway behind him, and he watched her some more while she glanced to her right and her left. He had only a vague idea what she was seeing when she did this, or what exactly she had been moving toward in their conversation, but she had his full attention on several different levels.

"Shuah," she said finally, her eyes fully focused on him again. "But the fockin' tears won't be for him, I promise."

This is the oldest high-school girl on the fockin' planet, Jesus thought, and then he ran his thoughts forward to the business that had put them both off the side of the road in Kurtistown.

"Who should I be talkin' to?" he asked when he thought he was ready for the answer.

"Me," the girl said, her perplexing eyes fucking with Jesus again while she said it.

2

This fockin' puta is good, Jesus thought, *for a kid her age. Almos' smart, too, tryin' to control what happens to her like this.*

Jesus was sprawled on top of a queen-sized bed, content to let the *puta* lead the way. He was mildly irritated that things had taken this turn; he would have enjoyed forcing the fucking *puta* to do what he wanted. But it was hard to actually complain about what was going on right now, this girl absolutely gorgeous and ringing all the right bells while all he had to do was lie there and listen to the music.

The clothes had melted off the girl as soon as she closed the door behind them, the thin white top with spaghetti straps going over her head and the shorts and panties sliding off in the opposite direction. That left only a pink brassiere, her small breasts tucked inside it but not very far.

"Would you undo me?" she asked, turning her back to him for help even though they both knew she had needed no help when she had put it on in the first place. He reached around her and cupped both of her breasts with his hands for a moment, savoring their soft heft and the hard nipples which adorned them. Then he unsnapped the bra and the girl slipped it away and onto the floor with her other garments.

"Lie down on your back," the girl had said, and after Jesus followed that instruction, she had disrobed him from the waist down. The boots had gone first, top-of-the-line snakeskin with high heels that increased significantly the number of people Jesus could look in the eye, then the socks, then the blue jeans and the jockeys.

That left nothing between the girl and his erection except empty space, and then the girl eliminated even the space by taking his manhood in her mouth. Jesus had been embarrassingly close to climaxing immediately, but when he warned the girl she looked up at him briefly and smiled.

"No problem," she said. "You have plenty more where this one's comin' from." Then she went back to bobbing her head up and down, and a moment later she took his spend in her mouth like it was mother's milk and went right on going.

Which had led to where he was now, buried deep inside her as she slowly rose and fell, her eyes boring into his as she moved. She leaned forward finally, placing her hands on the bed on opposite sides of his head, and offered him first one hard nipple and then the other, rotating back and forth as she moved up and down on his cock, and he absorbed as much as he could until he was filled to overflowing again.

"Jeezus fockin' Christ!" Jesus said when he was finished.

"You like?" the girl asked.

"Si," Jesus said softly. "Very much."

"Good," the girl said. She moved her hips slightly, surrendering his wet cock, and stretched out on her back next to him.

You are something to look at, Jesus said to himself, *I fockin' swear to God.* He drank in the sight for a moment or two, and briefly considered pushing everything else back a notch while he fucked this girl more fully for a while.

He ultimately allowed that thought to evaporate, however, leaving his mind focused on the business at hand. He sat up on the side of the bed, pulled on his jockeys and jeans, picked up the boots and socks, and padded barefoot across the room.

He turned in the girl's direction as he opened the bedroom door, her warm nakedness still stretched out deliciously on top of the bed. *"Muchas gracias, mi'ja,"* he said. "You are one helluva fock, I kid you not."

Then he turned toward the open door and said, "She's all yours, amigos."

Nalani

1

Nalani woke up sick again, and she was halfway to the bathroom before she finally heard what her body was trying to tell her.

"Oh, God!" she said as she dropped to her knees and vomited into the toilet. "Oh, my fockin' God!"

2

Nalani had her face buried in a towel when she heard Coach's sharp retort. She looked up in time to see him crumple and fall to the floor, a pair of dark men she didn't know looming over him ominously.

Another man was striding toward her, a cold smile on his brown face and enough gold flashing around his neck to stock a new kiosk at the mall. She glanced back in Coach's direction, but he was motionless on the gym floor; then she applied the towel to her sweaty face again while the man finished his approach.

Nalani's brain had been freeze-dried since her morning epiphany in front of her toilet bowl. Her nausea had subsided enough to allow her to sleepwalk through her workout with Coach, but she had been unable to wrap her mind around a single cogent thought while she converted Coach's passes into field-goal attempts.

Which had been fine at the time, because even the thought of cogent thinking made her head hurt. But she knew it was time to pull her head out of the fog now, no fucking question about that, so she lowered her towel and quietly regarded the man in front of her.

"Come," he said, motioning toward the door on the far side of Coach with a short toss of his head. She was familiar with that head toss—the royalty among the local boys had exactly the same mannerism—and it never failed to rub her the wrong way. But she knew this was no local boy, so she let the gesture go by without comment.

"Where?" she said, even though she could have asked why instead and had briefly contemplated doing so.

The man slapped her with the open palm of his right hand, the strike so sudden she felt it on the side of her face before she saw him move. Her head snapped to the right with the impact, but she slowly moved it back to front and center and stared into the man's cold eyes again.

"Now," the man said, as though she had asked when rather than where. He motioned with the fingers of his left hand this time, his left arm extended insolently in her direction. This was another gesture she had seen before, another she never responded to when given the opportunity by a local prince.

She looked up at the man silently for a moment, then draped the towel around her neck and rose to her feet. They walked toward the door the men had entered, her leading the way and the man a step behind her. She looked at Coach on the floor as she passed by him; his eyes were closed, but she could see the gentle rise and fall of his chest. The other two men joined Nalani and her companion as she moved on toward the door and out into the parking lot on the *mauka* end of the gym.

Nalani shook her head slightly, thinking about the fed parked next to her Datsun on the *makai* end of the building. "Helluva bodyguard, right?" the man with the gold said, apparently able to read her mind.

"No need," Nalani said softly.

"That depends," the man said.

"On what?" Nalani asked.

"On your fockin' father," the man said, walking past her as they approached a new Chrysler and opening the rear door. She locked eyes with the man as she slid into the car, but she learned nothing more before he closed the door in her face. He walked around the car and slid into the seat next to her while the two shadows took the seats in front, the one behind the Ray-Bans in the passenger seat and the other at the wheel.

"Let me see your cell," the man said. Nalani dug it out of her gym bag as the car began to move and extended it in the man's direction.

"Throw it out the window," he said. As soon as he finished saying it, the window next to Nalani suddenly began to drop. When the gap was big enough, Nalani tossed the phone outside. Then the window rose again, and she refocused her attention on the man in the seat next to her.

The man reciprocated her attention but said nothing as the car rolled away from the parking lot. Nalani tried to read his black eyes but came up blank, so she eased back against the side of the car and waited for more information.

"Turn right at the highway," the man finally said.

"I knew that," the driver said. "What I need to know is where to turn off the highway."

"Don't we all," the man said. "I know it's past the park."

"Maybe the *señorita* knows the way."

"Maybe," the man said. "You know how to get to the Volcano golf course?"

Nalani reacted to this question slowly, as though walking face-first into the tradewinds as she did it, but her mind was finally cranking like the trades were behind her and pushing hard.

"Shuah," she said softly. "I know the way."

But that ain't all I fockin' know, she thought. She had suddenly been dealt a new card, that much was certain, and she was already deep into deciding how to play it by the time the Chrysler was rolling *mauka* on Highway 11, Hilo behind them and nothing but bristling potential ahead.

3

"What did you mean?" the guy with all the gold asked after they were inside the vacation rental, the driver looking at the golf course through the picture window in a comfortable living room and the scary one sitting at the kitchen counter with his Ray-Bans pointed directly at Nalani.

The gold guy had asked his question as though the comment about which he was inquiring had just been made, in spite of the fact that 20 minutes of driving up Highway 11 had transpired since Nalani had last spoken. Not that she was inclined to begin speaking now, in spite of the guy's question.

Easy does it, she thought as she looked around the room at her companions. She could see how the situation she was in could turn around and kick her in the teeth, but she refused to dwell on that vision; instead, she preferred to focus on what she might do to influence the outcome.

The gold guy was the man in charge, no question, and the driver gave off no vibes that indicated any danger beyond whatever the gold guy decreed. The guy with the Ray-Bans, though, that was something a lot more volatile—she felt the heat radiating from him and knew she was the object of it.

Very easy does it with that one, she thought, rolling the gold guy's question around a little more in her head before she tackled it out loud.

"If you don't kill my father," she said finally, "Sonnyboy's gonna do it, you know."

"I understand that part," the gold guy said. "What I wanna know, what makes you think I need to talk to you?"

"You have to ask, it's too soon to answer."

"What the fock does that mean?"

Nalani shrugged slightly, then glanced at the guy behind the Ray-Bans. "I need a shower," she said instead of answering the question. "I gotta keep him off me while I do it?"

The gold guy followed Nalani's eyes to the Ray-Bans perched at the kitchen counter. "Think you can?" the gold guy asked.

"Not," Nalani said. "That's why I brought it up."

The gold guy looked at Nalani like he had a learning disability where she was concerned, and then he looked at the guy behind the Ray-Bans. "Go ahead and take your shower," he said. "Ain' nobody gonna bother you."

4

Nalani was on the couch in the living room, her long bare legs stretched out in front of her while fatherhood scenarios ran around in her head. She could feel the eyes behind the Ray-Bans over by the kitchen counter crawling up and down her body, which she was actually thankful for because it had launched her current line of thought.

Shuah, she had said to herself, *could fockin' be you. Local girl kidnapped and raped, po' t'ing pregnant now, yeah?* There were things she liked about that story, but she didn't think about it long before she erased the guy behind the Ray-Bans from it and inserted the gold guy instead.

Gonna go that way, gonna go with the boss, she said in her head. But the questions continued to besiege her: Was that the best alternative? Was there a way to get more mileage out of this legacy dropped on her by her father?

Could always tell the truth, she thought. *Po' t'ing raped by her faddah.* But she wiped that scenario away even faster than the one starring the guy with the Ray-Bans because it made her a victim for too long—she was definitely leaning toward a story with a one-time-only punchline.

Which left her new boyfriend as the only realistic alternative to the people in the room with her right now, Pono plenty eager to play his part and the pregnancy that would result a story she knew everyone had already heard countless times. Which were two strikes against it, because Nalani had no desire to be tied to Pono in this way for the rest of her life any more than she wanted to be the latest chapter in a story as familiar as this one.

On the other hand, these guys here are good to go right now, she thought. She turned her attention to the gold guy sitting across the room from her, his eyes definitely on her just like the ones behind the Ray-Bans only without the danger signs.

Nalani rose from the couch and walked across the room. She could feel all six eyes in the room moving with her, but she walked by the four that didn't belong to the gold guy like they didn't exist. When she was standing in front of the gold guy, she extended her arms in his direction. He reached up, took her hands in his, and allowed her to pull him up on his feet.

"What's your name?" Nalani asked.

"Jesus," the gold guy said.

"Kiss me, Jesus," Nalani said, and that's what Jesus did.

5

It wasn't as bad as Nalani had feared. The men did what they wanted to do without touching her, Nalani having escaped to a vantage point near the ceiling where she coldly catalogued each transgression committed upon the vacant body she had left behind on the bed.

The one who had driven the car came almost immediately, but the one behind the Ray-Bans could not get enough of her, either unaware or unconcerned that he was hammering at the empty husk of the girl he had lusted for all day. He kept after her until his *compadre* was good for another go, and Nalani watched herself absorb their attentions simultaneously for a while.

Sooner or later, Nalani knew with absolute certainty, these men would make a mistake. She patiently watched and waited for it, and when it happened, she came down from the ceiling and fell on the men like God.

Geronimo

1

The woman from the feds was sitting in a metal chair next to Geronimo's desk when he came back from his basketball break at lunch, the game that day a better run than usual because Stefano was there for the first time in a long time and no one pushed the pace as well as he did.

Geronimo was contemplating the blessing this noontime game represented in his daily routine as he walked into the building, but he let those thoughts drift away as soon as he saw the woman.

"Hey," he said as he dropped into his chair.

"Good game?" the woman asked.

"Very good," Geronimo said, idly irritated that the woman was this familiar with his comings and goings but willing to let the irritation ride for a while.

"We have something like it in LA," she said. "Too bad I'm never there."

Geronimo looked at her with new eyes; she suddenly made more sense to him than she had before. "I should have known you were a baller," he said. "Everything I know about you fits together better now."

"You were thinking in a different context entirely," she said with a shrug. "Most people would have done the same thing."

"I'm usually better than most people."

"Yes," the woman said, but she seemed to be looking at the wall behind Geronimo's left shoulder when she said it. He waited for her to say something else, and when he grew weary of that he stopped.

"What's up?" he asked.

"I'd rather talk about you a little longer," she said.

"I don't think you came over here to talk hoops."

"You're right," she said, her brittle brown eyes focused on his eyes now instead of the wall. "The Mexicans snatched Dominic's daughter this morning."

The words hit Geronimo like a fist, knocking the air out of him for a moment. A vision of the girl standing next to her Datsun in Dominic's driveway flashed through his mind, and his stomach rolled so violently that he might have vomited had he been able to breathe when it happened.

"Fuck," he said when he could finally squeeze out a word of his own.

"No shit," the woman said, eyeing him soberly. "This is the kind of collateral damage you were talking about the other day, isn't it?"

"Yeah," he said. "But let's not jump too far ahead. There may not have been any real damage yet."

"That would be nice."

"Do you know why they took her?"

"I thought you were going to ask how."

"What difference does that make?"

She nodded glumly, closed her eyes briefly, and massaged both sides of her head with her hands. "They said they want restitution," she said when she finished her ministrations. "Or something better."

"I suppose Dominic went ballistic."

"Quite."

"Shit," Geronimo said. "What happens next?"

"Every time Dominic goes off, the guy cuts the connection. Right now we're waiting for another call."

Geronimo got up from his chair so he could walk around behind his desk while he chewed on this information. He felt like closing his eyes and massaging his own temples by the time he had it all processed, but he stood there and addressed the woman instead.

"What do you want from me?" he asked.

"Whatever you have."

"Part of this is bullshit, I can tell you that much for sure."

"Which part?"

"Maybe all of it."

"They don't want the money?"

"They'll take any money they can get," Geronimo said. "That's the name of this game, right?"

"But what?"

"They have to take him out. Everything else is window dressing."

The woman stared at Geronimo for an instant or two more, then stretched in her chair. He watched her long arms extend out to each side and her legs reach out in front of her, visions of hawks suddenly circling lazily in his head. Or something larger—eagles, maybe.

"That's the way I see it, too," she said as she rose from her chair. *"Gracias."*

"Now what?" he asked.

"Now we wait for the fucking phone to ring," she said.

2

Everyone in the room could hear the conversation the next time Dominic's phone rang, one of the feds having rigged it on a speaker system while they were waiting for the call.

"You ain' left yet, homes?" the voice said.

"Cut da fockin' sheet," Dominic said. "No way you fockin' watchin' me."

"No problem on this end, believe me," the voice said. "You're daughter is a fockin' *puta,* but we all agree she is a damned fine one."

Dominic's power of speech atrophied at that point as he struggled to find a way to reach into his phone and grab the throat the voice was pouring through with both hands. He changed colors, too, which Geronimo watched in amazement from across the room.

"You fockin' dead, I promise!" Dominic finally sputtered. "You all fockin' dead!"

"I think you're wrong there, *ese.* I think the first one gonna die aroun' here is this sweet little *puta.*" Then the connection went dead, and this time Dominic did throw the phone across the room. It bounced off the wall next to a picture of the Madonna which Geronimo imagined had been there since before the death of Dominic's wife.

"You fockahs do somet'ing," Dominic said, "or I gonna do da kine!"

"You know where they are," the woman said quietly, "please tell us."

"Fockin' find da moddafockahs!" Dominic shouted, referring to a task every phone in the room except Dominic's had been turned to since Geronimo suggested combing through the haystack of possible vacation rentals which might have replaced the hotel room the Mexicans had abandoned that morning.

Geronimo knew this was far from a hopeless task, even though their initial efforts had been fruitless. Someone looking for immediate occupancy was unusual in the world of vacation rentals, and someone who didn't know one from another was likely to start looking at the beginning of the alphabet.

Consequently, Geronimo was not surprised when one of the feds shouted, "Bingo!" The fed held up the piece of paper he had been scribbling on furiously. "Someone named Jaime Gomez rented this place this morning, occupancy starting today."

"Wheah?" Dominic asked, the word squirting out as if propelled through a small opening by inordinate pressure.

"Dominic!" the woman cautioned.

Dominic launched himself toward the fed with the paper in his hand, moving quickly for a man carrying that degree of bulk, but the woman was quicker. Dominic was almost airborne one moment, hurtling toward liftoff like a jumbo jet, then he was suddenly airborne for real as the woman swept his legs out from under him. He careened off an easy chair and a sofa before falling face first on the floor.

The woman followed him all the way down, until her knee was

digging into his massive back and her handgun was screwed into the side of his face.

"Chill," she said quietly.

Dominic made no response, but his body trembled like it might explode at any moment.

"Do you understand me?" she asked.

Dominic breathed deeply and nodded.

"We get that you're upset about your daughter," the woman said. "Now calm down and help us figure out how to get her back. 'Kay?"

Dominic nodded again, and the woman rose nimbly to her feet and reholstered her gun. Dominic rolled over and sat up, rubbing his chin. "What da fock was dat?" he asked.

"A girl can't tell all her secrets, Dominic," she said. "Now how are we gonna get that girl out of there?"

"Where?" Geronimo asked, reintroducing Dominic's initial query.

"Adjacent to a golf course in Volcano?" the fed with the paper in his hand said, the words strung together more like a question than a statement because the fed didn't know Volcano from the dark side of the moon. Geronimo asked for the address and got it, then let his mind wrestle with it for a moment.

"How much backup can we get from you guys?" the woman asked.

"As much as you want, believe me," Geronimo said. "But backup isn't the problem, is it?"

"No," the woman said. "The problem is getting in on them before they know we're there."

"Exactly," Geronimo said. "Any of you guys play golf?"

3

Geronimo knew the precautions were mandatory, but he keenly regretted the time they required. Eventually, access to the street in front of the house was adequately restricted and the bonafide golfers had been removed from the course. He moved down the fairway with Ralph Benedetto, the woman, and one of her feds until they were directly opposite the target house.

"I think it's over here!" he shouted, more for the benefit of anyone in the house who might be watching than for his companions because his companions all knew he had not hit a ball into the rough near the house.

Geronimo took the golf bag he was pulling with him as he walked toward the picture window facing the course, and his companions all did the same. When they were about ten yards from the house, the woman came up behind him so she couldn't be seen from the building and removed a walkie-talkie from her bag.

"Here we go," she said, which was supposed to trigger an advance on the front of the house from the cops on the street.

"Ain't no car in the driveway, boss," a scratchy voice responded.

"Fuck," the woman mumbled. Then she clipped the walkie-talkie to her waist and removed a shotgun from her bag. The three men dipped into their bags and came out with similar weapons, and they all moved without wasted motion in predetermined directions—Ralph to the left of the window, Geronimo to the right, and the two feds straight at it.

"Now!" the woman said when they were only a stride or two away from the window. All four of them fired a round into the glass, one on each of the four edges, and they followed the flying fragments into a rustic living room as the front door burst open and uniforms swarmed in from the street.

The room was not at that moment inhabited by Nalani Rosario or her abductors, so Geronimo raced across it to the nearest doorway and stopped inside a bedroom that had been used a little harder than originally intended.

"Oh, fuck," he said softly.

"What?" the woman asked from right behind him.

Geronimo ignored her question and scurried around the bodies on the floor between the door and the bed. He found nothing on the other side of the room or in the adjoining bathroom, and by the time he started back toward the woman, Ralph was coming up behind her.

"Nothing out here," Ralph said.

"What you see is what you get, then," Geronimo said, which was two nude male Latinos whose life had leaked out of holes in their heads—one shot through the left lens of his Ray-Bans and the other through the back of his skull, as though he had tried to outrun the bullet and failed.

Dominic
1

Dominic was methodically checking the water and feed in each of the tiny tin A-frames which sheltered his birds. He had worked his way to the last row when the fed busted around the corner of the house, a phone stuck in his ear and a dark cloud all over his face.

The fed put the phone away as he picked a path through the A-frames, but Dominic noted that the dark cloud didn't go anywhere.

"Wassup?" Dominic said when the fed was close enough to hear the question.

"Fuckin' retard lost your daughter," the fed said, his lips so tight they barely moved enough to let the words escape.

"What da fock you mean?" Dominic said, his fists clenching of their own accord and the desire to smash the fucking fed surging so swiftly that Dominic was up to his neck in it by the time he punched his words out of his own tight mouth.

"Slow down, Dominic," the fed said, assuming incorrectly that Dominic had access to his accelerator. Dominic launched a left hook that the fed ducked under just a trifle too slowly; it hit him high on his right cheek and knocked him on his ass in the chicken shit. The cocks in the vicinity raucously protested this intrusion, but neither of the men heeded their angry cries. Dominic focused instead on wrapping both of his hands around the fed's neck and pulling him off the ground, while the fed focused exclusively on trying to find a way to breathe while Dominic dangled him like rag doll.

"What da fock you talkin' about?" Dominic said.

The fed couldn't talk through the stranglehold on his throat, so he reached down for the .38 on his right hip instead. Once he had it in his hand, he stuck it under Dominic's chin and began to push.

Dominic eventually noticed the cold pressure of the gun, and when he did, he released his grip on the fed. "Jeezus Christ, Dominic!" the fed sputtered as soon as he had surrounded the requisite amount of air.

"What you wen do to my daughtah?" Dominic asked, the desire to hit still throbbing incessantly through his nervous system but the monitor tenuously back in place.

"I'm gonna blow your fucking head off, you ever do that again," the fed said. He started to reholster his handgun, but he was on his back in the shit again before he finished the process. Dominic bounced a crisp right cross off the fed's face this time and followed right behind it until his knee was in the fed's chest and his mouth close enough to the fed's to French-kiss him if he wanted to—which he did not.

"Nevah fockin' t'reaten me!" Dominic said. "Break yo' fockin' neck like not'ing! You heah me, moddafockah?"

The fed nodded blankly, but said nothing.

"What you wen do to my daughtah?" Dominic said again.

"Somebody snatched her at the gym," the fed said, and then he dialed right back to speechless until the trill of Dominic's phone infiltrated the thin space between them.

2

Dominic felt like he could swallow the phone whole, but he resisted the impulse to do so and continued to wait. When the phone finally rang in his hand, he responded with what he thought of as moderation.

"What you fockin' want?" he said.

"I swap the *señorita* for you straight up," the voice said in his ear. "Then we sit down and negotiate our future."

You no got one futuah, Dominic thought, but he didn't say that. "How we gonna do dat," he asked, "da fockin' feds all ovah me?"

"I don' know, *ese,*" the voice said. "You da man, right?"

Which you about to fockin' find out, Dominic thought. "Weah?" he said.

"Jus' drive south on Highway Eleven. We see you got no one followin' you, we'll tell you more."

"When?" Dominic asked.

"Whenever you want her back, homes. We ain' in no rush to get rid of her, you know what I mean?"

The phone went dead in Dominic's ear after that, and he felt like flinging it across the room this time. Instead, he lowered it slowly and looked at the drug bitch and her two stooges—and fucking Geronimo Souza, who had trailed in with the drug bitch for reasons Dominic had yet to decipher.

"He gonna tradah fo' me," he said to no one in particular.

"Where?" the woman asked.

"What da fock he doin' heah?" Dominic said, suddenly on Geronimo overload.

"Where do they want to swap?" the woman said, as though Dominic had said nothing at all about fucking Souza.

"Gonna tell me latah," Dominic said. "Gotta go *mauka* on Eleven, dey gonna check I got one fockin' tail."

"All they really want is to kill you," the woman said. "You understand that, right?"

"Dey welcome to fockin' try, I get my daughtah back."

"You're dead, no telling what happens to your daughter."

"So what you gonna do?" Dominic asked.

"Could put a beam on his truck and follow him that way," one of the stooges said.

"I'm afraid he's dead if he gets out of our sight," the woman said.

"We could stash one of us in the back of the truck," the other stooge said.

"Then what?" the woman said. "He shoots it out with the three of them?"

"You ain't gonna do shit!" Dominic interjected. "You all fockin' wort'less!"

"You kept the girl home like we told you to," the stooge who had lost the girl in the first place said, "this fuckin' shit would have never happened."

"Shut the fock up!" Dominic said. "Could watch yo' fockin' shadow wit'out losin' it, maybe it nevah hoppen eidah."

"Where have these guys been staying?" Geronimo said from the far side of the room. The conversation he interrupted drained away as everyone turned in his direction.

"We're on that," the woman said. "We think they checked out of their hotel room this morning."

"Then you know who we're looking for?"

"Probably. We know who they said they were, anyway."

"Then you know what they're driving, right?"

Dominic watched the woman look from Geronimo to the stooges, then turn toward him. "May we borrow your phone book?" she asked.

"Fockin' unbelievable," he said, but he pointed to the book next to the phone on the kitchen counter.

"Cross-check the rental-car companies with the names from

the hotel," she said, turning her attention back to the stooges. One of them got up, moved to the counter and started flipping pages in the phone book.

"Plus they're still fucking tourists, right?" Geronimo continued. "Where did they take the girl?"

"Kind of risky waltzing a sixteen-year-old girl into a hotel with three men, don't you think?" the woman asked.

"I'd say they moved to a vacation rental," Geronimo said. "Way more privacy."

"There's gotta be a lot of those," the woman said.

"Yeah," Geronimo said. "But you get some more people on the phones, it's only a matter of time before you find the one who rented to these fuckers."

"What da fock?" Dominic said. "I stand heah wit' my t'umb up my ass while you fockahs play telephone games?"

"Would you fucking cool it for a minute?" the woman asked, her Slice-A-Ma-Tic eyes trained full-bore on Dominic. "Maybe if I had a minute, I could think of a way to keep your sorry ass alive."

Chapter Six
Quarter Break

Jesus

Jesus was behind the wheel of the rented Chrysler instead of Jaime, the girl a million miles away in the seat usually occupied by Manuel—Jesus and the girl having advanced from the back mostly because neither Jaime nor Manuel could sit up straight anymore.

Jesus had given up trying to track the girl's thoughts as he drove back toward Hilo, but he watched her out of the corner of his right eye and buried himself in some thoughts of his own.

He had hit the floor in the living room as soon as the .45 boomed twice in the bedroom. When nothing else happened immediately, he turned and ran his eyes out the picture window behind him; in spite of the fact that golfers had been meandering by all day, he saw nothing but empty green. He knew already that the vacation houses on both sides of this one were empty, so the first thought he had while sprawled on the living room carpet with his own gun trained on the bedroom door was that he might have enough time to work through this situation.

Whatever the fock this situation is, Jesus said to himself when the next sound he heard was the shower in the master bathroom. He got up carefully and moved to the doorway, where he found Jaime and Manuel motionless on the floor between the door and the bed. The girl was not in sight, so he stepped around the men and kept on stepping until he could see inside the bathroom.

The first thing Jesus focused on was Jaime's .45, which was

resting on the lid of the toilet; the second thing was the steam pouring out of the shower and the girl dimly visible through a clear plastic curtain. She was standing directly under the nozzle, her face turned into the driving water as though she needed every last drop to do the cleaning job at hand.

Jesus entered the bathroom and picked up the .45. The girl had turned off the water by then, and Jesus watched her push the curtain out of the way. She stood there in front of him and worked with her long black hair, the water still streaming from it and running down her back.

What the fock kinda kid is this? Jesus thought, but he had no questions about the kind of kid she looked like standing there with the nipples hard on those pert breasts and the sleek wet bush dripping water between her legs.

"We gotta move, you know," she said as she stepped out of the tub and reached around him for a towel.

"But you had time for a shower?" Jesus asked.

The girl glanced slowly in the direction of Jaime and Manuel, then brought her gaze back to Jesus. "Fockin' pigs were all over me," she said quietly, as though that said it all—which, somehow, it did. Jesus knew he had left his own traces on the girl, but she apparently did not include him in the same category as the others and he requested no revision of that status.

He watched her dry herself quickly; then he watched her dress the same way. "One thing," she said, standing next to the bodies in front of the bedroom door while she ran a comb through her wet hair.

"What?" Jesus asked.

"*I* choose the people I fock, yeah?" she said.

"Yeah," Jesus replied slowly, thinking the girl might still have a punchline for him she hadn't delivered yet. But she snatched his answer out of the air and walked away with it, picking up her sports bag when she got to it and stopping only when she was planted in the front passenger seat of the Chrysler.

Which is where she was now, the thin edge of the situation blunted a little with the golf course 15 or 20 minutes behind them. Jesus was uneasy, though; he was missing something right in front of his face, but he didn't know what it was until the girl finally spoke.

"The car is hot by now, you know," she said, looking away as she said it as though any temperature the Chrysler might or might not have made no difference at all to her.

"What do you mean?" Jesus said, but he finally saw behind the veil as soon as the words were out of his mouth. *They find the hotel three Latinos checked out of this morning,* he thought, his mind finally wrapped around it, *they find the rental car. They look hard enough, they find the fockin' vacation rental, too.*

"Big Island, my ass," he said, thinking not for the first time that the only thing big about this place was its appetite for ice. The girl apparently took his comment to be the answer to his own question because she added nothing to it, her eyes still lost in scenery she had probably driven by thousands of times already in her long kid life.

"You're almost focked," the girl said a few minutes later, wrapping her voice around exactly what he was thinking. But her assumption that she was somehow home free rubbed him the wrong way.

"You're not?" he asked.

"I'm the victim," she said.

"You can be victimized a lot more than you have been so far."

"Shuah," she said, looking at him for the first time in a while. "But you need me if you're gonna get this thing done and get yourself out of here after."

"You can do all that?" Jesus asked.

"Yes. If I want to."

"Do you want to?"

"I don't know," the girl said, her voice a little softer and thicker than it had been before. "Do I?"

"Sure you do," Jesus said, trying to sell it a little without selling it too much. "You make this happen, you definitely improve your situation around here."

The girl played with that in her head for a while, her eyes almost crackling in front of him. "I don't trust you yet," she said finally.

"Trust ain' got nothin' to do with it," Jesus said, amping the pitch up a little more, "'Cept you can trust me to waste your sweet ass you fock with me. And I can trust you to do the same, based on what I seen so far."

Neither of them spoke for a mile or two after that, which got Jesus to thinking about where the fuck he was going as the foliage along the road began to dissipate in favor of the southern edge of the town.

"I have a cousin with a boat you can use to get to Maui," the girl said suddenly. "But you would still need another name to fly out of there."

Among other things, Jesus said to himself, *this is one smart fockin' kid. But she has no idea how many people I can be when the need arises.*

"No problem," he said aloud. "Meanwhile, we have to dump this rental car."

"You take me back to the gym, we can pick up my car."

"Then what?" Jesus asked.

"Then I show you how to do my fockin' father," the girl said, her cold eyes bearing in on him so hard while she said it that Jesus had to think twice to remember who the fuck was going to do what to whom.

Dominic

1

The cops and the feds were all stuck at the house with the bodies on the floor like they had been snorting molasses all day, but Dominic was not similarly encumbered. He bounced as soon as he determined that Nalani was not on the scene, furiously speeding *makai* on Highway 11 even though he had no specific destination in mind.

He was rolling down the slope through Mountain View when his cell phone rang, and he hit it so hard when he pounced to answer it that it slipped onto the floor of the truck between his feet.

"Fock!" he shouted. He swerved off the highway in front of the Mountain View version of Verna's Drive-in and slammed to a stop. An instant later, he had a working phone in his hand.

"What?" he said, his anxiety boosted by the fact that he didn't recognize the number on his phone.

"It's me," Nalani said quietly.

"What da fock is up, girl? You okay?"

"Yeah," Nalani said, her voice sounding old and tired by the time it reached Dominic.

"Wheah da fock you at?"

"Three or four miles past the zoo," Nalani said.

"What da fock?" Dominic sputtered.

"Fockah spooked now," Nalani said slowly. "He dumped me out here and split."

"You hurt, girl? You okay?"

"I'm fine, I promise. I just need one ride, that's all."

"Gimme fifteen minutes," Dominic said.

"One thing," Nalani said.

"What?"

"You got the fockin' feds with you now?"

"Fock, no."

"Good," she said. "I can't handle them right now, you know."

"Fo'get all dese moddafockahs," Dominic said. "Got you now, I promise."

"Hurry, yeah?" she said, and Dominic put his phone down on the empty seat next to him and hurried.

2

Dominic made no concessions to the new conditions when the road turned to gravel shortly after he shot past the zoo, the truck still hurtling forward at its maximum speed and Dominic still trying to make it go faster.

He drove without thinking, his fury flowing freely as the truck obliterated the distance between himself and his daughter. What he needed to know he knew without thought—that this violation of his family by some fucking Mexican would be totally avenged, and that he would be utterly invincible in the process of administering that vengeance.

The truck sped up a short incline and almost flew by Nalani's Datsun in the dip on the other side. Dominic stood on his brake pedal and fishtailed to a stop three or four yards from the car, alarm bells ringing through the red rage in his head.

What da fock? he asked himself, the Datsun tilting the picture of this scene he had already drawn in his mind almost beyond recognition. He boiled out of the truck, but he had the nine he kept under his seat firmly in his right hand by the time his feet hit the ground.

Nalani was leaning against the hood of her car, her face lit with a strange glow Dominic had never seen before. He was trying to decipher that expression when something invisible slammed him in the chest, knocking the air out of him and bouncing him off the side of his truck.

He heard a sharp crack reminiscent of gunfire, and the next thing he knew he was flat on his back in the gravel. His head was tipped in Nalani's direction, and he could see individual rocks in front of his face if he focused his eyes just right even though he couldn't feel the gravel directly under him. He felt nothing but the panic of breathlessness, the cold realization that the law of one breath effortlessly and unthinkingly following another had somehow been repealed. He tried to wrestle the air around him back into his lungs, but he couldn't open his hands or move his arms, and when he tried to ask Nalani for help, he discovered that speech had been abolished.

Dominic watched unblinkingly as Nalani moved from the side of the Datsun until she towered over him, the strange glow still pouring out of her. She stood there silently until he succeeded in breathing again, then she stood on his right wrist while a dark man with several layers of gold flashing around his neck walked up beside her.

The man pointed a gun at Dominic's eyes, but Nalani intervened. "Not," she said, and sweet hope suddenly swept over Dominic like a wave.

"Let me do it," Nalani said next, and Dominic struggled to decode the words—he heard them clearly, but he did not understand them. The man slowly extended the gun in Nalani's direction, as though he had his own problems with interpreting the words.

Nalani took the gun in both hands, raised it to her lips and gently kissed the tip of the barrel. Dominic followed these movements from his vantage point on the ground, but they made no more sense to him than the words that had preceded them.

What da fock? he said, although he was not sure if he said it aloud or to himself.

Neither Nalani nor the dark man with all the gold replied, but Nalani slowly lowered herself until she was squatting by his side. Dominic stared directly into her hot eyes, and he was still contemplating that heat when she jammed the gun against his testicles.

The sharp pain in his genitals jolted Dominic into clarity; suddenly the door to absolute understanding swung open in front of him.

"Not," he whispered, his voice so faint he wasn't sure the word had actually escaped from his mouth.

"Oh, yes," Nalani said, and Dominic saw her lips tighten before his ears suddenly filled with thunder and fire coursed through his groin. He screamed—*like a focking woman,* he thought suddenly, the thought slipping through a crack in the pain and chaos surrounding him. He hated himself for the scream, but he was powerless to stop that first one and all of the screams that followed it.

The gun in Nalani's hands roared repeatedly, each time ripping a new roadway through Dominic's genitalia, and each time he responded with another scream until the screams finally all ran together. He poured every last feeling in his mutilated body out through his scorched throat, and when he was empty, he fell into a bottomless pit while his daughter crouched implacably at the edge of the abyss and watched him slowly disappear.

Nalani
1

Nalani reached over when she was sure her father was gone and picked up his nine where it had fallen next to his body. When she rose, she had a gun in each hand.

"What the fock was that?" Jesus asked.

"None of your focking business," Nalani said, moving a step or two away and raising Dominic's nine.

"Now you're gonna do me?" Jesus asked calmly, like he was asking about the price of admission to the zoo.

"Why not?" Nalani said.

"Why would you, first of all."

"You fed me to your focking pigs, that's why."

"I know," Jesus said. "That was wrong. I owe you for that."

"How are you fockin' gonna pay for it?"

"I don't know. I'll think of something, believe me."

"You can't, you know. No fockin' way."

"Fine," Jesus said. "Some things can't be undone, I grant you that. But you still don't wanna kill me."

"Why not?"

"Won't do any good, for one thing. There are more of me where I came from, and they'll be fockin' angry when they get here."

"If you can't tell 'em, how are they gonna know who they're angry at?"

"They know who fingered our ice to the feds," Jesus said. "They'll come in and sweep the fockin' board clean."

"Everyone but me, I think," Nalani said. "I'm the poor kid victim, yeah?"

Jesus stood there and continued to regard the three eyes pointed in his direction, the hard brown ones on Nalani's face and the black one at the end of her right arm. She watched him shake his head slowly and start to grin.

"You are really something else," he said. "I've never met anyone like you."

The gun was beginning to fatigue Nalani's arm, but she knew she could hold it up for as long as she needed to so she stood there without a word and waited for the rest of the pitch.

"You'll lose a lot of family," Jesus said next, "even if it comes down like you think it will."

"Fock my family," Nalani said.

"Plus you'll miss the chance to hang with me. What a team the two of us could be!"

Fock the team, too, Nalani thought, but then Jesus moved. She squeezed the trigger, but she was too slow to hit him with anything but the sound when the gun went off. He was inside her right arm before she could react, his right fist buried in her gut. She gasped and crumpled on top of her father while both guns clattered from her grasp.

Jesus reached down, wrapped both hands around her neck, and

lifted her into the air so he could stare into her eyes. "I should fockin' wring your neck," he said as she struggled to breathe. "I swear to God I should."

He threw her against the side of Dominic's truck and watched her slide to the ground. When he saw that she was breathing again, he picked up both guns and started to walk to the Datsun.

"Get up," he said as he moved, "and get me off this fockin' rock."

Geronimo

1

"That fucking Rosario just took off," one of the feds said from the doorway at the front of the house.

"It's not like we have an army at our command out here," the woman said. "Let him go for now."

Geronimo listened to this exchange from his vantage point at the entry to the bedroom with the bodies on the floor. Ralph was on the phone to get a crime-scene team rolling, and the woman was standing just inside the doorway with one ear on Ralph and the other one on the fed at the front door.

Geronimo turned away and started across the living room, but the woman's voice caught up with him after two or three strides. "You leaving?" she asked.

"You're gonna need the techies to figure this shit out," Geronimo said. "I sure as hell don't know what happened."

"You don't think you can catch up with him, do you?"

"Who?"

"Don't get cute. You know who."

"Considering my car is all the way over by the pro shop, no. But what's the point of standing around here with my thumb up my butt?"

"Tell me about it," she said. "Bobby, would you give him a ride to his car?"

"No problem," the fed at the door said, and a couple of minutes later Geronimo had his own rig cranked up and headed full-tilt down the hill toward Hilo.

Geronimo's head was spinning just as fast as the Explorer was rolling, and he let it whirl unchecked. He thought of the woman in Volcano as he roared past that turnoff, which led to thoughts of Denise and the demolition of the connection between them apparently well underway.

Then he thought of the Japanese bookmakers—and whatever else they were—and the game the next day that could get him out from under their weight or bury him almost beyond reclamation.

As soon as Geronimo wrapped his mind around that thought, his phone rang. He fumbled for it in spite of the fact that he was driving too fast for conversation, and after a clumsy moment he had his former bookie in his ear.

"Funny you called right now," Geronimo said after the exchange of greetings.

"Yeah?" Robbie said.

"I was just thinking about you."

"Me, or the fockin' Japs?"

"It's getting harder to see the distinction all the time, Robbie."

"You better look a little closer, Gee."

Geronimo considered that comment for a moment, but he didn't need much time to remember who was on the other phone. "Why'd you call, Robbie?" he asked.

"What you got on the Lakers?"

"I thought I was out of your hands now."

"How much?"

"Fifteen."

"So the Pistons win, you owe thirty?"

"You're pretty good with numbers, Robbie."

"You got the thirty?"

"What'd I say the last time you asked?"

"The last time it was fifteen, Gee."

"The Lakers can't keep losing," Geronimo said. *And neither can I,* he added to himself.

"That's what I fockin' thought," Robbie said, and it didn't take Geronimo long to figure out that he wasn't talking about the Lakers.

"Why'd you call, Robbie?" Geronimo asked again.

"To make you an offer you don't wanna refuse, brah."

"What?"

"I'll take thirty on the Pistons."

"The Lakers lose, I get the money to pay the fucking Japs from you?"

"Yeah."

"The Lakers win, I'm even with the Japs but I owe you the thirty."

"Yeah."

"If I thought the fucking Pistons were gonna win, I would have bet on them in the first place."

"Get away from the Japs, Gee."

"Robbie, you're a Jap."

"You know what I mean."

"Do I?"

"You better. Those fockin' fools don' play, brah."

Geronimo turned down the volume on the conversation, mulling it over soundlessly as his Explorer plowed past the Verna's in Mountain View forty or fifty miles over the speed limit. *Shouldn't be driving this fast with one hand,* he thought idly, and then he let his mind wander away from the money for a moment while he reconsidered the game itself.

The Lakers can't lose, he reminded himself. *Except the sorry mother-*

fuckers would have been swept already except for that one miracle shot. How the fuck are the Pistons doing it?

The answer to that question presented itself almost as soon as the question did, and Robbie's proposition suddenly began to glow in the dark of Geronimo's busy mind.

"Fucking Detroit's the better team, isn't it?" Geronimo said.

"I have no fockin' idea, brah."

"I don't know why I didn't see it sooner. The Lakers have the players, the Pistons have the team."

"Whatever you say."

"I think I'm gonna take you up on this, Robbie."

"I'll do it on one condition only, brah."

"Name it."

"This is last bet I ever take from you, win or lose."

"You can't make a dime by refusing to take bets, Robbie."

"Last one ever, Gee."

"Agreed," Geronimo said, although he wasn't at all convinced that he meant it by the time the word spilled out of his mouth.

"Good," Robbie said, and then the connection went dead and Geronimo had two hands available again for guiding his rig down Dominic Rosario's invisible trail.

2

Geronimo was the first cop on the scene, the blue light flashing on top of the Explorer and the siren screaming. He had been two or three minutes past the turnoff to the zoo, cruising at half his earlier speed to nowhere in particular, when he caught the squawk. He U-turned at Puainako and maxed out his rig until he rolled up on Dominic's truck in the middle of the gravel road.

The old farmer who had made the nine-eleven call was still there, leaning against the front fender of a beat-up flatbed truck and smoking a hand-rolled cigarette.

"Everything's still the same as it was, right?" Geronimo asked.

The old man nodded, drawing deeply on his cigarette and blowing the smoke out slowly. "Nevah touch not'ing," he said.

"You didn't check to see if he was alive, maybe?"

"Looked like he look right now. You t'ink he's alive?"

Geronimo looked down at Dominic's body, but it didn't take him long to get his fill of the view. "Somebody sure as hell didn't like him," he said quietly, the observation bothering him somehow. He rolled the tape of what he knew about the scene in his head, and only the wound in the middle of Dominic's chest fit that picture.

"Plenny people like dat, I promise," the old man said.

"You knew him?"

"Piece a sheet moddafockah, yeah?" the old man said. "Shoot him myself, evah get one chance."

"Why is that?"

"Fockin' drugs."

Geronimo nodded, those two words telling him everything he needed to know. "Nobody else around when you got here?" he asked. "A car driving away, maybe?"

"Not," the old man said. "Just him, like dat."

The others started arriving then, first a uniform Geronimo didn't know and then Stefano right behind the uniform. Stefano took one look at the body and turned toward Geronimo, his eyebrows raised. "How far the mighty have fallen since Saturday night," he said.

"This look right to you?" Geronimo asked.

"Some kind of a message, maybe?" Stefano said. "You fuck with us, we'll shoot your fucking balls off?"

"Maybe," Geronimo said softly.

"You don't sound convinced."

"Are you?"

"No," Stefano said. "I'm not."

Geronimo nodded, his mind sorting rapidly through the pieces of the puzzle he already knew, and one question or maybe two jumped to the top of the list of missing pieces and stayed there no matter how many times he turned it all over in his head:

Where is Nalani Rosario, he asked himself, *and what the fuck is going on?*

Kitano

1

"You want to get involved?" Kitano asked in Japanese, even though he knew the old man's answer in advance. But the old man took his fucking time with the reply, of course, which Kitano also had known would happen in advance.

The old man was in his bath, a daily ritual Kitano had lost patience with months ago. *Could he fall and hit his fucking head on the tub?* Kitano wondered. *Could he overdose and drown, maybe? How many ways might this fucking ritual be made to turn in my favor?*

Thoughts like these had been springing up in Kitano's head with more regularity on this trip to Hilo than any of the trips before it, and he was hard-pressed to understand why. This one was no different than the others, that was certain, except that Kitano's discontent continued to accumulate from one trip to the next.

Nothing is changing but me, Kitano thought while he waited for a response from the old man. *Is this a weakening,* he asked himself, *or an awakening? Should I continue to wait, or should I act?*

When the old man finally spoke, Kitano was sponging the soap off the old man's withered shoulders. He listened to the Japanese coming out of the old man's mouth, but he heard the words in English now and rolled them around in his mind in that language rather than the original.

Fuck no, he doesn't want to get involved, Kitano thought. *No percentage in it—better to wait and see what happens. Let Rosario and the feds muddle through the thing with the Mexicans, then deal with whoever is still standing.*

The only thing bothering Kitano about the entire scenario was the fact that Rosario had not been the source of their information about the snatch of Rosario's daughter and the current negotiations swirling around it—Rosario apparently closer now to the feds than he was to the old man.

Probably knew we wouldn't do a thing, Kitano thought, *but still—the guy was two or three times too full of himself, and if he survived this scenario, he would need to be cut back a size or two. Or cut all the way back to the ground and replaced, assuming a replacement could be found.*

One thing about this fucking business, Kitano said silently as he helped the shriveled old man out of the tub, *a replacement can always be found.*

2

Kitano was ready to jump out of his own skin when the phone rang. *I don't know how much more of this shit I can stand, old man,* he said to himself as he picked up the phone, one aspect of the shit to which he referred being the way the old man was constantly underfoot and another being this interminable interlude in fucking Hilo.

"Yes?" he said into the phone, his eyes on the old man dozing in Kitano's favorite armchair.

"All hell breakin' out ovah heah," a voice said in his ear, the voice low like it had to watch out who could hear it.

"What, exactly," Kitano said.

"Two da kine Mexicans dead out Volcano-side somewheah, and Rosario dead out past da zoo."

"Rosario is dead?"

"Yeah."

"Now what?"

"Everybody lookin' fo' da daughtah, mebbe on da Kona side now."

"Why?"

"Somet'ing about how da last Mexican gonna get off da rock. Fockah ain't gonna fly out, I promise."

"What? He's gonna hop a boat to LA?"

"Not. Mo' like Maui, dey t'ink."

"Maui? What the fuck good would that do? I would think the feds can cover the airport on Maui just as well as the airports here, wouldn't you?"

"Don't fockin' ask me, brah. Not paht of da high command heah, you know."

"No fucking kidding," Kitano said as he hung up the phone. The old man opened his eyes and fixed them on Kitano, Kitano suddenly feeling like a fly in the presence of a spider that had been around for a good long time. He summarized the call in Japanese for the old man, and several silent moments later the old man used the same language to issue Kitano's instructions.

You're so fucking slow, old man, Kitano thought, and while he began to implement the old man's orders, his mind continued to ponder ways the old man could be moved out of the fucking way.

Jay-Jay

Jay-Jay couldn't remember a night with the same degree of potential for delight, and he hummed his way around his house as he got ready for it. *Like I have said so many times before,* he said to himself again, *you can't fucking beat this business.*

Jay-Jay's pursuit of Kapua had been proceeding nicely, the pump almost fully primed now. Still, he was in no hurry for consummation; he loved the long preliminaries every bit as much as the months of fucking to follow. Now the girl was on her way over again, and he was tantalizing himself with visions of the liberties he would take this time around.

He had nearly brought her to orgasm during her last visit, his practiced fingers playing with her skillfully while he suckled her beautiful breasts, but he had managed to stop just in time. *Maybe tonight I'll let you have it,* he thought. Maybe *I'll sip at that sweet fountain tonight; maybe I'll show you what the tongue you've been sucking can do where it really belongs.* But as soon as he finished thinking all this, he knew there was no fucking maybe about it.

He hurried through his shower, and was almost dressed when the doorbell rang. "And away we go!" he said, for some reason thinking of the funny fat fucker who used to say the same thing on television.

Bet you were never going anywhere this fucking good, were you, big guy? he thought as he strolled across the living room, opened the front door, and ushered his princess inside.

Chapter Seven
Time Out

Nalani
1

"You sure this heap gonna make it?" Jesus said from the passenger seat of the Datsun as they rolled up on Honokaa, Hilo an hour behind them and Nalani's cousin with the boat still almost an hour ahead.

Not, Nalani said to herself. *Lightning might fockin' strike us, yeah?*

"What?" Jesus said after what seemed like several moments went by without a response he could hear. "You ain' gonna talk now?"

Nalani gave that question the same treatment as the one before it as she abandoned the highway at Tex's, followed the arrows around the building, and parked in front of the garden showcasing local shrubs.

"Who told you to stop?" Jesus said.

"You wanna drive, get behind the wheel."

"She speaks," Jesus said. "Now that we're here, I guess I could eat."

Nalani climbed out of the car and headed for the restroom, food the last thing on her mind. She knew Jesus was somewhere behind her with a "what the fock" expression on his face, but that was the next-to-last thing on her mind. She had to wait in line to pee, several Japanese women from the tour bus in the parking lot ahead of her, and when she was finally done, she washed her hands and face and stared at herself in the mirror until she knew for sure what she was thinking about the first thing on her mind.

Jesus was leaning against the driver's side of the Datsun with his phone to his ear when she came out of the restroom. *Can't leave the car, yeah?* she said to herself. *Maybe the kid'll drive off an' leave your sorry ass.*

"What the fock's a *malasada?*" Jesus asked when she walked up to the car.

"A mouthful of heaven," Nalani said, although the thought of the drive-in's signature pastry made her stomach roll.

"You could be talkin' 'bout me," Jesus said.

"It's deep-fat fried, you know," she said. "You wanna stick your thing in the fryer, maybe?"

"I don' think so. I stick it someplace hot, I feel like it—but not that hot. What's fockin' good to eat here?"

"Everything."

"Get us something," he said, dropping the phone into his pocket and coming out with a twenty. She took the bill and turned back toward the building again, a message flashing through her eyes as soon as he was in the wrong position to read it:

I've got something for you under my seat in the car, she thought, her mind racing back to her decision in the restroom. *It's something more than you can fockin' chew, I promise.*

2

Nalani drove carefully, the road dark and twisty and blanketed here and there with fog. Her mind felt the same way the road looked, sometimes clear and crisp but other times almost impenetrable.

She had been confident about the eventual outcome of any collaboration with her cousin, this particular cousin one of the relatives who wanted her the same way her father had. She saw Jesus coming up on the wrong side of the boat at some point and herself living happily ever after. Now, she saw nothing but the spin of another curve ball coming at her.

"Is that cactus out there?" Jesus asked, looking out his window at the hill slanting up into the night.

"Yeah."

"I thought we were in the tropics over here."

"We have six or seven different climate zones on this island," Nalani said. "Tropical is only one of them."

Jesus drifted back into silence as Nalani continued to drive, apparently lost in his own cactus-inspired thoughts, so she kept hammering away at the information currently at her disposal. Every new pitch was a new opportunity to hit the ball out of the fucking park, that much she knew for sure, and she fought to keep her eyes on the prize as she sliced through the murky night.

3

Nalani found the driveway on her second try, if driveway was the word for this slight grassy path through the trees. She made her way slowly, her headlights funneled by the foliage like she was driving through a leafy green tunnel. After what seemed like an hour or more, even though she knew it couldn't have been anywhere near that long, she came up on a small cabin almost buried in the trees and a new rental car stopped right in the middle of the slim track she had been following.

"Here we are," Jesus said quietly.

"Where do you want me to park?" Nalani asked.

"Here is good," he said as he reached over, turned off the ignition and removed the keys. "They're taking your car out when they leave."

"Who is?"

"You thought my nearest backups were in LA? I wouldn't come over here that fockin' thin, believe me."

Nalani looked at him as hard as she could in the darkness of the car, and after a moment or two he responded. "Relax, mi'ja," he said. "Won' throw you to the wolves again." Then he opened the door on his side of the car, unfolded himself from his seat, walked around and opened Nalani's door.

The door of the cabin opened as Nalani slipped out of her seat and four men fanned out, two on each side of a small front porch. Jesus walked between them and entered the cabin, Nalani followed silently in his footsteps, and the four men followed in hers.

"She has a bag in the car," Jesus said, and one of the men broke away and went outside. Nalani studied the interior while the man was gone, and she was finished well before he returned. The cabin had one large room in it, with what looked like a bathroom off to one side and a kitchen off to another. A bed big enough for two or three people filled almost half of the space, with the rest invested in a small table with a couple of chairs near the kitchen and a long couch along the opposite wall.

When the man returned with Nalani's bag, he walked across the room and dropped it on the bed. Jesus handed him the keys to the Datsun. "You know where to drop it?" he asked.

"Si," the man said.

"Go back to the hotel when you're done and wait," Jesus said. The man nodded and turned back to the door, and this time when he went out another of the men went with him.

Fock, Nalani thought as the men left. *I should have tried harder to come up with the gun.* Then she shrugged so slightly that only she noticed it and turned her attention to the situation in front of her.

"This is Nalani," Jesus said. "These are Rico and Luis."

Nalani looked at the two men and they looked blankly back at her until all three of them returned their attention to Jesus. "I need some sleep," Jesus said. "Don't let her out of your sight. My little lady friend wants to shoot my fockin' ass."

4

The first thing Nalani saw when she opened her eyes was the last thing she had seen when she closed them—the one called Rico tipped back in a kitchen chair with his hands locked behind his head and his cold dark eyes staring at her relentlessly.

Jesus and the one called Luis were sprawled on top of the bed to Rico's right, both apparently still asleep. Nalani glanced in their direction and then back at Rico. "You never sleep?" she asked from the couch where she had spent the night.

Rico blinked, but nothing else in his tilted presence changed.

"Whatever," Nalani said. She got up, moved briskly to the bathroom and closed the door behind her—or would have if Rico's foot had not suddenly appeared in the way.

"The door stays open," he said, nudging it gently in that direction with his foot.

"No fockin' way!" Nalani said, but she stepped back in response to the pressure on the door as she said it.

"The door stays open," he said again. "You heard the man."

"Gotta watch me fockin' pee?"

"He said to keep my eyes on you."

"You do whatever he fockin' says?"

"Si."

"What if it makes no fockin' sense?"

"I do what he says."

Nalani shook her head slowly and began to calculate how badly she needed to urinate at that exact moment. When the numbers indicated she had no choice, she grabbed a towel from the rack next to the shower stall, spread it across herself as she sat on the toilet and tried to ease her shorts and panties off without exposing herself to the man at the door.

Hope you fockin' like this, she said to herself while she peed. *You're fockin' gonna pay for it, I promise.* When she was done, she worked her garments back into place, rose and returned the towel to the rack.

Her stomach was touchy again, but she would have choked on the vomit before she allowed Rico to stand there and watch her heave into the toilet. She stepped to the tiny sink, washed her hands and face and then turned toward the door. Rico stepped aside and she walked by him, and she kept walking until she was standing on the small porch in front of the cabin.

She heard Rico move to the doorway behind her, but when he spoke the voice came out of Jesus. "Reminds me a little of home," he said.

"Oh," Nalani said, startled a little. "I didn't know you were there."

"There are so many things you don' know, *mi'ja.*"

"Why do you call me that?" she said, her eyes still pointed at the thick foliage in front of the cabin and Jesus still invisible behind her. "You think I'm a *puta,* yeah?"

"No," Jesus said. "I did, but I don' no more."

"Why not?"

"You kick ass," he said. "For a kid."

"Fock you," she said as she stepped off the porch and wandered past where the cars had been and into the brush. She listened vaguely as he followed behind her, breathing deeply, drawing the fresh morning in through her nostrils and expelling the morning nausea out through her mouth.

"Not, you know," she said after several silent minutes.

"What?"

"It's nothing like LA out here."

"LA's a fockin' garbage pit," Jesus said, moving within range of her peripheral vision to the right. "It ain' home."

Nalani looked at him discreetly, but his eyes were focused on whatever it was in front of him that had reminded him of Mexico. *Kind of a funny guy,* she thought as she watched him. *Here's hoping he never gets fockin' home from here.*

Jesus

1

Jesus leaned back in his seat as the girl drove through Waimea, or was it Kamuela? "Why the fock this place got two names?" he asked.

"Long story, you know," the girl said as she chased the Datsun's headlights down the main drag.

"You got plenty of time, *mi'ja.*"

"I'm not your *mi'ja,* you know."

"You know what that means?"

"I'm nothing to you in that tone of voice."

"You're whatever to me I want you to be," Jesus said. "Maybe you should try to remember that. I have to remind you, I promise you won't like it. *Mi'ja.*"

The girl shut up after that, and Jesus let her drive in silence. *Don' fockin' care why the place has two names, anyway,* he said to himself. *What I care about here is something else entirely.*

It didn't take long to reach the fork in the road he had been told to watch for, one route rising high to the right toward Hawi and the other drifting down to the left on the way to the Kona coast.

"Go right," Jesus said as soon as he saw the fork, and he nudged the girl a little on her right cheek with her father's nine to indicate how much he wanted her to fuck with his directions.

"We have to go left to get to my cousin's," the girl said, but she turned to the right as she said it.

"Fock your cousin. He can't carry me all the way to LA, he can't do sheet for me."

"He can get you to Maui, I promise."

"Then what? I walk up and get on a plane, looking just like the guy from the Big Island they already got a flyer on?"

The girl looked at him briefly and then put her eyes back on the road, nodding slightly as she drove. Jesus took that to mean she understood his point—not that he gave a fuck one way or the other if she understood it or not— but he was already on to the essentials of the situation at hand.

Trouble with these fockers, he said without a sound, *they think only one thing at a time. Ain' nearly enough to keep up.* The Datsun continued to climb into the night as he worked through his thoughts and the girl worked through hers, Jesus deciding who to fly in to give him a new face and the photo ID to go with it while the girl decided who the fuck knew what.

2

"I really hate this fockin' island," Jesus said into his phone. "It's so fockin' hard to take care of business here."

"Whaddaya mean?" Ortega asked, Ortega probably out by the fucking pool with bikinis parading back and forth in front of him while Jesus was stuck in the woods with a kid he was reluctant for some reason to look at wrong.

"I mean the fockin' cops know who you are, you can't fockin' get outta here. You start somethin' with the Japs, make sure you can keep our boys under the radar when you do it."

"No shootouts on Main Street," Ortega said.

"Correct. Someone sees a bunch of Mexicans leaving the scene, you'll all be in the same fockin' boat I'm in."

"You mean the same fockin' boat you might have been but ain' exactly in after all."

"Fock you, *cabrón.*"

"In the ass, *ese?*"

"Si."

"Gracias, amigo."

"Just don' do something gonna ID your ass."

"Got it," Ortega said, and Jesus unglued the phone from his ear. He was standing in the rough track that passed for a driveway in front of the cabin, his eyes on Nalani 15 or 20 yards away in a grove of trees that filled the air with a sweet, fresh fragrance—a magical scent that spoke to him like a memory of another time and place in his life that he could not quite recall.

The sense memory was unsettling, and so was the girl. In fact, Jesus noted that very few of the thoughts which ran through his head—or of the things which popped up in front of his face—made him anything but uneasy. The only exception he could think of was the game that afternoon, the outcome of which was preordained, but even that had been producing a tiny tremor in his alert system based on the fact that his peerless all-stars from LA had somehow managed to come up short almost every fucking time in the series.

Jesus watched Nalani breathing deeply as she stared off into nowhere, and he eventually found himself mimicking her. It didn't take him long to learn why she was doing it—the air seemed to rejuvenate his spirit when he drew it in and held it for a while, and a little of the tense unease he had stored away leaked out every time he exhaled. He continued to emulate the girl, breathing in and out according to her rhythm, until the sound of the phone jarred him back inside himself and his precarious position on the tiny rock inexplicably referred to locally as "the Big Island."

Geronimo

1

Geronimo watched the daylight die from the front seat of his car. He was parked along the bayfront with his nose pointed at the ocean, the swells rolling in gently as the dusk advanced in front of him, but he could assimilate none of the cool tranquility of the water.

"What a fucking day," he said aloud, even though he was the only person on the planet close enough to hear it. He had been riding an adrenaline buzz since the moment he had run into the DEA woman after lunch, and he was still wired with it. Mentally, though, he was too tired to think straight. He knew there was something he should be considering, something right in front of his face, but the more he chewed on it the less of it he could see.

"Two heads are better than one," he said idly, wondering whom he could enlist to help him with the thinking, and a moment later a name popped into the one head he already had at his disposal. Then he had to think about where Sonnyboy might be, and when an idea about that finally emerged, he had to call information to get the number there.

Eventually, he managed all that and a phone started ringing in his ear. "Yeah?" Sonny said after three or four rings.

"I thought you might be there," Geronimo said.

"Gee?"

"Yeah."

"Wassup?"

"How's your aunty?"

"Never says a thing, you know? I think she's been waitin' for this since day one."

"Probably," Geronimo said. "Everybody knows she wanted Buddy out of the shit; she made that perfectly clear."

"No shit."

"What about his boy?"

"He knows something's up, that's for shuah."

"God, this shit reeks."

"Why'd you call, Gee?" Sonny asked.

"The other day, when you said you were out now," Geronimo said. "That for real?"

"There is nothing more real than that, brah."

"Then I could use your help."

"Never said anything about going over to your side, Gee."

"The Mexicans snatched Nalani Rosario today, Sonny. I need to find her."

"Fock," Sonny said softly. "Come on over."

2

Ten minutes later, Geronimo was parked on a gravel driveway, and Sonny was seated next to him. "What do you know?" Sonny asked.

"We found two of them shot to death in a vacation rental out past Volcano, but the third one and Nalani were gone when we got there. A little later, Dominic got hit three or four miles past the zoo."

"Dominic's fockin' dead?"

"Very. Took one in the chest and several in the groin."

"What the fock?"

"Yeah," Geronimo said as his phone began to ring. "I know." Sonny watched him pluck his phone from his hip, study it briefly, and put it to work.

"Hey, Ralph," Geronimo said, and then he listened intently for a couple of minutes before promising to stay in touch and slowly lowering the phone to his lap.

"What?" Sonny said.

"They found the rental car the Mexicans were driving. No sign of Nalani."

"Where?"

"Parking lot down on the bayfront. Right in front of the fucking shave-ice place."

"You think they're on foot now?"

"Doesn't seem too likely, does it?"

"Not," Sonny said. "Where did they snatch Nalani, brah?"

"The gym. A fucking fed was sitting right outside when they did it."

"How far is that, from the gym to the shave-ice place? Maybe ten, fifteen blocks?"

"Something like that, yeah."

"Send somebody to check the parkin' lots, Gee. The girl drives a beat-up Datsun, right?"

"Right," Geronimo said, finally catching the same wave Sonny was riding. Sonny leaned back in his seat with his eyes closed while Geronimo went back to his phone. A few moments later, Geronimo put the phone back on his hip and Sonny opened his eyes again.

"Good one, Sonny," Geronimo said. "They're using Nalani's car now. But where?"

"Maybe the wrong question, Gee," Sonny said softly. His head was still resting on the back of his seat, but tilted slightly in Geronimo's direction now. "You know who this fockah is, right?"

"We know who he said he was when he checked into the hotel they were using before today."

"Right," Sonny said. "Then the question is how the fockah's gonna get off the rock."

"Shit," Geronimo said, and he took his time saying it. "I knew it was right in front of me."

"Nalani doesn't hook him up, no way he's gonna make it."

"Well, he can't fly out, true. But he could charter a boat on his own, maybe."

"Not," Sonny said. "Fockahs booked out way in advance, brah."

"You're right. He has to go private, and he's nothing but a fucking tourist. Who's he gonna know?"

"Only question you gotta answer now, Gee, is who the fock does the girl know who has a boat that can go to Maui."

"If we're right, I already know one thing, maybe two," Geronimo said as he fired up the Explorer.

"Yeah?" Sonny said.

"I know he can't kill the girl for a while yet," Geronimo replied, a tentative grin cracking his face like his face hadn't seen one for several weeks, "and I know they're headed for the Kona side."

"Gimme one minute, brah, I'm gonna come with you."

"You sure?"

"Yeah," Sonny said as he climbed out of his seat. "Just remember what I told you before, brah."

"What's that?" Geronimo said, eyeing him carefully where he stood just outside the door.

"You don' know this girl."

"I know she's just a kid, Sonny."

"Maybe," Sonny said, his quiet voice dropping down another decibel or two. "But whoever shot Dominic's fockin' balls off didn't fly in all the way from Mexico to do it, I promise."

3

"Please tell me you're not packing, at least," Geronimo said as he turned off the road about halfway between the boat basin and Hawi.

"That's illegal, yeah?" Sonny said from the passenger seat.

"Right. You being such a law-abiding citizen and all."

"Absolutely."

"Seriously," Geronimo said. "I appreciate your help with this. Just remember it's only your brain that I want involved. Anything goes ballistic, stay out of it."

"Low profile all the way," Sonny said through a grin.

"It's just that I'd have a helluva time explaining how I got a private citizen shot in the ass on this expedition."

"I'd have one hard time explaining it myself."

"I'm serious, Sonny," Geronimo said, even though he was laughing out loud by the time he was done saying it.

"Gotcha, brah," Sonny said, turning his attention to the dilapidated frame house in front of them. They were parked behind a new Ford pickup that stood out in the unkempt yard like it had been parked there by mistake, but Geronimo knew the same Rosario cousin owned both the house and the truck, so he climbed out of his Explorer and headed for the door.

The door opened before he got to it and Gappy stepped outside, Gappy the name everyone called him by even though he had been Julio before Dominic had accidentally knocked one of his front teeth out of his mouth while wrestling in the yard when they were both still teenagers.

"Got one fockin' warrant, Gee?" Gappy said.

"I'm not here to look around, Gappy. I'm trying to find Nalani."

"You t'ink I snatched da kine?"

"I didn't say anyone snatched her. How'd you hear about that?"

"Fock you, Gee."

"She wanted a ride to Maui, right?"

"Yeah."

"When?"

"Shoulda been heah couple houahs ago."

"You haven't heard from her since that first call?"

"Not."

"Fuck," Geronimo said, and then he took a moment off to think.

"What da fock's goin' on?" Gappy asked.

"Did she tell you Dominic's dead?"

"Fock, no!"

"These guys aren't playing, Gappy. Don't fucking try to cowboy this situation if they show up here."

"You know me, Gee. One lovah, not one fightah."

"What's the number of your cell?" Geronimo asked, and when he got the answer he punched it into his own phone until Gappy's began to ring. "Now you have mine," he said. "Use it immediately if you hear from her again. Don't fuck around with this, I'm telling you."

"Got it, Gee, I got it."

"I hope so," Geronimo said as he turned toward his rig.

"You t'ink she's okay?" Gappy asked.

"As long as they needed your boat, I thought so," Geronimo said. "If that's no longer part of the plan, I don't have a fucking clue."

4

"Now what?" Sonny asked.

"Let me check in before I answer that," Geronimo said, punching up his phone as he drove up the hill toward Waimea.

"Got no fockin' clue, yeah?"

"None whatsoever," Geronimo said before Ralph started talking into his ear. When Ralph was done, Geronimo dropped his phone into the tray between the seats and turned his attention back to Sonny.

"You know your cousin up here in the homelands on the edge of town?" he said.

"Shuah," Sonny said. "What am I gonna do, forget him?"

"How 'bout we stay there tonight?"

"You think Nalani's more likely on this side, yeah?"

"Yeah."

"That cousin doesn't like you too much, you know."

"I know," Geronimo said. "Maybe he likes you enough to make up for it."

"Not."

"It doesn't make sense to drive all the way back tonight, then turn around and come back tomorrow."

"Why don't you splurge? Stay at Waikaloa, maybe."

"You think I can float either the Hilton or the Marriott on my expense account?"

"My treat, brah. Got another cousin at the Hilton who might hook us up one sweet kama`aina kine deal."

"Plus you fucking drug lords are all rich, while we poor public servants can't put two dimes together."

"Plus that."

"You're on," Geronimo said. He swung off the road at the first wide spot in the shoulder, U-turned, and drove without another word toward the ocean.

Robbie

Robbie was in the front passenger seat of the first car, which was the bad news because he had no desire to be in this particular vehicle and thought it was speeding in the absolutely wrong direction.

Meanwhile, John was in the seat right behind him. That was the good news, because John was nothing but a faggot to everyone else in that car and in the car behind it. *If this shit turns the wrong way,* Robbie thought as both cars rolled into the night, *the fockahs will never know what hit 'em.*

John was badly outmanned and totally outgunned, of course, which Robbie knew was more bad news, but he saw no advantage to dwelling on those unfortunate facts so he kept his mind on other things. His phone was ringing constantly, for one of those things, tomorrow's playoff game continuing to attract wagers; and then there was the way Kitano and the old man kept pulling him into their Big Island drug interests whether he wanted to be involved or not. Whenever the phone died down for a moment, Robbie's mind jumped immediately to careful consideration of where he wanted to land when the current crisis finally played itself out.

Robbie guided the driver to Gappy's place after they flashed through Waimea, the dark night deepening around them while they drove posing no problem for Robbie at all. "The next place on the left," he said aloud when Gappy's place was the next place on the left, but he followed that instruction with a new one as soon as he saw Geronimo's Explorer in the driveway.

"Drive right on by, brah," he said.

"What's going on?" Kitano said from the seat next to John, but the driver made no response except to keep the car pointed at Hawi instead of turning off at Gappy's.

"Fockin' cops," Robbie said.

"How did they find out?" Kitano asked.

Robbie figured Kitano didn't really expect him to know the answer to that question, so he didn't offer one. "Pull over," he said to the driver when they reached a spot where the shoulder provided room enough for both cars. The driver followed that instruction, too, and the second car did the same without even hearing it.

"This cousin called us," Kitano said as a prelude to proving Robbie wrong about his expectations. "Who do you think called the fucking cops?"

"Not the cousin, that's for fockin' shuah," Robbie said.

"Who does that leave?"

"Maybe nobody did it. The cop in question is one smart moddafockah, I promise." *In certain areas, anyway,* Robbie added to himself.

"It would take more than brainpower to get to that house before we did," Kitano said.

"Fockah knows the families involved," Robbie said. "If he asks himself the right question, he's gonna give himself the right fockin' answer."

Kitano responded to that in Japanese, which chapped Robbie a little until he realized that Kitano was talking into his phone. "We're staying over here for now," Kitano said when he switched back to English.

"Not," Robbie said. "It's better if I go back."

"Go to Waikaloa," Kitano said, Robbie's comment apparently too low to register on Kitano's sound system.

"Which hotel?" the driver asked as he U-turned from the shoulder and headed back toward Gappy's place.

"The Hilton," Kitano said.

Robbie sat silently as the heat slowly rose in his cheeks. He was grateful for the distraction when his phone rang again; he was taking another five hundred on the Pistons by the time Gappy's driveway flashed by his window, the driveway there much emptier without Geronimo's Explorer than it had been with it.

Chapter Eight
Overtime

1

"Who you got on the game today?" Sonny asked. He was rubbing his wet head with a towel thick enough to cushion a fall from the vaulted ceiling of the suite provided by one of his cousins the previous night.

"That's a long story," Geronimo said.

"What you mean?"

"I've got 'em both."

"What for?"

"Take my word for it, you don't wanna know."

"Whatevah you say, Gee. You hungry?"

"I haven't been hungry for months."

"Gotta start the day right, brah. Got one killer buffet here, you know."

"That's a little spendy for me."

"No problem," Sonny said. "Cuz hooked me up."

"Get outta here. She comped us for breakfast on top of the room?"

"Shuah. Thought you were cute, brah."

"Plus the room was just sitting here."

"Plus that," Sonny said. He disappeared into the bathroom for a moment, and when he returned he had traded the towel for a loose-fitting t-shirt with Haole Hunter emblazoned across the front of it.

"What are you going to do if you find one of those?" Geronimo asked.

"Depends," Sonny said.

"On what?"

"On gender. Gonna give the boys some lickin's, I promise."

"And the girls?"

"I give the girls whatever the fock they want," he said with a smile bright enough to light the suite they were in and the one next door. "But right now, brah, I'm gonna give you one killer breakfast."

"I guess I could eat," Geronimo said as he followed his unlikely benefactor out the door.

2

Robbie was standing at the omelet station watching his eggs coalesce around his vegetables when Geronimo and Sonny walked up the buffet line. John was digging through the fresh fruit four or five steps to Robbie's right, Kitano was heaping salmon onto his plate two steps to Robbie's left and three or four more Japs—Robbie had lost track of exactly how many had come down from the rooms—were at the special section on the far side of the alcove dedicated to food the hotel imagined might be familiar to Japanese tourists.

"Ever notice how small the Big Island is?" Geronimo said when he and Sonny arrived where Robbie was standing.

"Yeah," Robbie said, embracing first Geronimo and then Sonny. "I notice it more every fockin' day."

Kitano ate the space between the salmon and the omelets while the greetings transpired, until he was standing at Robbie's shoulder with his plate in his left hand and a question on his face.

"This is Kitano," Robbie said. "A business associate. These are two of our clients, you know."

"So sorry," Kitano said, smiling coolly in Robbie's general direction. "I didn't catch their names."

No fockin' shit, Robbie said to himself, a flutter loose in his stomach that suddenly made his omelet obsolete. "Geronimo Souza, Sonnyboy Akaka," he said aloud.

"So nice to meet you both at last," Kitano said, suddenly nothing but hard lines in his face where the question had been. "But so strange to meet you together like this, isn't it?"

"Not really," Geronimo said. "We've known each other all our lives."

"I see," Kitano said. "Still, your paths would seem to have diverged enough to make this particular intersection unlikely."

"I don't think so," Sonny said with a smile Robbie knew from years of observation masked a dangerous edge. "You're the only thing 'unlikely' in this fockin' picture, you know."

"I suppose you might see it that way," Kitano said, his voice as soft as his face was hard. "But what have we got here—a cop, a drug dealer and a bookmaker? That's a little strange, especially considering all three of you live on the other side of the island."

Robbie tried to look ahead to where this conversation was going, but he reaped nothing from the effort. He glanced at John next to the fruit bar, and Geronimo followed his eyes and nodded a wordless greeting.

"This side of the island attracts a lot of people who don't live here," Geronimo said next, glancing over his shoulder briefly as several men holding plates of Japanese delicacies fanned out behind him. "You and the rest of your entourage, for example."

"Of course," Kitano said. "You and Sonny here don't really look like tourists, though, do you?"

"Neither do you and the other fellas," Geronimo said. "But here we all are. I guess you're right—it is a little strange."

"Exactly," Kitano said. "Like I said, good to meet you. No

doubt we'll be seeing each other again." Then he walked toward the seating area, his entourage trailing behind him.

"Why'd they drag you two over here?" Geronimo said as he watched Kitano move across the room.

"Same reason you dragged Sonny over, I think," Robbie said.

"Nobody dragged me, brah," Sonny said. "I don't fockin' drag worth a shit, I promise."

"For shuah," Robbie said. "What was I thinkin'?"

"What's up with your face?" Geronimo said in John's direction.

"What, this?" John said, putting his hand next to his battered nose. "Bumped into someone's foot the other day."

"Lots of random bumping going on around here lately," Geronimo said.

"This foot belonged to a guy who spoke Spanish."

"I know a few of those," Geronimo said. "But the number seems to be going down rapidly."

"I don't have a problem with that right now, believe me," John said.

"Almost met last night, you know," Robbie interjected.

"Really?" Geronimo asked.

"Fockah got a call from the cousin. Your car was in the driveway when we went by."

"I figured it was something like that," Geronimo said. "Where is this fucking dance going to end?"

"Dance?"

"Dominic does Buddy, the Mexicans do Dominic, now the Japs wanna do the Mexicans. It's the fucking Texas Three-Step."

"Texas doesn't have a Three-Step, brah," Sonny said with a grin.

"They have a Two-Step. Plus we're talkin' about a Four-Step, you know."

"Four?"

"Shuah. The fockin' Mexicans wanna do the Japs for droppin' the dime on the drugs, I promise."

"Fucking Four-Step, then," Geronimo conceded. "So what are you, the guide?"

"Yeah," Robbie said.

"And John?"

"The fockin' Japs make me nervous."

Geronimo looked from Robbie to John with the hint of a smile on his face. "You gotta talk to your boyfriend, John," he said. "Guy's seriously confused about his own ethnicity."

"I think he's right," John said, and there was not the slightest trace of a smile on his face when he said it. "No way he's one of those fucking guys." Then all four of them turned toward the table around which Kitano and his entourage had assembled and saw Kitano staring back at them silently while he made the salmon disappear from his plate.

3

"How'd you get this number?" the voice on the phone said.

"Your man Ortega here," Kitano said, motioning with his head in the direction of the compact man in nothing but flowery swim trunks and muscle seated on the sofa in front of him—even though he knew the voice on the phone had no way of seeing a fucking thing.

"How'd you get Ortega?" the voice asked.

"All it took was a blonde in a bikini," Kitano said. "We sent her down to the pool, and Senor Ortega here followed her right back to our room. It was easy, let me tell you."

"You're in the same fockin' hotel?"

"I know. This island is unbelievably small, isn't it?"

"What do you want?"

"We need to meet, talk over a few things," Kitano said. "Before something stupid happens."

"I can only think of one thing I wanna talk about," the voice said.

"What would that be?"

"My fockin' drugs, homes. What the fock you think?"

"I thought you might be capable of thinking farther ahead than that," Kitano said, and he let that dangle there for a moment before he continued. "But we can start with your drugs, sure. Where and when?"

"If I wanted to talk to a fockin' Jap, I'd talk to the one in charge."

Here we fucking go, Kitano thought. "That's one of the things I want to talk about," he said. "The conversation goes right, I might make a change in the leadership around here."

"Why would I have anything to say about that?"

"Because I don't want to be fighting with you while I do it. And because this change could be mutually beneficial."

"How?"

"The new leadership might look favorably on restitution for your product, for starters."

The voice said nothing in response to that, but Kitano thought he could hear the wheels turning at the other end of the conversation. "And looking a little farther ahead than that?" the voice asked after the wheels had apparently turned long enough.

"Fighting over this market is counterproductive," Kitano said. "We hook up, certain benefits accrue. Both here and beyond."

"Beyond?"

"The whole fucking Pacific, *amigo.* This place is just the tip of the iceberg."

"The Pacific don' have icebergs."

"You know what I mean."

"I do?"

"We both know you didn't start this shit just to pick up the Big Island. Honolulu is next, right?"

"Is it?"

"I would think so, yes. And that's going to create some significant static, if everything stays like it is right now. So how 'bout it?"

"How 'bout what?"

"How 'bout we get together and talk?"

"We talkin' now, homes."

"Face to face."

"Trouble with that is, I don' trust your fockin' ass."

"Fine," Kitano said. "Let me trust you, then. You pick the place."

"I'm out in the fockin' woods above Hawi," the voice said. "You wanna drop by, Ortega knows where it is."

"When?"

"Whenever. I ain' goin' nowhere."

"He's going to want to hear it from you," Kitano said. He handed the phone to Ortega, who mumbled a few words into it that sounded to Kitano like Spanish before he handed it back.

"He's good to go," the voice said when Kitano had the phone back to his ear.

"Excellent," Kitano said.

"One question."

"Yes?"

"How you know we won' light up your ass when you get here?"

"The same way you know I'm not bringing an army with me."

"What way is that?"

"We don't have a fucking thing to gain by doing it."

"See you when you get here," the voice said, and then the phone went dead in Kitano's ear. He clipped it to the pocket of his walking shorts and turned toward the Mexican still sitting quietly on the sofa.

"Let's go," Kitano said.

"He tol' me tonight, late," Ortega said.

"What if I'm afraid of the dark?"

"Then we stay here," Ortega said with a shrug, "and watch the pretty *señoritas* play in the pool."

4

Neither of them had spoken for a while because neither of them had a thing to say, Geronimo sitting behind the wheel of his Explorer and Sonnyboy in the passenger seat as they rolled into Gappy Rosario's driveway again.

"Tell me one more time why we're here, brah," Sonny said when Geronimo brought his rig to a stop.

"Oldest rule in police work," Geronimo said. "You don't have a clue where to go next, just go back where you were and start all over again."

"If you say so," Sonny said, his voice trailing off like it didn't really agree with itself.

Geronimo allowed himself a slight grin as he opened his door and climbed out of the car. *I know,* he thought. *Sounds lame to me, too.*

"The truck's not here, you know," Sonny said as he hit the driveway on his side of the car.

"Finc with me if I never see Gappy again," Geronimo said. "A little bit of him goes a long way."

"You're back in his driveway, brah."

"He's not the only person who lives here," Geronimo said. By that time, their paths had converged from their opposite sides of the car and they were approaching Gappy's shabby front door.

Geronimo raised his fist to knock and the door opened in front of them as though his fist had magical powers, something he knew from hard personal experience neither of his fists actually possessed. Geronimo lowered his hand as the woman who had opened the door began to fill the doorway.

"What you want, Gee?" the woman said. "Gappy not heah."

"Fine with me, Delores," Geronimo said. "I've seen enough of Gappy."

Delores absorbed that information without a visible reaction, apparently content to stand there and stare at Geronimo until he evaporated. Geronimo stared back, trying unsuccessfully to see a trace of the Delores Delgado he had known as a kid in the huge woman in front of him.

"Why you got him wit' you?" she said, looking over his shoulder at Sonny.

"He's trying to help me find Nalani," Geronimo said. "I was hoping you'd do the same."

"No can tell you not'ing, Gee."

"She called here, right?"

"Nevah talked to me, you know."

"Gappy say anything?"

"Said she comin' ovah."

"When did he call the Japs?"

"Why you t'ink he called da Japs?"

"They got here right after we did, Delores. Did you call them?"

"No way."

"You think Nalani called them?"

"Not."

"Who's that leave?"

"He nevah said not'ing, I promise."

"Can you tell me anything that might help?" Geronimo said. "Anything at all?"

"No t'ink so, Gee."

Geronimo started to turn away from the door, but Sonny stopped him with a hand on his shoulder. "You close to this girl, Delores?" Sonny said.

Delores looked at Sonny for a moment before she answered, as though calculating the cost per word. "Not," she said when the moment ended. "Nobody close to da kine no mo'."

"Now that Dominic's dead, you mean?" Geronimo asked.

"Not," Delores said slowly, her eyes moving from Sonny to Geronimo. "Not since her mama wen die."

That answer apparently drained everyone's diaphragm because no one said anything else for a while. "Can go now?" Delores said when the time finally came for someone to say something again.

"Yeah," Geronimo said. "*Mahalo,* Delores."

"Shuah," Delores said as she stepped back into the house.

"Hey," Geronimo said as the door began to close.

"Yeah?" Delores said.

"You take care, okay?"

Delores stood there for a moment, regarding Geronimo like he had just spoken to her in a language she had never heard before. Then she closed the door and left the two men standing where she had found them.

"What made you think to ask her that question?" Geronimo said as he turned toward his car.

"Like I keep tellin' you, brah," Sonny said softly. "You don't know this girl."

"I know the motherfuckers snatched her, Sonny. And I know whose fucking job it is to find her."

"Oh, yeah," Sonny said through a grin. "You fockin' know that, brah."

5

Kitano thought the Laker overload in the room when the game came on was funny, Ortega and two more Mexicans all on the LA bandwagon no matter how flat the tires had become. Kitano would have preferred by far to be on his way to the rendezvous with the leader of this unruly assemblage, but it didn't take him long to decide that the game was a better alternative than anything else available.

Kitano watched the proceedings with significantly more interest than usual, the usual being no interest at all. This time he had the handle to a drug cop riding on the game, which he found compelling enough to actually justify watching grown men comport themselves like kids.

Which they were doing, both on the television screen and throughout the room around it, the Mexicans apparently believing their entreaties might traverse the Pacific Ocean and more than half of the North American continent if they ratcheted up the volume enough. Kitano responded to the bedlam around him with silence, even though the Pistons gave him reason to cheer immediately and followed that with unlimited free refills until the final breath had been squeezed out of the Lakers.

The bookie and the bookie's faggot came into the room as the game ended, and Kitano allowed himself a quiet grin in their direction. "Your old buddy the cop now belongs to me," he said.

"To you?" the bookie said.

"To us," Kitano said, but he eyed the bookie silently for a moment before he said it.

"Whatevah," the bookie might have said next, but he didn't try to say it loud enough to rise above the collected wailing of the Mexicans, so Kitano couldn't use his ears to verify what his eyes were telling him.

"Watch your fucking tone," Kitano said, assuming from the tilt of the bookie's head what the tone had been even though Kitano hadn't heard it. He laced his own words with enough volume to get them twice as far as they needed to go, but the bookie stood just inside the doorway with his blank eyes beaming absolutely nothing in Kitano's general direction.

"Who the fuck do you think you are?" Kitano said, this time so loud that the Mexicans shut their mouths and turned to watch.

"Nobody, yeah?" the bookie said, nothing wrong with the volume now that the room noise had been dialed back.

"I wouldn't forget that if I were you."

"I think if you were me, brah," the bookie said after thinking it over for a moment, "you have no clue what the fock you might do." Then he turned and walked back out the door, the faggot following in his footsteps like walking around in circles was the most natural thing in the world.

6

Jesus listened to the crackling commentary on the game while he finished fumbling with the gun, the radio at least sparing him the agony of seeing what he was hearing. He chambered a round and returned the gun to its spot against the small of his back, reassured that if he should happen to need it he wouldn't come out shooting blanks like his fucking Lakers had just done.

"Can you believe that?" Luis said from the edge of the bed.

"We got a choice?" Jesus asked. "Fockin' Pistons."

"How much you lose on the series?"

"It ain' the money, homes; it's the fockin' aggravation."

"Fock the aggravation. I los' five gees on those fockin' losers."

Tell me about it, Jesus thought, his eyes moving idly to the girl working at the small kitchen sink while his mind returned to the impending visit by the Jap. The girl was the more pleasing object of attention by far, the view from behind her almost as stunning as the one from in front, but Jesus knew where his thoughts belonged and he put them there.

"What you gonna do, boss?" Luis said quietly.

"About what?" Jesus said.

"About either one," Luis said, as though he knew where Jesus had both his mind and his eyes.

"Time will tell, *ese.*"

"How much time we got?"

"We never know the answer to that one," Jesus said softly, trying to read from the rear how closely the girl was tracking this conversation. "We fin' that one out when the fockin' buzzer goes off."

Luis nodded in response to that, but Jesus had no idea why. *I said the sky was falling,* Jesus said to himself, *the focker would nod his head like that.* Meanwhile, his thoughts drifted back to the gun he had prepared and the visitor for whom he had prepared it.

Focker better not fock with me, Jesus thought. *No way I'm in the fockin' mood.*

7

Robbie was certain he had enough electrical current running up and down his spine to power a light bulb if you could find a way to screw it in, and he knew from extensive personal experience that he had an aperture or two that might suffice.

Kitano was really pushing his buttons now, dragging him along even though Kitano had Ortega to show him the way. *Got one fockin' bad feeling 'bout this shit,* he said where only he could hear it. *Something is comin' down, I promise.*

John had been left behind this time, Kitano in the front passenger seat with the muscular Mexican behind the wheel and Robbie stuck in the back alone.

The first thing I gotta do, Robbie thought, *is fockin' make it through all this, whatever the fock it is.*

The second thing, though, was right behind the first. Robbie knew there was a second thing, and that he definitely had to do it, but he was in no position to forecast what that thing was going to be. This rubbed him the wrong way, which was more stimulation than he could stand with his nervous system already on tilt.

Ortega had them up on the high road above Hawi, a route Robbie was more familiar with in the light of day than in the car's overworked headlights. He struggled at first to keep himself oriented, but gave it up after a while in favor of coasting above the wheels of the car with his eyes closed. This took the strain off his eyes but did nothing to ease his worried mind, so he was more than ready for something to happen by the time Ortega slowed the car down to a crawl and turned off into trees that allowed scarcely more illumination than Robbie's eyelids had permitted.

Ortega stopped the car suddenly for no reason Robbie could immediately discern, but flashlights appeared on both sides as soon as the car was motionless. "Everybody out," Ortega said as he opened his door and followed his own directions.

"What the fuck is this?" Kitano said.

Ortega leaned back into the car, his blank face illuminated slightly by the dome light. "The man ain' gonna let you roll up on him blind," he said. "Everybody out."

Kitano continued to hesitate until the door next to him opened as if by its own accord. He looked up at the silent man with a flashlight in his hand looming over him in the dark, and after a frozen moment he climbed out of the car. As soon as he was done, Robbie followed suit

"Assume the position," the man with the flashlight said as soon as they were both outside. Robbie placed both hands on top of the car and stepped back until he was leaning forward. Kitano watched him do it, then duplicated the movements. Ortega walked around the front of the car and patted them both down thoroughly, a process Robbie might actually have enjoyed in slightly different circumstances.

"Follow the light," Ortega said when he was done. One of the men with a flashlight moved off to Robbie's right, Kitano moving slowly behind him and Robbie trailing at the same pace as Kitano.

"Keep up," Ortega said from a step or two behind Robbie, and when Kitano increased his speed a little Robbie did the same. The man still at the car cut the headlights, and Robbie suddenly could barely see Kitano's back two steps in front of his face. Then Ortega said something in Spanish, and lights came on ahead and slightly to the left of the men.

The new source of illumination was a small cabin that Robbie had not seen before the lights kicked on. He watched the door open and a man emerge as they approached, but that image didn't hold his eyes very long. What took its place was Nalani Rosario, who turned out to be standing in the doorway when the man moved out onto a small porch in front of the cabin.

What the fock? Robbie asked himself, but he didn't offer himself an answer because none came to mind. The bare porch light would have been unkind to most people, Robbie thought idly as he stared at the girl, but Nalani turned it to her advantage without any visible effort.

That's one fockin' beauty, you like the type, Robbie said silently. Which Robbie did, in much the same way as he appreciated fine art. But he didn't have much time to savor the sight, because Nalani stepped away from the door when the procession reached it and all of the men moved inside the cabin.

"So you're the man," Kitano said in the general direction of the gold-plated motherfucker who Robbie had recently met in Robbie's own living room.

"Long as you remember that, you be fine," the guy with all the gold said as he took a seat at a small wooden table.

"Isn't this room a little tight?" Kitano asked.

"Sit down," the guy with all the gold said, and Kitano sat down on the opposite side of the table. Robbie remained standing with a Mexican on each side of him, while Nalani leaned easily against the wall next to the door to the left of Ortega.

"You came out here to comment on the accommodations, *ese?*" the guy with all the gold said.

"You're right," Kitano said. "It was you I came to check out."

"And?"

"And I don't like this thing with the girl."

"What thing is that?"

"This is Rosario's girl, right?" Kitano said.

"There is no Rosario."

"Then he's the only guy on this rock who isn't looking for her."

"What does this have to do with you?" the guy with all the gold said slowly, easing back in his chair even though it sounded to Robbie like the guy's voice was tightening up.

"If we start to work together, why would I want this hanging over my head?"

"The girl is here, homes. You got anything else to talk about?"

"Not if you still think snatching her was a smart move."

"It got the job done."

"Maybe," Kitano said. "But you're not out of it yet, are you?"

"No," the guy said. "But it still seems like more my problem than yours."

"I'm just saying, it's going to be hard to work with you if you don't solve it pretty fucking soon."

"Kind of like it's gonna be hard to work with you, *ese,* you don' get out of this room alive. Everyone's got problems, *si?*"

This time it was Kitano's turn to sit back in his chair and simmer, and neither of them spoke while he did it. Robbie used the time to look at Nalani, and Nalani looked back like she had never seen him before. *What the fock is up with you?* he wondered.

"The thing is," Kitano said, his voice drawing Nalani's eyes away from Robbie, "the Big Island isn't all that big."

"No sheet," the guy with all the gold said.

"It's not cost-effective to fight over it."

"You win the fight, it might be."

"What I'm saying is, that would cost more than it's worth. Plus it takes our eyes off the prize."

"The entire Pacific, I think you said."

"Exactly."

"If the prize is worth a fock, so is the fight."

"You feel that way," Kitano said, "why am I here?"

"You here to talk about my money, homes."

"That's part of the same conversation."

"I'm listening."

"First thing I do after I move the old man out of the way is pay you for the shit Rosario fingered."

"How do I know you can move the old man?"

"I don't do it, you're still exactly where you are now."

"How long I gotta chill?"

"As long as you like what it's doing for you," Kitano said. "Just like any other deal you've ever made, correct?"

"Bueno," the guy with all the gold said, nodding his head slowly. "You wanna go for it, I'll stay out of your way."

"Good," Kitano said. "The only thing left to decide now is the girl."

"What about the girl?" the guy with all the gold said, and Robbie could see the guy tighten up all over again while he said it.

"They have to find the girl," Kitano said. "There will be too fucking much heat running around here until they do."

"Maybe I ain' gonna like the heat coming down after they find her, *ese.*"

"Don't misunderstand me," Kitano said, his words air-conditioned cool. "I'm not saying they have to find her alive."

8

Jesus felt the heat drain out of his eyes as he stared at the cool Jap on the opposite side of the table. He knew there was something to what the Jap was saying, but he didn't like the way it sounded coming out of the motherfucker's mouth or the idea that the Jap thought he could tell Jesus what to do in the first fucking place.

"You ain' in no position to tell me nothing, homes," Jesus said, his words coming from a place just as cold as the Jap's now. "Look aroun' yourself, you forgot where the fock you are."

"I know where I am," the Jap said. "And you know I'm right. Is there anything else that needs to be said?"

Jesus looked at the girl before he answered, but the girl was staring idly at the Jap on the opposite side of room like the conversation at the table had been about tomorrow's weather forecast or the timing of the next tide. He followed the girl's eyes and recognized the Jap as the local bookie he had dropped in on earlier.

"One thing, maybe," Jesus said.

"What's that?"

"Why'd you bring him?" Jesus said, nodding in the direction of the bookie.

"He's my local expert," the Jap said with a shrug.

"The girl is mine," Jesus said, noting while he said it that the bookie was visibly less disinterested in the conversation than the girl seemed to be.

"Unlike Robbie there," the Jap said, "your expert is more trouble than she's worth."

"No, *ese,*" Jesus said as he reached behind his back with his right hand, produced his handgun and proceeded to point it at the Jap's blank face. "You're the one here more trouble than he's worth."

"She must be one phenomenal local expert," the Jap said quietly, looking from the gun to the girl and back again. Jesus had to admit that the Jap was cool, all things considered, which he admired all the way up to the moment he squeezed off the round in his chamber and totally obliterated the fucking refrigeration and everything around it.

The Jap stood up to the impact of the bullet about as well as Jesus expected—one moment he was sitting there with his slanted black eyes sticking out, the next he was sprawled on the floor between the table and the bed with space enough for a new eye in his face.

Jesus got up, walked around the table and looked down on the body. Ortega swore quietly in Spanish from his spot near the door, but Jesus let the curse drift off unattended while he stared at his handiwork.

"Why you did that, boss?" Ortega asked.

"Focker forgot who the fock he was," Jesus said. "I fockin' hate that sheet."

"Cost us some coin, though," Ortega said.

"No fockin' way," Jesus said. "You think the old man gonna roll over for this fock?"

"Sure as sheet won' be doin' it now."

"No," Jesus said. "But that ain' really the question, *ese.*"

"Don' look at me, boss," Ortega said. "No way I'm cleanin' up this sheet."

"Forget it," Jesus said. "That ain' the question, either." He looked at Ortega for a moment without speaking again, and Ortega looked back. When the moment was over, their eyes moved simultaneously to the only Jap in the room with a face still adhering to its original design.

9

Nalani felt all the eyes in the room rotate in her direction from Robbie's, but she didn't see them. She had her own eyes closed and her head tipped back slightly while she tried to think, knowing the position showed her fine features to maximum effect but far from certain that her face or any other part of her would matter much longer.

Robbie Tsubamoto should have continued to be the focus of attention on the other side of the room, of course, but once Jesus had looked her way, the rest of the room had followed. Jesus was still the key, as he had been from the beginning, but Nalani no longer knew anything else. The introduction of the gun into the conversation with the man now dead on the floor had shaken her grasp on her own situation so severely that she despaired of ever regaining her grip.

The silence in the room grew louder with every passing moment, but Nalani could think of nothing to say that might muffle it. She listened to the breathing around the room while she thought, everyone with a distinctly different sound plus one with no sound at all, but her mind continued to fire blanks until an unexpected voice intervened.

"Let's deal all the cards before we shuffle 'em," Robbie said quietly, and Nalani felt the focus of the room shift once more. She opened her eyes and waited intently for additional information, which suddenly seemed to be the prevalent posture in the room.

"Most people shuffle *before* they deal, homes," Jesus said.

"If the deck's stacked jus' right already, maybe you don't wanna shuffle at all," Robbie replied.

"This fockin' deck is stacked just right?" Jesus said, glancing at the body on the floor near his feet.

"Maybe," Robbie said. "We don't wanna miss anything here."

"I'm sure you don', homes."

"Shuah. But how much do you like missing anything?"

"I'm listening," Jesus said, and Nalani could see it was true by the tilt of his head as he sat in his chair at the table. *But no one is listening harder right now than I am,* Nalani thought.

"Kitano was a fockin' prick," Robbie continued, "but everybody knows that some of what he said was right on. The Big Island needs one organization, brah."

"That would be good, yeah."

"One supplier, one local face on the ground."

"Easier said than done, *ese.*"

"You gotta be local to put something like this together, I promise. You think I could fly to LA tonight and organize a network on the ground tomorrow?"

"Keep talkin'," Jesus said, leaning back in his chair now but his head still what Nalani thought of as tilted just right.

"You got two organizations right now," Robbie said slowly, picking his way along as though he had all the time in the world. "But neither one has a head, yeah?"

"Yeah."

"The right guy cuts the Japs out and puts Buddy's people together with Dominic's. All you gotta do, you keep the fockin' shit comin'."

"That we can do," Jesus said. "I suppose you're the guy can do the other?"

"Not," Robbie said.

"No?"

Robbie shook his head slowly. "Not alone, no," he said. "I can cut the Japs out, no problem, but you need someone to step up on both sides on the ground."

"Like who?"

"Sonnyboy Akaka, from Buddy's side."

"He says he won' do it."

"We make him an offer like in the movies, yeah? Maybe later he can walk—no fockin' way he can do it now."

"Who do we get from Dominic's side?" Jesus said.

"Her," Robbie said, and Nalani felt every eye in the room swivel in her direction one more time.

10

"She's just a fockin' kid," the gold-plated motherfucker at the table said.

"Not," Robbie said. He had enough butterflies fluttering in his stomach to raise his feet off the floor, but Robbie couldn't hear the beating of their wings so he was confident the Mexican couldn't, either.

"No?" the Mexican asked.

Robbie shook his head slowly, his eyes focused on Nalani on the other side of the room. The girl was looking back again, but not as blankly as before. This was the ticklish part, he knew, but it felt right to him—and his feelings were all he had to go on in his present situation.

There had always been something about this girl that bothered Robbie, and whatever it was had intensified as soon as he saw her standing in the cabin doorway when he and Kitano had first arrived. It wasn't her presence itself—everyone knew she had been snatched and whisked off somewhere. What struck him was the *way* she had been standing there, as much at home in that space as anywhere else he had ever seen her.

"Unusual kid, maybe," the Mexican said. "But she's still a kid."

"That's why we need Sonnyboy up front," Robbie said. "But she's the answer long-term, I promise. Right?"

He winged the last word in Nalani's direction, and she hooked the right answer to it and sent it back. "For shuah," she said.

Robbie returned his focus to the Mexican at the table, and what he saw encouraged him further. The Mexican's eyes were pointed at Robbie, but the man's mind was obviously somewhere else.

"You seen what hoppen to the las' Jap focked with me," the Mexican said when his mind came back to the same place as his eyes.

"Yeah," Robbie said.

"How you gonna move the old man?"

"That's my business, yeah?"

"Yeah," the Mexican said slowly. "But you ain' gonna have forever to take care of it."

"No need," Robbie said. "This time tomorrow, the deed will be done."

"This time tomorrow, you still gonna be where you are right now."

"You wanna wait," Robbie said with a shrug, "we wait."

"But what?"

"They're gonna send the troops out after him," Robbie said, glancing briefly at Kitano's lifeless body on the floor. "Mo' bettah I deliver the news."

"No tellin' how much news you deliver, we do it like that."

"If you move when I go, what am I gonna know?"

The Mexican mulled that over for a moment and then nodded his head slowly. "Gotta move anyway," he said, and then no one said anything for a while. Robbie stood stiffly in his spot in the room, his eyes on Nalani and her eyes on him, and he stayed like that until the while ended.

"Ortega will take you where you need to go," the Mexican said, which put Robbie half the distance he had to cover. "One more thing," Robbie said, his eyes still locked on Nalani.

"What?"

"Kitano was almos' right about her." The Mexican followed Robbie's eyes until both men were looking at Nalani.

"What?" he said. "She just walks?"

"Need one story whenevah, yeah? Mo' bettah now than later, I promise."

The Mexican rotated his eyes from Nalani to Robbie and back again while he contemplated the suggestion, and Robbie had to remind himself to breathe until the Mexican made his decision. "So tell me the story," the Mexican said when he was done, and that's the next thing Robbie did.

11

"Don't know why I didn't see it sooner," Geronimo said, the Explorer following its headlights toward Hilo almost on its own.

"Retarded, maybe," Sonny said from the passenger seat.

"It was kind of obvious, wasn't it?"

"No shit."

"It's not like I've never played the game."

"Takes a team to win, brah."

"All the shit going on right now, I can't believe we're sitting here talking about a basketball game."

"Maybe the more shit there is, the more we need the game."

"Maybe," Geronimo said. "I sure as shit needed Robbie last night."

"What do you mean?"

"I'd owe that fucking Kitano thirty grand right now except for Robbie stepping in."

"Fock, Gee. You think you might have a problem, maybe?"

"Who, me?" Geronimo said, but the trill of his phone saved him from saying any more.

"You sittin' down, brah?" Ralph said into his ear as soon as the salutations were out of the way.

"Yeah, but I'm driving."

"Maybe you better pull ovah."

"What the fuck is it, Ralph?"

"The kid's okay."

"What?" Geronimo said, his breath suddenly short and his confidence in his hearing shot to shit.

"Nalani Rosario. She's okay."

"Have you seen her?"

"She just came through the door, Gee."

"Nalani's okay," Geronimo said in Sonny's direction, relief flooding through him until the overflow started leaking from his eyes. "She's okay."

"Where are you?" Ralph said into his ear.

"Maybe fifteen minutes out."

"That's good."

"Why?"

"She won' talk to anybody but you, brah."

"What?" Geronimo asked again, a new trepidation beginning to infringe on his relief.

"She hasn't said anything yet," Ralph said.

"What the fuck is that about?"

"You get here, maybe we'll find out."

"I'm on my way," Geronimo said, glancing at Sonny briefly as he dropped the phone in his lap.

"What?" Sonny said.

"She won't talk to anyone but me," Geronimo said.

"You one special-kine guy, yeah?" Sonny said through a quiet chuckle.

"This shit's not funny, Sonny."

"I know."

"Whatever the fuck is going on, I'm glad she made it back."

"Maybe you should wait, brah," Sonny said, all of the humor gone from his voice.

"Wait for what?"

"To find out how far back she's fockin' come," Sonny said, and then no one said anything until Hilo showed up in Geronimo's headlights.

Chapter Nine
Double Overtime
1

"You okay with this?" Robbie said as Ortega rolled to a stop.

"Shuah," Nalani said. "I'm the victim, yeah?"

"Yeah," Robbie replied, thinking as he said it that he could easily be both right and wrong. He watched her slide out of the car, shoulder her bag, and walk toward the cop shop like she was heading for an early workout.

"Jeezus fockin' Christ," Robbie started to say, but Ortega said it first.

"She's something else, yeah?" Robbie said instead.

"No sheet," Ortega said, a note of sincerity in his tone that somehow sounded odd coming from one of the girl's kidnappers.

Shuah, Robbie said to himself as he watched Nalani walk into the building. *You're the fockin' victim, yeah?*

2

Nalani sat at an old wooden table and waited, her eyes closed and her mind wide open. She had a hard time believing the events of the last two days had actually transpired, even though she had played a featured role in some of them and had seen most of the rest from a front-row seat.

One thing's for sure, she thought with satisfaction so deep it seemed to seep from her bones, *my fockin' father will fock no more.*

"Good you still can smile," said the heavyset cop on the opposite side of the table.

Nalani opened her eyes slowly. She had not been aware of the smile on her face or the heavyset cop, even though the cop had brought her into the room and had been sitting there ever since. "Good to be back, you know," she said, hoping that explanation would satisfy the cop no matter how far short of the truth it might be.

"Fo' shuah," the cop said, his eyes friendly but insistent, like he had no intention of missing a thing while they sat on their opposite sides of the table and waited. *Gotta be more careful, girl,* she said silently to the only girl in the room. *This thing is a long way from ovah.*

Nalani let her eyelids fall again and returned to her thoughts, but she was so profoundly exhausted that she began to make a case for drifting into sleep instead of thought. She heard the door to the room open before she got very far into that argument, so she reluctantly put her eyes back to work.

What she saw made her sit up straight. Geronimo Souza was the first to enter the room, followed by Sonnyboy Akaka and a Japanese woman Nalani had never seen before. Nalani had been expecting Souza and could not have cared less about the Japanese woman, but Sonny was a genuine shock to her system; for an instant, she imagined that he had somehow materialized from inside her head and had not walked through the door at all.

The woman proceeded to the chair at the end of the table to Nalani's left and sat down in front of a typing machine of some kind, but the men stood side by side a step or two inside the door and regarded Nalani quietly.

"Not too sure about Sonny, Gee," the heavyset cop at the table said.

"I'd really like to have him here, Ralph," Souza said. "Can we leave it up to Nalani?"

"Whatevah," Ralph said. "The chief says anything, you come up with the answer."

"Do you mind if Sonny sits in, Nalani?" Souza asked. She studied him closely while the question rolled out of his mouth, and she was satisfied with what she was seeing by the time she heard the question mark.

She moved her focus to Sonny before she answered, and warning bells went off in her head. He was standing completely at ease, his eyes deep and playful as he stared back at her. *Gotta watch that focker,* she thought. *Sonnyboy's gonna be trouble, I promise.*

"Talkin' to no one but you, you know," she said quietly.

"That's not going to be possible, Nalani," Souza said, his voice just as quiet as hers. "Ralph and the recorder will have to be here, at least."

"Whatevah," Nalani said. She rose from her seat and directed her eyes at Ralph. "Would you get my bag, please?"

"I'm afraid you're not exactly free to go," Souza said.

"What?" she asked. "Now you're gonna kidnap me, too?"

"There is a lot we need to know that you can tell us," Souza said, his voice still low and his quiet eyes still sending the same unique Geronimo Souza vibe she had never encountered from anyone else.

Nalani returned to her seat, leaned back, and closed her eyes again. She tried to visualize what her face looked like to the men in the room, and the vision she came up with seemed to her to be adequate for the occasion. *Not that it's likely to matter much to this crowd,* she thought. *What's gonna matter here is how fast I can talk.*

She took a moment to soberly review what she was going to have to talk about. She could have just played the thing straight, of course, but that would have required an explanation of three shooting deaths with which she had been intimately involved. *No way,* she said where only she could hear it. *Much better to roll with Robbie's surprising plan for a while and see what happens.*

No one in the room spoke for a while, and no one seemed put out by the silence except the woman seated in front of the typing machine. Nalani could hear her fidget slightly every 60 seconds or so, but she heard nothing from the other side of the table or from the two men standing near the door until the men both moved to the table and sat down.

Nalani opened her eyes and located Souza next to Ralph and Sonny at the end of the table to her right. She was still dueling with Sonny's irreverent eyes when Souza broke the silence. "Do you mind if Sonny sits in?" he said for the second time.

Nalani turned her eyes to Souza but said nothing. After the nothing had lasted as long as he apparently desired, he broke the silence again by reciting her name, the date, the time and the names of the people present. "Please note," he added, "that Miss Rosario made no objection to the presence of Mister Akaka at these proceedings."

"Not," Nalani said softly.

"You do object?" Souza asked.

"Why do you want him here?"

"He knows things that I don't."

For shuah, Nalani said to herself. *But is that good or bad for me?* "You bring everybody in who knows things you don't," she said out loud, "we gotta move to the auditorium, you know."

"Yeah," Souza said, smiling easily. "But Sonny's insight is especially appropriate for this situation."

"You think you know the situation?"

"Not as well as you do, certainly. That's why we need to talk."

"Whatevah."

"Before we begin," Souza said, the concern in his voice sounding genuine to Nalani, "is there anything you need? A doctor, maybe?"

"Not," Nalani said. "I'm fine."

"Something to eat or drink?"

Nalani shook her head slowly, her eyes tied up completely with his in case the others in the room could be made to disappear by refusing to look at them.

"If that should change at any point in this interview, please let me know."

"Whatevah," she said again.

"Okay," Souza said, his eyes and his voice laced with kindness. "Would you try to tell us what happened to you, starting from the beginning?"

The beginning was one long fockin' time ago, you know, Nalani thought, but she shoved that thought aside in favor of unfolding the story she had worked out with Robbie one careful chapter at a time.

3

Geronimo knew he was weeping; he could feel the tears streaming down both sides of his face. What he didn't know was why.

"Adrenaline residue," the DEA woman said, sensing somehow these were not tears of joy. "It's like coming off a high."

"I thought you were the 'Just Say No' team," Geronimo said. "What do you know about highs?"

"I'm DEA," the woman said, her eyes drifting back to the transcript of Nalani Rosario's interview in her hands. "I know everything."

"So fucking true," Geronimo said, but the woman was back into her reading and gave no indication of hearing the sarcasm or even the words that had carried it. The four of them were sprawled around the table in the interview room—Geronimo, Ralph, Stefano and the woman, the three men waiting for the woman to catch up with the situation.

"Should be happy, you know," Ralph said. "The kid's okay."

"Is she?" Geronimo wondered aloud. "Sonny's not so sure."

"Sonny don' know shit, brah. Fock Sonny."

"Whatever," Geronimo said, his voice low and thick and his eyes still leaking water. He contemplated reaching into his back pocket for a handkerchief, but he didn't really feel like moving his arm that much, so he let the thought float away without acting on it.

"Interesting," the woman said, stacking the transcript neatly on the table in front of her.

"That's it?" Stefano asked. "Interesting?"

"You don't agree?"

"Sure, I agree. I was just hoping for something really profound, you being DEA and all."

"Of course," the woman said. "We do so suffer the burden of high expectations."

"What do we know for sure?" Geronimo interjected, his tolerance for repartee seeping out of him along with the tears.

"The kid fo' shuah snatched by three Mexicans," Ralph said. "Coach saw that part."

"And two of the three are dead now," the woman said. "I'm pretty sure of that."

"Rosario, too, for fucking sure," Stefano said.

"And the kid is back," Geronimo added.

"Plus we know what the kid said happened," the woman said, tapping the stack of paper on the table in front of her. "And that a lot of what she said is bullshit."

"Fo' shuah?" Ralph asked.

"I'm afraid so," Stefano said. "I don't see any of the shootings coming down the way she has them, for example."

"We are so fucking fucked," Geronimo said as he reached into his back pocket for the handkerchief, his arm functioning just fine as he methodically applied the material to his face.

"What do you mean, brah?" Ralph said.

"All hell's gonna break loose now, if it hasn't started already."

"That was always gonna happen," Stefano said. "Nothing changed."

"You're probably right," Geronimo said. He returned the handkerchief to his back pocket and sat there without speaking for a moment, his mind beginning to turn at closer to its usual rate. Everyone else settled into the same silence until Ralph's cell phone went off.

"Yeah?" Ralph said after he plucked the phone from his belt, and a moment later he said "Thanks" and put the phone down on the table.

"What?" Geronimo asked, suddenly anxious, suddenly ready to get up and go.

"One more thing we know fo' shuah," Ralph said. "They foun' the dead Jap up Hawi side."

"Just like Nalani said?" Geronimo asked, his mind racing up another notch or two.

"Yeah."

"All the bodies we have already," the woman said, "I wonder why the kid is still alive."

"What difference does it make?" Geronimo said.

"It might change the name of this game if we knew the answer to that question."

"No matter what you call it," Geronimo said, the words sliding off a sharp edge in his voice, "the game still stays the same."

The woman stiffened slightly in her chair, the edge in Geronimo's voice apparently leaving a mark, but she let whatever retort had been on the tip of her tongue dissolve without wrapping her voice around it.

"The only way this shit makes sense," Stefano interjected carefully, "is Robbie and the kid are part of the future somehow. Otherwise, they'd both be buried with the rest of the past right now."

"I'm with Skippy on this," Geronimo said. "The kid's the evidence; she's not the crime."

"You listen to that fockah?" Ralph asked.

"More every fucking day," Geronimo said, glancing at the woman as he said it. She glanced back with a question in her black eyes, but he let it bounce off unattended while he turned his mind back to the situation in front of them.

"Keli`i Ioane," Stefano said, picking the woman's question up where Geronimo had dropped it. "Everybody calls him Skippy. Think Cesar Chavez, then add guitar, ukulele, and vocals."

"Think fockin' local loser," Ralph said.

"Kind of controversial," Stefano said with a grin.

"So was Cesar," the woman said.

"Exactly," Stefano said.

"Past, present, or future," Geronimo said, hammering everyone back onto the situation again, "the motherfucker doesn't release anybody unless he already knows how he's getting out of here."

"It's gonna take a new face with matching ID," Stefano said. "You think he can get that here?"

"I don't see how," Geronimo said. "I couldn't do it, and I've lived here all my life."

"He's bringing someone in to do it," the woman said. "Your people at the airports need to watch the arrivals as well as the departures."

"Could be more than just an artist coming in," Geronimo said with a nod in Ralph's direction. "If I got into it with the fucking Japanese, I might call for reinforcements."

Ralph picked up his phone and jumped inside it, but Geronimo's mind had already skipped to another topic. "Where the fuck is Robbie?" he asked.

"We're looking, brah," Stefano said. "We'll turn him up pretty soon."

"What'd he say when you called?"

"Had to leave him a message."

"There isn't an easier guy to get on the phone on this whole fucking island, Stef. I'm getting a really bad vibe out of this."

"Big game yesterday," Stefano said with a shrug. "Lotta customers he needs to see."

"Believe me," Geronimo said, "I'm number one on that hit parade. Something is definitely up." *But where?* he thought. *Where are you, Robbie?*

4

"Gracias," Robbie said as he disembarked from the car in front of the hotel, but his mind was locked so tightly on his next few steps that he could not remember later what language Ortega responded in or if Ortega responded at all.

"Wassup, Robbie?" Sammi said from behind the registration counter, and Robbie heard that because he owed her a hundred on the game and he was walking right by her when she said it.

"Hey!" he said as he fished a Franklin out of his pocket and placed it on the counter. "You like da kine game, yeah?"

"Oh, yeah," Sammi said with a grin. "Shoulda bet da family fahm on dat one."

"Yo' family no got no fockin' fahm, Sammi."

"Mebbe dat's why I nevah do da kine," she said, her grin twice as wide as before as she snatched the hundred off the counter and made it disappear.

Robbie made himself do the same thing as soon as he could, and a moment later he was standing in front of the old man's door with a bodyguard on each arm.

The bodyguards both pawed him thoroughly, and Robbie assumed they were both eventually satisfied because they both eventually stopped. "The old man is here," one of them said when they were finished, "but Kitano is not."

No fockin' shit, Robbie thought, but he nodded in response and said nothing.

"Do you still want to go in?" the bodyguard asked.

He thinks the fockah can't speak English, too, Robbie thought, but he nodded again without a word. The bodyguard tapped on the door twice, opened it with a plastic card, stepped aside while Robbie entered the suite, and closed the door quietly as soon as Robbie was out of the way.

The old man was standing in the same place Robbie had last

seen him, staring through the large picture window at the suite's ocean view like he had to squeeze it until he got back every penny he had paid for it. Robbie stood just inside the doorway and waited, his mind mulling over what he needed to accomplish during this visit and the overwhelming unlikelihood of doing so if the old man really didn't understand English after all.

Robbie knew Kitano had thought the old man was finished and could easily be forced out of the way, but Robbie had serious doubts about that and was not proceeding from the same assumption. *Shuah,* he thought, *the older you get the weaker you are. But how strong do you have to be to grow that old in this fockin' game?*

The old man turned away from the window after a few moments of silence and motioned Robbie further into the room with a short toss of his head. Robbie approached him deferentially, stopping about ten feet away while the old man eyeballed him carefully.

"I have some bad news," Robbie said.

The old man continued to stare at Robbie without a word in any language, but Robbie was determined not to be the next person to speak so he stood in his spot on the carpeted floor and continued to wait.

"Fucking Mexicans?" the old man asked.

"Sir?" Robbie said, uncertain what the old man meant even though the words were both familiar.

"Kitano's not coming back?" the old man said.

"Not," Robbie said.

"Sit," the old man said, motioning to the sofa while he moved to the chair Kitano had typically used back when Kitano had been capable of sitting up straight.

"Thanks," Robbie said. He stepped to the sofa and eased himself onto it even though he knew that standing better suited his rolling stomach. The old man sat, too, and they slipped into another silent moment with their eyes doing all the work until the old man had apparently seen his fill.

"The Mexicans do it?" the old man asked.

"Yeah."

"Why is this bad news?"

"Not," Robbie said, but he considered the comment carefully before he said it. "Maybe for Kitano, yeah?"

"No," the old man said. "Kitano was dead when he left."

Robbie's stomach turned another time or two as he processed that remark, but he tried to keep his reaction out of his face until he settled back down again. He thought about asking the obvious—*you knew?*—but the obvious didn't need to be asked so he sat there without speaking and waited for the old man to continue.

"Why aren't you dead, too?" the old man said.

"I made a deal with the fockahs."

The old man nodded, his eyes still working overtime in Robbie's direction. "You start by taking me out?" he asked.

"Yeah."

"What then?"

"I take ovah local distribution."

"You can do this?"

"Yeah."

"No," the old man said, shaking his head slowly. "You're no killer."

"True," Robbie said. "But I know one."

"I see," the old man said, and then he stopped seeing for a moment. He leaned back in the chair and closed his eyes, and Robbie sat uneasily on the edge of the sofa and waited until the old man returned.

"You can do the other thing?" the old man said.

"What thing?"

"Front the Mexican shit."

"Not," Robbie said. "Not alone."

"Who do you need?"

"Sonnyboy Akaka," Robbie said, seeing no reason to mention

the participation of a 16-year-old orphan girl at this point in the conversation.

"That gets you one side," the old man said slowly. "How do you get Rosario's side?"

Fockah been payin' attention, Robbie thought with approval. *Heard everything two times, yeah?*

"Sonny carries a lot of weight," Robbie said. "If he's the one with the shit, I think everybody'll come over." Especially if he is working with Nalani Rosario, he added to himself.

The old man nodded and rattled something off in Japanese. Robbie shook his head slightly, and some words Robbie could understand rolled right in behind the ones he could not.

"The beast always eats," the old man said.

"Something like that," Robbie said.

"Why didn't they make a deal with Kitano?"

"They did, you know," Robbie said. "The thing blew the fock up."

"So you made the deal."

"Yeah."

"But now you're here."

"Yeah."

"So you are not to be trusted."

"I can be trusted to do what I gotta do to fockin' stay alive."

"You're not a *samurai,* then?"

"Not."

"The age of the *samurai* has been over for a long time now."

"There was never a time that I was gonna be one," Robbie said.

The old man nodded, his hard eyes closing once more and his voice sliding away into silence again. Robbie stayed on the edge of the sofa, comfortable with the discomfort of the position and the cautious buzz that came with it. After a while, his eyes wandered to the window across the room. He watched the night begin to lose its grip on the sky, a paler blue than the night's dark navy already intruding,

"What happened to the girl?" the old man said suddenly, bringing Robbie back to the edge of the sofa with a thud he hoped the old man could not hear.

"Why?" Robbie asked, even though he already knew the answer.

"Too crazy this way."

"Yeah," Robbie said. "She's at the cop shop now."

The old man shifted slightly in his chair, blinked once, and proceeded to turn up the intensity in his gaze two or three clicks. "She's in the deal?" he asked.

"Yeah," Robbie said.

"Why?"

"She's got the Mexicans still alive thinking like father, like daughter."

"What do you mean?"

"She shot two of them, you know."

"But she's okay."

"Yeah."

"I see," the old man said. "She has a tale to tell?"

"Yeah."

"And you have one for me."

"Yeah."

"So the police will find Kitano pretty soon."

Robbie nodded his response this time, more for the sake of variety than anything else; he still had many more yeahs where the others had been stored. The old man watched him closely from the beginning of the nod to the end before he spoke again.

"What do you want?" he said when he was ready for the answer.

"The same thing I have with the Mexicans."

"You already got it, why switch?"

Fockahs kicked sweet John in da face, dat's why, he said to himself, but he rolled out another reason for the old man. "I'm Japanese, yeah?" he said. "Fock da moddafockahs."

The old man rose from the chair and slowly returned to his spot in front of the window. The first hint of orange had crept into the several shades of blue in the sky, and Robbie sat on the edge of the sofa and watched the color intensify while he waited anxiously for the old man to sniff around at the bait a little longer

"You got a plan?" the old man said, the words bouncing off the plate glass in front of his face.

"Oh, yeah," Robbie said, and then he began the careful process of reeling in the line.

5

Robbie had plenty to do while he waited for John to get back from the Kona side with the rest of the old man's crew, but none of it engaged his mind so none of it eased his anxiety. He made several stops, picking up slightly more cash than he dropped off and throwing in idle chatter at no extra cost, but he was ready for solace long before his phone rang with what he hoped would be an offer of some.

"It's me," John said into his ear.

"Gimme twenty minutes, max," Robbie said.

"I'm not at home," John said. "I think I'm under hotel arrest."

"What the fock?" Robbie said, a cold chill running through him and his voice catching a little in his throat.

"What did you tell the old man about me?" John asked. "He apparently wants to keep me off the board for a while."

"Is the fockah there?"

"No. I think I'm right across the hall from him, though."

"The fockahs tell you to call me?"

"Yes."

"Fock," Robbie said, and then he traded saying things for thinking them.

"They want me to get off the phone," John said after a couple of minutes of silence.

"One thing," Robbie said. "How many fockahs you got in the room?"

"Three."

"How many can you handle?"

"One for sure, two if I get lucky. No fucking way on the third."

"Hang tight, brah. Gonna fockin' bring reinforcements, I promise."

"Sounds good to me," John said, his voice as free and easy as Robbie's was tight. Robbie savored that sound until the phone went dead, and then used the silence that followed to mull the situation over some more.

I fockin' know who, he thought, *but not how.* He kept after it, though, until he saw the way, and then he put his phone back to work.

6

The boy was asleep at Sonny's side, his warm head snuggled in tight under the arm Sonny had stretched out along the top of the couch. The old woman was still seated on the far side of the room, just as she had been before Sonny had left in search of Nalani with Geronimo, for all Sonny knew her silent eyes still staring across at him relentlessly. Sonny didn't know for sure and didn't want to, having closed his own eyes several minutes earlier in self-defense.

He found it more difficult to protect himself from his own thoughts, however, the primary offender being the one about his desire to sit on his ass in the bosom of Buddy Kai's family while both the Japanese and the Mexicans lined up to take a shot at him. *You know you gotta hit 'em first,* he kept thinking, *if you fockin' wanna win.*

This was the exact thought running through Sonny's mind again when the phone rang. The sleeping boy at Sonny's side didn't stir when the sound intruded, but Sonny did. He had dropped the phone on the couch to his left earlier, and he reclaimed it quickly to shut the thing up.

"Yeah?" he said into it, his voice tamped down low.

"We gotta talk, brah," Robbie said, Sonny thinking he had recognized the voice by the end of the second word.

"We do?" Sonny said.

"Kinda touchy, aren't you?"

"Spit it out, Robbie."

"You're on the fockin' hot seat, I promise."

"You think so?"

"I know so, Sonny. You're in the fockin' master plan no matter which way the shit goes down."

"You know the master plans, Robbie?"

"I'm up to my fockin' eyebrows both ways, brah."

"Fock 'em both, and fock you, too. Fockahs can't make me do shit."

"Can, you know. Too many people you care about, Sonny."

Sonny opened his eyes at that point, looking first at the boy next to him and then at the old woman in the chair across the room. As he had imagined, the woman's eyes were still locked on him—sad, silent eyes that never seemed to blink.

"What do you want, Robbie?" Sonny asked, taking on the old woman's gaze as he did it.

"Nothing, if you're gonna fockin' wait to get hit."

Sonny took that in but said nothing in response, looking as deeply into the old woman's eyes as he could. She looked back the same way, both of them seeing everything that neither of them said.

"Or what?" Sonny said into the phone.

"I need you right now, brah, you wanna hit the fockahs first."

Sonny took that in, too, and moved it around with everything he had learned during his years in the business with Buddy and everything his life had taught him before that. He didn't speak again for a moment or two, and neither did Robbie, but Sonny knew that his silence was nothing but a formality and suspected that Robbie knew it, too. *Fock it,* Sonny said to himself. *Even fockin' Robbie Tsubamoto knows what I gotta do.*

"What do you need, Robbie?" Sonny asked when he was done trying to dodge the inevitable.

"The fockin' Japs are holdin' John. I need to shake him loose."

"Where are you?"

"The Naniloa."

"I'll be right ovah."

"One thing I should say, Sonny."

"What?"

"I think we'll find three guys in the room and two in the hall. We can handle that?"

"If we get on top in the hall, fock the guys in the room."

"Fockahs gonna check for weapons first thing, you know."

"Whatevah."

"Thanks, Sonny," Robbie said, his voice only half as loud as it had been just a moment earlier. Sonny grinned slightly as he cut the connection and returned the phone where he had found it, but he said nothing more.

Don' thank me yet, brah, Sonny thought as he rose from the couch. *Don' fockin' thank me yet.*

7

"You think this gamble gonna pay off, *jefe?*" Ortega asked.

Jesus was deep inside his own thoughts when Ortega spoke, but his thoughts were on the same subject as Ortega's words.

"What gamble?" he said. "We got nothin' to fockin' lose."

"The girl and the Jap turn on us, we might wish we had put 'em down with that other focker."

"You don' think we can do that whenever we want? This is a free shot at the situation, homes. It don' work out, we still where we were."

"Which is where, exactly?" Ortega said, looking out of the window onto a street of nondescript houses similar to the one in which he was standing.

"Who the fock knows?" Jesus said, although he knew they were on the outskirts of Hilo somewhere. "Just one more street in paradise."

"When is Henriquez getting in?"

"She don' like it when you use that name."

"I got a lotta names for her she probably don' like."

"Eleven something. I need you to meet the plane."

Ortega nodded slowly at the window but said nothing for a moment. Jesus walked across the room and stood next to him, his eyes on the sky as it quickly added color to the palette of the night that was ending. "Ever notice how hard the morning hits the fockin' night here?" Ortega said.

"Everything else is like that, too," Jesus said. "First nothin' at all is goin' on, then the nex' thing you know the fockin' sky is fallin'."

"You think Henriquez get the job done?"

"*Si.* Focker make me look like J-Lo, she want to."

"She make you look like J-Lo, maybe I rethink my fockin' sexual orientation."

"Won' do you no good, *ese.* Gonna get me a rap star, I look like J-Lo."

"Henriquez do the ID, too?"

"The whole *enchilada.*"

"You make it out, who's takin' your place?"

"You," Jesus said.

"Gracias, jefe," Ortega said quietly. "I do a good job."

"Maybe," Jesus said, "you don' follow too many bikinis aroun'."

"She was fine, though," Ortega said with a grin.

"You think they're all fine."

"Si. But this one was super-fine."

"She got you pinched."

"She got us the fockin' Jap."

True, Jesus thought. *She did do that, as things turned out.*

"How much muscle we got comin'?" Ortega asked, his voice softly serious again.

Fockin' airport security, Jesus thought. "You'll have more muscle than hardware, homes," he said.

"Except for the girls in the bikinis," Ortega said, "this island could get fockin' old in a hurry."

"We got girls in bikinis back in LA," Jesus said. "We got beaches, too. We even got the same fockin' ocean."

"Yeah," Ortega said, the grin back in his voice the same way it was spread all over his broad brown face. "But these poor island people need our fockin' shit, *jefe.* Sometimes you gotta sacrifice for the common good."

"I heard that," Jesus said, but he didn't quite hit the playful note he had been aiming for when he started the comment.

"I know," Ortega said. "This could get ugly."

"This *will* get ugly," Jesus said.

"Don' worry," Ortega said. "Ugly is jus' fine with me."

That's why you're nex' in line, Jesus thought as he watched the red run over the sky on the far side of the window. *Ugly is jus' fine with us both.*

8

"You fockin' *pupule,* you know," Sonny said softly as he walked up to Robbie in the hotel's open lobby.

"So I'm crazy," Robbie said. "This is still the only thing to do, brah."

"I can think of plenty more things to do."

"You know what the fock I mean."

Sonny did know what the fuck Robbie meant, but he derived no consolation from the knowledge. It was just one more reason his head was beginning to hurt, the other being the bullshit victim story Nalani Rosario had laid out for the cops—Geronimo and Benedetto both appearing to embrace it like the words had come straight from the burning bush.

Gee should know better by now, Sonny thought, *but look what the fock I'm doing?* What he was doing was standing in the lobby while Robbie turned toward his cousin behind the counter and said something Sonny couldn't hear, but what was actually on Sonny's mind was the next thing on the morning agenda. The cousin spoke on the phone for a moment and shook her head before Robbie turned back in Sonny's direction.

"The ol' man is not receiving," Robbie said.

"He's gonna be, brah, if you wan' him to," Sonny said.

"You don't have to do anything, you know."

"No shit," Sonny said, but he knew why he was there. *If I leave the right fockin' message, maybe the Japs'll back the fock off,* he said to himself as they started down a wide hallway toward the elevators. *Fockin' gotta start somewhere.*

When they reached the gift shop, Sonny veered off, snatched a can of root beer out of a cold case, and paid the old Japanese woman at the counter.

"The thing is," Robbie said when they were moving down the hallway again, "if I'm gonna do this thing, I gotta have John."

"You think you're gonna have time to fock?" Sonny said, shaking the can in his hand briskly while his face broke into a grin.

"Not," Robbie said, his face briefly lighting up with a grin of his own when he said it. "But John kicks some ass, brah."

"No shit?" Sonny said, the soda can still moving up and down in his hand.

"What the fock are you doing?" Robbie said.

"You no like da foamy kine?"

"You're gonna have fockin' foam all over, you know."

"That's the fockin' idea."

"You're the *pupule* one, I promise."

"So John's a badass, yeah?"

"Way bad."

"It doesn't matter, you know. If we spring him, Robbie, get the fock out. What difference is it gonna make who brings the fockin' shit in? It's still gonna be shit, I promise."

"I know. But why we gotta take the shit and the moddafockahs, too?"

"You don't. Just stay the fock out."

As they approached the elevators, one of the doors opened. They waited for an old *haole* couple dressed in matching poolside outfits to exit before they entered. "It's not that easy, you know," Robbie said when the door closed behind them and they started moving up. "You try to stay the fock out, they're gonna come at you hard."

"That's the fockin' price I gotta pay, Robbie. You still can stay the fock out."

"Not," Robbie said, his voice only a notch or two above a whisper. "The cards have already been dealt, brah. Gotta play 'em now."

"How far you gonna go?" Sonny said as the elevator stopped and the doors opened in front of them.

"Whatevah it takes."

"We gotta put these guys down, they gotta stay down, you know."

"I know," Robbie said as he stepped into the hall.

Sonny reached out and placed his right hand on Robbie's nearest arm. Robbie stopped immediately and looked back over his shoulder. "You shuah?" Sonny said. "This is no fockin' game, I promise."

"Yeah," Robbie said, and then he moved on down the hall.

Sonny trailed after him, and they stayed in that formation until they reached two men standing at doors opposite each other in the hallway.

"You know the drill," the taller of the men said, and Robbie placed both of his hands on the wall near the old man's door and leaned on them.

"You, too," the shorter man said, and Sonny replicated Robbie's position as closely as he could—the only difference being that Sonny was holding a well-shaken can of root beer in his left hand and Robbie was not.

"He's busy," the taller man said when both of the men were finished with their frisks. "You'll have to come back later."

"I can see John, yeah?" Robbie asked, turning his head slightly in the direction of the shorter man.

"No," the shorter man said, his voice almost an exact replica of his partner's.

"How you do that, brah?" Robbie asked. "You open your mouth, and his voice comes out."

Neither of the men responded to Robbie's question, nor did either of them indicate in any way from that point on in the proceedings that Robbie was in fact standing in the hallway. Sonny looked into one set of slanted eyes and then the other, and quickly came to the conclusion that both sets were focused entirely on him.

"I guess we'll come back a little later," Robbie said, turning in the same direction all the eyes in front of him were pointed and slowly stepping out of the way.

"Shuah," Sonny said through an easy grin, and he snapped the top of the soda can in his hand while he said it. What happened after that happened rapidly, Sonny knew, but inside his own head it all unfolded in slow motion. First, root beer sprayed in all directions, and everyone but Sonny instinctively ducked away from it.

Second, Sonny rammed the hard edge of the foaming can

into the nose of the shorter guard until the nose started gushing blood almost as fast as the can was spraying root beer.

Third, the man's hands both flew to his face in a futile attempt to stop the blood from flowing while the guard on the other side of the hall produced a handgun and began to raise it in Sonny's direction. Robbie tried to voice a warning, but by the time Sonny heard it he was already inside the arm with the gun on the end of it. As soon as the taller man and Sonny were standing face to face, Sonny cracked his forehead into the guard's nose and started another geyser of blood. He backed the head butt with a short left punch that disappeared in the man's midsection, and the guard collapsed in a breathless heap at Sonny's feet.

Sonny followed him to the floor in hot pursuit of the handgun while the other guard filled one of his bloodstained hands with a gun of his own. That was the fourth thing that happened, but the fifth occurred almost simultaneously.

Sonny rose swiftly, whipping the taller man's gun upside the shorter man's head as though the choreography had been worked out in advance and rehearsed by them both. The shorter guard went down right on cue, his gun slipping from his grasp as he fell.

Onetwot'reefo'five, Sonny thought as he swiped at the blood on his face with the sleeve of his shirt, each number a syllable rather than a word as it raced through his mind. He picked up the second gun and compared it to the one he was already holding, and found them to be dissimilar in only one way—the one in his right hand had a sound suppressor attached to the end of it and the one in his left did not.

The taller bodyguard began to regain his ability to push air in and out of his lungs, so Sonny slowly extended his right hand in that direction first. Then he paused for a glance at Robbie, who was standing against the wall like he needed it to remain upright.

"Robbie!" Sonny said, his voice low but sharp.

"Yeah?" Robbie replied, jerking like the word had slapped him in the face.

"You fockin' shuah?"

Robbie blinked his eyes once and then directed them all the way down Sonny's arm to the guard stirring tentatively on the floor in front of the gun. "Yeah," Robbie said softly, his head moving up and down slowly as though he couldn't trust the word to make it all the way across the hall by itself.

Sonny promptly rendered the guard's newly found ability to breathe superfluous. The gun popped when it went off, but it was a moderate pop that seemed to Sonny an inadequate counterpoint to the hole that suddenly appeared between the guard's sightless eyes.

Sonny turned his attention to the shorter guard next, and when he squeezed the trigger for the second time the gun coughed out the same pop with the same result.

"Can you do something?" Sonny asked when he was done.

"Yeah," Robbie said again, the word on its own this time as Robbie kept his eyes fixed on the bodies on the floor.

"Look for the room key," Sonny said as he leaned in close to the door he believed stood between them and John and listened intently.

Robbie moved like he was fighting through a fogbank, but he eventually began to rummage through the available pockets until he came up with a pair of plastic cards. "Two, brah," he said, his voice catching a little in his throat before the words came out.

Sonny extended his left hand in Robbie's direction, the gun in that hand more trouble than Sonny thought it was worth. "Wipe it clean and drop it," Sonny said.

Robbie reached up gingerly and took the gun by the barrel, but Sonny kept his arm extended in Robbie's direction even after the hand was empty. "Gimme the cards," Sonny said softly as soon as he was certain Robbie needed the instructions. Robbie did as he had been told, both with the cards and the gun, and when he was done he looked up at Sonny again.

Sonny pocketed the key cards and reached down with his free hand, and Robbie allowed himself to be pulled to his feet. "You're gonna be fine," Sonny said, even though he had serious doubts on the subject, and Robbie responded by moving his head up and down as though his voice couldn't be trusted with a reply.

Stay the fock outta this shit, brah, Sonny said without another sound. *If we get badass John outta here, take him home and fock him.*

9

Robbie was standing in the hotel hallway with a pair of corpses at his feet and a blank expression on his face. He stared at Sonny for a moment, wondering idly as he did it how long they could linger there before the elevator door opened or someone walked out of a room.

"Gotta move, yeah?" he asked.

"Yeah," Sonny said. Robbie nodded slowly, but made no other response. After another frozen moment or two, Sonny spoke again. "Call the room, brah."

Robbie looked back at Sonny like Sonny had just flown in from a foreign galaxy. "How come?" he asked.

"Call the room," Sonny said again, checking the chamber of the gun in his hand. "Let me know when they answer."

Oh, Robbie thought as he punched his phone to life, his mind finally coming up with a picture that made sense of Sonny's instructions. *At least you'll know where one of the fockahs is gonna be.*

"Yes?" said a voice in Robbie's ear as soon as his call bounced back from the desk downstairs, the voice very similar to the voices recently abandoned by the bodyguards now stretched out silently on the hallway floor.

"Put John on the phone," Robbie said as he nodded in Sonny's direction. Sonny removed one of the key cards from his pocket and inserted it into the slot in the door.

"This is Tsubamoto, right?" the voice said. A red light started blinking near the door handle in the hallway.

"Yeah," Robbie said. Sonny switched cards silently.

"Quit calling here," the voice said. Sonny repeated the same maneuver with the new card that had failed with the old one and was rewarded with a green light this time. He cracked the door slightly, checked for a chain and found none, pocketed the key card, pushed the door open, and stepped into the room.

Robbie bit back his answer to the voice in his ear until Sonny's sequence was completed, but his reply had nowhere to go by the time he followed Sonny into the room. Robbie had barely cleared the doorway when he heard the gun pop again, and the guard standing between a pair of queen beds with the phone to his ear pitched suddenly to his left and bounced off the wall as though pulled off his feet by a puppeteer concealed in a hidden crawlspace above the ceiling.

The gun popped again almost immediately, and Robbie's eyes rocked slightly to the right in time to see another guard sprawl against an open refrigerator door and sink to the floor in a cascade of condiments.

Robbie quickly scanned the room in front of him, and when he didn't see what he was looking for, he stepped into the bathroom to his hard right and looked some more. He stepped back out a second or two later with his heart in his throat and a silent question on his face.

Sonny had moved to a door in the wall to Robbie's left by the time Robbie emerged from the bathroom. *Connecting rooms,* Robbie thought as he watched Sonny lean in close and listen for a moment. When the moment was over, Sonny tested the doorknob carefully, found it up to the task of opening the door, and followed the gun in his right hand into the room.

"Stop right there," said a voice which originated somewhere

beyond Robbie's field of vision, but Robbie knew the voice and the beautiful young *haole* who went with it.

"Easy," Robbie said quickly. "He's with me."

"I was hoping that might be the case," John said.

Robbie finished entering the room and finally got his eyes pointed in the right direction. "You okay, brah?" he asked.

"Yeah," John said, lowering the gun in his hand until it was pointing straight at the floor and turning his eyes toward the bed. Robbie saw Sonny doing the same and let his own eyes follow suit, which was when he noticed the third guard stretched out on top of the spread with his head turned at an odd angle—too odd to maintain life, apparently, as the guard emitted no vital signs that Robbie could discern from the doorway.

"Fucker wasn't into 'no means no' at all," John said quietly. "Didn't leave me much of a choice."

"You have anything in the other room?" Sonny said.

"No," John replied.

"Wipe the gun and leave it," Sonny said as he used the tail of his shirt to follow his own instructions.

"What about the ol' man?" Robbie asked.

"Up to you, brah," Sonny said.

"What do you think?"

"If you hit him, the fockahs will send somebody new fo' shuah. You already have a relationship with this guy."

"I'd say it's a little dysfunctional, though."

"I think that goes with the game, brah."

Robbie turned in John's direction and picked up a silent nod of agreement. "Okay," he said. "We let him ride." Then he walked out the door into the hallway, turned away from the bodies on the floor, and headed for the stairwell to his right, his old friend and his new lover trailing behind him like neither of them had ever wanted anything more in their lives than this opportunity to walk down eight flights of stairs with Robbie Tsubamoto.

10

Ortega dropped the window in his door as he rolled up to the gate at the entrance to the airport parking lot. "Pop the trunk, please," said a chunky woman in a security uniform.

Ortega hit the release lever for the trunk and waited quietly while a second security guard strolled to the rear of the car. He heard the trunk slam shut a moment later, and the chunky woman nodded at him. "You good to go," she said.

Always, Ortega thought, but he kept the thought to himself while he drove through the gate. The open lot sprawled out in front of Ortega for what looked to him like the equivalent of two or three football fields, but he was already at the end that he needed, so he slipped into the first open slot he found that faced the terminal.

Gotta love this fockin' Hilo, he thought as he settled down to wait. *How many airports can you sit in the parking lot and watch the incoming passengers ride the escalator all the way to the baggage carousels?*

Ortega eyed the uniformed cops lounging near the escalator while he waited, but neither of them could hold his gaze whenever a young woman appeared in his field of vision. He undressed each of the women in his mind and savored the results—or he did until he realized with a jolt that one of them was the object of his errand. She was long and blonde and California brown, as were the three surfer dudes moving easily behind her, and Ortega grinned as he watched them blow by the cops like the tourists they resembled.

Fockin' profilers, Ortega thought, wishing suddenly that he could say it where the stupid cops could hear it. *Muscle comes in any color you want, you willing to pay for it.* The woman veered toward the street in front of the terminal and raised a phone to her ear while the surfer dudes headed for the luggage, and Ortega's phone immediately began to vibrate.

"Looking good, Henriquez," he said as soon as his phone was connected to the one in the woman's hand.

"Don't fucking call me that," the woman said into his ear.

"Why not? Was your husband's name, *si?*"

"If I still wanted his fucking name, I wouldn't have killed the motherfucker."

"I guess not."

"What's next?"

"Rent a car and follow me out. I'm in a silver Buick."

"You can see the rental cars from where you are?"

"Si."

"Jesus Christ."

"That's Hilo, baby."

"Yeah, well, the sooner I'm out of this fucking puddle, the better I'll like it."

"What you mean? You in paradise now."

"Fuck paradise, Ortega," the woman said, "and fuck you, too."

"Any time," Ortega said, but he could see the woman closing her phone by the time he said it, so he stopped talking and went back to undressing her in his mind.

11

"Here we fucking go," Geronimo said as he hung up the phone on his desk.

"Whassup?" Stefano said.

"We've got five fucking bodies at the Naniloa."

"Shit," Stefano said. "Let's go."

"You can't be the next up to catch a homicide. How many you got going already?"

"I think they're all related, don't you?"

"Yes, I do," Geronimo said, and then his voice froze up and he didn't say another word until they walked up on the knot of people jamming the hallway on the eighth floor of the hotel. The attraction turned out to be two dead men with three eyes each, two of the eyes in each case having originated in Japan and the third apparently from a recently-fired Smith & Wesson found on the floor of one of the rooms nearby.

"I'm Souza," Geronimo said to a uniformed cop he didn't know standing on the edge of the crowd. "Are you the one who called me?"

"Yeah," the cop said. "Louie's in the room across the hall with the ol' man."

"What's this old man got to do with anything?"

"A woman and a girl came out of his room at the same time I got here. Maybe they heard something."

"Where are the other bodies?"

"Two shot in that room there, one with a broken neck next door." Stefano took that information and eased around the crowd with it until he disappeared inside one of the rooms the cop had indicated.

"You the first one here?" Geronimo asked.

"Yeah."

"You know who called it in?"

"A hotel guest from three or four rooms down."

"Louie talk to him already?"

"Her," the cop said. "Yeah."

"All the victims Japanese?"

The cop nodded, his eyes focused on the group of people in front of him.

"What's up with the root beer?" Geronimo said, his eyes lingering on a bloody can on the floor between the bodies.

The cop shook his head this time. "Looks like the whole thing started with a pop can," he said.

"Thanks," Geronimo said as he started in the opposite direction as Stefano.

"No problem," the cop said.

The first door Geronimo came to was propped open with the safety latch, so he pushed his way through it and walked inside the room. A panoramic view of the bay through the picture window on the far side of the room slapped him in the face immediately, and he took a moment to watch as an incoming tour ship labored around the breakwater on its way to the dock in Keaukaha.

The second thing Geronimo noticed was Louie Yamamoto, who was standing at the edge of the picture window but facing the wrong direction to enjoy the view. "What you got?" Geronimo asked while he surveyed the third thing he noticed—the old man sitting in an armchair with his eyes closed and the woman perched on the edge of a couch with a young girl at her side.

"What you see is what you get," Louie said. "Hard to say what it is."

"I'm Geronimo Souza," Geronimo said, focusing first on the old man. "Did you folks see or hear anything that happened in the hall outside this room?"

The old man made no indication that he heard the question, or that he was even aware that the questioner had entered the room. Louie rattled off a few words in Japanese, and the old man opened his eyes for the first time and regarded Geronimo quietly.

After another short burst from Louie, the old man shook his head and responded briefly in the same language Louie was using. "Saw nothing, heard nothing," Louie said.

"He doesn't speak English?" Geronimo wondered aloud.

"Hard to say. Hasn't so far."

"How about you two?" Geronimo said, turning toward the woman.

"We nevah see not'ing!" the woman said sharply, as though she had already staked out this territory and for some reason felt the need to defend it. Geronimo studied her carefully for a moment, cataloging the hard edges on her bony frame, the hollow cheeks, the agitated eyes, the tangled brown hair that hung dully down her back. He wondered idly how old this woman was, but knew from past experience that observation alone would never reveal that number.

You're younger than you look, though, aren't you? he said to himself as he turned his attention to the young girl. *And you're just the opposite, aren't you, sweetheart?* He felt a deep rage buiding as the girl looked back at him through round brown eyes that absorbed everything and revealed nothing, her face as composed as a finely crafted mask, Geronimo suddenly and inexplicably thinking of Nalani rather than the girl in front of him.

"Is this your girl?" Geronimo asked, his face flushed.

"Granddaughtah," the woman said.

"Why are you here?"

"Why not? Can be here, yeah?"

"How old is she?"

"Eleven."

"Why are you here?" Geronimo asked again.

"We got business here."

"What business?"

"He owed me money."

"For what?"

"Work."

"Don't fuck with me," Geronimo said. "I'm not in the mood for it, I promise you."

"How I gonna fock wit' you? Fockin' let me go."

"So he paid you the money?"

"What money?"

"The money you said he owed you. What money did you think I meant?"

"Yeah, he wen pay me."

"How much?"

"T'ree hunnerd."

"Let me see it."

The woman reached into a small purse clutched in her hands and produced three hundreds. "What you t'ink, I gonna lie da kine?"

"Do you speak Japanese?"

"What?"

"Do you speak Japanese?"

"Fock, no!" the woman said as she put the money away.

"Louie," Geronimo said, "can you run these two down to the station?"

"Shuah," Louie said. "You need a translator?"

"This motherfucker speaks English," Geronimo said. "Hold this woman until I get there, and see if Becky can get the little one started on an exam."

"What da fock you mean?" the woman said.

"Get 'em out of here before I lose it, Louie," Geronimo said, totally ignoring the woman in favor of locking on the girl's silent eyes. The girl stared back without blinking as the woman yanked her to her feet.

"What da fock dis is?" the woman said.

"Hush," Louie said. "I gotta cuff you?"

"Fock, no!"

"Come, then," Louie said, and he took the girl by the hand and crossed the room to the door. The woman followed after him, her nervous eyes dancing from the back of Louie's head to the front of Geronimo's and back again. When they were gone, Geronimo sat down on the couch and studied the old man for a moment or two.

"You're in some shit here, you know," he said when he had seen enough, but the old man said nothing.

"Seriously," Geronimo said. "If that exam shows what I think it will show, you're more fucked than she was."

The old man continued to watch Geronimo in silence, his quiet eyes revealing nothing but a calm intelligence that Geronimo found disconcerting considering the circumstances. *Why the fuck aren't you worried?* he thought, and the question was still turning in his head when the answer walked in the door with Ralph Benedetto.

"This guy is here for the ol' man," Ralph said, motioning to a Japanese man wearing a light gray business suit over a white shirt and a tie.

"What?" Geronimo said, rising from the couch with the question.

"Mr. Johjima needs to come with me," the man said in perfect English that Geronimo was still unable to fully comprehend.

"I don't think so," Geronimo said. "He's involved in at least two investigations here."

"I'm afraid you have no authority to hold him here," the man in the suit said. "Mr. Johjima has been recalled and must report to the consulate in Honolulu."

"What are you saying? This motherfucker has diplomatic immunity?"

"That is correct."

"What about your five dead citizens outside the door there? What kind of fucking immunity did they have?"

"I assure you that has nothing to do with Mr. Johjima."

"Fuck this bullshit," Geronimo said. "Nobody's going anywhere until we sort this shit out."

"Mr. Benedetto?" the man in the suit said.

"This shit's legit, brah," Ralph said quietly. "I'm comin' straight from the chief."

"Legit, my ass. They'd have to set it up in advance to get here this fucking fast."

"Whatevah. We still gotta let it go, Gee."

The old man rose at that point and shuffled slowly past Geronimo, Ralph, and the man in the suit on his way to the door.

"You sure as shit understand this, don't you?" Geronimo said sharply.

The old man paused at the door and turned in Geronimo's direction. "I understand numbers," he said softly, his words barely audible where Geronimo was standing.

"What is that supposed to mean?" Geronimo asked.

"Thirty thousand dollars, for example," the old man said. "I understand that very well." Then he turned away and disappeared into the hall. Geronimo watched him go, and then he watched the man in the suit do exactly the same thing.

"What the fock was that?" Ralph said when he and Geronimo were alone in the room.

"Believe me, boss," Geronimo replied, his face suddenly flushed again and his breathing restricted. "You don't fucking want to know."

12

"You fucked up," the old man said, his voice so soft that Robbie could barely hear it even with his phone jammed as far into his ear as it would go.

"Not," Robbie said, reaching for a note of confidence in his voice that turned out to be just beyond his grasp. "You took him, I took him back. End of fockin' story, yeah?"

"No," the old man said, and the phone connection dissolved in Robbie's ear. Robbie lowered his phone to his lap and let his gaze drift out the window to his right.

"Not a happy camper?" John asked from behind the wheel. He had Robbie's Mustang stopped behind a flatbed truck at the light at Kawailani, but he hadn't glanced at the light or the truck since the call from the old man had come in.

"Not," Robbie said, turning toward Sonny as he said it. Sonny was lounging in the back seat like his mind was on a conversation transpiring in another time zone.

"What do you think?" Robbie asked.

"Whatevah," Sonny said. "Up to you, brah."

"He has at least half a dozen guys on the Kona side still," John said as he eased the Mustang forward. "Plus who knows how many where those motherfuckers came from."

"Wassup with the Mexicans?" Sonny said, his question right on point even though he still seemed unconnected to Robbie.

"We're cool right now, I guess," Robbie said.

"Later?"

"Later they're gonna want the cash."

"You gonna pay it?"

"Fock, no."

"Then sit these fockahs down, brah."

"Together?"

"The sooner, the better, I promise."

"We're gonna need a fockin' army if these moddafockahs freak out."

"Nobody's gonna freak out," Sonny said, "if we stay on top of this fockin' wave."

13

Geronimo kept cramming what he knew into the box in his mind labeled "What the Fuck?" and one of the pieces kept rising to the top.

"What?" Ralph said as the hotel elevator doors whispered shut in front of them.

"We need to talk to Sammi downstairs," Geronimo said.

"We got her statement already, brah. Said she didn't know anything, yeah?"

"Yeah, well, her cousin remains the best connection to these fuckers we have."

"Robbie?"

"The very one."

"Where the fock is that guy?"

"I don't know, boss," Geronimo said, "but I think I know where he was when all this shit came down around here."

"Why do you think that?"

"It's more of a feeling than a thought."

"The fockah dropped outta sight, that's fo' shuah."

"And then there's the thing with Nalani. How the fuck did he spring her loose?"

"I know, brah. The whole thing feels funny."

"Okay," Geronimo said when the elevator stopped and the doors opened. "Let's find out if I'm right." He led the way to the registration counter and stopped at the end of a short line of people waiting for Sammi's attention.

"We don't have to wait in this line," Ralph said.

"Trust me," Geronimo said. "We wanna wait in this one."

Ten minutes and several surreptitious glances from Sammi later, they reached the front of the line. "What I can do fo' you guys, Gee?" Sammi said.

Geronimo declined to answer immediately, and Ralph followed Geronimo's lead. Sammi looked from one to the other nervously, back and forth, until Geronimo finally spoke. "I know Robbie was here, Sammi," he said. "That's not the question."

"What da question is?" she asked.

"We know he's no killer. You tell me who was with him, we can forget about Robbie."

Sammi didn't respond immediately. Instead, she stood behind her counter and chewed on her bottom lip while her eyes continued to bounce from Geronimo to Ralph and back again.

"Spit it out, Sammi," Geronimo said after a silent moment or two, and that's what Sammi finally did.

"Sonny," she said. "He wen come wit' Sonnyboy Akaka."

14

"Sit still!" Henriquez said when Jesus reached for his phone. Jesus had been sitting still for an hour already with Henriquez fussing over him like a mother hen the entire time, so he was more than ready for a break.

"Hold up a minute," he said, and the way he said it shut Henriquez up before she whined any more. "Yeah?" he said into the phone.

"The fockin' shit's goin' down," a voice said in his ear.

It took him a minute, but Jesus hooked the face of the Japanese bookmaker to the voice before he answered. "What sheet?" he asked.

"The shit with the Japanese."

"So?"

"So you said you had something for those fockahs, yeah?"

"So did you, I remember it right."

"We jus' took out five of them at the hotel. It's gonna get fockin' hot now."

"You didn't get the ol' man?"

"Not."

"He gonna hit back?"

"Fock, yeah, we let him find us."

"Where that gonna hoppen, homes?"

"We'll send you a guide, you tell us where the fock you're at."

"You tell us where to pick the guide up. How 'bout we do it that way?"

"Whatevah," the bookie said.

15

"Howzit, baby?"

How the fock did he find me? Nalani wondered. She rolled her head in the direction of the voice but didn't bother to open her eyes. "I'm fine," she said softly. "You?"

"I've been missin' you like crazy, girl," Pono said. "You're fockin' hard to find, you know."

"I know," Nalani said, opening her eyes just as Pono kissed her gently on the forehead. "You heard what happened, yeah?"

Pono dropped into the empty space next to Nalani on the

couch in Aunty Minnie's crowded living room and wrapped his long left arm around her shoulders. "Yeah," he said. "You really okay?"

Nalani nodded, tucking her head into his chest as she did it. He countered that move by adding his right arm to the hug, and she was just beginning to snuggle into the warm comfort of the embrace when the phone rang in the kitchen.

"Nalani," one of her cousins said. "Phone for you."

"Can you bring it here?" Nalani asked.

"Not," the cousin said, her head sticking through the kitchen doorway. "It won't reach that far."

"I'll be right back," Nalani said as she rose from the couch and padded slowly to the kitchen.

"Thanks, Cuz," Nalani said, the soft grin on her face masking her concern about the call. "Yeah?" she said into the phone.

"Nalani?"

"Yeah?"

"Robbie."

"Wassup?"

"We need to get inside your house, girl."

"What?"

"We might need Dominic's guns, that's why," Robbie said.

"The Japanese or the Mexicans?"

"Maybe both, Nalani."

Nalani turned to look over her shoulder into the living room as she rolled Robbie's words around in her mind for a moment. Pono was ogling her from the couch with a grin on his face that might have made her laugh out loud had she been in the midst of a lighter conversation on the phone, but as things stood she pulled back her response to the briefest of smiles and a wink.

The moment with Pono passed. Nalani knew she was ready when he began to disappear right before her eyes—he was still there on the couch, but the couch seemed to recede until she could no longer see who was sitting on it.

"Robbie?" she said when Pono was no more than a spot in front of the wall.

"Yeah?"

"Come on ovah."

16

Sonny soundlessly surveyed the occupants of the car and shook his head almost imperceptibly—almost, but apparently not quite, because the girl sharing the back seat of the car with him picked the movement up even though her eyes appeared to be closed.

"What?" she said, her deep brown eyes definitely open now and fixed on him like twin tracking beams. Sonny looked her over deliberately, and had to admit when he was done that Nalani hit the beauty bulls-eye from a lot of different angles.

"This is not a fockin' beauty pageant, you know," Sonny said.

"What?" she said again.

"It's not basketball, either. The fockin' game you're flirtin' with here is nothing like any game you ever played."

"You have no idea what games I have played, Sonny—no idea whatsoevah."

"Shouldn't be here, you know," Sonny said to Robbie, who was looking in on the conversation from the front passenger seat while John pushed the car toward the house the girl had formerly shared with her father.

"Who?" Robbie asked.

"All of you."

"But me especially?" Nalani asked.

"You got a three-pointer yet?" Sonny said instead of answering.

"Now you wanna talk fockin' hoops?"

"Why not? You're a hooper, yeah?"

"I was, maybe."

"What do you think you are now?"

"Nothing to you, I promise."

"Yeah," Sonny said, turning away from Robbie and the girl and focusing on the view through the window on his side of the car instead. "You, especially, shouldn't be here."

17

Sonny was lounging against the side of Robbie's Mustang when his phone rang. He was watching the others move Dominic's arsenal from the house to the trunk of the car, but his mind was locked on how to keep this crew and the guns in the wrong place at the right time.

"Hey, Gee," he said into the phone, moving away from the car and his companions as soon as he saw who was calling.

"What the fuck are you doing?" Geronimo said, the words coming out about as hot as Sonny had anticipated.

"Whatevah I think I gotta do, brah. No more, and not one fockin' thing less."

"You thought you had to kill five people at the Naniloa?"

"Not."

"What? They're not really dead?"

"I didn't kill all five."

"Jeezus fucking Christ, Sonny!"

"You gonna fockin' help, or jus' stand over there and holler?"

"Help do what?"

"Put the milk back in the fockin' nut."

"You've lost your fucking mind, Sonny, I swear to God."

"Whatevah. You wanna help, pick Robbie up."

"We're already looking for that idiot."

"He'll be at Dominic's place until dark, Gee. You need to pick the fockah up, I promise—and the boyfriend, too."

"And you, Sonny."

"Later, brah. I got a few more things to do. Can I count on you wrappin' Robbie up?"

"I'm on my way right now."

"Thanks, Gee," Sonny said, and then he cut off his phone, returned it to his hip, and walked back to the car.

18

"Can you drive me to the mall?" Sonny said.

"Not," Nalani replied.

"Fockin' drive me to the mall, girl," Sonny said, which was the way he had planned to say it in the first place.

"You can't tell me what to do, you know."

"Think again, Nalani. You're missin' something here."

To Sonny's surprise, she did exactly that—she thought it through again, and this time she walked across the kitchen, pulled a set of keys off a hook on the wall, and walked out the door into the carport.

"Why her?" Robbie asked from his seat next to John at the kitchen table. "Anybody could do it, yeah?"

"Forget Nalani, brah."

"I've got some things goin' you don' know, Sonny."

"I take a hike, you've got nothing goin'. Forget the fockin' kid." *Forget everything,* he added to himself as he handed Robbie his phone. Robbie took it, but the look on his face made it clear that he didn't know what to do with it.

"Call the ol' man," Sonny said.

Robbie entered a number and listened for a moment. "Gettin' voice mail, brah," he said.

Sonny reached for the phone and Robbie returned it. "This is Sonnyboy Akaka," Sonny said after the tone. "We need to talk, you know."

19

There were two voices in the old man's head when the call came in, and he had to shut them both up to listen to the message. The first voice was calling for the sky to fall on the people responsible for the deaths of his crew in the hotel, but the second wanted to know who was going to take care of business on the island if he wiped out all of the locals he knew.

He listened to the message twice, but it turned out to be exactly the same both times—nothing, really, just the name. But the name belonged to exactly the right person, so the old man was leaning heavily toward returning the call when the lawyer who had picked him up at the hotel came back in the room.

"Is there anything else that you need?" the lawyer asked.

"No," the old man said, even though it wasn't true.

"Just let me know if that should change before we have to leave for the airport."

The old man nodded, the lawyer departed, and the name from the message returned to the front of the old man's mind—Sonnyboy Akaka. *Yes,* the old man thought, *we do need to talk.*

20

Nalani had her father's Escalade on the speed limit exactly, which was exactly where Sonny wanted it. He sat to her right and watched her drive, and she did it as though completely unaware of his attention or even his presence in the car.

The Escalade made Sonny smile when he took the time to think about it, Dominic having bought it mostly just to show that he could. As far as actual driving was concerned, Dominic had much preferred the Chevy truck now sitting on a police lot somewhere while the investigation of Dominic's death continued.

"What?" Nalani said, apparently more tuned in to Sonny's presence than he had imagined.

"Your father ever drive this thing?" he asked.

"Not."

"Funny guy, your father."

"Fockin' funniest ever."

"Why did you kill him?"

"Why do you think I killed him?"

"Please," Sonny said, stretching the word out a little.

"What the fock difference does it make to you?"

"None. Just curious, that's why."

"Fock you, Sonny, and your fockin' curiosity."

"You can't fock curiosity, you know."

"Double fock you, then."

"I didn't know you swore so much."

"You don't know anything about me, I promise."

"I know you can hoop, girl."

Nalani rolled her eyes at that, but the high school in Kea'au flashed by on their left as she did it. "Saw you drop the fifty over there," Sonny said, referring to a game that no one who had seen it was likely to forget. "You're goin' dee-one if you get a three-pointer."

"Whatevah."

"Go back to bein' a kid, Nalani. This other shit is going no-where, you know."

Nalani made no response to that for three or four minutes. Sonny continued to watch her drive, and she had them solidly entrenched on Highway 11 before she spoke again. "I can't go back," she said, her voice so low Sonny could barely hear it. "I never was a kid."

21

Jesus hated his new look, which was just fine with him.

"Bueno," he said, but Henriquez didn't bother to reply. She was bent over the document she was forging to prove that Jesus was in fact the old man he now appeared to be, which was also just fine with him.

The thing that was not fine with Jesus was the *fandango* flourishing in the space reserved for his business on the Big Island. *Fockin' locals,* he thought as he studied his new reflection in the mirror. *Can't live with the fockers, can't live without 'em.*

"Where you supposed to pick up this fockin' guide?" he said.

"In front of the movie theaters at the mall," Ortega said.

"How well you like it, homes?"

"Not worth a sheet."

"That's about how well I like it."

"Maybe we reshuffle the deck, *ese.*"

"That's what I'm thinkin'," Jesus said. "How 'bout you go over alone? You pick this guide up, bring the motherfocker here."

22

"Pull ovah," Sonny said.

"Droppin' you by the theaters, yeah?"

"Not. Drop me here."

Nalani pulled into a slot near Hilo Hattie's and stopped, the theaters tucked around the edge of the mall behind them. Sonny opened the door on his side of the car but didn't get out right away. "Go back to your aunty's," he said.

Nalani stared at him but said nothing. "I'm serious, you know," Sonny said. "Stay away from the house."

"Why?" Nalani said, the shadow of a smile emerging in the back of her eyes as she continued to stare at him.

"Gee's gonna be there."

"That's what I fockin' thought."

"This shit is not for you, girl."

"Only for you, yeah?"

"Not," Sonny said as he climbed out of the car, possibly talking to himself more than the girl. "It's no fockin' good for anybody, I promise."

23

Geronimo pulled his Explorer in tight behind Robbie's Mustang and parked. By the time he was out of his rig, Robbie and John were coming through the door into the carport.

"Wassup, Gee?" Robbie said.

"Good question," Geronimo said. "It's on my list for you and John."

"What?"

"Please spare me the dramatics. You know why I'm here."

"Why, maybe," Robbie said. "What I wonder is how."

"You wonder long enough, it'll probably come to you," Geronimo said, and then he stopped talking for a while so he could think instead. That was easier said than done, though, because the din of the frogs was thick enough to cut with a knife.

"I guess what they say about the fockin' frogs out here is true," Geronimo said. "This is the worst I've heard."

"Fockin' Sonny," Robbie said, apparently disinterested in discussing the rapid proliferation of Coqui frogs around Pahoa.

"He's doing you a favor," Geronimo said. "Get Nalani out here."

"She's not here."

"So she's with Sonny, right? Where'd they go?"

"What the fock do I know?"

"Where'd you think they were going?"

"Makes no fockin' difference what I thought, yeah? You takin' us in?"

"Yeah," Geronimo said. "We need to talk about the thing at the Naniloa."

"You won' fockin' believe it, I promise," Robbie said, and there was something in the look that went with the words that had Geronimo believing it already.

24

Sonny walked across the lot with the Sears entrance to his left and the corner of the mall shielding the theaters to his right. He veered left and entered the store, in no particular hurry as he picked his way through the major appliances lined up as if especially for him. He glanced at the stickers on the dryers as he went by because he had seen that the old woman in Keaukaha could use one even if she had never been willing to accept it from her son, but his mind was more on what the Mexicans were likely to have in store for him than what Sears had in stock.

"Hey, Sonnyboy!" said a salesman Sonny almost recognized.

"Howzit, brah?" Sonny said, even though he couldn't put a name with the face and had no compelling reason to try very hard to do it.

"Great!" the salesman said. "Anything I can help you with?"

I need plenty of help, I promise, Sonny thought, *but you don't have it.* "Jus' lookin' today," he said.

"Big sale starts Friday," the salesman said. "You might want to check it out."

"Fo' shuah," Sonny said. *If I can still shop by Friday,* he said to himself, *I'm fockin' gonna do it.* A moment later, he was past the salesman and into the mall. The ticket windows to the theaters were right in front of him now and the entrance from the parking lot off to his right, so he drifted in that direction until he was outside again.

He walked to the curb and waited, and after 30 seconds or so a silver Buick pulled up and stopped. The car was empty except for the driver, so Sonny opened the front passenger door and slipped into the seat.

"Ortega?" he asked.

"Si."

"Sonnyboy Akaka."

"Si."

"Robbie was hoping you'd bring an army, you know," Sonny said as he looked Ortega over, the first thing he saw being Ortega doing exactly the same thing to him.

"Slight change in plans there, homes," Ortega said. "Gotta take you to it."

"You fockin' got one?"

"We have one," Ortega said as he eased the Buick into motion. "Small, but good. Is this the time and place to use it, though?"

"I have thc fockin' answer if you want it."

"We know what you think, homes. Let 'er rip."

"Not."

"No?" Ortega said, his eyes distracted from his driving briefly while he turned in Sonny's direction. Sonny shook his head slightly but said nothing more, so Ortega went back to driving until he eased the car to a stop alongside a new Chrysler in a driveway off Haihai Street.

"Why you here, you don' wan' the army?" Ortega asked.

"Robbie wanted it," Sonny said. "I'm not Robbie, brah, I promise."

25

Nalani slipped the Escalade into gear as soon as Sonny entered the Sears store, but she didn't point the car toward Aunty Minnie. Instead, she drove around the corner of the mall and parked in the first slot she came to with a view of the entrance in front of the theaters.

She waited patiently for Sonny to emerge from that entrance, and her patience was eventually rewarded. She watched him walk to the curb, and she was still watching when he climbed into a new Buick that stopped in front of him. She started rolling when the Buick headed back in the direction from which she had come, and she could still see it when it turned *mauka* on the highway even though she was five cars behind by then.

She had to run the light to make the same left-turn arrow the Buick used to get on the highway, but she got hung up when the Buick turned off at Kawailani. *Please, God,* she thought after choking back a series of epithets, and her forbearance paid immediate dividends when she got off the highway in time to see the Buick turn left on Kilauea.

Nalani had another anxious moment when the Buick disappeared up Haihai, but she drove right past Ortega and Sonny disembarking from the car in a driveway only three or four minutes up that street. She allowed herself a silent smile as she continued up the hill in search of a place to turn around, the Jesus on her mind not the one directly descended from the God who had guided her to this place.

26

Sonny knew Jesus wasn't the blonde woman at the light table in the small dining room or any of the surfer dudes working with the guns at the counter in the kitchen, so the old man sitting on the living room couch under white hair and whiskers had to be the guy.

"Paradise has taken a fockin' toll on you, brah," he said when he walked in the room.

"Fockin' tell me about it," Jesus said while Sonny and Ortega fanned out and took chairs at opposite ends of the room.

"A four-soldier army, yeah?" Sonny said.

"Five," Jesus responded, nodding in the general direction of the woman at the light table. "She's as good as those three put together, and they ain' bad." That reference was to the surfer dudes in the kitchen, but they either didn't hear it or didn't disagree enough to dissent.

"Sonny here don' wan' an army, though," Ortega said. "Says that was Robbie, *ese.*"

"You draw a distinction between the two of you, homes?" Jesus asked.

"Forget Robbie," Sonny said. "Robbie's off the fockin' chart."

"Fine."

"The girl, too."

"Really?"

"Nalani fo' shuah."

"Fine," Jesus said again.

"No problem?"

"I got you, it's no problem."

"You got me," Sonny said, "you pay the fockin' price."

"Which is what?"

"Two things. Make peace with the fockin' Japs, number one."

"Heard that one before, homes. Guy who said it is dead now."

"He was the wrong guy, yeah?"

"Way wrong," Jesus said. "But you ain' necessarily right."

"Whatevah."

"Jus' for the sake of discussion, what's number two?"

"You eat the fockin' money."

"That's a lot of money."

"True. But it's gonna cost you way more than it's worth, I fockin' promise."

"Really? I think you're the only guy I'd have to worry about, and I've got you surrounded by my little army here right now."

Sonny surveyed the other people in sight from where he was sitting and nodded his head slowly. "The thing is, that ain' enough to keep you alive," he said.

"You can get to me before these guys can take you out?" Jesus said. "And you can fockin' do me when you get here?"

"Fo' fockin' shuah."

"I don' think you're that fockin' good, homes."

"What you think don' change what is."

"I'd kinda like to see you try."

"You can, you know. It's up to you all the way, brah."

"Say I wanna pay your price. Fockin' Japs ain' exactly on my speed dial, you know."

"Leave that to me."

"I decide to do that, what's next?"

"We wait for the fockin' phone to ring."

"I could do that for a while," Jesus said as he glanced at the woman. "I'm outta here when she gets done."

"Won' take long," Sonny said. He leaned back in his chair and stretched out, but he wasn't quite as much at ease as he appeared. He knew a call from the old man was coming—no anxiety there at all—but what he didn't know for sure was what to do about the girl in the Escalade who had followed him all the way from the mall.

27

"So what do you have so far?" the DEA woman said.

"Nothing," Geronimo said. "I know they were in the hotel, but so far I can't prove they were on the eighth floor when it happened."

"I understand why Tsubamoto might have been there, but what was Akaka's motive for being involved? I don't get that."

"That's a good question. The first rule of street fighting, maybe."

"What's that?"

"He who hits first lasts longest."

"That make sense to you?"

"Sonny's probably the best street fighter on the island," Geronimo said slowly. "Yeah, I can see him hitting those fuckers first."

"What do you see him doing now?"

"He called it 'putting the milk back in the nut.'"

"Nuts have milk?"

"Coconuts do."

"Duh," the woman said with a grimace. "Wouldn't that be kind of hard to do?"

"Extremely."

"It would involve both the Japanese and the Mexicans, I would think."

"I would think that, too. My only question is where."

"Apparently, the choices are rather limited as far as Johjima is concerned."

"What do you mean?" Geronimo asked, sitting up straight for the first time in the course of the conversation.

"He'll probably be on the next plane out of here, don't you think?"

"Jeezus," Geronimo said as he rose to his feet and came out from behind his desk. "I might have thought that if I could fucking think at all."

The woman got up and matched Geronimo stride for stride, and when he stopped at Ralph's desk, she stopped, too. "You going with?" he asked.

"Do you mind?" she said.

"No," he said.

"Wassup?" Ralph interjected.

"We need to talk about Sonny, boss," Geronimo said.

"He's a suspect in a multiple homicide, yeah?" Ralph said. "There's nothing more to say at this point."

"I think there is."

"Fockin' say it, then."

"I think he's gonna try to put a lid on this situation."

"What makes you think that?"

"That's what I'd try to do in his place."

"You ain' Sonnyboy, Gee."

"I realize that," Geronimo said. "But I know him."

"What do you want?"

"I want us to leave him alone while he tries to do it."

"Not," Ralph said, but he gave it a minute or two of thought before he said it. "If we find him, brah, we gotta pick him up."

"That your final answer, boss?"

"Yeah."

"Then take me off the fuckin' clock," Geronimo said as he turned and started for the door.

"What do you mean?"

"I'm goin' home sick for the rest of the day," Geronimo said, and he continued to walk away with the woman less than a step behind him.

28

"You want the guy who hit you in the fockin' hotel," Sonny said into the phone a few minutes later, "that's me. Forget Robbie Tsubamoto."

"I decide to go in that direction," the old man said into Sonny's ear, "I will forget no one."

"Not," Sonny said. "You're gonna forget everything you know, you go in that direction. You could be dead right now, yeah?"

The old man said nothing to that, which Sonny took to be a good sign. *Maybe the fockah can see the obvious,* he thought while he waited. He glanced around the room, wondering idly what this conversation sounded like to the Mexicans and their hired guns as they sat around and waited for the punchline.

"What else?" the old man said when he finally said something, which Sonny took to be another sign of the old man's ability to see the obvious.

"You want the guy who can handle the shit here," Sonny said, "that's me, too. The thing you gotta do, you gotta decide which guy you want. You can't get them both."

"You are willing to do it?"

"If you're willing to pay the price, yeah."

"And the price is what?"

"Make peace with the Mexicans, number one."

"Why would I do that?"

"Because that's what I want."

"What is the other thing?

"Forget the fockahs in the hotel."

"That's a lot to forget."

"Not," Sonny said, "if you really think about it."

Once again, the old man got quiet at exactly the right time, and Sonny allowed himself an optimistic thought or two while he waited. "Say I want to move in this direction," the old man said next. "I'm not in contact with the Mexicans."

"Yeah, you are," Sonny said. "Just come on ovah."

"I'm afraid that isn't possible. I'm leaving for Honolulu soon."

"Hang on," Sonny said into the phone as he locked eyes with Jesus.

"Wassup?" Jesus said.

"He's leavin', too. If the two of you meet at the fockin' airport, nobody has to worry about nasty surprises."

"That could work."

"He's leavin, too," Sonny said into the phone. "How 'bout sittin' down at the airport?"

"I could do that," the old man said. "About an hour from now?"

"One hour from now?" Sonny said in the Mexican's direction.

"Henriquez?" Jesus said.

"Don' fockin' call me that," the woman said.

"You be done in an hour?"

"No problem."

"One hour from now," Sonny said into the phone.

29

"You ready to go?" Jesus asked.

"Not," Sonny said. "I'm afraid you've made the airport too hot for me."

"What?"

"Thanks to you, got cops all ovah the fockin' place."

"You wanna be dropped somewhere else?"

"No need," Sonny said. "But hang tight, yeah? Gimme five minutes before you go."

"Why?" Jesus said.

"Lemme check the neighbahood one time, that's why," Sonny

said, and then he walked out the front door before the puzzled expression on the Mexican's new face turned into more questions.

Where the fock are you at, girl? he said to himself as he walked down the driveway and out on the shoulder of the road. *Gotta be somewhere close enough to see the house, yeah?*

He looked up the hill before looking down and immediately reaped a reward for that decision—Nalani's Escalade was parked nose-out only four houses away.

What I gotta do to set this fockin' kid straight? he wondered as he covered the distance between the two driveways. He walked up to the car like it had been waiting for him all along, but he discovered that the question on his mind as he moved was alarmingly wide of the mark—he didn't have to set the kid straight; he had to fucking find her.

The Escalade was empty, and Nalani was nowhere in sight.

Chapter Ten
Sudden Death

1

Nalani had a good view of the dining room and a fair view of the living room beyond that from her vantage point on the lanai. She knew she had been lucky so far—lucky to have stuck with the Buick all the way to this house, and now lucky that the sliding glass door she was looking through was only almost covered by a long drape.

She watched the hot blonde working at the table in the dining room with ease, and with a little more effort she watched the three men in the living room on the far side of the woman. At first, the men confused her—one of them was Sonny, of course, and one of them was the man she knew as Ortega, but she thought initially that she had never seen the third man before.

That thought didn't stick for long, though. First she noticed that the jewelry on the old man with the white hair and whiskers belonged to someone she knew, and then the old man got up and moved. He looked a lot like an old man, sure, but he moved like a mountain cat—just like the guy she knew who owned the bling the old man was flashing.

Cute, Nalani said to herself. *Almost ready to get off the rock, yeah?* The question was barely out of her silent mouth when the blonde woman got up from the table and Sonny walked out the front door of the house. Nalani's first reaction was to start moving herself, but she knocked that response down and stood on it.

Fockin' wait, girl, she thought, and while she did what she was thinking, she continued to peer into the house. She watched the blonde woman walk into the living room and hand Jesus a laminated card. He studied the card for a moment, and then nodded at the woman and cracked a smile that didn't belong on an old man's face.

The woman returned the smile, stretched her arms above her head for a moment and plopped down on the couch Jesus had recently abandoned. Then three *haoles* she hadn't seen before entered her field of vision from the left, each of them carrying a suitcase and a California tan. *Where the fock are they comin' from?* she thought while she watched them cross the living room and walk the luggage out the front door of the house. Ortega followed after them, which left only Jesus and the blonde.

Oh, yeah, Nalani said to herself. She raised the Glock she had found under the front seat of the Escalade in her right hand and tried the sliding door with her left. The door responded, sliding easily and without a sound, so she soon had it open enough to allow her to enter the house. But when she reached for the drape hanging in front of her, a strong brown hand clasped her wrist and pulled her away from the door.

2

Nalani gasped as soon as Sonny put his hands on her, and the sound apparently made it around the drape in front of the door because the conversation going on between Jesus and the blonde suddenly disappeared.

Sonny yanked the girl away from the door with his hands around both of her wrists, and when he had her tucked in close to his body he whispered directly into her ear. "Gimme the fockin' gun," he said softly, and he slid his right hand from her wrist to the weapon while he said it.

Nalani surrendered it immediately, which turned out to be barely soon enough. Sonny jammed it into the waistband of his surfer shorts against the small of his back, and he had his shirt flowing over it by the time Jesus opened his mouth on the other side of the drape.

"Step inside," Jesus said.

"Cool it, brah," Sonny said. "It's me." Then he pushed the drape aside and nudged Nalani through the door. "Fockin' kid can't get enough of you, yeah?"

Jesus was standing slightly to the right of the door, but all of the action came from the left. The blonde knocked Nalani off her feet with a sharp blow to the side of the girl's head, and Sonny stepped away and let her fall. The blonde kneeled over her and checked for weapons, then rose with a shrug.

"She's clean," the blonde said.

"What the fock is up, homes?" Jesus said, his face clouding over like his own personal weather front was about to roll in.

"You tell me, moddafockah," Sonny said. "She didn't come to see me, I promise."

"Fockin' girl still wants to kill me."

"What was she gonna do, hug you to death?"

"I think she was gonna shoot me."

"She didn't have a weapon, remember?"

"I find that a little hard to believe, homes."

"Check her yourself, you don't believe it."

"Oh, I believe she doesn't have one now. What I'm wonderin' is what the fock hoppened to it."

"Could check me for it, you know, if you want a fockin' broken arm."

The storm clouds on the Mexican's face intensified right before Sonny's eyes, but Ortega and the surfer dudes picked that moment to walk back in the house and Nalani began to recover her senses on the floor. Sonny tried to put those slight distractions to good use.

"Nothing fockin' changed here, brah. Let me handle the girl."

"Nobody's gonna fockin' handle me," Nalani said as she rose from the floor, and Sonny slapped her hard across her face in response. The blow rocked her back on her heels and put her head on a swivel, but she bounced right back with her eyes blazing.

"I've been hit by better men than you, you know," she said, and Sonny hit her again. This time blood began to flow from the girl's nose, but she drew herself up like she had made a personal decision to bleed.

"Not, you know," Sonny said. "Ain't nofockin'body better than me."

"Get her a wet cloth," Jesus said, and the blonde moved off to the kitchen. Ortega and the three surfer dudes filed into the room behind Jesus, but he kept his focus on Nalani until the blonde returned with a washcloth. He took it from her and applied it to the blood on Nalani's face.

"Hold this," he said when he was satisfied with his work, and Nalani raised one hand to keep the cloth pressed against her nose.

"What the fock you doin' here, *mi'ja?*"

"What you fockin' think?" Nalani said through the washcloth. "Maybe get one farewell fock?"

"Think about it this way," Sonny said. "She's just here to give me a ride."

"Last guy made me feel like you do," Jesus said, the storm clouds still roiling behind his eyes when he looked Sonny's way, "I put a new eye in his fockin' forehead."

"Been there, done that," Sonny said. "You wanna talk story or fockin' take care of business?"

"Maybe you the fockin' business needs the most attention."

"Not. Your business is at the fockin' airport, brah."

Jesus teetered on the brink of exploding for a moment, and Sonny watched him do it until the Mexican settled down on the side of commerce instead. "You one lucky motherfocker, homes," he said.

"Whatevah," Sonny said.

"Here's how we're gonna do this," Jesus said. "Henriquez takes me to the airport, Ortega keeps an eye on you and the girl. Everything goes down like it should, you guys walk."

"Good one, brah," Sonny said. "Only we're walkin' right now."

"I don' think so."

"Your call, you know. You still have the same choice as before."

"What? You fockin' take me out?"

"Fo' shuah."

"That shit don' really work, homes. I don' fockin' believe it."

"Whatevah."

"What I believe don' change what is, is that how you said it?"

"Exactly."

"Ortega," Jesus said, acknowledging the presence of the men behind him for the first time.

"Yeah?" Ortega said.

"Shoot this motherfocker," Jesus said, and then no one said anything for a while. What happened instead of conversation was this: Jesus crumpled toward the floor with a scream when Sonny took out his right knee, but Sonny was down there in time to catch the falling Mexican. By the time the move was finished, Sonny had Jesus in a choke hold and was wearing him like a cheap raincoat.

Ortega had a gun in his hand by then but didn't know at first what to do with it. "Put that thing away," Sonny said. "Let's get this fockin' program back on track."

"How 'bout I shoot the fockin' girl, you don' let him up?" Ortega said.

"Could, you know," Sonny said, "you want this one dead. What do you think, boss? You fockin' believe this shit now?"

"Put the gun away, Ortega," Jesus said gingerly, working the words through Sonny's hold on his throat.

"You sure, *ese?*" Ortega asked.

"I'm sure," Jesus said, but Sonny could feel the crosscurrents still surging through the Mexican unchecked. He tightened his hold a little, and the tension slackened slightly.

"One more time," Sonny said quietly.

"I'm fockin' sure, Ortega," Jesus said, and this time Sonny started to believe it. Ortega put the gun away somewhere; when Sonny glanced up, Ortega's hand was empty.

"Don't mess up his fucking face," the blonde woman said from the side.

"No way," Sonny said. "Gotta walk outta here, yeah?"

"If I can still walk, motherfocker."

"Old age is a fockin' bitch, I promise," Sonny said. "Give him a hand, brah."

Ortega helped Jesus rise to his feet, and Sonny came up behind him with Nalani's gun pressed to the back of the Mexican's head. "No worries," he said. "Nobody gets frisky, we got no problem here."

"Now what?" Ortega said, his voice flat but his eyes showing plenty of juice.

"Go get your car, Nalani," Sonny said. "Pull up in front, yeah?"

Nalani stood with her face still buried in the washcloth and stared at Sonny, but she eventually walked around Sonny and Jesus, through the other men and out the front door.

"Henriquez, right?" Sonny said to the blonde woman.

"No," she said.

"Lead us out to the car. Ortega, give this fockin' old man a hand. You three follow Henriquez."

Sonny was certain he had spoken clearly enough for everyone to hear the instructions, but nobody moved. He added a little pressure to the gun at the back of the Mexican's head and waited to see if that message got through.

"Do it," Jesus said, and that's what everyone did. Jesus was able to walk after all, but he leaned heavily on Ortega while he did it. They all proceeded slowly across the house and out the door, and by the time they reached the cars in the driveway, Nalani had the Escalade stopped in the road in front of the house.

"Tell the rest of these fockahs to wait here," Sonny said.

"Wait here," Jesus said, and everyone stopped except Sonny, Jesus, and Ortega. They slowly worked their way to the end of the driveway, walking backwards now so Sonny could keep an eye on the Californians as they moved.

"'Kay," Sonny said when he reached the Escalade. "Take him back, Ortega."

Sonny slipped into the seat next to Nalani as the Mexicans started back toward the house. "Drive," he said, and for the first time that Sonny could remember the girl did exactly as she was told.

3

"Can you work with that focker?" Jesus asked as he folded himself into the front passenger seat of the Chrysler in the driveway.

"Si," Ortega said. "Be a helluva lot easier than working against him, that's for sure."

"I guess," Jesus said. "If it was me gonna be here, though, I'd have to shoot the focker sooner or later."

"I'm making no promises about that, boss," Ortega said with a smile. "But he's a lot handier than anyone else I've seen around here, you have to admit."

"I don' have to admit sheet," Jesus said. "But you might be right there, homes."

"Good luck at the airport," Ortega said.

"Miss Don't-Call-Me-Henriquez here has taken all the luck out of it."

"Then good luck with the old Jap."

"She's takin' all the luck out of that, too. You're the one needs the luck."

"Well, fock you, then. I take it all back."

"I'll call you from the airport," Jesus said. "Let's go." Henriquez heard the part of that directed at her and backed the car into the street, headed it down the hill, and didn't stop driving until she reached the security gate at the airport.

4

"Where to?" Nalani asked as she drove down the hill toward Kilauea.

"Where the fock did I tell you to go?" Sonny said.

"Aunty Minnie's."

"Bingo."

"Fockah needs to fockin' die, you know," Nalani said as she made the right turn when she had used up all of Haihai Street and headed for the entrance onto Highway 11.

"That's not your fockin' job."

"I'm the one he focked ovah, Sonny."

"I know," Sonny said softly. "But you can't get unfocked, Nalani. You gotta move on. Let the rest of us carry the fockin' weight."

"You fockahs gonna let him walk away clean, yeah?"

"Not," Sonny said as he raised his phone to his ear. "This moddafockah is walkin' nofockin'where, I promise."

5

"This better be fucking good, Sonny," Geronimo said into his phone.

"You at the airport yet, Gee?"

"What makes you think I'm going to the airport?"

"I think you got skills, that's why," Sonny said, his grin coming through loud and clear over the phone.

"Yeah, I'm here."

"Is the old Jap there?"

"Why?"

"Why didn't you hold him after the hotel shit, brah?"

"He's fucking untouchable. But yeah, he's here."

"Gonna have some company *wiki wiki,* Gee. You can touch this fockah, I promise."

"Tell me it's the Mexican."

"Good one, brah. He's gonna show white hair and whiskahs like one old fockah, got ID to match. You see him sit down with the Jap, bust his fockin' ass."

"How'd you make this happen?"

"I got skills, too, you know. You got Robbie and John?"

"Yeah, we got 'em. But we need you, too, Sonny. Anybody sees you, we gotta bring you in."

"Ain' nobody fockin' gonna see me yet, Gee. I'll come in when it's ovah."

"Sounds like it's pretty much over now."

"Maybe. These guys still might try to fock each other, you know."

"I know."

"Call me when you have the moddafockah."

Geronimo listened to the connection disappear and returned his phone to his hip without a word of explanation, but the DEA woman wouldn't let him get away with it.

"Was that Akaka?" she asked.

"Yeah," Geronimo said.

"Why'd he call?"

"To give us the Mexican, believe it or not. The guy's coming in to meet with Johjima on their way off the island."

"Seriously?"

"Seriously."

"You gotta love that."

"I'll love it if it actually happens," Geronimo said, his eyes directed at the woman but his focus on the old Japanese man slowly walking up the stairs to the departure gate on the left edge of Geronimo's peripheral vision.

6

"You know what to do, right?" Jesus said as the security guard opened the trunk of the Chrysler.

"I know what to do," Henriquez replied.

"It's not do or die. You get a good opportunity, take it. Otherwise, fock it and make your connection to LA."

"I fucking do this for a living, Jesus. I know what to do."

"You're good to go," said the security guard standing near the driver's window, and Jesus was thinking the exact same thing. The hardest part had been getting Henriquez on the right flight to Honolulu—they had been lucky there. But that was in the bag now, and most likely so was the fucking Jap because Henriquez was always good to go.

Henriquez parked in the first open slot they came to and got out of the car. Jesus got out, too, and slowly limped around to the driver's side. "Just wondering," Henriquez said. "Why did you decide against the deal with the Japanese?"

"What deal would that be? He takes one side of the fockin' street, we take the other? Believe me, this fockah don' wan' no deal with us."

"I see what you're saying. I guess you don't want one, either."

"Do we have another operation anywhere we gotta kiss someone's fockin' ass to make it happen?"

"Not that I know of."

"Then why the fock would I start now?" Jesus said as he climbed behind the wheel.

"I thought it was something like that," Henriquez said, and then she turned and walked toward the terminal. Jesus treated himself to a moment of enjoying her progress, her tight butt and long legs set off perfectly in a short white skirt and her tanned arms swinging freely from a sleeveless red blouse.

Bitch travels light, Jesus thought as he watched her. *Light and fockin' lethal.* When she entered the terminal and moved out of his line of sight, he backed out of the parking slot, piloted the car through the lot, and pointed it at the Kona side of the island and his direct flight from the airport there to San Francisco.

7

"He didn't show," Geronimo said into his phone as he watched Johjima's plane taxi to the runway.

"You shuah, brah?" Sonny asked.

"Nobody huddled up with him here, and nobody answering the description you gave got on the plane with him."

"I was fockin' afraid of that."

"No shit."

"Better call the Kona side, Gee. They didn't focking give him that new face for nothing, I promise."

"On it like a bonnet," Geronimo said. "That's not the problem."

"What's the problem?"

"If the fucker doesn't wanna do the deal with Johjima, what does he want?"

"You know the fockin' answer to that, brah. Only one other thing he can do."

"How many more Mexicans are we talking about?"

"Fockah named Ortega is the only one I saw," Sonny said, "but he has four Californians here, too. On the Kona side, I don't have a clue."

"Californians?"

"Blonde, tan fockahs who look like they rode in on a wave."

"We're looking for one Mexican and four California beach boys?"

"Not. Three *kanes* and one *wahine,* and the *wahine* is hot for a *haole.*"

"A blonde you would look at twice, you mean?"

"Or more."

"Tell me she wasn't dressed in red and white the last time you saw her."

"I think so—white skirt, red top. You saw her?"

"Someone who looked just like that got on the same plane as Johjima."

"You shuah? Gotta be a lotta blondes around, you know."

"I sure as shit looked at this one twice, Sonny, and I don't even fucking like blondes."

"Maybe it doesn't mean anything, yeah?"

"Like a coincidence, maybe?"

"Yeah."

"Right," Geronimo said. "Like I really believe in those."

"I know," Sonny said.

"At least she can't be armed, right?" Geronimo said, trying hard now. "She had to pass through security before she got on the plane."

Sonny made no response to that, and it didn't take much silence to rattle Geronimo's cage. "What?" he said.

"Fockin' Mexican said she was better than all the dudes combined," Sonny said quietly. "She might not need a weapon."

"Which raises an interesting question," Geronimo said, his voice quiet now, too, while he thought about the 30,000 reasons he had to root for the blonde and the single reason he had to try to prevent a crime from occurring.

"No shit," Sonny said. "Maybe the moddafockah ain't quite as untouchable as you thought."

"Whatever," Geronimo said. "Do you have a number for him?"

"Don't tell me you're gonna warn the fockah."

"I think that's my job here. Don't you?"

"If it is, your job is focked, Gee."

I can't argue with that, Geronimo said to himself, but what he said aloud was this: "Give me the number, Sonny."

"What are you gonna do next," Sonny said after he rattled off the number.

"Take a chopper to Kona."

"Let me check the house they were in one time first, yeah? If we're lucky, it might save you the trip."

"Get back to me, Sonny. I mean it. I'll wait at the chopper pad for a while, but not very long."

"No worries, brah," Sonny said with a chuckle. "We're a fockin' team, I promise."

"Please don't remind me," Geronimo said, and then he cut the connection and clipped his phone to his belt.

"What was that about Kona?" the DEA woman asked.

"Looks like we're at the wrong fucking airport," Geronimo replied.

"What was the interesting question?"

"I could tell you, but then I'd have to kill you."

"I wish I had a dollar for every time I hear that fucking line," the woman said. "You watch too many movies, Souza."

"No," Geronimo said as he started for the helicopter dock. "I don't fucking watch enough."

8

Jesus was streaming by the bay with downtown Hilo up ahead on his left by the time he was sure about the car on his ass—or sure enough to kick in his insurance policy at the very least. The car was a new Chrysler, probably a rental just like the one he was driving, and it had followed him out of the parking lot at the airport and through one right and one left so far.

He knew Kilauea was off to his left somewhere, so he turned in that direction right in front of the market. The street showed up approximately where he thought it would be, but it was one-way going the wrong direction. He crossed it and hooked the next available left, and the Chrysler behind him did exactly the same thing. Jesus kept his eyes on his mirror while they made the turn, and his new companions looked to him like they were all Japanese.

Jesus reached for his phone and punched in a speed-dial digit, which put Ortega in his ear with very little delay. *"Si, jefe?"* Ortega said.

"I think I've got some fockin' company," Jesus said. "I'm bringin' them by in a couple of minutes."

"What are they driving?"

"A Chrysler sedan a lot like ours, only white."

"You told me no shootouts on Main Street, *jefe.*"

"We don't have much of a choice—and that ain' Main Street you're on."

"Bring 'em by. We'll be ready to welcome them."

Jesus dropped the phone on the seat next to him and continued to drive, the street he was on climbing gradually just like Kilauca had done when he had used it to get to the house.

If I'm right, Jesus thought, *this street will end at Haihai.* A couple of minutes later, the street did exactly that. Jesus turned to the right and climbed uphill some more, and the white Chrysler made exactly the same maneuver behind him.

"You fockers wanna follow me?" Jesus said as he reached the right house. "Fockin' follow this!" As soon as he was past the driveway, he slammed on his brakes.

The driver in the next car was quick—he got his car stopped before it rammed Jesus from behind. That did him little good, however, because Jesus popped his car into reverse as soon as he was stopped and hit his accelerator hard.

The collision that resulted wasn't really much because the cars were too close together when Jesus made his move, but it turned out that the collision was not the primary problem facing the occupants of the trailing car.

9

Eleven-year-old Jimmy Hirata heard the rending sound of metal ripping and scrambled to look out his bedroom window. He had been in a funk ever since his mother had banished him to his room an hour earlier, but he saw that things were looking up as soon as he got his eyes on the scene in the street.

Two new Chrysler sedans were mashed together, which he ordinarily would have considered pretty cool, but this time four men with guns were boiling out of the house across Haihai from Jimmy and that was *way* cool. The driver of the front car was hitting the road the same way, and Jimmy was pretty sure the men rolling out of the rear car were sporting weapons, too.

Fock, yeah! Jimmy said to himself, the scene in the street suddenly kicking into obscurity all thoughts of the video game from which he had been banished. *How cool is this?* he thought as the guns began to roar and bullets ripped into bodies almost at random—one moment a guy would be standing there pumping lead like it was water and the next he would be jerked off his feet in a splash of blood.

Jimmy watched the show with a grin on his face, relishing the action almost to the final frame—right up to the instant that one of the rounds fired from the far side of the street pierced his bedroom window, penetrating his left eye profoundly enough to pull down the curtain on his own private drama forever.

10

Jesus took inventory as soon as the gunfire died away, surveying the Japs first just in case. There turned out to be four of them, all either dead or dying in the street, so Jesus turned his attention to his own people.

One of the surfer dudes was dead in the ditch, but the others were up and moving to the Buick in the driveway. Ortega was leaning on the hood of the car as the Californians climbed into the front seat and got the car running, blood streaming down his arm and pooling in the gravel at his feet.

"Gotta go," Jesus said, conscious of the cars backing up on Haihai in both directions and the sound of sirens already in the air.

"You hit, *jefe?*" Ortega said.

"No," Jesus said.

"Go without me, then. You might still make that Kona flight."

Jesus limped past his lieutenant and climbed into the back seat of the Buick. "Get in," he said through the open door.

"I can't do you much good," Ortega said with a weak smile.

"Get in," Jesus said again. "You've already done plenty." He slid across the seat to the opposite side, and Ortega climbed in and shut the door behind him.

"Turn down the hill," Jesus said, and the surfer dude behind the wheel followed that directive until a Cadillac SUV slammed the Chrysler into the ditch at the end of the driveway.

11

Sonny rolled right on by the stopped traffic on Haihai without slowing down, swerving to the left and continuing up the wrong side of the street until he reached the house. When he saw the Buick heading out, he punched his accelerator and ran right up the smaller car until it was under his wheels almost on its side in the ditch

Sonny climbed out of the Escalade and walked to the nearest

door of the Buick. He opened it, grabbed Jesus by the shirt with both hands, and pulled him out.

"What the fock is wrong with you, homes?" Jesus sputtered, raising a hand that still had a gun in it as he spoke.

"Put that thing down before the cops fockin' shoot your ass," Sonny said. "Gimme a hand." He reached into the car for Ortega, and after a clumsy moment Jesus leaned in and helped. They pulled Ortega out, then went to work freeing the two surfer dudes in the front seat.

"How the fock did you live this long, homes?" Jesus asked as he propped himself against the Escalade and eyed the cops arriving on the scene from both directions.

"I have no fockin' idea, brah," Sonny said. "No fockin' idea at all."

12

Johjima watched the plane turn in over the island and then settle itself down on the runway just like it was supposed to, which brought the hint of a smile to his face. *One more successful landing,* he thought, thinking about a lot more than the plane's safe arrival in Honolulu.

The smile dried up and blew away as soon as he checked his phone, however, the message from his source in the Hilo police department—the good one, the one not even Kitano had known about—exactly the opposite of what he wanted to hear. He responded to the news about the shootout on Haihai Street with a call to his people still in Kona as he entered the terminal, but his phone rang in his hand as soon as he cut that connection.

"Yes?" he said, using English because he didn't recognize the number.

"This is Geronimo Souza."

"Yes?"

"Where are you right now?"

"Why?" he said as the blonde woman in front of him dropped her purse. He stopped as the woman bent low to retrieve it, thinking idly that some people might have enjoyed his vantage point on the process.

"You may be in some danger," Souza said, but the blonde came up from the floor with a sharp chop to Johjima's throat and the old man immediately lost track of both his phone and the passage between his mouth and his lungs.

The blonde followed him all the way down to the floor as he fell, and he saw into her cold blue eyes for an instant before she pinched his nostrils shut, planted her mouth over his lips and began to blow.

Why are you doing this? Johjima thought. *Nothing is getting through.*

"Help me!" the blonde said, rising above him slightly to speak. "Call nine-one-one!" Then she returned, blowing nothing into his mouth again.

I don't know who you are, Johjima whispered in English into the woman's incessant mouth just before he lost forever the power to form words in any language, *but you are very, very good.*

13

Geronimo knew he was hot around the edges and that hot was the wrong temperature for this interview. He got up from the table in the interview room and walked around for a moment to cool off, breathing deeply and massaging his temples in exactly the same way the DEA woman had been doing it earlier.

"Believe me, homes," Jesus said from his seat at the table, "I know how you feel."

"The woman you sent after the old man got the job done," Geronimo said in an attempt to clear out the one thing sticking in his craw. "Pretty slick job, too."

"How you know that, *ese?*"

"I was talking to him on the phone when it happened."

"I have no idea what you're talkin' about, but she sounds like my kinda woman."

"I'm sure she is," Geronimo said. He moved back to the table and reclaimed his seat opposite the Mexican. Ralph was still seated to Geronimo's right, the woman recording the interview to his left.

"Once again," Geronimo said, "you understand that you have a right to counsel during this interview?"

"That's right, homes, dot all the eyes and cross all the tees."

"Do you waive that right?"

"Fock, no."

"Have you retained counsel?"

"*Si.* But it'll take him a while to get here."

"Fine," Geronimo said. He raised his hand and pointed at the door, and a moment later a cop in a uniform came in and escorted Jesus out of the room.

The woman from the DEA entered as the men left and took the seat at the table vacated by the Mexican.

"Thank you," Geronimo said to the recorder. "You're through for now."

The woman nodded and departed, leaving Geronimo in the same hot funk that had been swirling around him all day.

"What's wrong, brah?" Ralph asked.

"What's fucking right?" Geronimo replied.

"We've got that fockin' Fernandez in the building, nothin' wrong with that."

"Not for too much longer, you know."

"What the fock are you talkin' about?"

"Run down the list against him, and I'll show you."

"Okay," Ralph said. "Let's start with the most recent."

"Self defense," Geronimo said, his eyes closed and his head propped up by his hands as he rested his arms on the table.

"Fock, no!" Ralph said.

"I think you better get used to it. We're gonna hear it a lot in the very near future."

"What about the kid across the street?"

"We might get something to stick on somebody for that, but it won't be Fernandez. He was on the wrong side of the car."

"Rosario?"

"Nalani sticks with her current story, we have no witnesses."

"The guys at the golf course?"

"Ditto."

"What about the kidnapping, then?"

"She was too scared to get a good look at any of them at first, and then she was blindfolded."

"Coach saw the fockahs, yeah?"

"Yeah, but the only ones he can positively ID are the dead ones. Fernandez was at the back of the line when they punched Coach out."

"What about the Japanese guy out in the woods?" the DEA woman interjected.

"According to Robbie, we haven't caught the guy who did that yet."

"You're talkin' the worst-case scenario, brah," Ralph said. "It ain't necessarily gonna go like that."

"You're right," Geronimo conceded. "But my money would be on the worst-case scenario, if I were still a betting man."

"When you were still a betting man," Ralph said, "you couldn't bet worth shit."

"Good point," Geronimo said, but what he thought was this: *Where'd you get that information, boss?*

"What about your locals?" the DEA woman said.

"Unless one of them rolls on the other," Geronimo said, "we don't have shit there, either."

"Kind of hard to believe you could know as much as you do and not be able to prove any of it."

"Fuck," Geronimo said, opening his eyes and sitting up straight in his chair. "This thing isn't even over yet, you know."

"Fock it isn't," Ralph said. "We have everybody here who ain't dead, brah."

"I don't know, boss. We saw a whole crew on the Kona side that hasn't made an appearance yet."

"True," Ralph said softly. "So what do you think that means?"

"I don't know," Geronimo said as he rose from his chair and headed for the door. "That depends on who's been told what."

"You lost me again, brah," Ralph said.

"The old man obviously sent the troops after Fernandez when he left the island. I'd like to know if he found out what happened to them."

"What difference would that make?"

"He might have given the rest of his troops marching orders."

"Won't it be a little hard to ask him about it? Him bein' dead and all."

"No shit," Geronimo said, but what he was thinking as he walked out of the room was this: *On the other hand, it might not be too hard to ask his fucking telephone.*

14

Geronimo sat at his desk with his phone to his ear for almost 15 minutes before his cousin in the Honolulu homicide division came up with Johjima's cell phone, but he had the numbers he wanted only a minute or two after that. It turned out that Johjima had retrieved one call and made another after his plane was on the ground, and then Geronimo's call had come in and the old man had retired permanently from telephone communication.

Geronimo thanked his cousin and began to try the two numbers not his own as he retraced the steps he had taken to reach his desk. He started with the more recent call, which turned out to be to the Waikaloa Hilton. "There's the call to the fellas on the Kona side," he said for his own benefit as he cut that connection. "If I were still a betting man, I'd bet the call he received before he made that call was the news about Haihai Street."

He punched in the remaining number as he walked back through the door of the interview room, but he stopped abruptly when a cell phone on the table began to ring in concert with the tone in his ear. He watched from behind as Ralph reached down and picked up the ringing phone, and when Ralph said "Yeah?" Geronimo heard it twice.

15

Nalani sat on her haunches with her back against the trunk of a tree and watched the sun glint off the water in front of her. She had been in the same position doing the same thing for almost an hour, and the same thoughts had circled through her mind the entire time.

She was due back at police headquarters for another fucking interview soon, but she knew she was lucky to be out at all. *That's more than the others can say,* she thought, which was part of the problem. She needed to talk to someone involved, and all of the candidates for that conversation were otherwise occupied at the moment—and probably would continue to be for the foreseeable future.

She knew she had Sonnyboy Akaka to thank for the respite from Geronimo Souza she was enjoying at that very moment, Sonny the one who had made sure she was home with Aunty Minnie and her cousins before the firestorm on Haihai Street exploded. But Sonny wasn't the one she wanted to talk to at this point—his opinion was already perfectly clear. She needed some time with Robbie Tsubamoto or, believe it or not, Jesus Fernandez.

The problem she wanted to discuss was where the fuck things stood at this point because Nalani could no longer distinguish up from down as far as the overall situation was concerned. She knew she still enjoyed victim status with the cops, but she feared that distinction was wearing thin and might not continue to cloak her satisfactorily. But beyond that uncertain knowledge, what?

She listened to the water while she watched it, filtering out the sounds emanating from the other people using Coconut Island behind her. The sound seemed to soothe her as she soaked it in, the waves lapping quietly at her feet as she waited for enlightenment.

Maybe Jesus is still the key, she thought, *just like he was before.* Sonny had been true to his word about Jesus so far—the motherfucker wasn't walking, at least not yet—but he also wasn't talking, and Nalani had a lot riding on what the Mexican ultimately decided to say to the cops.

Turned out to be a strange one, she said to herself, reflecting on the way Jesus had blotted the blood from her face in the house on Haihai. *There are times when I almost like the motherfucker.* Nalani paused every time she came around to that thought and let it percolate for a moment, but when the moment ended, she knew again that she had no need for an attitude adjustment—even when she almost liked Jesus, she wanted him a lot more dead than alive.

Meanwhile, was she really going into the drug business—and if so, with whom? The guy she wanted dead? Robbie? Sonny? All of the above? No—she already knew the answer to one of those. If Sonny was in, Nalani was out, no question about that.

And what about this legacy left by her father? Not the fucking drug business, the real legacy—the one she was carrying around inside her now and would be for longer than she could stand to contemplate. She couldn't bear to think of aborting the child—not because of her faith, since her Catholicism was less than an inch deep, but because the baby contained a piece of her mother, the same mother who had been killed too often already.

Nalani wrestled with these questions while the waves murmurred at her feet until it was time to return to the cop shop, and when she got up to leave, she had the answers she needed tucked away in a safe corner of her weary mind.

16

"Got a minute, boss?" Geronimo asked from the doorway of the interview room after cutting his connection to Ralph's phone.

"Wassup?" Ralph asked, looking over his shoulder.

"Got something I need to check out before Nalani comes back in."

Ralph rose from his seat, walked past Geronimo, and led the way to his office. "Did you just call me?" he asked as he sat down behind his desk.

"Yeah," Geronimo said. "But I didn't know it was you until you answered."

"You got the number from the old man's phone."

Geronimo nodded but said nothing.

"That's pretty good police work."

Geronimo nodded again and said nothing some more.

"Now what? You wanna know why, yeah?"

"I don't give a fuck why you did it. There's only one thing I want to know."

"What's that?"

"Who did Johjima point his shooters at after he got your message?"

"How the fock would I know that?"

"All he had to go on was whatever you said, yeah?"

"All I told him was what happened to his crew on Haihai Street."

"You better use your lifeline, you sorry motherfucker. You don't want that to be your final answer, I promise."

"I don't know what you're fishing for here, Gee."

"I think you do. You pointed him at Sonny, right?"

"Sonny and Fernandez both. Why wouldn't I? They're both fockin' pieces of shit."

Geronimo drifted off with that information for a moment, and he was nodding his head when he came back. "Call the shooters off, boss," he said.

"You think I run the fockin' organization now? I'm just a spare-change guy, believe me."

"I don't."

"You don't what?"

"Believe you."

"Why not?"

"You're in charge of the Drug Task Force, boss. You're not a nickel-and-dime kinda guy. Plus you slipped up with that crack about my betting. That's not exactly common knowledge."

"Fock you, Gee. Believe whatevah you want."

"Call the shooters off, Ralph, or I let the chief sort this shit out."

"You need to think this through before you go crazy here, you know."

"What's there to think about?"

"You're the one who hates collateral damage, yeah? Collateral damage fockin' loves chaos, Gee."

"So all you're doing with this is keeping things in order."

"Same thing you're trying to do, really, only my way actually works."

"And it's more lucrative than my way, I imagine."

"Definitely."

"Is this a recruitment pitch, boss?"

"It could be."

"Did the old man really have immunity, or was that just you?"

"What difference does it make? Any immunity he did or didn't have was obviously no more than partial at best."

"Answer the question."

"That was just me. You happy now?"

"Yeah, I'm fucking ecstatic now."

"So what's next?"

"You call the shooters off. After that, I'll let you know when I figure it out."

"So I'm at your beck and call now, yeah?"

"Only if you want to be, boss. It's entirely up to you. You prefer to work it out with the chief instead of me, just say the fucking word."

17

Geronimo sat behind the wheel of his Explorer and watched Louie Yamamoto lead Sonny and Jesus Fernandez across the parking lot. Louie opened the back door when he got to the car and stepped aside. "Have a seat, fellas," Geronimo said, and that's what the fellas did.

"Thanks, brah," Geronimo said. "I appreciate this big-time."

"No problem," Louie said as he closed the door behind the men and headed back to the building.

"No need," Geronimo said as his passengers started to buckle up. "We're not going anywhere."

"Wassup, Gee?" Sonny said.

"We need to talk. Just the three of us."

"What do the three of us have to talk about, homes?" Jesus said.

"The immediate future."

"What other kind of future is there?"

"Exactly."

"So talk."

"If everything stays the way everyone is playin' it right now, we won't be able to hold any of you much longer. Even if we come up with some charges, you'll get bail."

"That works for me," Jesus said.

"Maybe, maybe not," Geronimo said. "It looks like Johjima sent his remaining shooters after you two right before he died. I'm trying to call 'em off, but I can't guarantee it."

"Why would you wan' to?" Jesus said. "You let 'em do us, you get rid of us and them both when you catch 'em."

"Gee's got a serious phobia about collateral damage, brah," Sonny said. "Like the kid you fockahs shot on Haihai Street."

Jesus nodded soberly in front of that information, but only briefly. "Why both of us, though?" he said. "We ended up on opposite sides over there, *ese.*"

"Let's just say the old man's source of information had an agenda of his own," Geronimo said. "He thinks you're both pieces of shit."

"So what's the plan?"

"I get the feds to ship you back to LA today," Geronimo said. "That should keep you out of the line of fire. The only catch is the feds have to think you're playin' for their team now."

"That ain' hard to do, homes," Jesus said through a grin. "What do I have to do for you?"

"You give me the straight scoop on Nalani Rosario. I want to know exactly what happened to her."

"And what she did?"

"And what she did."

"Off the record?"

"For the ears of this assemblage only."

"I can do that, homes," Jesus said. "I can do that in two fockin' languages."

18

Ralph clipped his phone to his belt when he was through with it and walked out of his office. He didn't like the position he was in one bit, but he could imagine worse and wasn't without resources for coping with it.

Luckily, he said to himself, Geronimo is only half-smart. Once he got onto me, he should have stayed all over me. Instead, his best investigator had given him enough room to get himself out of this fix—all it had taken was a single phone call.

Now I go to Waikiki for some well-deserved vacation, he said to himself, many watery miles away from whatever happens to noble Geronimo Souza.

Ralph understood Geronimo's problem—he can't really see me as a bad guy after all these years of seeing me as something else. Ralph didn't suffer from the same difficulty—he could see things as they actually were. And except for Geronimo, things were perfect right now. There was a hole in the top of the natural order of things in the island's drug trade, and Ralph knew exactly how to fill it. That was one of two things he knew, the other being how to neutralize Geronimo Souza before Geronimo Souza fucked the whole thing up.

19

"Where you gonna send me, brah?" Sonny said. "Disneyland, maybe?"

"To tell you the truth, Sonny," Geronimo said, glancing at Jesus and then the parking lot on the far side of the car window, "I haven't figured that out yet."

"Just send me out the door, Gee. I'll take it from there."

"If anything happened to you as a result, Sonny, I'd never forgive myself."

"The moddafockah can get to me inside, you know. I'm better off out than in."

"Who are you talking about?"

"Fockin' Benedetto, who do you think?"

"I didn't say anything about Ralph."

"No need. I know what this is about, Gee. It's personal between him and me."

"Then you know more about it than I do."

"Don't turn your back on him now, yeah? You have more to worry about here than we do."

"He's dirty, Sonny, but no way he's *that* dirty. He's not gonna hit a cop."

"Whatevah," Sonny said. "I can walk?"

"I can do that."

"In exchange for what?"

"You don't owe me, brah. If anything, I owe you."

"I can live with that," Sonny said. *Assuming I can live at all, of course,* he added where only he could hear it.

20

"Let's walk," Geronimo said as Nalani entered the interview room. "You've already spent more than enough time in here, yeah?"

"Are you sure this is appropriate?" Nalani said, mocking him a little with the way she said it as she turned and walked out the door.

"Maybe you can render a verdict on that when we're done," Geronimo said, mocking her a little in return. He set a leisurely pace and she matched it stride for stride, neither of them speaking until they stopped at the corner across from St. Joe's gymnasium to let the new Buick that had come out of the parking lot behind them make a left turn.

"What do you want?" Geronimo said as they started across the street.

"What kind of a question is that?" Nalani said.

"Do you know the answer to it?"

"I don't know," she said, looking at him hard while she said it. "Not really. Why do you ask?"

"Because I'd like you to come out of this experience with something that you want."

"Do you think you know what the experience was?"

"Yes. I think I know it all."

"Who was your source? Jesus?"

"Yes."

"Jesus doesn't know it all. For that, you'd have to talk to God Himself."

"Or you."

"Or me," Nalani said.

"I'm talking to you now," Geronimo said.

"True. But I don't think I'm talking to you. Not about that."

"Who, then?"

"No one," she said after thinking her answer over for a while. "It's nobody's business but mine and God's, anyway."

"That's fine," Geronimo said. "Let's go back to talking about what you want."

"When were we talking about that? I don't know what I want, remember?"

"I know some things you can't have. We could start by talking about them."

"What would be the point?"

"They might provide a frame of reference for the original question."

"You're the one who scheduled this interview. Talk about whatever you want."

"Apparently you wanted to shoot Jesus on more than one occasion," Geronimo said. "You can't have that—he's off the island now."

"That doesn't mean I can't shoot him, does it? That just means I can't shoot him here anymore."

"I guess you're right. I stand corrected. How about this one—you can't have a role in the drug business here, no matter what you may have been told earlier."

"Why would anyone ever tell me something like that?"

"I talked to Jesus, remember?"

"Like I said, Jesus doesn't know everything."

"Fine," Geronimo said, speaking so softly that Nalani might not have heard it at all if she hadn't been watching his lips form the words. "Whatever you say is fine, Nalani."

"You were right," she said. "I did think of something I want."

"What is it?"

"I want to move off the island."

"When?"

"Now."

"Where?"

"I'd say LA, but you'd get the wrong idea. Anywhere, really."

"I don't see why that can't happen, if you really want it."

"I do."

"You'd be totally alone, you know."

"I always have been alone," she said, and then everything turned upside down. It started with sunlight glinting off glass which she glimpsed from a car at the intersection half a block or so ahead of them. Then she heard a loud crack and Geronimo crumpled to the concrete with a quiet cough, as though he had simply missed his step. Nalani heard the squeal of tires from the intersection, but she was reaching down to help Geronimo rise and did not look up. That's why she saw his aloha shirt morph from mostly light blue to entirely dark red right before her eyes.

Chapter Eleven
Post-game Cool-downs

1

Nalani and Pono arrived at the little church in Keaukaha slightly late, which is how they happened to walk in at the same time as the *haole* artist Nalani had met during one of the art celebrations in Volcano. *I came late intentionally,* Nalani thought as she briefly locked eyes with the woman and nodded in recognition. *How about you?*

The woman returned her nod as they stepped through the door, but they said nothing to each other. Nalani and Pono took seats in the back pew, but the pale artist remained standing just inside the door.

The room was ringed by members of the police force in dress uniforms standing rigidly at parade rest, even though a separate memorial service had been held downtown for the cops the previous day.

The priest at the front of the room was droning on as though he knew things about Geronimo Souza the others in the room did not, which Nalani found doubtful at best. She leaned back and closed her eyes, but that turned out to be a mistake—the first thing she saw was Geronimo bleeding on the sidewalk in front of her, his life ebbing away again as she watched helplessly one more time.

As the priest continued his attempt to put Geronimo's many friends and relatives to sleep, Nalani kept her focus on the people in the room with her.

Sonnyboy Akaka was seated in the first pew, Buddy Kai's five-year-old son up close under Sonny's right arm and Denise Souza sitting stiffly on his left, and Robbie Tsubamoto and his lover turned up a few seats over in the same row.

As Nalani prepared to start a scan of the second pew, the ceremony took a radical turn. The priest stopped talking and people started singing, various combinations of relatives laying down several songs in Hawaiian that spoke to Nalani profoundly even though she was not fluent in that language. By the time Sonny got up, Nalani was properly primed for the experience.

Sonny sounded a lot like the other singers until he slipped into a falsetto so pure that gods might have infiltrated the congregation just to hear it. His voice soared above the room and lifted everyone with it, the spirits of everyone rising until unified with Geronimo and the rest of Geronimo's line who had preceded him—all of the people for whom empty chairs had been placed at the front of the sanctuary and whose names Nalani knew had been chanted before her arrival at the ceremony.

Then everyone rose and joined hands, and Sonny led the entire assemblage through a song written by a queen at the end of an era now gone for more than a century. Nalani knew the words to this song and joined in the singing, as did Pono beside her in his clear, strong baritone, some of the words in Hawaiian and some in English, and tears rolled freely down both sides of her face by the time they were finished.

2

"I'm right around the corner," the blonde on Benedetto's arm whispered in the vicinity of his right ear. "We're almost there, honey."

Benedetto wrapped his big right arm around the blonde's thin shoulders and squeezed. "No offense, baby," he said, his words a little thicker than the words that came out of his mouth back on the Big Island. "But you are hotter than any of the pros on this fockin' street. I kid you not, baby."

"Oh, you big tease," the blonde said as she kissed him sloppily on his right cheek. "You know that isn't true, but I love you for sayin' it anyway."

"No, I mean it. We get to your place, I'm gonna prove it, too."

"Oh, honey, the way you talk," the blonde said with a giggle, all the while putting one high-heeled foot in front of the other and moving them steadily down the alley.

Sonny leaned in the shadows against the side of the building and watched the couple advance, and when they reached him he stepped forward with a pair of Franklins in his right hand. The blonde slipped out of Benedetto's clumsy embrace as soon as she saw him, snatched the money out of Sonny's hand, and continued down the alley without a word.

"What the fock's up?" Benedetto said.

"You, Ralph," Sonny said softly.

"Sonny? What the fock are you doin' here?"

"You focked up, you know."

"Says who?"

"You should have hit me first, not Gee."

"What the fock difference does it make?"

"If you had hit me first, you sorry moddafockah, you'd still be alive right now."

"You don' make any fockin' sense, as usual. I am alive right now, you stupid fockin' *kanaka.*"

"No, you aren't," Sonny said, and he started pouring .22 rounds through the silencer on the end of the gun in his left hand until he proved himself right.

3

"No, I insist," Robbie said. "You gotta take it."

"Thirty thousand dollars is a lot of money, brah," Sonny said.

"It's not mine; it's Gee's. Don't you think he'd want Buddy's kid to have it?"

Sonny looked at Robbie for a moment, then moved his gaze to John. "Don't look at me," John said with a shrug. "I agree with him."

"So do I, actually," Sonny said. He took the paper bag with $30,000 in it out of Robbie's hand and wrapped Robbie in a hug that lasted long enough to say everything he could think of to say.

"*Mahalo,* Robbie," Sonny said when the hug ended. "I mean it."

"Take care," Robbie said, and then he turned and walked to one side of his Mustang while John walked to the other. Sonny watched them get in the car and drive away, and then he took the paper bag inside.

Time to go to work, he said to himself as he picked up his phone and started matching sellers with product for the rest of the warm, wet Hilo night.